GREG MUTTON

Chronicle of the Twelfth Realm

BOOK 3:

HUNT FOR

Cover design: Gail Rust.
Original Image: Shutterstock
ISBN: **978-0-909497-17-0** (paperback)
978-0-909497-16-3 (Ebook)
First Edition 2020
Body Text Font: Calibri 11.5 pt

CAST OF CHARACTERS

Abraham Family

Jason: Patriarch & father of Jeffery & Aaron
Amanda: Matriarch & Mother of Jeffery & Aaron
Jeffery: CEO Abracorp & father of JT, Salina & David
Sonia: Professor of Horticulture, mother of JT, Salina
                 & David
John (JT):   Captain ECS Valiant
Salina: Marine Biologist
David: Financial controller Abracorp
Aaron: Freebooter Trader, estranged brother of
                 Jeffery

Coalition Space Corps

Skye Wilson: Fleet Admiral
Simon Morris: Rear Admiral, Deputy to Wilson
Sam Grogan: Admiral – Commander Space Corps
Alan Dean: Captain – Adjutant to Admiral Morris
Sol Radchak: Captain – Commander Space Corps training

Crew ECS Valiant

JT Abraham: Captain
Jarad Cross: First Officer
Greg Holgate: Tactical Officer
Amy Rodregas: Chief Engineer
Colin Bryant: Sensor sensor/defence officer
Sharon Holm: Communication officer & linguist
Helen Tradeski: Weapons Officer
Dave Carmelli: Second Weapons Officer
Holly Morgan: Navigation Officer

Freebooter Characters
Freebooter Trade Ship (FTS) Condor

Aaron Abraham: Captain and CEO AA Trading
Petra Mannix: First Officer
Kate Albrecht: Second Officer
Simon Holm: Navigator
David Cross: Tactical Officer
Dianna Holland: Chief Engineer
Colin Anderson: Engineer
William Croker: Sensor Officer
Phillip Harper: Cadet

FTS Albatross

Steve Harris: Captain
Greg Lewis: First Officer
Zab'ata Gollti: Second Officer

Other Freebooter Characters

Henry N'Gabo: Proctor AA Trading
Jacinta N'Gabo: Henry's Wife and Medical Technician
Allen Grainger: Freebooter Prime
Grace Grainger: Alan Grainger's wife and First Lady of Argos

Other Characters

Salim Malik:	President Earth Coalition of Planets
Silas Greenbach:	CEO Greenbach Technology
Kratc Dokad:	Admiral – Krell Imperial Navy
Damien Albrecht:	CEO Vision Cruise Lines
Eugene Sarclan:	Former CEO of Sarcorp (liquidated) – dissident
Anthony Crompton:	Director Coalition Intelligence Directorate (CID)
Ivan Klastok:	General – Commander Coalition Army
Damien Albrect:	CEO Vision Cruise Lines
Janice Barker:	CID Operative
Dr Anton Alvaris:	CEO Omnicron and Security Consultant
Wu Chan:	Emissary of the Mechanista

Inter Realm Characters

Eldrac-Tar:	Senior Eldoran Councillor
Jok-Tar:	Son of Eldrac-Tar
Zal-Tar:	Daughter of Eldrac-Tar
Mondrac:	Eldoran Council Member – half-brother to Eldrac-Tar
Zarof:	Leader of Galdor
Nefaris:	Queen Regent of Nileros
Tocmal:	Admiral – Commander Reglaos armed Forces

ACKNOWLEDGEMENTS

Again I must thank all those in my advance team for their input, insight and effort. These people know who they all are and how grateful I am for their advice. I must particularly thank Michelle; she has been indispensable in polishing this, and other, books. Her knowledge, insight and feeling have been a huge help. She and others look at my raw manuscripts and make comments that I take into the initial editing process. That's not to say we always agree, but these ideas always produce a thought process in me, and this is what we writers all need.

As with the first two books cover design has been by Gail Rust and she always delivers what I see. This cover is a scene from the final confrontation and was designed at the height of the COVID lock down, here in Australia. We only met once face to face but her initial design was so close. A couple of phone calls and emails and she nailed my vision perfectly, thanks Gail.

I welcome a new member of our advance team, Suzanne. She is, now, the final stage in our editing process, and misses very little. She has really helped to polish and make my books more enjoyable, I thank her for all her hard work.

It would be remiss if I didn't include the two most important people, my wife Debbie and step son, Tim. They are my sounding boards, grammar masters and story line editors; they are my toughest critics and my strongest supporters. Without them I couldn't do what I do.

Thank you for purchasing my books, I hope you enjoy.

"The most difficult thing in life is to know yourself."

Thales (c. 624-546 BCE)

A year had passed since the battle of the Exodus gates had taken place.

Many believed that this victory would bring stability, but instead of ushering in an age of peace, there was still a great deal of unrest.

The Coalition of Earth Planets had been thrown into turmoil with the mass rebellions that started a few years back and, while most had been quelled, Ummah was still in a state of upheaval. Initially, the military sat back as things unfolded. The imposition of extreme interpretations of their guiding religious texts had led to constant rounds of executions. Finally, General Al'Hadi had seen enough and he acted, decisively. His forces overpowered the insurgent army and martial law was enacted.

It took several months before the majority of the Jihadist leadership was either dead or in custody - the rest fled to the outer provinces or off-world. The ruling Council of Imams met and decided that there was only one person who could unite their now fractured culture - Salim Malik, President of the Coalition. General Al'Hadi and Malik had been in constant contact during the uprising so the Council tasked him with convincing Malik to return.

Malik was torn between the need of the Coalition - now experiencing the greatest trade and cultural expansion ever - and his people, who had suffered greatly at the hands of the rebels. He and Al'Hadi spent many hours discussing possible alternatives, all the while knowing his people were looking to him for guidance and protection. It was with a heavy heart that he had requested Sam Grogan to meet with him at his residence.

Malik stood gazing out the window of his office, drinking in the beauty of the ocean view - something he would not see for quite a while if he returned home. Ummah was a largely marginal or desert planet. He remembered the rolling dunes outside his home city with some nostalgia; there was great beauty in this memory, and deep down he missed his home.

His thoughts were interrupted by a knock at his door, he shrugged and turned. 'Enter' he said as he moved to one of the leather armchairs. The door opened and Sam Grogan, Fleet Admiral of the Coalition Space Corps, and Commander in Chief of Coalition Military entered the room.

'Mister President, how are you today?' Sam asked, not wanting an answer. The President had been distant lately, something Sam was grateful for. His tolerance for political machinations diminished every day.

'Admiral, thank you for coming,' Malik invited Sam to take the chair to his right. 'We will be joined by the leader of the Coalition Council shortly but I wanted to have a quick discussion, with you, before she arrives.' Sam looked at his Commander cautiously; Malik had a reputation for intrigue. 'You are aware of the problems on Ummah?'

Sam nodded 'Yes Sir. The Corps is assisting in searching for any rebels that have escaped off-world.'

'Yes, I am aware of that; and the General is grateful for your assistance.' Malik paused, gathering his thoughts. 'The General and I have been in constant communication, as there are some problems he doesn't have an answer for.'

'I am sorry... I'll come to the point. General Al'Hadi and the ruling Council have asked me to return to Ummah to form a new Government and start rebuilding our society. I am torn whether to accept or not... that is why I have asked both you and Madam Collard here today to discuss options. I specifically asked you here to sound you out on my possible successor.' He took a breath, allowing Sam room to interrupt.

'Mister President you can't be serious. Look, we have had our differences but if I have to work with politicians, I would rather my boss be you than any of the other clowns I deal with. Please reconsider.'

Malik smiled at the words. 'Sam, I thank you for those words but it may be the only option for my Ummah. My people won't accept military rule for long and another uprising will inevitably take place unless we rebuild the government. I thank you for your candour and, believe me; I call most of the Council a lot worse than clowns. I too hate all the politicking that goes on, but I believe this is something I should do, for the good of my people. I would like your input into who should succeed me.'

'But surely Mister President; that will be the responsibility of the Council.'

Malik shook his head. 'Well actually no. I have been working through the constitution, and the recommendations made by the founders of the Coalition are quite specific,' he handed Sam a data-pad. 'Please read this before we talk more.'

Sam activated the pad and read through the document on it. He had to read it twice before the implications sank in. He looked up and Malik spoke; 'now take a look at the file marked 'advice.' Sam read the file before placing the pad on the table before them.

Sam's face showed his concern. 'This was written by Argort?'

Graham Argort was the most respected constitutional scholar in the Coalition. The Council always sought his advice on constitutional matters. Sam shook his head in disbelief.

'Yes, I asked Graham for his opinion months ago, that is his response. So, in the event of a President resigning, he or she must select a replacement to complete their term... in this case for 25 years. I have a few candidates I think could take over but only one who I believe should... and that is where I need your help.'

'Who, Mister President, who is your preferred candidate?'

Malik cleared his throat before he spoke; 'Jason Abraham.' He looked intently at Sam, waiting for a reaction.

Slowly Sam digested this and finally spoke, 'I appreciate why.

Jason has experience in interplanetary relations, Abracorp has operations on many colonies and they have a reputation of fair dealing. Also, he has dealt with the majority of the Council, but will he agree?'

'That is another area I need **your** help with. You have strong relations with the family and are well acquainted with Abracorp. I firmly believe he is the only person who can rise above the pettiness of our politics and finish the job. Will you help me, Admiral?'

At that moment, there was another knock at the door; it opened and Madam Collard entered.

The leader of the Coalition Council was a tall elegant woman of indeterminate age. She had silver hair that she wore tied back. Her high cheekbones and full lips gave most people pause to look at her but her eyes were and had always been her most striking feature. They were steel grey and penetrating - laser-like.

As the leader of the Council, she had great responsibility and she bore this with integrity. When she moved it was with such grace and poise that she seemed to float into the room. Malik and Grogan stood as she entered, the President indicating she take the chair to his left.

'Madam Collard, thank you for coming... you know Admiral Grogan?' Malik opened the conversation.

'Yes, how are you, Admiral?' Madam Collard's voice was melodious and clear, a hint of an accent betraying her French heritage.

She came from a successful industrial family on Rogan, one of the most distant colonies - it was this distance that had forged a cohesive and ingenious society. Anything needed from Earth or any other colony took many years, in the early years of settlement. Her great, great grandfather had started the family business out of necessity. If something broke that far out, you had to fix it yourself - or go without. Rogan had become a shining example of human ingenuity and determination.

Yvette Collard had been selected by the Rogan Government to represent them at the Coalition General Assembly eighty years ago, a task she'd tackled with outstanding success. Not long after she was chosen as a permanent member of the Council and now held the leadership position.

Over the years, she had proven herself to be a brilliant political strategist and a ruthless adversary - someone not to be taken lightly. But her time was coming to an end. In five years her mandatory retirement would come into effect. Still, it was widely accepted that she would be the next Rogan Ambassador to the Coalition so her influence would be felt for many years to come.

'Well, thank you, Madam, and yourself?'

'Very well, and I must congratulate you on your actions during the recent crisis. It is a relief that we can rely on our military again.' A compliment, or veiled criticism, one never knew with her. 'Now, Mister President, what do you wish to discuss?'

Finally, the question that would test the President's mettle. Collard always found a way for every situation to benefit her and this would be no different.

'Madam, no doubt you are aware of the situation on my home world.'

'Most definitely, Mister President, a most disagreeable situation. I trust everything is starting to return to normal.' Collard's voice gave nothing away; she sounded concerned but, cautiously distant.

'Somewhat, but there are some matters we must discuss. General Al'Hadi has been in contact and asked that I return to Ummah and form a new Government. He doesn't believe that a long term Military Junta is in the best interests of our people. His reading of the mood of the people tells him that I am an acceptable interim leader. He believes I am the only person acceptable to all and, therefore, able to bring stability... the Council of Imams agrees with him on this.'

Malik paused, allowing her time to respond. Collard said

nothing so he continued, 'I have studied the options and, considering that this is an unprecedented situation, I have sought the finest counsel in my deliberations.' He handed her the data-pad. 'Please read the information so we can continue.'

While she was reading an aide entered with a tray that contained a fresh pot of coffee and a plate of biscuits. They all took a mug of the offered coffee and the aide left, only when the door was securely closed did Madam Collard speak.

'This is interesting, have you made your decision?' She sat back and waited for Malik to answer.

'Not yet... there are many things to consider. As you can imagine this is a very heavy decision I face, and I want your counsel on the matter. Admiral Grogan has given me his ideas but I am interested to hear yours, Madam.' Malik had turned the tables skilfully. She had no option but to speak her mind.

'President Malik, if this were me I would follow my heart. If my people needed me I would do everything in my power to help them but... I must say that I, and the Council, have been impressed with your performance in this office. You would be hard to replace, and this is something I do not say lightly. While I would rather you stay as President, the final decision must be yours.'

'Thank you... but how do you think the Council would respond?'

'Don't worry about the Council; they are more concerned with their own agendas You have the advice from the one person the Council will ask so there will be no issue but, you will need to decide soon. We must make the necessary arrangements.' There was a hint of warning in her voice.

'Whatever I decide, you will be advised by the end of the month, ten days from now.' President Malik committed, 'I only ask that this conversation remains confidential, agreed?'

'Agreed,' Madam Collard and Grogan answered, simultaneously.

'Thank you both; your confidence and discretion are

appreciated.' Malik ended this conversation and proceeded to other business. 'Now, there is some other business we need to discuss. Admiral, what progress in filling the senior flag positions?'

Since his promotion, Sam Grogan had been exceedingly busy, he needed to fill two senior flag positions and the file of suitable candidates was thin. The role of Fleet Commander-Logistics - Simon Morris' role - had been the most urgent and seven candidates had been screened, from this only two were selected for consideration.

As this was a role that included a great deal of politics in dealing with the Council for funding and budgets, the candidates were passed to the Council standing committee for comment. This had taken up a huge amount of time and finally, after Madam Collard, herself had intervened; a Four Sun Captain had been selected only a week ago.

Captain Anthony Hubbard had been the prime candidate. He had excellent qualifications in logistics, was one of Morris' senior supply chiefs and his father was an ex-Council member, so Anthony was known to most of the Council. He had been approached and had signalled Grogan, only this morning, of his acceptance.

'Excellent Admiral!' Madam Collard seemed genuinely happy with this news 'I have worked with Anthony. He's excellent in the political arena and continues his father's legacy... he is incorruptible. But that still leaves what I believe as the most critical post, your old one. Who do you have for this?'

'Yes, that's somewhat of an enigma. I've been looking at our candidates, all Four Sun Captains, all with some actual battle experience but I keep coming back to one. So far I haven't had an opportunity to discuss anything with him. My suggestion for this post is John Abraham. He has an excellent record and is a lateral thinker, something that has proved extremely useful lately.' Sam waited for a response.

'Now that is out of left field.' Madam Collard was taken by

surprise. 'Not long ago he was investigated for disobeying orders, and yes, he was exonerated, in fact, I still believe we should decorate him for what he did. Then only what, twelve months ago, he was promoted to full Captain. Now you suggest he is the best candidate to replace you? There are still two other Admirals, shouldn't they be considered?'

'Neither have the battle smarts that Abraham has demonstrated. Look, I believe that for too long these positions, even my position, have been given for the wrong reasons. Until recently we haven't needed real fighters. Peace has made us soft, and many promotions never happened, leaving us with a huge gap in senior rank. To be blunt, Madam Collard, any promotions that did take place were more of a political appointment.

'For the last 150 years, we have, sadly, let the Corps degenerate. Promotions were rare, with no planning for senior rank succession. We have let our fleet degrade so much that it is only a token operation... something I have been warning about for quite a while. The fact that Freebooters are now more powerful than the combined fleets of the Krell Empire **and** the Coalition is a testament to that. Hell if it wasn't for them, we'd be in a world of hurt now.'

Sam was on dangerous ground now, but these things needed to be said. 'Take Vice Admiral Icaron... why the hell was she given the rank? She has no battle experience, she's rarely seen the inside of a battleship let alone fought in one, but she is Katsu Icaron's daughter; tell me I am wrong.' His eyes flared as he looked directly at Collard, Malik sitting back, watching how this panned out.

Collard seemed ready to explode but instead, she calmed down and responded 'Yes, I agree that was a mistake; but Admiral, you don't have to deal with Katsu. He is a real pain in the proverbial especially when he starts on his minor colony and repression rant. That's why she was promoted... and, in hindsight, not our best decision. But what about Vice Admiral

Rogaris... isn't he senior?'

Sam couldn't believe his ears 'Yes he is senior, but he's three hundred and forty years old. I don't think he's been off-world in nearly a century and to be honest, nobody knows what he does except annoy the staff at the Academy. No, Madam, the real talent in our entire military is in the junior ranks and we need to fix that **now**.'

Madam Collard turned to the President. 'Mister President, what is your view?'

'I concur with Sam. For too long we have paid lip service to our military, thinking it was an anachronism; just a token force. How wrong we were.' He slowly shook his head, emphasizing the error of those decisions. 'In truth, if it hadn't been for Captain Abraham and Captain Radchak, we would have been in deep trouble. I think it is time to stir things up, bring in some new blood but... will he accept?'

'Only one way to find out... ask him,' Grogan replied.

The meeting continued for a few more minutes before President Malik thanked Madam Collard for her input and again agreed to have an answer to her in ten days. She bowed, slightly and left the two men alone. Malik asked Sam to arrange meetings with the Abrahams regarding both matters and they tentatively scheduled that for Friday, two days away.

Sam went back to his shuttle but was surprised to find Madam Collard was waiting for him.

'Admiral, I need to go to Perth and I was wondering if I could travel with you?' Sam felt the hairs on his neck stand, a warning he knew he should pay heed to.

'Of course, Madam, I would welcome the company.' Sam stood aside for her to board.

On the shuttle they took their seats, Collard spoke first. 'I do hope you have something stronger than coffee, on board. As much as I do admire our President, his religious restrictions are a bit much, at times.'

Sam opened the cupboard by his seat and produced two

glasses and a bottle of well-matured Bourbon.

'Sometimes one does need something a little stronger. Here's to change.' They raised their glasses and sat back, savouring the excellent spirit.

'Admiral, what is your take on the President's dilemma?' Direct as ever, Collard went straight to the issue.

'He has some sober thinking to do. Look, you understand my view of politics, but I must say he has been a great leader. I never thought I would say this but I will miss him if he decides to resign.' Sam didn't want to give any indication he had more information.

'So... he didn't discuss his chosen successor with you?' Now the real reason for her company was clear.

'Madam, even if he did, I can't discuss it with you... it would have been a privileged conversation. All I will say is, it appears he has a couple he is considering, he only wanted my input from a military perspective. He'll inform us when he's ready.'

Collard simply smiled 'Sam, you would make a great politician. Let me know if you ever tire of playing soldier, I think you would fit in very well.' The rest of the hour flight was spent in small talk and ended with Sam and Madam Collard agreeing to meet when a decision on Captain Abraham had been made.

***

The Coalition task force comprising of three Hood class cruisers reinserted into normal space outside the Jupiter Station exclusion zone. Captain Solomon Radchak was in command of the group as it returned from scouring the Shadow sector of the outer rim. Their mission had been to check coordinates Jok-Tar had supplied regarding the possible location of Balerophon. Six months in that area, was bad enough, but the information hadn't panned out. Even though they had found traces of Trisidic radiation, and some evidence that humans had been in that area, Balerophon still eluded them. Sol was exhausted, his mood deflated as the group entered Jupiter Station's control area.

Jupiter Station to approaching vessels, please identify yourself.

'Jupiter Station, this is Coalition task force Paladin, Captain Solomon Radchak commanding the cruiser Wilson. We request transit through your sphere of control.'

He was rewarded with *Wait one.*

Sol was not in the mood for bureaucrats, deciding that a tactical retreat was a much better alternative he beckoned to his second in command. 'Number one, you have the con... I'll be in my ready room.'

'Aye, Sir. I have the con;' Daniel Akaido replied.

Daniel was not particularly tall, slightly over one hundred and seventy centimetres, but he was a particularly fit individual preferring the gym to the many other distractions on board. He had short-cropped black hair, tanned skin, and almond-shaped eyes. He had joined the Wilson after the inter-realm conflict as First Officer and had formed a firm working relationship with Sol during this mission. Both men had desperately hoped that they could find the elusive Balerophon, but it was not to be.

Task Force Paladin, this is Jupiter Station. You were not expected for another two weeks.

Daniel knew how his skipper felt. Six months in the proverbial Bad-Lands and now they had to justify their early arrival to some snotty-nosed bureaucrat who, in all probability, had never left the Solar System. But Daniel had greater tolerance than Sol and he set about explaining their early arrival.

Please hold at the outer mark, the Station replied.

Ten minutes later, *Task Force Paladin, this is Commander Hargraves, Commander Jupiter Station, please hold while we complete our scans.*

Six months in some of the worst space in the galaxy, cosmic storms, huge gravity wells, and many weird spatial anomalies were constant trials. Plus there were some rather nasty and unfriendly outposts to deal with; and now they were at the mercy of some spit and polish paper pusher. The crews were tired, everyone just wanted to return to earth and get off the ship, shore leave had been non-existent for the whole mission.

Fifteen minutes later, the Commander of the Station came back on the com.

Task Force Paladin you are cleared to proceed. Keep speed below point three of light during your transit of Jupiter Station Controlled space.

Daniel answered calmly 'Thank you Commander, Paladin proceeding.'

At that precise moment, Sol re-entered the Bridge, thankful they had been cleared to proceed 'Number one, let's give them a flypast... let them see what they've been holding up.'

'Yes, sir' Daniel replied. He nodded to the Navigator who transmitted the new course to the rest of the group.

The task force's new course took them to within one hundred kilometres of the Station, close enough for the bureaucrats to have a first-rate view, but not close enough to frighten them, too much.

As the three ships transited the Station, Commander Hargraves stared at the fly past, astonished at the sight. 'Coms; call Space Corps Headquarters, now.' Hargraves couldn't believe these ships were still able to navigate space.

Twenty minutes later, Sol received a call from Admiral Grogan; he took it in his ready room. *You have some damage, Captain, care to elaborate?*

'Not now, Sir. I only want my people back home and on-planet. We can discuss the mission later if that's OK.' Sol was at the end of his tether. Not only did they not find Balerophon, but they also ran into a heap of trouble, lost one ship and the remaining three appeared like they were only fit for scrap.

Steady, Sol. When did you last sleep? Grogan could tell from his voice that Sol was on the edge.

'No idea... I'll sleep when we dock.'

No, you won't, Captain. You hit the rack now, that's an order. If I find out you don't sleep till Mars I'll kick your arse back to the Bad-Lands, understand? Grogan didn't like speaking to Sol this way but it was the only way he would rest. *I have sent a copy of this order to your number one. If I need to, I'll order him to have you sedated.*

'OK, sir I'll get some shut-eye.'

Good. I'll make sure that there are transports ready when you arrive at Mars, Grogan out. Sam cut the connection.

Again he gazed at the damage to the three ships. A cold shiver running down his spine as a thought crossed his mind, the last time he could recall damage this bad was when JT brought the survivors of the Zyralin 4 debacle home. He knew he wasn't going to like the story behind this.

His intercom buzzed and a rather gruff male voice spoke.

Admiral, Captain Abraham is here.

'Send him in.'

Captain Johnathon Thomas Abraham the fourth, tall, powerfully built and handsome, or at least that was the consensus of the female members of the Admiral's staff. It was his deep brown eyes that fooled everyone, eyes that seemed lazy, almost docile but they never missed a single detail.

'You wanted to see me, Admiral?'

'Yes, John. Take a seat. Care for a drink?' Sam was stalling, still trying to find the words he needed. He poured two glasses of Bourbon and handed one to his guest. He turned the view screen towards JT 'Sol ran into some trouble.'

'Shit!' was all JT could say as he viewed the damage. 'What happened?'

'We don't have the report yet, but it has to be bad, I don't think Sol has slept for a week by the sound of him. I ordered him to bed before he collapses.'

Sam stood and quietly took a swig from his glass, 'Captain I need to talk to you about something important, **and** I want you to wait till I finish before you say anything... think you can do that?'

'I'll try, Sir.'

"That's all I ask. As you are aware we have been through the wringer, lately. One thing that has been rammed home is our lack of talent, in flag positions.' Sam took another swig, and continued.

'Captain I have known you for most of your life. I watched you grow up and I have followed your career, to date. You have never flinched from your duty, you have never complained when the shit hit the fan and you have always looked outside the box in tight situations. Hell... what you pulled at Zyralin 4 was out there, but it worked... and I believe that manoeuvre saved Petra and her crew in the Eleventh Realm. It has even become part of Battle Strategy at the Academy. It has shown us that we need thinkers like you, in senior ranks.'

JT wasn't sure where the Admiral was going with this, 'Admiral, all I did was follow my instinct. I didn't do anything brilliant.' He spoke quietly, his mind calling for caution.

Grogan responded, enthusiastically. 'But you did, that bloody idiot Dean nearly got everyone killed, but you took command and saved over six hundred from certain death. Captain, I need you here, on my team. I am offering you my old role as Commander, Space Corps. The role has been authorized and will carry the rank of Rear Admiral. You will be second in command to me but, you will have complete autonomy on running the Corps.'

JT started to say something but Grogan held his hand up.

'Captain the Coalition almost got its collective arse kicked to hell and back. For too long we have put the wrong bums on the wrong seats, and senior command simply got old... myself included... we need new blood and we need it **now**.'

'I don't know what to say.' JT was stunned. 'What about the Manta project, I'm fully committed to that, at the moment.'

These words gave Grogan a glimmer of hope.

'Are you telling me, that no one in your crew can take that over? Come on John, I'll bet there are at least half a dozen, equally involved who could easily take over. Am I right?'

JT slumped back in his chair. One of his key leadership tasks, he believed, was to make sure that he, the Captain, was not necessary. This conviction came from his father, his grandfather and right back to the original John Thomas Abraham, they all believed that any organization was only as strong as the people in it and that any leader should be the least necessary person in the organization. A good leader should always strive to surround themselves with the best people; people capable of filling the leader's shoes if needed. JT had carried this philosophy into his military career with great results

'Yes, sir you are correct... anyone of my Bridge crew could replace me. I don't know if I am ready for this... hell, I'm only sixty-three. There hasn't been an Admiral that young...ever!'

'So you'll be a first, what's wrong with that? I understand you want to be out there,' Grogan pointed to the sky through the generous window behind his desk. 'But I believe that with you in this role, many more will go out there but more importantly, return home.' Grogan sat, his sales pitch over. It was now up to the young man before him to decide.

***

Sol woke to a knocking sound - someone was at his door. He slowly returned to consciousness.

'Enter.'

Commander Akaido entered. 'We have arrived at Mars Dock, sir. We have been ordered to disembark for transport to Earth.'

'How long was I out?'

'Twenty-two hours, Sir. I was under strict instruction not to wake you... Admiral Grogan was most insistent.'

Sol waved him to silence 'I guess I needed it, Dan, thanks. I'll have a quick shower and be ready in a few minutes. In the meantime, can you download all the data from the mission; I think I'm going to need it.'

Sol returned to the Bridge twenty minutes later, looking much refreshed. Except for Dan Akaido, the Bridge was empty.

'Everyone off the ship?'

'Yes, sir, everyone has already left for Earth. The Admiral is

15

waiting for us, here on the Station, it appears he wants a quick debrief before we leave.'

'Well, if you have all the data, we better not keep Admiral Grogan waiting.'

'All here,' Dan held up his data-pad. They left the ship and went to the Station Administration office.

Half an hour later, they were waiting outside a small conference room in the Administration section of Mars Dock. Most dock admin complexes were dull and boring but not Mars Dock, this one had a little character. Instead of the usual pictures of old space ships and images of work taking place on them, the foyer here was filled with many different works of art. Paintings, sculptures and even tapestries representing many of the colonies as well as some indigenous art from various non-human cultures were on display.

To one side was a substantial transparent display case filled with models and replicas of ancient sea-going Earth naval ships. From old sail-powered vessels to the last of the giant super battleships, all phases of Earth's naval development were portrayed.

They were so engrossed, admiring the models and replicas; they didn't hear the receptionist approach. 'Our dock manager wanted to show what she believes the human race represents. What, do you think?'

'Exceptional... beats looking at old star-ships any day,' Sol replied.

The receptionist smiled 'Thank you, I'll tell her. The Admiral is ready for you. If you will follow me' she turned and led the way. Opening the door to the conference room she stood aside as the two men entered, then closed the door behind them.

Someone was sitting in a chair on the opposite side of the table, looking intently at the images of their task force, the back of his chair to them.

'You certainly got your arse kicked, by the looks of that.' The figure in the chair said.

The voice was familiar but Sol couldn't be sure. Then the chair turned to face them, 'Nearly as much as when I kicked it on the range.' There before them, in full three Star Burst, Rear Admiral bling was JT Abraham.

'JT, what the hell; you can be shot for impersonating an Admiral.' Sol moved closer to his friend as he spoke, 'and you didn't kick that hard, I had to let you look impressive.'

'OK, first, these Star Bursts are real... I am a Rear Admiral, second, what happened out there?'

'No, come on. What has happened back here, why are you an Admiral?' Sol probed, still unable to believe his eyes.

'Admiral Grogan promoted me, seems they want to inject some new blood into the senior ranks, he really should have been a salesman after the job he did. Anyway, I thought about it and decided to accept so now I'm in command of Space Corps. So that's my story, now tell me what happened.'

Sol shook his head, trying to clear his thoughts. 'We were following the Eldoran's Balerophon lead. We found out the hard way just how dangerous Shadow Sector can be. No bloody wonder navigation is restricted. We were hit with a couple of huge cosmic storms that played havoc with our systems... then we got slammed by those mysterious gravity wells that we have only heard about.

'After that we got lucky, we picked up what turned out to be a Trisidic trace. We followed it to a binary system where we found some evidence of Human activity on two of the planets. It seemed fairly recent too, so we started our search. We split up and eventually found what we believe to be a drive trace from a Trisidic powered ship. Then all hell broke loose... we were attacked by Tragarian Raiders.'

'Come on, Sol,' JT challenged as he pointed to the screen. 'Tragarian Raiders don't have the firepower to inflict **that** much damage.'

'I agree, usually, they detect ships our size and they run like the wind, but not this time.' Sol continued. 'We first encountered two and they came straight at us. We responded and smashed one but the other accounted for the Cargan... they just blew her apart.

'We regrouped but there were now five of them, and they were spoiling for a fight.' He hesitated for a second time, reliving the events he was describing.

'I've never seen anything like it. Their shields were all but impenetrable and their weapons... their weapons passed through our shields like they weren't even raised. The only thing that saved us was the absorption field, but even that has limits. We eventually destroyed two more... then they turned and left. We did what we could to repair our ships and got the hell out of there. Anyway, everything's in the data.' Sol sat quietly, staring at the screen, almost in disbelief.

JT stood and turned the screen off. 'Time to go, Captain; we need to take this information back to Earth and try to find out what happened to your group... and more importantly why the Raiders suddenly have such vastly superior weapons.'

Admiral Abraham, Captain Radchak, and Commander Akaido left the conference room and took the short walk to the transport pod.

The pod stopped at a shuttle bay and they boarded the Admiral's personal shuttle. They moved into the passenger area, Sol taking in the plush surrounds; deep leather chairs, thick carpet, and a well-stocked bar and kitchen area. The attractive female aide handed the Admiral his data-pad and retreated to her station, in the office section.

'Not bad.' Sol whispered, 'being promoted has its perks.'

JT grunted as he pored over his pad. The pilot wasn't visible - the Command Section was separated by a bulkhead and substantial door.

'Now, before you say any more,' JT explained, 'this is my private boat. I have had it for nearly six years but never used it, so would you rather we used a standard transport or will this do, for now?

'Sorry Sir, this will do fine.'

JT chuckled, 'easy... I'm only starting to get used to this Admiral gig myself, so drop the Sir, for now.'

Sol grinned. 'Just a small personal question... how did your father take this promotion?'

JT looked a little sheepish, 'I haven't told him yet. Hell, it only happened two days ago! As soon as I heard the condition of your task force, I came straight out here... but I'll probably tell him this weekend; Grogan and Malik are coming to Lucknow for the weekend and I've also been included... at Grogan's insistence.'

'Oh really, what's the chance of getting a seat at that? I don't want to miss it.'

JT handed his pad to Sol. 'Certainly, read this and agree,'

Sol took the pad and read the file he paused and read it again. 'Are you serious?'

'Totally,' JT spoke to Akaido as he stood. 'Commander, I apologize but I need to have a few minutes alone with your Captain. Please help yourself to a drink or ask my aide for anything you need. Sol, come with me.'

Sol stood and followed JT back to his office. The shuttle left Mars base and was now headed for Earth, accelerating to point five light speed. The whole journey would be in normal space and at this speed; it would take a little over fourteen minutes to reach earth, a far cry from the first Mars' expedition. That mission, from Earth to Mars, took seven months.

JT closed the door and took his seat behind the desk while Sol took one of the two armchairs opposite. 'Look,' he began, 'we both have complained for years at the quality of who was in the Flag posts. Wilson, Morris, and Grogan were the last of what seemed a dying breed; Flag Officers who had seen any sort of action. Grogan convinced me that by taking this job I could shape the future of the Corps, but I can't do it alone, too much to do. That is why I'm offering you this promotion. We make a great team and honestly, the Corps needs you to do this job.'

Sol read the file again, 'OK, I accept.'

'Excellent!' JT opened a drawer. He took out a small box and handed it across the desk. Sol opened it and stared at the contents. 'Well Admiral, aren't you going to put them on?' Sol gazed at the insignia for a few moments before finally removing his old Captain's suns and replacing them with the twin starbursts indicating his new rank of Vice-Admiral.

JT stood and held out his hand. 'Congratulations, Admiral; welcome to the team!' The two shook hands and JT clapped his old friend on the back. 'Now to work, you'll need to look for your own staff as soon as possible... any ideas?'

'Not really, I need some time to collect my thoughts.'

'Good answer; we can work through it with Sam this weekend.

Now, fill me in on the Tragarian issue... we've both had run-ins with them and never had any problems with their weapons.'

For the remaining nine minutes of the trip, Sol gave JT as close a blow by blow description of the encounter as he could, finally realizing just how fast it had all happened. The data from the ship would give the actual timing, but Sol's recalling of the incidents gave JT the impression that each had only taken minutes, not hours. If this was borne out by the data, then the Coalition had some grave issues to face.

***

Aaron Abraham stood in his office on the Twelfth Realm portal, cursing silently. He hated this job; stuck in this office, dealing with the most tedious and boring administrative issues, things that Henry N'Gabo, his company Proctor, always did.

Aaron was a Freebooter trader; roaming the galaxy making deals, uncovering new trade opportunities, and leaving all the administrative details to Henry. He stared out of the view port, not looking for anything in particular, but wishing he was out there, in Condor, doing what he loved.

But since the battle for the Twelfth Realm had taken place; he'd been saddled with the job of managing the inter-realm portal traffic and trade, shackled to the office. Petra had been away for six weeks dealing with issues about her inheritance; and this didn't improve his mood either.

She needed time to deal with the aftermath of the death of her father, and it had been a shock that he had left her everything. Even though she knew she was an only child, she had never considered any inheritance. Colin Mannix had many business operations ranging from engineering to agriculture; construction, to finance. Petra's inheritance was substantial and complex.

She and Aaron had taken residence at the portal and had been there for six months when she received a communique from a firm of lawyers on Earth. They advised her of her inheritance and requested she attend their offices to discuss her options.

21

Petra had no idea what she wanted to do and Aaron suggested she take Henry with her - after all, he handled all the company business. Petra agreed, contacted Henry on Argos, and made the arrangements.

Two months later, the first time that Henry had available; they had met at Perth Space Port and taken a shuttle to Guatemala City and the head office of Mannix Intergalactic, her father's company. They'd hoped that everything could be sorted out in a day or two but when Henry understood the size and complexity of the operation; he knew they would need much more time. In addition to this, Aaron and Petra were due to marry in four weeks and that added another set of complications.

Under Freebooter law, any two people who enter into a relationship agreement must have their affairs in order and have clear, and documented arrangements on division or amalgamation of assets - if not, the relationship agreement could not be ratified. In the case of Aaron and Petra, it was even more complicated as Petra's inheritance was governed by Coalition laws and regulations and as it turned out, Aaron's interest in Abracorp made the issue even more complex and confusing. Henry's call, this morning, to discuss the situation had only added to his foul mood.

Henry thought that they may be able to devise a workable solution, but he needed some help. He suggested they discuss it with Aaron's brother and father. Abracorp was one of the largest conglomerates in the Coalition and Henry surmised it would have the legal clout he needed. Aaron agreed and resigned himself to the fact that this weekend at the family compound would be all business.

Just then his assistant hailed him over the com system, informing him that his nephew was calling. 'Put him through,' Aaron accepted the call.

Aaron, JT here. How's the life of a portal manager? JT opened with the wrong issue.

Aaron barked his answer. 'Fucking great, I think my right hand will fall off with all the signing I do... damn, I envy you out there where I belong. What can I do for you?

Sorry, I didn't realize you were having a hard time. Sol has returned from the Bad-Lands and I was wondering if you could ask the Eldorans to take a look at the data he has?

Strange request, Aaron thought 'Can't your people look at it? Why do you need Eldoran input?'

Can't say here, but if I send the data will you look at it and call me back? We're about to land on earth.

Aaron was intrigued. 'OK, send it through.'

Sending now; Abraham out, JT cut the connection.

Abraham out; young John's getting a bit up himself, Aaron thought. Then he spotted a data stream being downloaded. He spent the next hour dissecting the data, not able to believe the result. In the end, he requested a priority comm link to Mondrac on Eldora and waited anxiously for a reply.

Finally a reply; *Aaron, Mondrac here, good to hear from you. How, are the wedding plans coming*? Even with the best Eldoran comm system, there was still a delay of two minutes, making the conversation slightly disjointed.

'Mondrac, as always it's great to hear your voice, my friend. Wedding plans? Well, I don't know what happens on Eldora but here it is all done by the women... we males are only along for the ride. I have some data I would like you to analyse for me and before you ask, I want you to do it without any background information. Can you do that for me?' Aaron waited for a reply.

Of course, sounds intriguing, I could use a bit of intrigue... Eldora can be so boring.

'This could be serious Mondrac, thank you.'

Think nothing of it, send the data through I will start working on it immediately.

Aaron compressed the data, encoded the transmission, and sent it. 'I'm leaving for Earth in a few minutes Mondrac but you can reach me on my private comm-link at any time.'

Of course, I will call as soon as I have any information. Mondrac broke the connection.

Aaron looked at the time on the desk readout. The simple short conversation had taken fifteen minutes - time to go, he thought to himself. While he had transferred command of his beloved Condor over to Captain, Katherine Albrecht, he had kept the yacht for himself; replacing it with a new runabout for her use. He left his office and walked directly to the hangar.

It was not a long walk, less than two kilometres; but it gave him time to think, and calm down. His mind kept going back to his early days as a trader. The adventure, the risk, and the sense of being alive - this new job seemed to suck all that out of him. His mood was not getting any better when he heard a female voice call his name. He stopped and looked around; there standing at the hangar view port was Jacinta N'Gabo, Henry's wife.

'Jacinta what are you doing here?'

Jacinta N'Gabo was tall, with long curly black hair that fell below her shoulder blades. Her eyes were a sparkling shade of steel grey and always seemed to radiate happiness. She was a voluptuous woman who was comfortable with, and proud of her femininity; one of those women who would always catch any man's attention, but was never smug about her attractiveness.

'Aaron Abraham, you're better looking every time I see you. If I were thirty years younger that young lady of yours would have some competition!' She reached out and embraced Aaron, her hugs were always welcoming and motherly. 'Henry called and said that the job here was going to take some time, so I decided to catch the next available ship here and surprise you both. Now, where is that man of mine? He has some intense making up to do, and I do mean intense.' They both laughed and Aaron planted an affectionate kiss on her cheek.

'He's on Earth... helping Petra sort out the legal issues with her inheritance and our marriage.'

Aaron sounded flat and this worried Jacinta. She had first met Aaron when Henry started working for him many years ago. He reminded her of a lost boy, so she made it her duty to mother him. As the friendship grew between Aaron and her husband, he became another member of the family. When he made Henry company Proctor, she could not have been more pleased. While the position did carry some considerable financial gains for them, she was mainly pleased about how these two worked together like Ying and Yang, it was a partnership made in heaven.

She smiled. 'Well, we better go there. I assume you won't mind giving an old lady a lift?'

'Old! Jacinta N'Gabo you will never be old and yes, I would welcome your company... follow me.' Aaron turned and led her through the airlock doors, down the ramp, and finally to Junior. 'You can sit at any of the Stations, or I can show you to a cabin if you prefer?'

'No, I have never been on the Bridge of a space ship, this will be interesting.' She sat at the sensor console.

'What about your luggage?'

'It will be waiting in Perth when we arrive, I sent it on ahead.' She smiled, sheepishly.

'What ship brought you here?'

'Albatross; that young Steve Harris is such a lovely boy.' Jacinta's smile was laced with wicked innuendo.

Aaron laughed. 'And I bet you had him wrapped around your little finger?'

'Why Aaron Abraham, I have no idea what you mean.' As she spoke, she felt something brush against her legs. 'So, this is the famous Prince!' She bent down and picked him up. 'My, what a lovely boy you are.' She set about stroking the now purring feline.

Aaron smiled and started working the initialization sequence - *trust that cat to find a soft touch*, he thought. He could have let George do it all but he desperately needed to feel a ship under his control again, even if only for a short time. Junior floated a few centimetres off the hangar floor as Aaron waited for permission to exit the dock. Finally, it was granted and he wasted no time in leaving. As he worked his way through the line of vessels waiting to access the portal, he glanced at the time readout on his console, almost twelve hundred hours. To facilitate the smooth operation of the portal in both directions a timetable had been devised and was rigidly enforced.

At 12:00 and 24:00 hours, the direction of traffic would change, giving equal priority to both, with thirty ships waiting to transit; the time would go very quickly.

' The portal business is booming,' Jacinta remarked.

It had been agreed, by all parties, that there would be a charge to transit the portal. Henry had been the one to work out the maths. The charge was based on many variables: energy use, maintenance, personnel, and a myriad of other inputs. Everyone who wanted to travel to, or trade with other realms, paid the charge.

What was not common knowledge though, was an initial legal problem with Coalition law. As the Cordoba Corporation owned the portal and they were being pursued for their involvement in the rebellion, the legal eagles had determined that the portal could not be used, without the express permission of Antonio Cordoba, or the Coalition Court of Justice. In the end, Jeff and Aaron had purchased the portal from Antonio; for a considerable sum. This meant that the new operation was a private undertaking without any official government support and, while Jacinta was correct - business **was** booming - the costs were similarly huge.

As part of Henry's agreement with Aaron, he had a ten percent share of all business operations--ten percent of the profit, and ten percent of any loss. So far this arrangement had made Henry and Jacinta quite wealthy, something that made Aaron very happy. Not only because it meant that he also had benefited, but mainly because he considered them his family and to see them and their two daughters doing well was one of his greatest joys.

'Yes you could say it has potential,' Aaron changed the subject, 'by the way, how are my two goddaughters?'

'They never stop fighting but try and intervene? Well, I'd rather fight a Zandian Sand Cat than referee them.'

'No, not my two gorgeous little girls? I don't believe it.' Aaron baited her.

'Gorgeous... ha! Tell you what I'll do for you, I'll send them for a little holiday with Uncle Aaron; after two weeks you can tell me just how gorgeous they are.'

Aaron laughed and changed the subject. 'I've programmed a couple of jumps to speed up our trip; the autopilot can take over for a while. I'm hungry, would you like some dinner?'

Jacinta agreed and they went to the galley to discover what had been loaded in the way of food. His mood lightened as he worked quickly to rustle up a fresh Caesar salad, accompanied by some beautiful Argosan lake salmon. He always found cooking to be a distraction; the process and the aromas coupled to brighten his mood. Jacinta helped, telling him about the girls and their exploits.

Mala, the eldest, was currently studying for her final senior school exams and was in the habit of locking herself away for days at a time only to surface with accusations of being starved and neglected and, after a usually dramatic entrance, proceeded to eat everything she could find and then disappear again.

Corrie was almost the opposite. She was an action junkie always doing something that her mother was sure was going to kill her. 'You know Corrie wants to be like you, she wants to go into space and become a trader.' Jacinta concluded.

'A great plan... she does have an aptitude for it and she thinks on the fly. I could help her, we could give her an internship, let her try out the life. If she works out we could sponsor her into the Academy,' Aaron pondered.

'Not with you, though. You're a push over, they both work you around their little fingers!' Jacinta laughed.

'No,' I was thinking of Katie Albrecht, she now captains the Condor and she'd be an excellent role model for Corrie, but we still have her doting dad to deal with.' Aaron knew how protective Henry was of his two daughters; one of them going into space - well it would be a hard sell. The rest of the trip was spent reminiscing and planning how to approach Henry. Aaron's mood had improved and laughter filled the dining area.

Approaching Saturn orbit, Captain, George's voice interrupted their fun.

'OK I'm coming back,' Aaron turned to his guest. 'Sorry to end this, I'm glad you decided to drop in, you always make happy.' He bent down and gently kissed Jacinta on the top of her head 'You always dig me out of a foul mood.'

On the Bridge Aaron busied himself checking the reinsertion details although there was nothing he could do; it was habit that made him do it.

Two minutes later, they re-entered normal space exactly where they should. Saturn was half a million kilometres to their starboard side and about ten degrees above their horizon. No matter how many times he arrived here it always filled him with awe. There was no base on the planet itself, only the Coalition Station in permanent orbit. He hailed it and gave their flight plan and manifest - standard protocol when entering the Solar System.

The base was now the initial control point for all vessels transiting the area and controlled all flight paths; clearance could take a while. Today, however, the response was quick, a flight path and speed restriction were transmitted. They were approximately 1.6 billion kilometres from Earth and their flight speed was authorized at point six of light. Aaron did the calculations quickly; allowing for acceleration and deceleration they should arrive in Earth orbit in under three hours.

He chuckled to himself - they had travelled fifty-three light-years in a little over an hour and this little hop was going to take three times as long; he loved the Eldoran jump drive. He busied himself setting the course and drive parameters into the nav and flight controls and didn't notice Jacinta enter the Bridge.

'How long to Earth?'

'Unfortunately three hours or thereabout. If you want to rest use one of the guest cabins, they have clothing dispensers so you can arrive in something new, if you want.' Aaron proposed.

'Thanks, a new outfit might be what I need, to show that man of mine what he's been missing!' She turned and left the Bridge leaving Aaron to his tasks.

When satisfied with the flight program, Aaron simply touched the 'execute' icon on the Command Console and Junior altered course and accelerated toward Earth, the Bridge door was closed so he could indulge in one of his passions; twentieth-century rock music.

Twenty minutes later he was enjoying his favourite guitar riff when the music when George's voice, broke through the music. *We are being hailed by Mondrac.* Aaron shut the music off and answered the hail.

'Mondrac, that was quick,'

My friend do you know Jok-Tar's whereabouts?

'Not at the moment but I should see him in a few hours, I believe he is on Earth. Why?'

Could you arrange for him to examine the damage from the data you sent me?

'I can try, but our engineers will be looking into it.' Aaron's interest was rising.

I understand, but they will not be looking for what I need. I am sending through some details of what I want him to look for... it will be unintelligible to your engineers, but Jok-Tar knows what to look for.

'Sounds ominous.'

It may be nothing, but I think we should rule out every possibility. Mondrac sounded uneasy.

'OK send the data, I'll make the arrangements.' Aaron agreed, realizing that Mondrac would not be drawn further on this issue.

Thank you, it may be nothing but we need to make certain.

Mondrac cut the link.

Aaron recorded the data as it was received, then copied it to a data-pad for Jok-Tar, and went back to his music, the cat purring contentedly on his lap.

***

Mondrac sat and stared at the comm unit, his thoughts confused and worried. If he was correct, then things were worse than anyone suspected. He knew what his next move must be but still, he hesitated, silently arguing with himself. He was so engrossed in his thoughts he didn't hear his half-brother enter.

'Mondrac, why are you so troubled?'

Mondrac stood and pointed to the view screen, at the far end of the room.

'Brother, this is what has me so concerned.' He brought up the data that Aaron had sent him. Together they stood and studied the simulation Mondrac had devised from the information.

When it finished, the head of the Tar clan turned. 'This cannot be correct... there must be a mistake!'

'I agree so I have sent a message to Jok-Tar asking him to inspect the source, hopefully, A-Bra-Ham will be able to arrange it. Until that transpires I can still make some inquiries myself; maybe I can find some more acceptable explanation.' They continued to watch the screen for a few more minutes until Eldrac-Tar took his leave and left.

'No time to hesitate, now.' Mondrac spoke aloud to himself and went back to the comm unit.

He selected a contact and requested communication. It took almost half an hour for the comm to be initiated, but finally, he was rewarded by the face of an old friend and sometime adversary appearing on the view screen.

'Kyralan, old friend, it is good to consult with you again.'

The face now on the screen was old. Kyralan was a Galdoran equivalent to Mondrac, he traded information. Since the rebellion led by Zarof had failed, he was now more of an elder statesman, trying to lead his people back from the precipice of civil war. While he had no official capacity, he was still the one Galdor turned to for guidance.

His tired face studied Mondrac before he spoke. *Mondrac, I am relieved you still can call me old friend, after all we have shared and faced lately.*

Like all Galdorans, Kyralan had a canine-like face, a long nose, which resembled a snout, and eyes set above it facing forward. Mondrac remembered him having dark brown hair, but now it was quite grey; another sign of his advancing years.

To what do I owe this call?

'We may have some problems, in another realm. I ask that you to view some data and give me your insight into what it may mean. Can you do that?'

Kyralan studied the image on his screen. Mondrac had been a solid friend and valued contact for many years; he had always been forthright in all his dealings but he sensed something different in this request.

I will be direct, Mondrac; what are you not telling me?

'Only what I do not know myself. The information I am acting on is limited... I only suspect things and, as we both are well aware, suspicion is not evidence or truth. The data appears to be from an encounter in the Twelfth Realm. What that encounter was or who was involved, in truth I do not know. All I have are the readings contained in the data are familiar... only I cannot recall where I have seen this before and, as I believe you have much more experience in matters of this kind; I thought you may be able to clear the issue for me.' Mondrac waited for a reply.

Kyralan considered the request and finally agreed; Mondrac transmitted the data and they agreed to talk again in two cycles, Galdoran time - approximately three days Earth time.

Jason and Amanda Abraham had decided to return to Caprica, but a last minute problem called for Jason to meet with some off-world company executives. Amanda left Jason at Jupiter Station and continued with the journey.

It had been six months since she had last visited. She and Jason had decided that, for the foreseeable future, they would be staying on Earth so some things needed to be organised. Her cats for one - she missed them and had decided to bring them back to Earth - after all they had travelled extensively with them over the years. The quarantine issues had been finalized and she had just sent them up to the ship. Her final activity was to visit the maintenance agent who was managing their small estate. That meeting only took half an hour and she called the ship as she left that office. Captain Starling answered.

'I am going to the shuttle pad now, Captain. We can leave as soon as you are ready.' She informed the ship.

Of course, Ma'am... we'll be ready when you arrive. The comm unit replied. Amanda arrived at the pad, boarded her shuttle, and left the planet. She had mixed feelings, Caprica had always been her dream retirement destination but, as is sometimes the case, the dream was better than reality. Still, they could always return for a vacation.

Captain Jennifer Starling had been in charge of Jason and Amanda's yacht for twenty years and considered it to be the best job she had ever had. Her employers were first-class; treating their employees like family - every member of the crew felt the same. The ship itself, while classified as a yacht, was a converted military frigate. It still had all the weapons and defensive systems, something most crews on private yachts never experienced.

Starling was in her quarters, dressing for duty when the voice of second in command, Arnold Coutriver, hailed her.

Mrs. Abraham's shuttle is on final approach.

'Thanks, Arnie, I'll meet her. We leave as soon as she is settled,' Jennifer said as she walked toward the door. She took the pod to the shuttle bay, arriving as Amanda's shuttle was locked into its berth. The bay doors closed and the ship started to move out of orbit. Amanda walked into the waiting room.

'Jennifer, we're already underway?'

'Yes, ma'am... orbit control has given clearance... someone is arriving shortly and I got the impression that an armed private vessel was not what they wanted to show.'

Caprica was one of three **Peace Planets**. When it had been founded, a policy of zero tolerance to weapons was enshrined in the articles of formation. There were no planetary defences and no vessel was allowed to hold active weapons on board. The latter rule had been relaxed, somewhat, over the years as a number of the retirees that called Caprica home, had armed yachts--so long as the weapons were offline, there was no issue.

'Must be something big, I wonder who could be coming here?'

'We might just catch a glimpse of them. The outer marker is still ten minutes away. Come to the Bridge, we'll use the main view screen, maybe we can find out who all the fuss is about,' Jennifer said conspiratorially.

They took the pod to the Bridge where Jennifer set the view screen to watch the planet. Seven minutes later they were almost at the outer mark when, suddenly five substantial ships dropped out of Displacement, above Caprica.

Almost instantly they started bombarding the planet, huge energy blasts ripped through the atmosphere, smashing into buildings, seemingly at random. The destruction was massive; buildings collapsed; fires started and thousands died in the first attack.

'Jennifer, what's happening,' Amanda cried, 'who's doing

this?' Starling was busy trying to focus on the ships - she wanted to catch their markings, their identity would be necessary for Space Corps to chase them down.

'I don't know, Arnie how long till we can initiate a wormhole?'

'Seven minutes, Skipper.'

'We may not have that long, sound Battle Stations.' One of the ships was altering course toward them. The interior of the ship suddenly changed to red as Battle Stations was called. Although this was a private yacht, Starling still drilled her crew like the military, forty seconds later all Stations were ready, shields were energized and weapons powered up.

'Skipper they're firing!' Coutriver exclaimed.

Three torpedos slashed across space between the two ships, the shields operated perfectly, the torpedos detonating harmlessly, but the attacking ship was overtaking them, rapidly.

Amanda was transfixed, staring at the screen. The ships were making another run on the planet. 'Jennifer we've got to do something, we can't run while all those people are being killed. We have to help.' She called out.

'Sorry ma'am, I have to ensure your safety, otherwise, I answer to your husband.' Starling knew she was in a bad place.

'If we don't do something, you'll answer to me.' Amanda's tone stopped Jennifer cold. 'Now turn around and **attack that damn ship**, at least we can give them a bloody nose.'

Starling stopped and turned to Amanda; her eyes said it all, 'Yes ma'am. Weapons, do you have a firing solution?'

'Yes, Skipper, come to course one-eight-five by zero-three-three... they still haven't raised their shields.' The reply came from the youngest member of the crew.

'Navigator, change course,' the ship started to change its heading immediately. 'Weapons, fire at will.' Starling ordered.

Ten seconds later, the young officer, Michael Galloway, tapped his console and a full spread of six torpedos shot out of their tubes - moments later they impacted the enemy vessel. The result was better than they could have anticipated, the forward section of the ship was torn apart, the ship started to yaw as Galloway sent a second salvo, of three, toward it. This time he hit the engineering section and that ended its life.

'Well done young man. Now Jennifer, let's find another target.' Amanda seemed to be enjoying herself.

Starling powered the Displacement drive down and turned the ship back toward Caprica; all but one of the other ships had disappeared. 'Full sensor sweep' she called as a second attacking ship changed course and turned to face them; this one was raising its shields. Galloway locked his target and fired the forward blasters; they lit up the shields brilliantly.

'Their shields are holding, Captain.' He said.

'Keep firing... they can't last long.' Starling was beginning to enjoy the challenge of battle.

Galloway obeyed, this time with blasters and their ion cannon, the opponent returned fire, their blasters flaring brilliantly on the yacht's shield wall. The space between the two ships was sizzling with the amount of energy being unleashed.

'Our shields are holding at seventy percent.' Galloway called.

Locked in a deadly ballet, the two ships frolicked around each other, looking for any advantage. Ducking, weaving, zigging and zagging, engaged in a constant bizarre dance; one that could end in death and destruction in an instant.

'Keep firing,' Starling called back.

Inevitably one had to lose this battle - their opponent finally zigged when he should have zagged and exposed his weakest shield point - the aft section of his ship. Galloway seized the opportunity and tilted the scale in their favour with another spread of torpedos. Of the six, four were stopped by the shields, but the other two broke through. One hit aft of the Bridge, the other forward of engineering, but that was enough. The ship lost directional control and started rolling and its shields were now down. Even though their adversary was all but defenceless, Galloway fired another three torpedos. All three found their mark... finishing the battle decisively.

'Arnie, where is the next one, give me a full sensor sweep.' Starling called.

'They're gone,' Coutriver sounded uncertain with his answer.

'Contact the planet. Find out what we can do to help.' Starling was already programming the emergency hail.

All ships, all ships. This is CPV Charlotte calling all ships. Mayday; mayday... We are in Caprica orbit... the planet has been attacked with possible severe damage. We request all ships respond. Mayday: Mayday. The call was then put on an automated emergency transmit, it would keep being sent until she cancelled it.

***

Aaron's music was interrupted, again. *An emergency mayday has been received*, George's voice said *from CPV Charlotte, on Caprica.*

Aaron was dumbfounded... Charlotte was his father's yacht but he was on Earth, 'George, open a channel to them,' he called. George complied and opened the comms to Charlotte.

'Charlotte, this is FTS Condor Junior, please respond' Aaron waited for a response, 'George, what is the comm dwell?'

Approximately 35 seconds.' Aaron thought as he watched the time, intently. After 40 seconds he repeated his hail, again he waited. Another 40 seconds and he tried again, this time he got his response.

FTS Condor junior, this is Charlotte, we need help. Where are you?' Starling replied, her voice clearly showing the stress of the moment.

'Starling, this is Aaron Abraham, where we are, is unimportant, what's going on?'

Captain, we were leaving Caprica when a total of five ships materialized and started strafing the planet, it's bad... can you help? She had just finished when another voice came on the comm.

Aaron immediately recognized his mother, *Aaron; am I glad to hear your voice, now listen and don't interrupt. We need medical and rescue assistance and a few of the Coalition's warships won't go astray either.*

'Yes I understand, but what are you doing there, what happened?'

Don't worry about that, start things moving. Amanda snapped and cut the comm link.

'George, contact Space Corps... tell them what we know and get them moving.' Aaron instructed as he started calculations for a jump to Caprica - he needed to change course for the best insertion point. He set the program into the nav system and pressed the execute icon. The ship responded immediately, accelerating and changing course.

'CPV Charlotte, this is Condor Junior, please respond.' He called into the comm.

Junior this is Charlotte, go ahead.

'Charlotte, we have sent information to Space Corps and are awaiting their response. We have altered course and should be with you in about ninety minutes, do you copy?'

Junior, this is Charlotte. We copy. Thank heavens you're so close.' Starling sounded relieved.

George's voice entered Aaron's head. *This jump is incredibly deep, are you sure you want to do it?* He was correct, to reach Caprica so quickly, Aaron was planning a very deep subspace jump which would take them close to the null point - the point of no return.

Inter-realm travel depended on it, null was the point where all realms intersected and had to be crossed to transit between them. This was always done with utmost precision, the slightest mistake, and you could end up somewhere totally different from where you intended - many ships and lives had been lost this way. What Aaron planned, was to drop deep, almost to the null interface, and back out again - risky, but he was confident he could do it. He rechecked his calcs and sat back.

Condor Junior, this is Captain Kaddin of the Krell Imperial naval vessel, Roharg, can we assist?

'Roharg, this is Junior. Kaddin what is your disposition?'

We can be on-site in less than two earth hours, can you use our assistance?' Like Junior, Roharg had been equipped with the Eldoran jump drive as part of the agreement with the Eldoran Council. Two hours meant they were probably the closest help available.

'Thank you, Kaddin. Your assistance will be invaluable. I'll be there when you arrive.'

Things were looking better, now. Roharg was the Emperor's flagship and had a fully equipped medical centre, something Aaron was certain they would need.

Jacinta stepped back on the Bridge, 'What's going on? I was nearly thrown out of the bath when we changed course!'

'A problem on Caprica... the planet has been shot up by someone and, my mother's there. I've changed course so we can assist - looks like Henry's getting a reprieve on his making up!' Aaron tried to make the moment light, but failed.

'What do you mean shot up, is anyone hurt?'

'I don't know, but we are possibly the closest ship. Sorry for the delay.' He felt bad but, his mother's safety was paramount in his mind.

'Aaron Abraham, I may not be a star ship captain but I know a little about astrogation. We are in Earth's solar system, at Displacement eighteen Caprica is what, six days away...' her voice trailed off, 'we're not using Displacement... are we using that new jump drive?'

'Yes, we'll be there in a little under ninety minutes,' Aaron said as they both felt the ship start its deceleration, 'we'll jump in eight minutes. You might want to sit down... it can be a bit unnerving, the first time.' He didn't explain how deep the jump was going to be or the risks that posed, he hoped he'd got it right. Eight minutes later the jump drive energized and the view screen went black - no turning back now.

'So this is what subspace is like?' Jacinta thought out loud.

'More or less... black and empty,' Aaron was almost dismissive, his mind elsewhere.

'OK, what is your plan, when we arrive?' Jacinta stood, hands-on-hips, staring at Aaron.

'I honestly don't know. I haven't thought that far ahead.'

'Well, top marks as a concerned son, but I would say an F in organization. Aaron, they'll need medical help... don't forget I wasn't always a wife and mother; I am a qualified Med-tech. What facilities does this boat have?'

'Not much, we have a small infirmary, just aft of the cabins, but it's only designed to serve the crew, no more than ten. I think it only has two beds.'

'I don't care about beds, what about medical supplies, what do you have?' She was getting feisty now.

"Again, I don't know. Maybe we should go and look.' They left the Bridge and headed to the infirmary. It turned out to be very well stocked with everything she thought would be needed.

Jacinta was puzzled, 'you've got enough here for a ship ten times as big, why?'

'Better ask your, husband, he purchased all the gear in here... I think he got a package deal when we built Condor. I remember him saying we got two of everything.'

For the better part of an hour they catalogued the inventory, their work was interrupted by an alarm, five minutes till reinsertion to normal space.

The moment of truth, Aaron thought, *if I got it wrong who knows where we'll be*. The seconds slowly counted off, the timer on the view screen. As the counter reached zero, he felt the familiar static electricity and then they reinserted back into normal space.

Aaron waited for the view screen to return. Finally there, above them was a planet. The nav data cleared and confirmed they had indeed arrived at Caprica, he wasted no time in hailing Charlotte.

Starling answered and told Aaron his mother had taken some of her crew and two shuttles and gone to the surface, to help where she could. Charlotte had remained in orbit in case the attacking force returned.

'You did an excellent job, Captain,' Aaron commended Starling, 'two of them down and no damage... I'm impressed, pretty good for a pleasure boat Skipper... well done.'

I'm not too sure... I don't think Mister Abraham will be too pleased. I'm supposed to look after his wife.

'I take it Mother was insistent about helping?'

Yes, very much so. Starling appeared to be worried at her actions.

'Then don't worry, she'll handle him. Again, fantastic job... I'm going to take Junior down to the surface... we have medical supplies and my passenger is a Med-tech. Oh, by the way, there will be a Krell cruiser arriving soon... the Roharg, Captain Kaddin is commanding. They have a full medical facility and personnel... Junior out,' Aaron cut the comm, and set the yacht on a fast descent, time to find out how effective Tocmal's new coating really was.

***

Junior's message was received at Space Corps' Headquarters in Perth. The young ensign, who received it, logged it and placed a copy in Admiral Abraham's tray. It sat there for nearly two hours before anyone noticed it.

Lieutenant Brogan, one of the new attaches to the senior staff, picked it up and decided to quickly scan it. Admiral Abraham was not back at HQ for several days, and he wanted to make sure any important issues were dealt with. His blood ran cold when he read the contents, 'what fuckwit received this?'

The ensign looked around 'I did, sir. Is there a problem?' he said quietly.

'Did you bother to read it?' The lieutenant was pissed now, 'There has been an attack on one of the Peace Planets, and all you do is file it?' He reached for the comm unit and called Admiral Grogan, when he answered, the Lieutenant read the message - the silence on the other end of the comm said it all.

40

Finally, Grogan spoke, quietly 'Lieutenant, I'm on my way down. Contact Admiral Abraham and inform him of the situation.' Sam stood and almost ran to his door, but stopped at his secretary's desk. 'Captain, call the President and route the call to my private link, I'm going to the Ops centre.'

There had never been an attack on one of the Peace Planets. They were neutral ground, totally unarmed, and, as the name implied, peaceful. Sam was entering the Ops centre when the President's call came through.

'Mister President, there has been an attack on Caprica... I don't know the details yet... but I hope to know more very soon. I thought you should be informed.'

Thank you, Admiral. I will call senior members of the Council to the chamber. You can contact us there when you know more. Malik closed the link. The next call was going to be worse - he selected the code for Jason Abraham and initiated the link.

Jason was sitting at his desk when the call came through, he recognized Sam's code and accepted the call, 'Hello, Sam. I wasn't expecting to hear from you until Friday,' Jason said.

'Jason... I... umm...' Sam stumbled for the right words, 'Caprica has been attacked... it appears that Amanda is still there. Aaron's on his way... he should be there by now... that's all I know.' Grogan's voice was edged with concern.

What do you mean, an attack? Jason fired back.

'I don't know... Aaron's information came from Charlotte... evidently five ships, origin unknown, materialized above the planet and strafed the surface. We have no more info than that, sorry.' Sam felt helpless, he needed more information, but nothing more had come through.

Space Corps from ECS Cutlass, respond. It was JT's shuttle, now Sam had another issue, how to keep his new Admiral where he needed him, at HQ.

'Cutlass this is Admiral Grogan... location?' Sam was biding time, trying to work out what to say.

We,re about ten mintes from Earth, what's the flap about?

Sam explained to JT what he knew.

Admiral, I believe that Condor is approaching Jupiter, we could divert her here; that way we have a much faster response.

'Good idea, you arrange it and meet me in Ops when you land; Grogan out,' Sam said, relief etched into his face. The minutes ticked slowly by.

Ten minutes later the ensign called out, 'Sir, we're getting something from Caprica.'

'On the screen,' Grogan called. What was displayed was horrific. Barton, the largest city on Caprica, was a mass of rubble and debris, fires everywhere. The footage was coming from a drone that Aaron had sent to reconnoitre the damage - it was the only way he could stop his mother from diving headfirst into the mess. The scene changed and panned out over the countryside, many houses and estates had sustained damage, but the one the drone now concentrated on had been obliterated.

This is Aaron Abraham, on Caprica. This drone is surveying the damage and, as you can see, the city is devastated. We don't know how many are dead or injured, but we assume it will be millions. The Roharg has arrived and we're setting up a field hospital, but what we need urgently is search and rescue people and equipment, heavy lifting and earth moving gear. Roharg has dispatched its fighters so the planet should be well covered, should the attackers return. We've had a quick inspection of the two ships Charlotte destroyed and it appears that they were Tragarian Raiders. The transmission paused as the drone passed to another site. *Two other cities, Capricornia and Fitzgerald were also hit, the damage is much less but still significant. We'll try to get more information and report again, in one hour.*

Sam, and everyone in the room, sat and stared at the view screen. Finally, he turned to the Lieutenant 'Get me the disposition of all ships we have in the vicinity. Send this report to the Council... the President will want to see it.'

Then the ensign called 'Sir, Jason Abraham is calling.'

'Put him through.' Sam waited till the link was established, 'Jason, we have some news, not good but fortunately, I believe Amanda is fine.'

Excellent, I'm on my way... we may break a few flight regs... but you can sue me later. We'll be there in fifteen minutes. The link was cut.

By the time Jason arrived many things had happened. Omnicron had responded to the call for assistance - they were terraforming a small planetoid only two parsecs from Caprica. As luck would have it a new shipment of earth moving equipment had just arrived and hadn't even been unloaded - it was immediately diverted to assist. Three Freebooter ships were also reasonably close and altered their course to join the rescue mission.

Jason was escorted to the Ops centre as all this was happening. Seeing so much activity did nothing to quell his anxiety, fortunately his grandson arrived moments later.

'Jason,' Sam called, 'things are well underway. We have dispatched SAR teams and heavy equipment is due to arrive in a few hours. Aaron has arranged for several Freebooter ships to assist and Caprica civil emergency teams are starting to organize.'

'What about Amanda?'

'She's fine, my friend, organizing everyone; but what else would you expect?' Sam was grinning; both men knew what an organizer she was.

'Damn fool woman, she should have high tailed it out of there when she had the chance.'

'Then you can tell her that, Pop.' JT chimed in.

'Yeah, I'm going to tell her that!' Jason countered 'I think not, I like all my bits as they are.' He and JT laughed, knowing that Amanda would be extremely displeased, if they chided her over these actions. He turned to Grogan 'Do we know who attacked?'

Sam's face showed his concern as he brought images of the

damaged vessels on the screen, 'Look for yourselves,' He said, both JT and Jason were speechless.

'Not possible... Raiders have never come this far from the Bad Lands,' JT said quietly.

'That's why I want you out there. Condor is loading supplies and Captain Albrecht has agreed to take you both, so get moving... she is due to leave in an hour,' Sam ordered.

'Actually, I think Admiral Radchak should go... with all that is happening, I will be more useful here.'

'Agreed, make it happen.' Sam smiled inwardly, *only two days into the job and he is already thinking like an Admiral.*

***

The next two weeks were frantic, rescue teams worked around the clock desperately trying to locate any survivors. Barton was a total loss, nothing was left standing and survivors were few. Fitzgerald and Capricornia fared much better with only minimal damage, and their casualties were light with few fatalities. The Barton death toll was a different story, the initial estimate was two million, and still, no reason for the attack could be found.

Of all the estates surrounding Barton, only the Abraham compound was destroyed. The others had superficial damage only. Jason and Amanda spent the two weeks working with planetary officials, helping to coordinate rescue efforts. The remains of the two Raider ships were placed on a heavy transport and sent back to Star Base 602 for analysis - Sol accompanied them.

Aaron, Jason, and Amanda were sitting in the lounge area of Junior when Jacinta arrived back from the hospital, 'I don't think I can do much more,' she said, 'the locals are organized and, with all the Corps' personnel arriving over the last week, I'm now redundant.'

'We're the same,' Amanda added, 'the last two days I haven't had much to do, maybe we should go, let the pros handle things, now.' Aaron and Jason agreed and two hours later, Junior left Caprica orbit and jumped for Earth.

4

Two weeks passed very quickly, on Earth.

The initial relief for Caprica took days of constant effort - logistics had to be arranged and personnel transferred. Neither Sam nor JT got much sleep for that period, or for the remainder of the first week. The second week was spent answering the politician's questions - Sam was relieved to be able to delegate this to JT.

The trouble that JT ran into was the lack of concrete information. No reason for the attack could be ascertained and, despite an intense search, no trace of the three surviving ships could be found. Some of the more forthright representatives started to question the ability of the Corps, and its value. JT didn't let this go and had several pointed discussions with them regarding their inaction over the years and their constant trimming of budgets.

He made the point clear that if the Council had more foresight, an attack of this nature could have been avoided. If the Corps was stronger, JT argued, they may have been able to stop it before it happened. His point was taken and the critics eventually agreed that there needed to be a program of upgrading the fleet and personnel.

Sir, Admiral Abraham is here. Sam's adjutant announced over the intercom.

'Send him in.'

The door opened and JT entered. Sam was sitting in the lounge with Madam Collard opposite in one of the armchairs. 'Take a seat, John.'

'Thank you, sir, Good morning Madam Collard.' JT shook her hand.

'I believe that congratulations are in order?' she said.

'What for, Madam?'

'Young man, not everyone can handle Hiro Tanaka the way you did. I hear you even got him to agree to an increase in personnel numbers for the Corps. Believe me, that is quite an achievement. Well done.'

'Thank you Madam, but all I did was to point out the obvious.'

'You will learn that to some of our Councillors, the obvious can be extremely difficult to see. Now, Sam tells me you have some information I need to hear.' The next half hour was taken with JT giving her an impromptu briefing on the latest findings from the two ships they had at 602. They had managed to retrieve the data core from one, but it was heavily encrypted, so any information would take time. The best news was that they now had the nav data, unencrypted, so the initial starting point was now revealed.

'That is great news,' Madam Collard broke in excitedly. 'Now we can send a retaliatory force, really do some damage to these Raiders,' In the years he had known her, Sam had never seen Collard so excited about anything - she was always measured and contained.

JT shook his head. 'Not that easy Madam.' He stood and moved to the sideboard to pour himself a coffee, 'Anyone else?' Both declined so he came back, coffee in hand. He looked at Sam who simply nodded for him to continue.

'Madam, what I am about to tell you is classified and must remain so, for the moment.' He waited for this to register. 'Task force Paladin was sent to the Bad-Lands to trace Balerophon... you know this already,' Collard nodded. 'What hasn't been released, as yet, is that they ran into some very strong Raider forces. One ship was destroyed and the other three severely damaged; and by severely I mean **write-offs**.'

Madam Collard's face showed her shock at this revelation. Paladin was considered to be one of the Corps' strongest groups.

'How did this happen, why wasn't the Council informed?' she

demanded.

'How... we don't know. It appears that the Raiders had some highly advanced weapons and shields; we're looking into this, both here and in other realms. We suspect they may have come from either Galdor or Nileros but, we can't confirm this. Why didn't we inform the Council? That was my call and I still don't want it to be made general knowledge; CID requested we keep it in house, for the moment.' JT stopped, trying to gauge what was going on in her mind.

Collard smiled 'I take it that you don't consider me a security threat?'

'To be honest, Madam, I don't think anyone on the Council would be but, we must work with our intelligence guys... at least until we have more information.'

JT sat back, still trying to gauge her mood. Although he had met Madam Collard previously, she was still an enigma. She always played a complex game and held all her cards close to her chest. He couldn't find even the **slightest** tell.

'So the rumours of at least one Galdoran ship escaping into our realm are true?' she probed, gently.

Sam answered. 'Again, we don't know for sure. We suspect that may have happened but we have no concrete evidence, only conjecture, and suspicion. Out of all the protagonists in the battle last year, there are two people we can't account for and two ships. But, and I emphasize; we have no real evidence they are here... hell, they could be anywhere in the twelve realms.'

'So where is Paladin and what's happening with it?'

'Paladin is in a secure dock, our experts, and some from Eldora have gathered data... hopefully, we can decipher it all and find a way of defending our ships... the weapons they used against Paladin were incredible. So you can appreciate why this needs to remain classified.' Sam stared at Collard, an intensity JT hadn't seen in him before.

'Of course Admiral, she assured him. 'As the leader of the Council I have, at times, had sensitive information... I know the drill, gentlemen. Thank you for this; I look forward to my next briefing.' She stood, leaving both men in no doubt that she expected to be kept fully informed.

***

Junior reinserted into the Solar System 11.00 hours on Wednesday, April 8, 2922. Aaron contacted Jupiter Station and was ordered to dock - to file the correct flight plan and would be required to face a review board before he could continue to Earth.

'**Fucking bureaucrats**,' he yelled as the comm went dead. 'They don't get their bloody paperwork and they throw a hissy fit!'

'What's all the yelling about?' His mother spoke as she entered the Bridge, Aaron explained the delay.

'Jason, call someone and fix this - I will not be held up by stupid bureaucracy.'

'OK, OK...leave it with me.' He said as he left the Bridge. Fifteen minutes later Jupiter Station called with Junior's clearance and confirmed their priority course to Earth, complete with Displacement approval. Aaron wasted no time and set the coordinates into the nav computer. He punched the execute icon, Junior's Displacement drive energized and they left Jupiter quickly behind, as Jason returned to the Bridge.

'Who did you call, dad?'

'Well, I called Sam Grogan. He called Malik and Malik called someone else: situation resolved. Oh, by the way, all charges have been dropped.' Jason seemed to get some perverse pleasure out of the last few words.

'What do you mean... **charges**... what bloody charges?' Aaron fumed.

Jason chuckled, 'Evidently you changed course and left the Solar System without proper clearance; this displeased the commander on Jupiter Station. Anyway, doesn't matter now, all is resolved.'

'OK, Perth space port here we come.' Aaron was still seething at what had transpired. The trip to Earth was only twenty minutes, at Displacement 2, just enough time for Aaron to calm down, with deceleration, landing clearance, and other contingencies it took just over 45 minutes before they were on the ground. A ground car met them on the apron and transported them to the terminal. Here Jacinta and Aaron left to find her luggage and have it transferred to Junior, while Jason and Amanda were taken to Corps' HQ, at Sam Grogan's request.

They left the car at the entrance and were met by one of Sam's aides. She conveyed them to a secure section of the building and to a meeting room, where she offered them coffee and asked if they wanted any food. All this attention was making Jason uneasy, usually this much courtesy meant something bad was coming down.

The aide left and Sam entered the same moment. 'So glad to see you are safe, back here. How are you, Amanda?'

'I'm fine Sam, a little upset at the loss of the house; but furious that so many died. Do you have any answers?'

'None, as yet... but we're working on it,'

Standing in the doorway was Salim Malik, President of the Coalition. He walked into the room and greeted both Amanda and Jason. 'I am so glad that you were not harmed, Amanda, this was a terrible business,' he said sincerely.

Jason looked hard at the President, perplexed at his arrival 'Salim, we have known each other for a long time, what's really going on here? The President doesn't come to Perth to greet a couple of refugees'

'I'd hardly call you two refugees, but there is something I need to discuss with you, and I think you both need to hear it.' They all sat as Sam closed and sealed the door. 'Jason, Amanda, as you know there has been a bloody rebellion on Ummah... many of my people died. General Al'Hadi has restored order and routed most of the dissidents... we are trying to capture them as we speak.' He turned to Sam who simply nodded.

'The problem is with military rule, the General doesn't believe it is the right thing and, quite frankly, I agree. The ruling Council has been disbanded, a number of them were complicit in the rebellion, and the General has asked me to return and form a new government. He believes I am the only person who is acceptable to all factions.' Malik hesitated, trying to find the right words.

'But Salim, you still have 25 years as President, can't you find someone else to form the government?'

'No my friend... believe me, we have examined every aspect of this, there is no other option. I have consulted with several people, Madam Collard, the Admiral, and others; there is a simple solution... I need to name someone to replace me for the duration of my term.'

'Surely this is for the Council to decide?' Amanda inquired.

'No,' Sam entered the conversation. 'The constitution is clear... the President has the right, indeed the duty to choose his replacement, in an event like this. Unfortunately, there is no precedent... this is the first time we have had this situation.'

Malik held his hand up 'Please, allow me to finish,' he turned his attention toward the Abrahams. 'Jason, I am asking **you** to complete my term as President.' The room fell silent at his words.

Jason sat, dumbfounded. Finally, he spoke. 'Salim, I don't know what to say.'

'Do not answer now, you will need time to discuss this, both of you,' he glanced to both Amanda and Jason. 'But, I need an answer by Monday; I must give the Council my decision.'

'I understand,' Jason nodded, the enormity of the request filling his mind. 'This is something we need to discuss with our family as well. You will have an answer Monday, Salim.'

'Thank you; I will await your decision.' Malik said as he stood, 'I am truly grateful that you were unharmed, Amanda.' He turned and left the room; almost on cue Sam's aide called to say that Aaron was in the outer office.

'It's time to go,' Jason said as he took Amanda's arm. 'Sam, what are your thoughts?'

'They shouldn't matter but for the record, I think you would make an excellent President. You have experience with the Council, you are recognized on most colonies and you have the acumen for the job, the only issue is... do you want it? Only you can answer that.' Sam said as the door opened again, and they left the room.

The trip to Orange was a quiet one, Jason and Amanda went straight to a cabin and didn't come out until Aaron announced they were back at the compound.

***

Jeff took a taxi back to the Abracorp office - his trip to the construction dock had taken longer than he had planned. He paid the driver and took the elevator to his office, he still had a few things to finalize before he could leave. His secretary was at her desk when he entered. 'Chloe, why are you still here?' He noted the time was after 6 pm.

'Waiting for you... your father called earlier, looking for you, I told him where you were and he left, he seemed a bit upset.'

'With all he has been through in the last two weeks, I'm not surprised. Anyhow, off you go, enjoy the weekend. I have about half an hour and I'll be gone too, thanks Chloe,' he said as he went through to his office.

There had been a few design changes to the main reactor compartment on Galileo, it was now to be equipped with jump drive technology, and that's where the problem came from, and why he had to go to the dock. He called up the revised schematics and began his analysis. Only he couldn't get a handle on the problem so he sent the drawings to the holo-projector.

Maybe if I see it in three-D, I'll understand, he thought. The projector room was two floors down so he closed the console and locked his office, whatever happened he wasn't coming back here tonight.

As he entered the projector room he moved to the control desk. 'Computer, display Galileo reactor drawings Golf Romeo

51

one eight seven to one nine three and organize into a holographic simulation.' It only took the computer a few seconds to arrange the display; now before him was a ten percent sized image of the reactor room.

Still nothing. 'Computer, enlarge to thirty percent.' The image before him enlarged - now the problem was evident. Somewhere in the design process, somebody had drawn a bulkhead support running right through the **middle** of the reactor core. Jeff swore to himself - this simple, but obvious mistake would take several weeks to rectify.

'Computer enhance grid twelve and send this simulation to the design team with a **please explain**, also ask for the explanation to be on my desk no later than Tuesday morning. Sign the transmission **JT Abraham, Managing Director**.' Jeff noted the acknowledgment on the screen so he closed the console.

Someone's head was now on the block - this was a stupid mistake that shouldn't have happened, he shook his head in disbelief and took the elevator to the roof where the shuttle was parked. *Time to forget this week and go home*, Jeff smiled at this thought. While the Coalition Council had approved construction, Jeff couldn't shake the fear that, with all the new technology now becoming available, Galileo may be nothing more than an expensive white elephant.

***

Jeff's trip home was uneventful, mainly on autopilot. As he descended to his designated landing pad he identified five other vessels already parked. He recognized his brother's yacht and David's shuttle; the other two he assumed were Petra's and Salina's - the fifth, a new shuttle - one of Abracorp manufacture. But he was confused as to who it belonged to. It was painted in Coalition livery with the insignia of a Rear Admiral.

Wonder who the brass is, he thought as he settled his shuttle on the ground.

He left it parked on the apron, he was too tired to worry the ground staff over parking and, by the looks of things they had

52

plenty to do. He took the pod to the house and was greeted by laughter and the sound of popping champagne corks, Sonia had heard the pod arrive and met him as he exited.

'Welcome home, darling! We have some very exciting news.' She took his arm and guided him into the family sitting room... everyone was there, replete with a glass of champagne. JT stood as his father entered, still in his uniform - he walked over to Jeff.

'What's this?' Jeff touched the rank insignia on his son's collar. 'They will court martial you for impersonating an Admiral.'

'No impersonation, I'm now in command of Space Corps.'

Jeff shook his head. 'When did this happen... how did it happen?' He stopped and stared at his son. JT was different; somehow, he seemed a little... Jeff couldn't put his finger on it, but there **was** a difference. He held out his hand. 'Congratulations! Now you'd better tell your old man what this is all about.'

'Shortly,' JT laughed. 'Now I'm going to change... I only kept this on so mum could watch your reaction.' He was still laughing as he left the room. Jeff watched his son stride down the hall, still trying to figure out what had transpired.

He was interrupted by his father at his side. 'Jeff, can you and Sonia come with us, to your study. I need to discuss something with you.'

The four went across the wide entrance hall to Jeff's study. Jason closed the door before he proceeded to tell Sonia and Jeff what had happened in Perth. 'I have agreed to give him an answer by Monday.' He said as he finished his revelation.

'How do you feel about this, Mum?'

'I don't know, with all that's happened I don't know whether I'm coming or going. But, I do believe that your father would make a great President.'

Jeff moved to his sideboard, everyone else had a glass in their hand and he felt the need for a good belt. 'Whatever you decide Dad, we'll all support you... you know that.'

'But what about you, the workload, can you cope?'

'It really won't be that bad. The Manta project is rolling along on its own, now. We have some issues with Galileo, but that was to be expected. The other operations seem to be running smoothly, so I don't envisage any real problems. You will be missed, make no bones about it, but maybe this should take priority.' Jeff smiled at his father. 'Life certainly throws a few curve balls,' Jeff said, raising his glass in salute.

Amanda and Jason returned to the sitting room. As they entered, they saw Aaron, Petra, Henry, and Jacinta sitting to one side, deep in conversation - Aaron beckoned his father over.

'Dad,' he started, 'Henry thinks he has a solution to our problem, but we would appreciate your input.'

'OK, Henry, let's hear your answer?'

Henry took a couple of seconds to gather his thoughts and answered. 'Aaron's situation is quite clear... while he has citizenship of Argos and is, therefore a Freebooter, he also retains his Coalition citizenship by way of his Earth birthright... and as his affairs have been well managed, in both locations, he doesn't seem to have any problems.

'Petra, on the other hand, may have some issues. Her mother remained a citizen of Varga even though she lived most of her life on Argos. Petra was born on Argos and automatically was granted Argosan birthright, effectively making her a Freebooter citizen. Her father, Colin Mannix was born on Earth and remained a citizen of this planet, and the Coalition, all his life. As his daughter, Petra can claim Earth citizenship by way of parentage, but she also has Argosan and Vargan citizenship. I think there is a part of the Coalition Constitution that deals with this sort of issue but I can't seem to find it. You served on the Council, can you shed some light on where we go now, Jason?'

Jason smiled 'I know where you are coming from, and I think you are correct. Let me make a call, there is someone who will have the answer.' He stood and left the group.

As he reached the door Jeff and Sonia came back in; 'Jeff, I need to use your study for a couple of minutes.'

Jason closed the study door and placed his call. Almost immediately it was answered 'Graham, this is Jason Abraham, how are you?' He exchanged some small talk with the person on the other end before he got to business, 'Graham, I have a small constitutional issue I would like your take on.'

The person Jason called was Graham Argort, the same constitutional authority Malik had used in his Presidential deliberations. They spoke for nearly twenty minutes before the situation was clear.

Jason closed the conversation. 'As usual, Graham, your counsel has been invaluable. Can you please draft your answer, send it to me ASAP and your account to Abracorp, I will personally endorse it.'

They said their farewells and Jason returned to the sitting room, as the others were moving to the terrace for dinner. He caught Henry and spoke quietly to him. 'You were correct... there is a precedent... I will have the resolution shortly.'

Dinner was a buffet of cold meats, salads, and fruits. When everyone had their plates and had taken their seats, Jason spoke. 'Tonight has been interesting, to say the least. As I am still head of the family, I think we should discuss what has transpired.

'The most pressing issue is the pending wedding and a possible derailment of it because of Petra's inheritance. I have called Graham Argort on the matter and he has agreed to send us his interpretation of the constitutional issues. Don't worry,' he said raising his hands, seeing the collective concern on the faces around the table, 'there are precedents and he has the solution so the wedding can proceed as planned.' The news brought a collective sigh of relief; many months of planning and effort had gone into it, and a last-minute hitch was not what anyone wanted.

Jason paused and took a sip of water. 'The other issue is not so easy to fathom. President Malik has asked me to complete his term, as President. He believes he needs to go back to

Ummah and help rebuild, after the rebellion. Now, before you all start anything, we need to discuss this as a family as it will have implications for each of you if I accept.'

He sat and allowed the discussion to start - it ranged from one of enthusiasm to why bother, the personal views each held of politicians became evident. Finally, Jason had had enough.

'Thank you all for your input... it has been of no help at all, but at least you now understand the gravity of this decision. For Abracorp, I can see some difficult issues. I'll need to distance myself from all aspects of the company, so I won't be available for meetings or advice. Jeff, you need to understand this and make the necessary arrangements.'

Jeff nodded solemnly at his father's statement. He did indeed realize what this could mean and he wasn't too keen on the ramifications.

Jason sat down as Phillip entered the room. 'Mr. Abraham,' he spoke directly to Jason, 'you have a call from Mr. Argort, and he would like to speak with you, Aaron and Petra.' Jason excused himself from the table and beckoned the other two to follow him.

They entered the study and Jason accepted the call, the screen changed and Argort now filled it. He was an old man; some believed him to be as old as the Coalition. His body was thin and hunched as he sat in his wheelchair, his long grey hair hanging limply down his shoulders.

Jason greeted the image, 'Graham, thank you for responding so quickly.'

No need to thank me, yet. I have derived a solution and it will be sent to you, as requested. But I thought it might be a good idea to discuss the options, face to face. Argort began to summarize his findings. For the next half hour, they discussed the various options until finally agreeing on the most advantageous solution.

Petra's situation gave few problems to their coming marriage. Her father was born on Earth and her mother on Varga, both members of the Coalition and, even though Petra was a citizen of Argos, she could claim Coalition birthright from both parents.

Surprisingly Aaron was a real problem. He was, by birthright, a Coalition citizen but he had relinquished this when he became a Freebooter. Add to this the fact he had business operations on Coalition, Krell, and some non-aligned worlds, his citizenship could prove to be problematic. One redeeming factor was that, although he was now a citizen of Argos, he had never actually completed the formal change documentation required to completely rescind his Earth associations; as well he held the largest shareholding in Abracorp. This revelation stunned and astounded Aaron.

Argort's solution was simple - Aaron had to formally renew his Earth citizenship before any marriage being enacted. The issues that his Freebooter standing might raise were largely negated by Henry. Having a Proctor run his Argosan and other off-world operations meant he had no conflict of interest and even his trading operations were covered. Finally, it was decided that Argort would prepare the necessary documents; Aaron and Petra would meet him the following Monday and make the necessary authorizations and signatures, then Argort would file the documents. Any documents filed by Graham Argort were never held up by red tape, bureaucrats knew all too well the ramifications of that. They all thanked Argort for his efforts and the call ended.

'Dad, I don't understand how I came to own so much of Abracorp?' Aaron inquired as they walked to the study door.

'Maybe you should discuss that with your brother. You wait here... I'll send him in... believe me, you two have much to discuss.' Jason escorted Petra out of the room. Aaron nodded and closed the door behind them, he went to the sideboard and poured two glasses of brandy and waited for Jeff to appear. Moments later Jeff opened the door and came in. He took the offered glass and sat opposite his brother.

Jeff opened the conversation. 'Dad tells me you're confused

about your shareholding in the company?'

'Confused is an understatement. From the figures Argort has, I appear to own **forty percent**... as much as the rest of the family combined! How did that happen?'

'Simple. While you were gone your share of the profits kept building until it became a problem. I couldn't contact you and when we tried you didn't respond so we had a meeting and thrashed out a solution, Argort was the legal counsel we contracted, so everything was above board. I was granted power of attorney *in absentia*; we decided to invest your funds back into the company. You were issued shares per the value of your investment, plus we used any residual funds to purchase additional shares as they came available.

'The result is you are now the largest single shareholder of Abracorp. I was going to discuss this with you when you first came home but things got out of hand and there seemed to be bigger issues to sort out.' Jeff stopped and raised his glass. 'Now you know.'

Aaron shook his head in disbelief. 'Henry's going to have a fit. He has to give Argort a full accounting and valuation of our business operations off-world; this will set him off.'

'He just spent the last three days with David, so believe me; he knows, but we have a much more critical issue, the one we have both been avoiding... why we fought all those years ago.' Jeff began his recollection of the incident.

Thirty-eight years ago he had been approached by someone who claimed to have some information about wrongdoing by Aaron. Jeff decided to meet with this person who turned up with recorded images and documentation that suggested Aaron and Sonia were having an affair. They had met several times, surreptitiously in various places. There had been two meetings at the Hilton hotel in Sydney... both times Aaron had booked a room. There had been visits to several high-end merchants and finally the revelation that they had purchased something expensive from another merchant in Adelaide.

There was never any specific evidence, or proof, just enough information to raise Jeff's suspicion. Finally, after a particularly grinding week for both the brothers, Jeff had confronted Aaron and the fight had ensued. They had come to blows with both sporting black eyes for a week or two. This was when Aaron had left, vowing never to return. He had cleaned out his primary account and hopped on the first ship he could buy passage on, and disappeared.

'How could you even think I would do that to you, let alone believing Sonia would be part of it?' Aaron's voice echoed in the room.

'I don't know. I had been away a lot, you were always here and you and Sonia were so close. Then the so-called evidence I was shown, I'm sorry but I jumped to the wrong conclusions.' Jeff said quietly, obviously embarrassed by his mistake.

'You know what we were doing? Take a look on the mantle, what's there?'

Jeff let his eyes wander to the spot indicated, there on the mantle, was the model of his first command, **ECS Leeuwin**, during his tour with the Corps. The model was one of a kind, encased in a glass bottle made like one of the ancient ship-in-a-bottle models - except this one floated on a miniature anti-gravity field. Sonia had given it to him on the day he retired and took his position in the company, one week after his brother had left.

'We were meeting over **this**,' Aaron stood and walked to the fireplace, touching the item that filled the mantle, 'we wanted to have it made to celebrate. I had the contacts that could do it but Sonia wanted it to be a complete surprise.' Aaron almost spat the words.

'It took us six months to find the right person to do it,' Aaron continued, his voice noticeably calmer, 'and then we had to compile all the data he needed. We had to find all the components and have the power supply manufactured and certified. Yet all the time you thought we were having an affair?'

Aaron sat, seemingly deflated; '**Now** I understand.'

Jeff looked to his brother, sadness etched on his face. 'I know. I put it all together many years later, and found out what had truly happened... but it was too late. I don't know what else to say but believe me, there isn't a day that passes I don't wish I could change history, go back in time and give myself a good smack in the face.'

Aaron put his glass down, a half-smile crossing his lips 'I think I did that before I left.' They both had a chuckle at the comment. 'And even after all that you still did what you thought was best, with my holding. Maybe it wasn't all bad. I think I've become a better person because of all my travels and I wouldn't have met Petra if I'd stayed here. I think we should leave the past where it belongs, I only have one question, who was the person with the information?'

'Crompton, Anthony Crompton.'

Aaron smiled. 'So the lying prick was involved with the old black hat brigade.'

'I never met him, in person, so he doesn't know I sussed him out. One day we'll use that to our advantage, make him squirm and jump through our hoops.' Jeff said with conviction. He drained his glass and held his hand out. 'All I can do is apologize for being such an arsehole... I'm truly sorry.'

Aaron took his hand, 'forget it, the past is the past, we can't change it. The future is what we need to work on now; hang on... does Sonia know?'

'No, I've never had the guts to talk to her about it.'

'Probably best if she doesn't find out, she'd skin us both alive if she did.' Aaron stood and went to the door, 'Time to re-join the others.'

It was past 11.00 pm when Aaron and Petra bid the others goodnight, signalling that the evening was about to end. They now had one of the executive suites on the second floor.

Petra led Aaron to the door. 'I took some ideas from Condor, in here.' she said as she opened the door, waiting inside was

Prince; he stood on his back legs and stretched up to Petra. She reached down and picked the cat up, he settled instantly in her arms and started purring, 'OK, now for the tour.' She revealed.

She led Aaron through the apartment, which had been made up of two executive suites. They had two bedrooms, two bathrooms, a dining room, a full kitchen, study, lounge, and a sitting room. The latter overlooked the lake and would give them great sunrise views. The bathroom attached to their bedroom was sizeable; it had all the usual bits and a huge spa. 'Maybe you should fill the spa.' Petra suggested, her smile leaving no doubt what was on her mind.

Aaron complied and opened the taps. He moved to the bedroom, noticing a door at one side, he opened it and walked into a huge wardrobe and dressing area, already filled with clothes. 'You've been busy,' he said as he took in the number of clothes in the room.

'Don't be too sassy... half of what is there is yours, take a look.' Petra called from the lounge. Aaron took a long look at the contents and it was correct, almost half the space was taken by male clothes, 'After our soak, you need to try some on, make sure I got the size right.'

Aaron walked back to the bathroom, the spa was now full so he removed his clothes and stepped in. The water was perfect so he set the program and sat back to enjoy the sensation. He opened his eyes; Petra was standing at the side, naked with her hands on her hips 'When were you going to tell me it was ready?'

'I had to make sure it was perfect.' Aaron offered in his defence.

'Bullshit,' Petra protested as she stepped in. 'Now, how glad are you, to see me?' She moved over to Aaron and straddled him. She put her arms around his neck and gave him a long and passionate kiss. 'Quite a bit, from what I feel.' She tittered as she squirmed against him. 'So, my love, how much did you really miss me?'

Aaron thrust his hips upward, entering her vigorously 'This much' he moaned.

'Oh I think you need to miss me a lot more,' Petra whispered as she nipped his ear. 'But not so quickly.' She disengaged from Aaron and lay back in the water, the bubbles frothing around her. 'I think slow and long is what I need tonight.'

And that is what happened - they made love for the next two hours, in the tub and finally the bed. Eventually, they fell asleep in each other's arms in the early hours of Saturday morning.

It was early in the morning, on Eldora.

Mondrac was awakened by his communicator's insistent tone; he reached from his bed and activated it. Immediately the view screen was filled with the face of Kyralan; a grim and troubled looking Galdoran if ever Mondrac had seen one. 'A very early call, old friend... I take it that you have some urgent news,' he said as he rose.

Yes, I do, but I need to meet with you, to discuss it in person.

'Of course, where do you propose we meet?' Mondrac was intrigued and a little concerned; Kyralan was acting strangely indeed.

Tallos, in one cycle, can you be there?

Mondrac agreed and Kyralan cut the transmission.

Mondrac sat back, this was unlike Kyralan; his behaviour was cause for concern. He decided to call the dock master to reserve a ship for his journey when a small icon glowing at the bottom of the view screen, caught his eye. He tapped the icon, an encoded and encrypted message opened.

The encryption was a standard commercial version but the encoding he only used with one person and not for many, many years. His heart was filled with trepidation as he entered the code key and the message began to compile. The face of Kyralan again filled his screen.

My friend, please forgive my theatrics, but I believe we have opened a Sudris nest, with the data you sent me, so please disregard any conversation we have had. These words amused Mondrac, Sudris was a dangerous reptilian creature only found on Galdor. Like an earth snake it had an extremely venomous bite but, unlike snakes, it could fly. Kyralan was extremely phobic about these creatures. For him to even mention this was a testament to his perception of danger.

The message continued. *You must take the information in the file attached to this message to the Twelfth Realm; they must receive it urgently. I feel that their survival, and indeed ours may depend on it. Please be careful, what we have uncovered is far worse than I could have imagined.* Then the screen went blank.

Mondrac sat, bewildered. What could be so bad that it caused the reaction that he had just witnessed? *Kyralan is always so calm and measured.* The thoughts only further deepened his concern.

The file had automatically downloaded to Mondrac's data pad; he opened it and began to delve through the contents. Half an hour later he shook his head in disbelief. 'Is there no end to the stupidity and treachery of those two?' He said out loud. He knew he had to find Eldrac-Tar. Knowing where his brother spent most nights, he walked directly to Morlan-Tar's sleeping chamber and used the door annunciator to contact his half-brother.

A few seconds later, the door opened and Mondrac was admitted to the room. Morlan-Tar's sleeping chamber was divided into three sections; the first was the entry and reception area, replete with a lounge and various chairs for guests; Mondrac waited for his sibling to appear.

'Mondrac, you look wretched, what is wrong?' Eldrac-Tar observed as he entered the room.

Brother, I have received some information, information that must be brought to the Twelfth Realm with extreme urgency. I need a ship, one that will not raise suspicion... can you assist?'

Eldrac-Tar smiled, he knew exactly what Mondrac was asking. 'Of course, I will arrange it immediately, but why the urgency and secrecy?'

Mondrac answered solemnly. 'We thought the war for the Twelfth Realm was over, but we were wrong, it may have only just begun.'

These words brought a cold shiver to Eldrac-Tar's body; he simply nodded and beckoned Mondrac to follow. They walked in silence to the study where he busied himself at his console. Mondrac stood and took in the room; he was constantly amazed at how much influence the humans were having on his culture. This room was evidence, with many relics from Earth's history proudly on display.

Eldrac-Tar finished his work and stood, 'Your ship is arranged,' he declared as he turned the screen so that Mondrac could see the image. The ship was different from anything Eldora had constructed before. Instead of being an ovoid shape, it was long and sleek with wings that swept back and slightly up. 'This is our newest vessel, she has recently completed the final trials and passed every test, she will serve you well.'

'A different design... very different,' Mondrac noted.

'Yes, we went back through the ancient tomes of our past looking for inspiration, finally, it was an ancient human shape that took our eye, an old airliner, I think they called them. In its time it was revolutionary... the first supersonic passenger aircraft... Concord. We did make many changes to the design, but we were inspired by the basic shape, and here is the final product... Duramot.'

'You gave the ship a name?' Mondrac was surprised; Eldorans had not named inanimate objects for many millennia. 'Brother you are certainly adopting many human traits!'

'Yes, although we are a far more advanced species, I sometimes feel that it is we who are the children and humans the educators. It is all so fascinating,' Eldrac-Tar spoke enthusiastically. 'You should prepare for your journey... Duramot will arrive here shortly.'

Mondrac nodded and left the room. He collected the few items he would need for his journey and returned to the study; Eldrac-Tar was talking to someone sitting at his desk.

'Brother, this is Goran-Esk, Commander of the Duramot.' Eldrac-Tar introduced his guest.

Mondrac bowed slightly and replied in the traditional Eldoran manner. 'I, Mondrac, recognize you Goran-Esk. I hope my request of you is no imposition.'

Goran-Esk was slightly taller than Mondrac - his eyes were a deep blue, something uncommon in Eldorans. His hair was long, as was the tradition of Eldoran males, but was tied behind his head, something of a new fashion with younger males. 'It is no imposition, Mondrac. I welcome the opportunity to utilize my new vessel. Eldrac-Tar has informed me that you require some discretion in this journey; believe me, this new ship is exactly what you need.' He sounded confident, even slightly arrogant when he spoke of his ship.

'Trust me; it may be tested to its limits, so we need to exercise extreme caution.' Mondrac's voice was filled with trepidation. 'If our enemies discover what we are doing they will stop at **nothing** to contain this information. I hope your ship is as good as you say.'

The room fell silent, Goran-Esk gleaned that Mondrac was serious and he knew enough about the man to realize that if he was concerned, then everyone should be very wary.

'It is time for me to go,' Goran-Esk turned toward the door. 'I have to oversee the final preparations for our venture. I will see you tomorrow.'

***

Saturday, April 11, 2922, greeted everyone at Lucknow with low cloud cover; rain was forecast and eagerly anticipated. Earth's flirtation with weather control had proved to be disastrous and, once again, Mother Nature was in command. Part of Abracorp's agricultural business was the storage of enough water to drought-proof each operation, even so, rain was always a welcome event.

Not for JT - this morning he wanted to show Aaron how much progress he had made with restoring some of the old cars that had been found in the Bunker. He was fast realizing that with his new position, it would become even more difficult to give the project the time he wanted. He stood at the window, staring at the sky. 'Fucking weather,' he mumbled.

'That will be enough of that language, young man,' Amanda said as she entered the room.

'Sorry, Gran, I didn't hear you come in.'

'Don't worry; it won't rain until this afternoon. You'll still have all morning to play.' She went to the buffet that Phillip had laid for them, took a plate and added toast, bacon, and a generous helping of scrambled eggs. Next, she poured a cup of Earl Grey tea, added a slice of lemon to it, and sat at the table.

'We're not playing,' JT protested. 'The automobile is one of the most important developments in human history... it gave people the freedom to move far and wide... some even say it was responsible for the development of much of the interior of America and Australia. We must restore them for posterity,' he said passionately.

'If I remember my history it was also responsible for changes in morality and part of the cause of the baby boom in the 20th century,' Amanda baited her grandson.

'Gran, a bit rich, don't you think?' JT replied, indignantly. 'I didn't think you would discuss **that** sort of thing.'

Amanda laughed. 'Do you think your old Grandmother was some sort of vestal virgin? I can assure you, young man if I was you wouldn't be here today.' She was enjoying making JT squirm. 'I'm only kidding, but you must admit the fact that the car did give people other opportunities than mere transport. I believe you even have an old Sandman in your collection?'

'Yes, it was an example of what the surfing generation used to follow the surf and be able to rest in the back. A great idea that achieved a cult following.' JT sounded slightly pompous as he made his point.

'Did your research also reveal their more colloquial name?'

'What other colloquial name?' JT hadn't found any other reference in the manuals and advertising material he had found in the Bunker archives.

Amanda smiled. 'Where has education gone? **Shaggin'** wagon is what they were more commonly called... do you need me to tell you why?'

JT surrendered. 'No, I get the picture.'

'What picture?' Aaron asked as he and Petra walked into the room.

'I was educating your nephew in on the folk history of one of his new toys, that's all,' Amanda said, a wicked grin on her face. 'I take it you are going to play with them, this morning?'

Petra answered. 'You couldn't stop him even if you tried. Even I'm not enough of a distraction.'

One by one the rest of the family came to the table, except for Jason. JT posed the question, 'where's Pop?'

Amanda sat back and looked at everyone before she answered. 'He has a lot on his mind, he took one of the horses and left about 5.30 this morning, Phillip packed him some food, so he'll be OK. He needs some time to think.' Everyone was quiet, they all realized the weight of the decision Jason needed to make.

Aaron was the first to break the silence. 'OK JT, what's the agenda?' The rest of breakfast was taken up planning what they would do for the rest of the day.

With breakfast over, JT and Aaron left for the Bunker and a quick tour before taking a shuttle to Dubbo and JT's complex. The main house was set away from most of the other buildings, a modest five-bedroom dwelling that JT intended to live in when he got the chance. The other buildings were set up next to what JT called his race track; he explained that this was the most essential part of his plans.

JT and the design team had pored over old videos of car races and, somehow found several old plans for tracks. Like true zealots they devoured any information they could find on the subject. Finally, they had sat down with an architect who designed the track that was now nearing completion. It contained many features that JT had loved from the old videos including a fast banked corner section, flat sections, and even a six hundred metre mountain as part of the track. The mountain had been particularly taxing - permission to terraform to that extent had been incredibly difficult - but not impossible.

The surface of the track was the most troublesome part. In the old days, they used asphalt, a by-product of the petrochemical industry; but now with no such industry and no roads, it took some clever chemical engineering to develop an acceptable alternative. Finally, with all the approvals obtained, construction had commenced and was progressing well ahead of schedule.

JT was animated as he took Aaron on the tour. 'Down here, is Pit Straight. We will have all the different marques and teams housed here. All garages will be built in the old company styles and colours; everything will be as authentic as we can make it!'

Although it was still a construction site Aaron could picture what JT was aiming for and it would be impressive. 'Here's Gordon: Gordon, this is Aaron, I told you about him.'

Gordon Simpson was managing the operation for JT and was almost as obsessed with the result. 'Pleased to finally meet you... it seems you have a lot to answer for. According to John, you're the one who got him interested in these things.' Gordon offered his hand to Aaron. He wasn't a tall man but he was solidly built and his hands showed he was no stranger to working with them. He had brown hair and a boyish face, Aaron liked his first impression.

'Guilty as charged. You have done a fantastic job in such a short time.' Aaron was truly impressed with what had been achieved, especially when the bureaucratic problems they had faced were included in the mix. 'What sort of fuel are they allowing you to use?'

'Hydrogen... we're building new engines to work with hydrogen. We'll head over to the factory complex; you can see first-hand what we are doing.' Gordon ushered them to a boxy looking vehicle 'We'll take this; it was called a Sport Utility Vehicle, or **SUV**, back in the day. We've converted it to run on hydrogen... works bloody well too.'

They took their seats and Gordon started the engine - the sound was a muffled rumble and they could feel the vibration of the old engine through their seats. '6.5-litre diesel engine, we've done a bit to it,' he explained, 'added a second turbocharger and a few little tweaks... goes like a rocket.'

To prove his point, Gordon smashed the accelerator and the large vehicle responded, tyres smoking and screaming as it leaped away from the parking spot. Gordon had an almost evil grin on his face as he threw the big unit into a drift around the end of the garage site, caught it, and fed in more power. The factory was less than a kilometre away but Aaron thought it was the most exciting couple of minutes he'd ever had.

The factory was huge, over a square kilometre in one building, and one of five in the complex. 'So, what's the purpose of this?' he asked as they left the vehicle and walked into the factory entrance.

Gordon answered, 'this is where we will build the cars for the track, as well as restore the originals.'

Aaron was confused. 'I thought you would only be using the cars from the Bunker, why build new ones?'

'Bureaucracy, politics and red tape,' JT said as they walked through the enormous but empty area. They entered a room that was set up for meetings; a central table with ten chairs, a sideboard, and a wall mounted view screen. They took seats around the table.

'We ran into an almost impenetrable wall of bureaucratic posturing. The original vehicles are so rare that no-one would give any official approval to use them, so we decided to work the private ownership angle. That was shot down as, technically, they are all owned by Abracorp and it would take a full board meeting to sort it out; but then Dad stepped in and helped. Eventually, we were granted permission to run them for displays only, no actual track racing. It was Gordon who came up with the idea of building replicas and the project took off. The actual ownership of the originals is still being sorted; the lawyers are having a field day.

'Anyway back to where we are. We aren't allowed to use proper gasoline... pollution and all that... so we eventually came up with a solution; actually an old idea. For the original vehicles, and that includes the larger ones you know... trucks, cranes, and the others, we will use Biodiesel and for the cars ethanol, both made from plants. We only have authorization for 20,000 litres a year so we won't be able to run them much, probably only a couple of times a year. The race cars will run on hydrogen so we have no restrictions.'

'Why is it so important to go to these measures?' Aaron inquired. 'Surely having a few running would be enough; and why the race track?'

'That is where it gets interesting,' Gordon began as he opened a drawer on the sideboard. He produced a file which he passed over to Aaron.

'Apparently the economy of Earth is in a bit of a mess. Most colonies are mainly self-sufficient and, except for companies like Abracorp and Greenbach, not much is happening to generate income for the government. The Council believes we need to encourage more visitors to Earth... but why would people come **here**? Most people now want things that can be provided off-world, or by free space operations.

'When we were negotiating with the various bureaucracies, we were approached by some of the Council members who felt that this was an attraction that they could market to other worlds. What you have in that file is the result of our investigations and a proposal from Vision to develop vacation packages. Read it.'

Gordon sat back as Aaron opened the file and began to read. JT stood and left the room, returning shortly with a coffee pot and three mugs.

It took Aaron twenty minutes to digest all the information in the file. 'You certainly have done your homework, looks like a prospectus to me, though. What's the pitch?' He sat back in his chair, waiting for the others to respond.

JT spoke frankly, 'OK, there is a pitch. We need some capital input to finish everything. I've funded it to date but it is now becoming a financial strain... I don't have your resources. I thought that as you were always so passionate about cars, you would be interested.'

Aaron stared intensely at both of them. 'What's the current ownership, how much do you need, and what's in it for me?' JT and Gordon relaxed and both smiled, at his words. 'I didn't say I was in, I need to know details so I can decide.'

'Currently, I own 80%, Gordon has 10%, and the other 10% is held by a trust for employees.' JT took another file from the same drawer and handed it to Aaron. 'That details the financials and the capital requirements until project end. The second part is the ongoing commitment for the first two years; after that, we should begin to see positive cash flow.'

Aaron whistled softly. 'That's a bucket load of capital you need.' He read the numbers a second time. 'OK, **assuming** I am interested, what's in it for me?' He was deliberately pushing JT, trying to discover how astute he was.

JT passed another thin file over. 'The first sheet details our projections for the first five years, based on our discussions with the parties we have mentioned; I think this will show you the returns are strong. The second sheet is the share offer for your involvement.' He stopped - the pitch was over - it was now up to Aaron to peruse the final documents.

Aaron went over the documents again, carefully scrutinizing the details. Finally, he finished and closed the file. 'OK, I'm interested. But I'll need to run it by Henry; now how about the rest of the tour?'

The mood changed, everyone relaxed as they left the room and entered the factory. They boarded a small transport and weaved their way through the various production stations. Not all were manned as actual production hadn't started, but with the injection of more funds, this would change rapidly.

'Each vehicle will be a replica of the original,' Gordon said. 'While we will have some common parts, the important things will be replicated. Engines, transmissions... even suspensions will be copied from the originals, with some improvements in materials. Each vehicle should give the same drive and feel as the original.'

'I take it that's why there are so many interested in coming here, to drive one of these?' Aaron was genuine in his curiosity.

JT nodded in agreement. 'But before we go any further, I think you should see this.' They stepped off the transport and entered a smaller room. 'A simulator,' JT proclaimed, proudly. 'Before anyone can drive, they must pass this; and believe me, it is not easy. Want to try?'

'Why not,' Aaron's smile showed how keen he was.

'I'll run you through the basics,' Gordon said as Aaron took the seat. It wasn't as easy as it first appeared. Coordinating clutch, accelerator, gear changes, and steering was far more difficult than Aaron had thought – a few crashes testament to the problems that faced drivers of old. After half an hour he was more confident with his ability.

'I think I'm getting the hang of this!' He grinned from the cockpit of the simulator, 'I think I'm ready for more!'

'OK, you asked for it,' JT sniggered. 'This is a simulation of the track we are building. First let the simulator take you through a circuit, at a familiarizing speed, then we'll ramp it up to what the experts of old could do. After that, it's all yours, but remember; you'll feel the same g-forces that the real thing can produce, so be careful.'

JT was grinning like the proverbial cat; as he fed the program into the system. The track they were building had elements of some historic tracks. Daytona, one of the most famous of the old American tracks would be replicated in the centre of the complex, banked corners and all, and could be used as-is or incorporated into several other configurations. The mountain was a replica of Mount Panorama, old Australia's most famous track. The rest were parts taken from other old-Earth race tracks; when completed there would be over twenty kilometres that could be configured into many different circuits.

JT selected a fairly easy configuration and started the simulation. The track he chose was 3.2 kilometres long and had sixteen turns as well as two long, fast straights.

Aaron studied every detail on his slow familiarization lap. When he finished the speed built as the simulator took him through a hot lap at full race speed. This was different, Aaron was thrown around as the cornering speeds and g-forces were transferred through the cockpit. He watched every movement he could, memorizing brake points, turn-in points, and when the unit accelerated and braked.

In the end, JT spoke to him. 'Are you sure you're ready?'

'Sure, ready as I ever will be!'

'OK, watch the lights and when they turn green go for it,' JT called. This time he added the soundtrack to the simulation, at full race volume.

Aaron sat still, his right foot pressing the accelerator, bringing the engine to red line as the light turned yellow. Two seconds later it turned green; he dropped the clutch and the race was on.

He shifted up through the gears until he was at the first brake mark; downshifting as he braked hard. Too hard, he discovered as the simulator started to move into a slide. Aaron corrected and brought it back under control, accelerating through the corner.

The rest of the lap was much the same - untidy. Aaron's ears were ringing from the sound of the engine, transmission, and the protest from the tyres as he threw the simulator round the track. Finally, he was through the last corner and he slammed the accelerator to the floor and flat shifted through the gears till he shot over the finish line. He continued around the track again, simulating a cool-down lap. Finally, he stopped and the simulator went dark.

'How'd I go?' he called as he unbuckled the harness. Suddenly he felt pain - pain in his arms, his legs, and his back - more pain than he thought possible.

'Well if you were driving Gran to town, she would have been a little concerned. Take a look at the comparison,' JT handed him a data pad. The comparison showed the facts.

'How could I have been **that** slow' Aaron griped. 'I feel like I ran it on my own.'

'Now you can see why we will not offer anyone a drive... everyone must pass this first. You did pretty well; only fifteen seconds behind the base mark. A couple of days in this and you should be able to hold your own.' Gordon seemed impressed. 'My first time I crashed, took me two days to match your time. Well done.'

Aaron climbed out of the simulator and winced. 'I forgot... no inertial dampening. These things really throw you around,' he said as he tried to massage some circulation back into his right shoulder.

'That's nothing, try doing a full race simulation. I did, and could hardly walk afterward!' Gordon declared, a wicked smile crossing his face. 'So before anyone qualifies to race, they will need to complete a full training package. But, how'd it feel?'

'Awesome, fucking awesome, I don't think I've ever had so much fun!' Aaron's joy was impossible to hide he was grinning from ear to ear. 'When can I do more?'

'Soon, Aaron, but we need to show you the rest of the facility, and we have a lunch appointment, remember?'

Aaron agreed and they left the sim room and took the transport trolley through the rest of the factory.

It was truly a remarkable operation. In less than a year they had erected the buildings and partially completed the fit-out. Everything required was either manufactured or assembled here. Tyres, engines, chassis, body; all had their specialties, and the facility catered for this - even fuel was produced on-site, at a separate facility.

Bureaucratic oversight was evident with inspectors constantly wandering around. Strangely JT seemed to welcome this activity and when Aaron asked, he explained.

'It shows that the administration is serious about the project. If we do it right now, we will have no troubles when we start to market the idea.' His logic was sound, as many times in the distant past projects had ground to a halt when bureaucrats deemed they had been left out of the loop. It was much easier to include them in the process than to fight them at the conclusion.

The tour took another two hours with Gordon giving a constant commentary. They stopped briefly at each new station as he explained the operation and the challenges they had overcome in resurrecting some of the ancient technologies.

Aaron was particularly taken at the engine section, where he met Ivan Kasparitz, an engineer and metallurgist who was the brains behind the new hydrogen-powered engines. His luck was holding as they entered the section, as Ivan was about to run a newly completed engine on the dyno. Aaron felt a slight tremble through the floor as the 6-litre V8 engine was started.

They sat at the back of the room watching as Ivan ran it through a series of power runs, stopping occasionally to make a few adjustments before returning to repeat the tests. Finally, he was satisfied with all the settings and he saved the program and idled the engine down to allow it to normalize.

Aaron read the results: 685 HP, a little under 520 kW. He marvelled at how much the small power source had contributed to humanity, but thought back to his run in the simulator and realized that it was much more than transport. It was a passion, an escape that had been part of mankind's love affair with the old automobile.

Aaron and JT boarded their shuttle to return to the house for lunch. JT spoke as they cruised on autopilot, a leisurely 100kph showing on the flight log. 'Aaron we need more than capital. Gordon is great at what he is doing, but he freely admits he doesn't have what will be needed to get the operation up and running and keep it that way. I don't enough time and now I will have even less… I was hoping that you could step in.'

'JT, I'm not the right guy, I know very little about the marketing side of things but I may know someone who can help. The truth is, I'm bored with the Portal stuff, all I do is sign things, but we'll need someone who can handle all the other stakeholders, diplomatically,' Aaron's reply was honest.

JT sceptically raised one eyebrow. 'I don't understand, you have successful operations on, what, twelve planets? You have a freight company that is the second-largest Freebooter operation; even an engineering company that could almost rival Abracorp and you still don't think you're the right guy?

'Correct. The only reason I now have all these is Henry; he is the real brains behind the company, he runs the whole thing. Me? I'm a Freeboot Trader… a good one, make no mistake… but a trader. I'll talk to Henry… he'll know the right person for the job.'

They arrived back at the compound and, after a quick clean-up, joined the rest of the family for lunch. Jason had returned from his early morning ride and looked much more relaxed, as if a weight had been lifted from his shoulders.

He stood at the head of the table as everyone else sat. 'I have reached a decision,' he revealed 'I'm going to accept the appointment to complete Malik's term as President.' He let his gaze flow over his family, knowing that whatever their political disposition, he would have their support.

Jeff rose and went to his father. 'Typical bloody Abraham… when the shit hits the fan, we're the first to run headlong into the fray. You know we'll all support you.' He held his hand out to congratulate Jason.

After lunch, Aaron spoke, at length, to Henry who agreed to take the Dubbo project on. He had a couple of protégés, who would, in his words, excel in the role Aaron had described, they agreed to the usual 10% terms. In the end, both JT and Aaron agreed to split Henry's share and the new company ownership ended as JT & Aaron with 35% each, Gordon, Henry, and the employee Trust with 10% each.

Everyone felt upbeat. The year was progressing well and the future looked bright. Little did they know, however, that events were already coalescing - events, that if left to run their course, could change the face of the Coalition and humanity; forever.

lanet Betanna lay deep within the worst part of Shadow sector, more commonly called the Bad-Lands.

The surrounding space was its best asset, for anyone wanting to hide. Constant cosmic storms, huge and unpredictable gravity anomalies, and thousands of rogue meteors made this a dangerous and potentially deadly part of space. Only the foolhardy, or those who needed to hide, ever ventured here.

Betanna, a young M class planet with a volatile, but breathable atmosphere and, most importantly liquid water, orbits a star similar to Sol, Earth's sun. It was constantly racked by massive storms and atmospheric conditions that made flying a survival exercise. Lightning strikes were recorded in the thousand per hour band and made life above ground interesting, if not downright suicidal.

Its ability to conceal was the reason Tragarian Raiders had used it as their base for over two hundred years. The nature of the Bad-Lands and continuing evolution of Betanna was so inhospitable that no Coalition vessel had ever attempted to come close, until now. The four cruisers that had been detected at the outer limit of the Raider's detection zone had been given a royal bashing - one destroyed and the others feebly limping back to their own space to lick their wounds. Normally this would have been cause for celebration, the first time any Raider group had soundly defeated a Coalition force; but the mood in the audience chamber was sombre.

Eight months ago - Betanna time - newcomers had arrived; a ship of different and advanced design. The first meeting had been more of a confrontation, with the newcomers having more advanced technology but the Raiders had numbers - after some mild confrontations, a truce was forged and discussions had commenced.

The newcomers offered new weapons and drive technology in return for a safe haven, but their truly alien countenance caused much suspicion in the Raider ranks. At first, no agreement could be reached. The Dog Heads, as the Raider Leadership referred to the newcomers, demanded too much. The stalemate held for weeks until a human arrived in a second ship and entered the discussions.

She was exceedingly beautiful and a skilled negotiator. Her name was Nefaris and she requested private discussions with Darius Tragarian, the Raider's leader. Darius agreed and all other members of both delegations left them alone. Ten hours later, they sent for the others, announcing that an agreement had been reached. The Galdorans (Dog Heads) and Nilerans - as the humanoids were called - were given a section of Betanna to inhabit and the new alliance began.

Two months later Sarclan had returned. He met with Darius and they agreed to continue to work together. So far their loose agreement had benefited both sides and, over the years a weak bond of trust had emerged between the Raiders and Sarclan's people. Now with the additional members joining the cartel, and their technology, the future was looking secure.

Sarclan's huge ship, Balerophon, was grounded in a remote area of Betanna, an area that had a significant and complex cave system. To facilitate upgrading the Raider fleet, part of this was converted to workshop space and work on the upgrades commenced.

With twelve ships now equipped with the new weapon and drive systems, the time was ripe to test them. It was almost fortunate that the Coalition Task Force, Paladin, had stumbled along when they did - they were a perfect test for the new ships.

The Audience Chamber, as Darius liked to call the cave, was huge. One hundred metres long and over thirty wide, the roof soared another sixty overhead. Stalagmites and Stalactites grew from the floor or hung from the roof, adding to the grandeur. The lighting was designed to highlight the most impressive geological features of the area giving it a sense of solidity and power.

The main entrance was through two massive metal doors that spanned nearly ten metres and stood twenty high. Two thirds into the room was a raised section of floor, artificially constructed to house Darius' *throne*, where he now sat with Nefaris to his right. The doors, operated by an elaborate mechanical mechanism, slowly opened and in strode Sarclan, looking as belligerent as usual.

'Who sent those ships to Caprica?' Sarclan bellowed as he strode towards the throne.

'I did,' snarled Zarof, who was standing to the left of the dais.

'Then you are as fucking dumb as you are ugly! Why did you send those old units?' Sarclan called

'It was an easy target, no defences. Why risk our best ships on an errand to deliver a message.' Zarof moved closer to the throne, trying to absorb some authority from it.

'Then, Jackal head, tell me how in hell, did you manage to lose two ships and miss the primary target?' Sarclan spat at Zarof. 'The mission was a total failure, you idiot.'

Zarof glared down at Sarclan, 'What do you mean? We obliterated the target and destroyed the city as you requested... how is that a failure.' Zarof refuted, with conviction.

'The primary target wasn't there. All you did was blow up a house and you lost two ships to a fucking private yacht, not even a warship. Talk about useless, you give that word a new meaning.' Sarclan turned away from Zarof, an insult in Galdoran culture.

Zarof was about to respond when Nefaris moved between them. 'Now, gentlemen, please let's keep our heads. Eugene, as I recall,' she gestured to Darius, 'we supplied the ships. Zarof planned the attack, but **you** supplied the intelligence. Surely the blame must be levelled at whoever gave you the information?

After all, we didn't know who the target was... just the location on the planet.' Her voice was calming and seductive, almost hypnotic, as she diffused the situation.

Darius rose from his throne. 'Not true,' He was tall, solidly built with long grey hair. His face bore the marks resulting from his mutiny all those years ago, with a long scar running down his left cheek. His eyes were soft and deep blue, something that was out of character with the rest of him. 'The target was Jason Abraham, I believe,' he stared at Sarclan, 'a personal vendetta from the distant past.' He turned dismissively and sat back on his throne.

Sarclan smiled. 'Still sharp, Darius... yes, Abraham was the target, but not for revenge. I still have sources on Earth and I can assure you: this man is our **greatest threat**. Listen... I will only tell you this once,' he locked eyes with each, in succession, until his gaze fell on Zarof, 'and I will speak slowly so the less intelligent can understand.'

Zarof growled at this insult, but a hand on his arm from Nefaris calmed him. 'Please continue, Eugene,' she said as she resumed her place beside Darius.

'The rebellion on Ummah failed, dismally. If you recall, I said it was a mistake to involve those religious nutters in this. Now Malik is being recalled to the planet to form a new government, leaving the Presidency vacant...'

'That is our chance, the Coalition will be leaderless. We should strike now!' Zarof called.

'No, you fool! This is why I wanted Abraham killed... Malik has nominated him as his replacement. With his grandson heading Space Corp and their company churning out their new space ships at an alarming rate, Jason Abraham as President is the worst situation for us. Do not underestimate him or his family... they have a long history of beating the odds... I advise you to take care with them. If Abraham accepts the appointment, that fucking family will be the most powerful dynasty in the galaxy... but... if you had done your job, this wouldn't be an issue.' He finished vehemently, glaring at Zarof.

The final insult was too much for Zarof; he drew a long double-bladed weapon and leaped to attack. Sarclan was ready - he had already palmed a small disruptor. He fired--the full blast slammed into Zarof, dropping him in mid-leap.

Sarclan snarled. **'That's** how I deal with a disobedient dog. When he wakes, tell him that,' He turned and strode out of the room.

Tragarian stood and moved to Zarof's side. 'He's going to have a hell of a headache when he comes round.' He signalled for two guards to remove Zarof. 'Take him to the med centre; and be gentle,' he added as they started to haul Zarof away. He turned to Nefaris 'Sarclan is right, this is a bad situation; we'll need to be far more careful.'

***

Jason grumbled as he gazed out of the window. The day had dawned grey, the sky filled with dark, pendulous clouds. So far, the weekend on Earth had gone smoothly.

'This is unseasonal weather,' he was watching the sky when the other men joined him in the study. At that moment the skies opened and torrential rain began falling, so heavy that the furthest anyone could see was the fountain in the centre of the garden. 'A good day to stay indoors,' he said with a wry smile.

'Yeah, climate change can be a bitch,' Jeff spoke quietly. 'Still, it gives the environmentalists something to whinge about.'

Aaron didn't understand. 'What do you mean, climate change?'

Jeff explained 'Ever since the ecological disasters, back in the 24th century, everyone believed that the planet would be in an ice age for several millennia, but it seems that old Mother Nature is hurrying things up a bit. The latest readings show that the northern ice sheet is receding much faster than anyone thought possible - some are even saying that we could see most of it gone within a few hundred years, and even some talk of beginning a re-population discussion.'

'That sounds positive,' Aaron observed. 'It may help with the economic problems JT told me Earth has.'

Jason stood, shaking his head. 'Not really. This was an argument used back before everything went to hell. They followed a badly flawed economic theory that guaranteed the destruction of Earth. Hundreds of years ago economists seemed to rule and they ascribed to a theory of endless growth... we all know how **that** ended. Just re-populating Earth will achieve little, if there is nothing for people to do. Let's face it; the old planet is at the arse end of the galaxy now.'

Aaron was still confused, so his father continued. 'It is simple. When the exodus took place, Earth was the centre of human existence, but as we went further afield it became too distant. Yes, in the initial stages, each colony was dependent, in some measure, on Earth and that fuelled our economy. Our companies made all the things that the colonies needed and Earth, itself, was the centre of our civilization.

'But, as is evident from past migrations, the colonies started to become more self-sufficient. Look at Abracorp... how many operations do we still have here and how many have we set up closer to our customers, the colonies? In reality, the only reason we are still here is the Coalition; they are our major customer here in the Solar System. I have spent the last year going over the figures. Earth operations are now less than 20% of the company's income base, and the Corps is around 80% of that. Years ago it was the opposite, and the projections are that it will continue to slide with other operations growing as their markets expand.'

'But surely the Coalition spend is enough to sustain Earth?' Aaron inquired.

'The Coalition is still based here, but it doesn't generate much in the way of income for Earth. Essentially, there is very little income from the Coalition except for the usual fees and taxes, and even these are in decline as more operational activities are decentralized. If you look at it purely from a business perspective, Earth is bankrupt or near to it. Jeff, what other industries does Earth have, besides Abracorp and Greenbach?'

'Not much, really; some agricultural and primary exports, but even these are reducing as the colonies get their programs under control. Most business is now generated from the colonies. But there is another issue... location,' Jeff hesitated and looked at his brother. 'Aaron, you may not realize it, but Argos is now the astronomical centre of human civilization. You can reach all colonies better from Argos than Earth... I believe that eventually, Argos needs to be the administrative centre as well.'

Aaron replied indignantly. 'No fucking way! Freebooters will never submit to Coalition rule.'

'Hang on, Aaron; I never said anything about rule, all I said was it was a better location for Coalition administration to operate from. Lines of communication would be better, it is more central so delays would be minimized, it makes more sense. How long does it take for you to reach... let's say, Ummah from Argos, and how long from here?'

'At normal cruise, seven days from Argos and twelve from here,' Aaron conceded, quietly.

'Exactly, and for freight, even longer! Earth needs to reinvent itself; it needs to become a destination of choice, or else it will end up as a poor backwater. From what I heard you three discussing,' Jeff looked at JT, Aaron, and Henry in turn, 'I believe that is what the Council needs to encourage.

'First Earth becomes a tourist destination, not just a historical anomaly; then we can begin new industries, complementary to tourism and the rebuilding process begins... an organic movement!' Jeff's voice was filled with enthusiasm, 'dumping people here with nothing to do is a recipe for disaster.'

'I take it you are talking about the Terrestrial Council, not the Coalition Council?' JT added.

'Yes, the Coalition Council has no input into Earth affairs. The Terrestrial Council handles all domestic issues, and you know how difficult it can be to work with... all that red tape and bureaucracy,' Jeff remarked. The conversation ranged over many topics for a couple of hours, making everyone silently glad of the rain; it had been a long time since they all had the opportunity to sit and discuss matters as a family.

JT was standing on the veranda at the rear of the house gazing over the fields now being prepared for winter crops when his communicator chimed. He checked the caller ID and sighed, as he accepted the call.

Sam Grogan's voice floated in the air. John, *Grogan here. How's the weekend?*

'Pretty good... relaxing I'd say.'

Excellent! We just had word from six zero two, Solomon has had some luck; he's on his way back so I've arranged a meeting for zero eight hundred tomorrow. See you then.

'Yes Admiral,' JT cut the connection.

He stood, gazing again at the field in front of him; a cultivation unit was standing at the far end, waiting for the ground to reach the optimum level of water saturation before beginning its work. Three small remotes flew out of the front section and went to different parts of the field where they landed and took samples. When analysed, the results would give the machine the time to commence work; a far cry from the days of old when a farmer would make these decisions based on intuition and experience and do the work himself. This technology was critical, as no-one wanted to do the manual work required for successful farming now.

JT decided to leave for Perth, mid-afternoon; a leisurely flight and good night's sleep before getting back into things. Aaron, JT, and Henry had drafted the agreement for the Dubbo operation and had left it up to Henry and Abracorp's lawyers to finalize the wording of the document.

Monday dawned bright and clear and held the promise of a fine day. Jason and Amanda had departed early to meet with President Malik; David and Selina had similarly, breakfasted early and left. This morning it was just Aaron, Petra, Sonia, and Jeff at the table.

The conversation was mainly around their meeting in Sydney with Argort to finalize their financial and corporate affairs before the wedding. Everyone was upbeat; the war was now in the past and everyone was now focusing on the future.

'Jeff, I have been thinking,' Aaron said, 'You know Debbie Harcourt, my PA on the portal?' Jeff nodded. 'I would like to promote her to the Manager role.' He waited for Jeff to respond. As they were equal partners this was a decision that they needed to make together.

'I know she's good but do you think she's ready for it?' Jeff asked. 'She is quite young?'

'I know she's young but I have been letting her take the reins lately. She's surprised me, I could do nothing better myself, so yes I think she's ready,' Aaron pointed out.

Jeff pondered this for a couple of minutes, 'OK,' he said at length, 'but you go back and spend a couple of weeks with her, as handover. And arrange to meet with her every quarter, for the next year, OK?'

Sonia stopped them in their tracks. 'Hang on a minute! Aaron and Petra are getting married in four weeks, we still have a huge amount to do, and you want to send him back out there for two of those? No way Jeffery... it will not happen, do I make myself clear?'

Both Jeff and Aaron knew better than to argue and sat quietly.

Finally, it was Petra who broke the stalemate. 'Wait a minute... except for our meeting with Argort this afternoon; I have nothing on until a board meeting on Friday. Aaron you're clear for this week so you and I will meet with Argort, then take Junior to the portal and be back by Thursday night. That will give you at least three days to ease Debbie into the role, sort out the paperwork, and transfer everything to her. Also, I'll be there to keep you on track. How's that sound?'

Jeff grumbled something, softly under his breath until a

withering look from Sonia stopped him. 'I suppose that will have to suffice,' he acquiesced begrudgingly, and then checked the time. 'I need to get going... our first group of students from Adelaide is arriving around ten. I'm looking forward to finally having them tour the Folly.' He stood and left the room.

Petra smiled at Aaron. 'Darling, could you prep Junior? I have a couple of calls to make and we need to get going, Sonia's given me the details of a couple of traders I want to see.' She stood, placed a gentle kiss on his cheek, and left.

Sonia offered him another coffee, and Aaron eagerly accepted. 'I'm pleased you're finally settling down, but where are you two going to settle? You have the apartment here, but have you discussed it?'

Aaron was surprised. 'No actually, it hasn't come up. I was thinking of going back to Argos. I haven't got a home there, so it might be time to do something about that, but aside from that I haven't given it much thought.'

Sonia frowned. 'Well, maybe you should. This venture with Johnathon will take quite a bit of time unless you are going to leave that to someone else.' She smiled, knowing that Aaron was as mad about this project as her son. 'And you will have some duties with Abracorp. So a base here makes perfect sense; plus Petra's now got her own business to work on. Think about it.' She finished and left him alone, to ponder.

He finished his coffee and left the room, he was about to enter the pod when Sonia called out. 'And don't worry about Prince. He and Amanda's two seem to be getting on fine, so leave him here this week!'

It was just after 09:30 when Petra boarded the yacht. 'I don't know how you do it? Three calls and over an hour of bullshit, may I have Henry please?' She begged.

'Over my dead body!' Aaron was adamant. 'He's the only reason I am still sane and not incarcerated. Tell you what, we'll talk to him when we get back, I'm certain he'll have someone who can slot in for you.

'OK, anyone Henry recommends would have to be better than the lawyers and accountants that I have met with so far, talk about bloodsuckers,' Petra muttered; running a corporation didn't suit her either.

***

JT entered the foyer of Admiral Sam Grogan's office and greeted the adjutant who indicated for him to go straight in. 'Morning' he greeted Sam and Sol as he closed the door behind him. Both men were grim-faced, something he had rarely seen in Solomon.

'Morning, JT,' Sol's voice was as grim as his face. Grogan nodded . 'Good weekend?' The question was irrelevant but asked in any case.

'Not bad, but from your faces I assume things are about to take a change for the worse.'

'Correct,' Grogan replied dismally. 'Solomon, will you brief Admiral Abraham?'

'Sure. As you know, we have dissected all the remains from the two Raider ships from Caprica; there is little of significance about them. One is of Coalition origin; the other we believe is an old Tellurian explorer. It did have some weapons upgrades, but nothing significant. No evidence of the new shields or weapons was found on either ship.'

He paused as he flipped through some of the images from the investigation. 'We did capture an intact data storage system and this is the gold we were after. One of the items is the exact location of the Raider base, Betanna, in the Bad-Lands.

'We were so close with Paladin, less than two light-years away, but that is not the real jewel. It appears that the Raiders have an ally; Sarclan. The data shows that he joined forces with them, officially, six months ago, but we know he's been working with them for much longer. Also, two unidentified ships arrived on Betanna prior to Sarclan officially partnering with Tragarian. These ships are very advanced, with technology that they agreed to share in return for a haven. From the descriptions of the crew, one ship was crewed by Galdorans.'

'Then the rumours are true! Zarof and Nefaris are here, and working with both the Raiders and Sarclan! But why attack Caprica?' JT added as he started the familiar Abraham pacing. 'It has no strategic significance and to lose two ships there... it makes no sense at all. Maybe we are looking at Caprica all wrong... what if there is a strategic issue we are missing?'

Sol shook his head. 'We can't find anything. Caprica is a retirement planet, and while the inhabitants may have been important in their day, they aren't now, most wanted to leave that sort of life behind, that's why they settled there'

'Then what are we missing... have you sent the data down to cryptology?' Grogan asked.

Sol nodded. 'Yes, they have had them for a few days... still nothing. It doesn't make sense. Maybe it was a training exercise or a propaganda stunt. Now we know who they have with them it could be a statement from Sarclan.'

'No, he's far too smart for that; this has all the hallmarks of amateurs... Sarclan wouldn't have a bar of this,' Grogan added.

While the others were discussing, JT was scrolling through all the damage images from Caprica. He kept going back to one and then he checked the date stamp.

'Sam, look at the date stamp on this. It was taken on the day after the attack.'

Grogan approached the screen. 'So what? It's just the date.'

'No, look at the destruction.' JT started to bring other images to the screen, forming a mosaic around the image. 'See the difference?' The central image was his grandfather's compound; the others were surrounding properties that had also been attacked.

'Well, I'll be!' Sam gasped. All the other properties had some degree of damage, mostly superficial; but the Abraham compound was destroyed.

'Everything... the house, the two guest houses, the staff quarters, the barn; even Pop's workshop was obliterated. Why target this so much?' JT was thinking aloud, 'I know Sarclan has no love for our family, but I don't understand the Raider's role in all this. They are mostly a pain in the arse, they have never come this far in and for what, to demolish a house?'

Sam sat back at his desk; he activated the intercom and called his adjutant to the room. 'Lieutenant, can you ask the chief cryptologist to join us?' The adjutant turned and went back to his desk. 'While we are waiting, how much do you know about Raider history?'

'Only what we learned at the Academy. The Montana was on a diplomatic mission and was attacked, the ship was destroyed and most of the crew died. Only the Captain and a few officers survived.' Sol repeated the scant information from his student days.

'Yeah, the official story,' Sam said. 'What **actually** happened though is something the Corps has covered up and hidden for over two hundred years. It was at the end of the war with the Empire. The Coalition was expanding and we had been in negotiations with both the Ulgans and Olaks; they had been adversaries for longer than anyone could remember.

'The strange thing is that both races share common DNA. A deal was struck, where Princess Natola of the Ulgans would marry Crown Prince Qetolk, of the Olaks, thus ending the war. Isabel Nolan, Captain of the Montana, had been instrumental in brokering the deal and was trusted by both sides, so the Montana and Nolan were dispatched to act as the Coalition guard to the dowry transfer.

'There were reports of the size of this dowry... no official records exist, but I can tell you it was **huge**. The First Officer of the Montana and Captains of two of the other guard ships, one each from Ulgan and Olak, conspired to steal it. Most of the crew of the Montana were involved, except Captain Nolan and her senior officers; they were marooned on a small M class planetoid, with full survival gear.

'The raid was successful, the dowry was stolen and the

perpetrators escaped. The princess was also delivered, safely, but without her dowry. In the end, the marriage took place and both races are now strong members of the Coalition.'

'Nice story, but what does this have to do with our situation?' JT queried.

'The First Officer on the Montana was Darius Tragarian.' Sam's words were greeted with silence. 'That information stays in this room, understand; now you both know exactly who we are dealing with.'

There was a buzz from the door and Sam tapped the icon to unlock it. The person entering was a young woman, no more than fifty; tall and elegant, she had dark brown skin and jet black hair that was held back under a scarf. Her dark eyes took in the room and she walked purposefully toward the three men. They all rose to greet her.

'Gentlemen, this is Maalai Bakshi, our lead cryptologist. Miss Bakshi, may I introduce Admirals Abraham and Radchak.' Sam waited as they shook hands, JT moving to arrange another chair for her.

'Please call me Maalai. What can I do for you, Admiral?' Her voice was soft and musical, with a slight accent pointing to her ancestry.

'How is the decrypting coming?' Sam was straight to business.

'Quite interesting, we have found a small file, heavily encrypted; hidden in one of the comm files. We are giving this our full attention.'

'A comm file, any idea of what it might hold?' JT asked.

'Not as yet but the file was part of the command to attack Caprica, so we assume this is some sort of target information.'

'Thank you. The contents of this file are most important, JT; work with cryptology and see if you have any information that can assist.

Sorry Admiral, but Miss Bakshi has a call from her office. The lieutenant's voice filled the room.

Sam indicated the comm unit to her. 'Maalai, please,' she took the call but put it on speaker, for all to hear.

Maalai, we have deciphered some of the message... a date range and a name, so far.

'Well, what does it say?'

The name's Charlotte Abraham, the date range from March 23 to March 29, 2922. That's all we have as yet

Maalai thanked her operative and cut the connection. She turned to JT 'Is Charlotte Abraham a relative, Admiral?'

JT felt a cold shiver ran up his spine. 'No, *Charlotte* is the name of my grandparents' yacht, but the date range is what's interesting. Sam' when did you have the conversation with Malik?'

'March 20, why?' Sam didn't like where this was heading.

'My grandparents were due to be on Caprica during that time, March 23 to 29, but as they reached Jupiter Station my grandfather received a confidential message. He was needed for a meeting, an issue with an off-world project and the others involved had decided to meet at Jupiter Station. He left Charlotte and my Grandmother continued to Caprica to attend to things there. Now, look at the images again.' He brought up the collage of damaged houses again. 'My grandparents were the target! Their house was destroyed and most of Barton as well. The only reason is to stop him from agreeing to Malik's request.' JT stopped and looked at the time, 09:30. 'Shit they are due to meet with the President in half an hour, at the Palace.'

Sam was already on the comm unit, calling Crompton 'Coalition intelligence, my arse!' He said to no-one in particular. Someone answered the call and Sam barked for Crompton. Almost immediately Crompton answered.

Crompton here; what can I do, he never got to finish as Sam cut him off.

'Crompton, shut up and listen! We have reason to believe the Presidential Palace has been compromised again. Do you have any operatives there?'

'Yes, three.'

'Here's what I want you to do.' Sam continued to issue instructions.

Strangely, Crompton agreed and cut his connection. While this was happening, JT had used his communicator to contact his office and arranged for a flight of Darts to proceed to the Palace. Also, he had asked for a team of ground commandos to be airlifted to the site, which would only take twenty minutes from the base on Madagascar. Finally, he called his father to find out which shuttle had been used to ferry his grandparents this morning.

When he had the information, he called the shuttle and spoke to the pilot, telling him to orbit where he was until the flight of Darts arrived to escort the shuttle the rest of the way. The fear was that not only was the threat to his family real, but the President was also in harms' way. Sam relayed the information to Crompton, who informed him that the President had been secured and was being evacuated as they spoke.

'This all means that the President's office and probably the whole complex may be compromised... the second time in a year. All the staff is now suspect and we have no clue how deep this goes,' As JT finished speaking, the adjutant announced that Crompton had arrived; he entered the room and immediately noticed the head of cryptology was present.

'Why is she here?' he demanded.

'She and her team are the ones who broke the code and warned us... that's why.' Sam barked back.

Crompton snorted but backed down. 'I've already started a full background check on all the Presidential staff as well as arranging for a full security sweep immediately. Just what triggered this?'

Sam glanced at JT, who shook his head. 'Sorry; but your security clearance isn't high enough.' JT's communicator chimed, he took the call and appeared relieved at the end of it.

'That was the Dart flight. The shuttle has been secured and is proceeding to meet with the President's transport, before bringing them all back here.' He turned to Crompton, 'When they arrive, you can ask them what this is all about.' He turned to Maalai. 'We have about an hour... maybe we should look at the rest of the file?'

JT followed Maalai from the office to Cryptology, where she introduced him to her team. She brought the team up to date with events and asked if they had any questions for the Admiral. JT was swamped with questions; finally, the team went back to their stations and started working furiously.

Maalai took him to the dining area and made a pot of tea. They had finished their second cup when one of her team came running in, they had deciphered the message. The answers JT had given to, what he thought meaningless questions, had given them hooks to work with and these finally located the key and broke the code.

JT stood quietly reading the message. It was incredibly accurate and contained details of his grandparents' flight plans, the location of their home on Caprica, as well as details of the main areas they visited in Barton. To collect this sort of information meant someone had been watching for a long time, or they had someone on the inside of the Abraham family. Neither scenario made him feel comfortable. He thanked the team for their efforts and turned to Maalai.

'Can you send this to Grogan?'

'Of course...and a copy to you?'

JT smiled, awkwardly. 'Maalai, thank you again, your team has done wonders. Perhaps we can catch up for coffee or tea when this all blows over?'

'I'd like that, Admiral.'

He turned and left for the elevator.

ondrac sat in his quarters.

The room was not large, but more than adequate for his purposes. He studied the furnishings and decor, his thoughts raising mild alarm in his mind. *So human,* he thought to himself, careful to cloak his thoughts lest they be overheard.

He was aware of an inclination his half-brother had to adopt many things he had seen, or obtained from the humans. The room was one example. It strongly resembled one of the rooms he had seen in some of the old entertainment vids Eldrac-Tar was so fond of. The entry portal had been replaced with a solid, ornate wood door that had to be manually opened. Indeed, throughout the Tar compound, he had seen many examples of this; portals replaced with wood or metal doors depending on the function of the room they accessed. He recalled his last conversation with his sibling, with some amusement.

You will need to visit my tailor, Eldrac-Tar had said, *unless you wish to be without clothing. The replication system on Duramot is for food and essential components only, it doesn't have the necessary raw materials to make clothing.* Eldrac-Tar seemed strangely pleased with this situation.

So Mondrac had taken his brother's advice and spent two hours being measured and fitted for clothing, something that normally was done by simply standing in a holographic chamber and the replication system doing the rest. He was unprepared for the tailor's next comment *you will have your new clothes tomorrow morning.* That would leave little time for any alterations, at least with replicated clothes they always fitted.

Three sharp sounds came from the door.

'Enter,' he called, gruffly. The whole human thing his sibling had going on was becoming tedious. The door flew open and the tailor pushed in a wheeled contraption. On it hung several sets of clothes, trousers, shirts, jackets, even boots - the same type of clothes his brother now wore.

'Our Sire thought you might like to have some more human attire for your journey,' he produced a box 'I have made the undergarments as well, all to your measurements.' The tailor was proud of his effort and even Mondrac had to agree, the garments were superb - just not what he was used to wearing. 'I'll leave you now, please try some on. If you have any problems, I can make alterations quickly.' He bowed slightly and left, closing the door behind him.

Mondrac shook his head, but selected a complete set of clothes and began to dress. Finally, he donned a pair of socks and pulled on the carved leather boots, standing and examining himself in the mirror.

'Not bad, maybe Eldrac-Tar is not so foolish.' The clothes were comfortable and serviceable, plus in these, he would fit in with almost every culture in the Twelfth Realm. As he was admiring himself, there was a quick knock and the door opened, in walked his half-brother and one of the domestic staff, carrying a large box-like object.

'Your luggage brother,' Eldrac-Tar announced proudly.

'My **what**?'

Suitcases, things you transport your clothing and personal items in,' Eldrac-Tar explained. 'You need something to carry all your fine new clothes in, and I must say you cut a dashing figure in that outfit.'

Mondrac was lost for words. He had never needed to transport clothes - that was what the replication systems were for. 'Brother, would it not be more efficient to use the replication system?'

'Please, Mondrac, humour me. This is all part of an experiment we are conducting so, go along with it, please.' Eldrac-tar seemed genuine in his request.

'Just this once... now I need to move. Time is short and we're already late.'

Eldrac-Tar smiled. 'All taken care of... Duramot has arrived at our landing area; once you pack we can get you away.'

The domestic assistant quickly and efficiently demonstrated the best way to store the clothes. In under ten minutes, Mondrac was ready, with his new clothes in one suitcase, and the boots in another.

They left the room and took a ground vehicle to the landing area. This was new - another of his brother's ideas - and resembled one of the ancient earth aerodromes he had seen in the myriad books in the clan library. They proceeded down a long, straight area that was covered with some kind of grey resin-like compound. Mondrac decided against asking questions; he needed to leave as soon as possible.

Moments later their destination loomed directly in front of them. It was a huge construction that seemed only to be accessed by two equally huge doors in the front. The vehicle stopped to one side where they entered through a small access door. Mondrac stopped and stared as he entered. There before him was Duramot, in all its glory.

It was long and thin with triangular wings sweeping back from just before the mid-point of the body. At the rear a tail, again triangular, the structure stood vertically from the body, protruding from the top and facing forward - a sinister-looking weapon. Under each of the wings hung a tubular structure and the leading edge of each wing revealed a deflector system.

'Beautiful, is it not?' Eldrac-Tar stated, not expecting any disagreement.

'Interesting, I would say,' Mondrac retorted. As he spoke, Goran-Esk approached them.

'Mondrac, welcome, if you would accompany me we can begin.' He directed Mondrac to proceed to an elevator that had descended forward of the wings. Mondrac complied and entered the small compartment. As it rose to the body he felt his brother's mind.

Travel with safety, brother. I await your return.

I thank you brother, for your assistance and courteous thoughts, Mondrac replied.

More surprises were awaiting Mondrac as he entered the ship; this was nothing like any Eldoran ship he had ever seen. They entered the control room or Bridge as Goran-Esk called it, and he could have been on any human or Krell ship. Consoles were everywhere, with people actively working them and even a holographic navigation system in the centre of the room.

Goran-Esk chuckled as he took his position in the Command Chair. 'You seem confused, Mondrac?'

'Somewhat... I have never seen an Eldoran ship like this?'

'The reason is simple... efficiency; allow me to explain. During the battle for the Twelfth Realm, Jok-Tar witnessed that the Humans and Krell reacted in battle much quicker than he could. It was something that he could not understand. In any situation, they had to view the situation, decide on an action, and then physically implement that action. Yet even doing all this, they responded to situations and threats faster and, more effectively than we did. We were only saved by the superiority of our weapons.

'On his return, we started to analyse his data and found that we were overthinking every action and considering multiple options. In reality, we were confusing ourselves. We have developed this trait over many thousands of cycles and it is now ingrained into our telepathic command structure. But we now see it is not always to our advantage. So we decided to experiment... we built simulators and trained our people to go back and 'react' not think, not to consider all possible options. The results were astounding. After only a few weeks of training, we saw huge improvements in reaction times. We had started to regress; to use our instinct not only our intellect.

'Now, on this ship, we have combined both operating systems

and we believe this will give us greatly improved reaction times,' Goran-Esk explained. 'Even the design was chosen for efficiency. Compared to our usual vessel this is comparatively small; we only have three hundred crew members unlike the several thousand we normally carry. But the shape has proven to be more efficient and easier to control in either a wormhole or during a jump. In all, this could be the most efficient ship we have built for many, many millennia.'

Mondrac was amazed; it seemed that the humans were teaching the Eldorans as much as the Eldorans were teaching them. After so many millennia, he now realized, Eldora had become stale and even a little arrogant. To be taught these things by a race they considered little more than children might be what Eldora needed.

Another thing Mondrac noticed was the total lack of view ports. The entire outer skin of the ship appeared to be one solid structure but here in the Bridge, he could see through the front, sides, and overhead. 'Goran-Esk, the structure appears solid and yet I can see outside, how are you achieving this?'

Goran-Esk handed the command chair to his subordinate and stood beside Mondrac, 'Simple; we use external visual sensors and display the real-time images captured by them on the surfaces in this room. It gives us an effective all-round view and we can do the same below and behind.' As he spoke, the floor disappeared and was replaced by an image of the floor of the building they were now exiting, giving the impression they were floating above it. 'Come with me, we will get you settled and tour the ship while we leave the planet.'

'Thank you, but first, may I see the flight plan?'

'Of course,' Goran-Esk moved to the nav console and brought up the flight plan they had filed with Eldoran control.

'Excellent, but might I ask for an unrecorded deviation?' Mondrac manipulated the console to show an alternative route. 'Can we follow this path, without any official involvement?'

Goran-Esk understood and agreed, after all his employer, and clan ally had suggested that Mondrac may have some *particular requirements.* He authorized the new flight plan without notifying orbital control. 'Shall we take that tour now?'

They left the Bridge and walked through the ship, Goran-Esk giving a complete rundown of his charge. Duramot was only 450 metres long with a total span of 289 metres, Mondrac learned. It was constructed around twelve decks and carried a complement of 350. Power was supplied by the two MAM reactors housed in the tubular structures attached to each wing; engineering was adjacent in the central hull. In Displacement mode, she could hold a factor of 30 for long periods and was equipped with the latest jump and inter-realm drive.

'Weapons are completely new... our main offensive weapon is the ionic plasma cannon on the tail. This is complemented by our usual energy projectors but we also have blasters... and torpedos, obtained from human technology. Our defence is primarily by a multi-phasic shield with a random harmonic and frequency modulation and energy absorption fields. Plus,' Goran-Esk boasted, 'the hull is made from the amalgam of human Acrilan and Reglaos resin, so even in the unlikely event something does penetrate our shields, the hull is built to take any punishment,'

Mondrac's interest was piqued by the shields 'Your new shields, where did this technology come from?'

'I don't know, I only know they work, and work well.' Goran-Esk hesitated as he received a telepathic message. 'I am required back on the Bridge, we will be inserting into the worm-hole shortly... your quarters are here.' He stopped a few steps on and indicated the door for Mondrac.

They parted and Mondrac entered the room. It was quite comfortable, even if a bit small compared to what he was used to on a normal Eldoran ship; still, it would be home for the next few weeks. He quickly unpacked his clothes, noting how the assistant had placed everything and consulted his timepiece. If his new flight plan was followed, they would be entering their first wormhole in a few seconds. Exactly on time, he felt the faint tell-tale disorientation of the insertion. This only lasted a fraction of a second but told him they were on track. Now there would be a fifteen-minute trip at Displacement 7.5 and then an immediate jump to the Tenth Realm.

He opened the small case he carried and removed a portable console. He composed a message and directed it through the ship's comm system and transmitted it in a nanosecond burst - hopefully the desired recipient was listening.

***

Four men stood behind the glass wall of the arrivals section of Perth Spaceport; Ivan Klastok, General and Commander of all Coalition ground forces; Sam Grogan, Fleet Admiral and Supreme Commander Coalition military forces; John Abraham, Rear Admiral and Commander Coalition Space Corps and; Anthony Crompton, Director Coalition Intelligence Directorate, they all wore grim faces as they watched the security team deploy.

Overhead, the first three fighters transitioned into hover mode and fanned out to cover the southern perimeter. Three more mirrored this move to the north - now the spaceport had 360-degree air cover. On the ground, Klastok's troops mirrored this formation as well as setting up sniper cover on the roofs of various buildings.

When he was satisfied, Sam Grogan activated his comm unit 'Postman, you may deliver the package.' He still didn't get why Crompton had insisted on these ridiculous code names. If anyone had infiltrated the Presidential Security Team they already knew what was going on - silly names would change nothing.

The next few minutes were the most difficult and dangerous. If there was to be an attack, it would come now. The rescue flight descended through the clouds and dropped quickly to ground level. Once hovering only a few centimetres above the deck, the controller directed both shuttles to a vacant secure hangar at the end of the terminal.

The four men turned and hastened towards that area, the security troops outside falling back to cover the hangar entrance. Inside there was a similar scene; security troops moved into the door-way to provide cover while the doors closed. With the doors closed, the troops formed a cordon around the shuttles, now settled on the ground and powering down. Access doors opened and the passengers began to disembark.

President Malik was unimpressed at being dragged out of his residence and transported half a world away, with little explanation. His eyes shone with quiet fury. 'I hope someone has a good reason for this!' he demanded, glaring straight at Crompton.

Sam Grogan interrupted. 'Mr. President,' he said his voice stern and commanding. 'Please come with us; all will be revealed soon. But for the moment we acted on a plausible threat to your safety.' He started to walk toward the rear wall of the building, the others following.

Once there, he took a small oval device out of his pocket and placed it into a receptacle that matched it. It began to hum and give off a dull blue glow. A few seconds later, a section of the wall - about 3 metres long - moved forward and then started to slide to his left, revealing a transport pod.

'Please Mr. President,' Sam said, standing aside to allow Malik to enter the pod. The others followed close behind. Once everyone was seated Sam retrieved his key and climbed aboard before closing the pod door behind him. The wall had already settled back into its place and to any visual inspection, it would look like it was just a wall - exactly what the designers had planned.

President Malik spoke, 'Interesting, Admiral... I didn't know of this area.'

'Not many people do, Sir. It's only for the direst of circumstances and, as we still don't know exactly what or who we are dealing with, I thought it prudent to utilize it. It may not be as comfortable as your usual transport, but it is secure. Our next stop will be Coalition Defence Operations. Then we can brief you on what we have found.'

The trip took 15 minutes. When they arrived the group was ushered into a room already set up for the meeting, waiting to greet them were Sol, Maalai, and Madam Collard. Sam introduced Sol and Maalai to everyone and indicated they all take their seats.

'Admiral, before you start, may I have a word with Mr. Abraham, in private?' Malik asked. Sam agreed and showed them to a small anteroom.

Once the door was closed Malik looked at Jason, 'My old friend I take it you were on your way to give me an answer, before all this happened?'

'Yes, Mr. President, I was.'

'Well, maybe we should settle that issue before we proceed further. Do you agree?'

Jason studied the man standing before him. They had known each other for over one hundred years, had many dealings together, and had formed a firm trust and friendship. He had watched Salim's political career with great interest.

'Salim, Amanda, and I... indeed the whole family... have discussed this at length and I must say that despite the diverse political views in my family, we will be sad to see you leave. But, if you believe I'm the one you wish to entrust your legacy to, I am honoured to accept.'

Malik smiled. 'Jason, you are the **only** person I trust to complete this work. Thank you, my friend.' They shook hands and then Malik embraced Jason. 'Believe me, by accepting you have given my people new hope. Now let's go see what this is all about.'

Returning to the others, Malik sought out the leader of the Council. 'It is most fortuitous you are here, Madam Collard,' he now addressed the whole group. 'Some of you do not know this but I have been wrestling with an issue; an issue that has great ramifications for the Coalition. My home... Ummah... has been through a great deal of turmoil lately. I have been asked to return and help set up a new government, one that will unite the people. My dilemma has been my Presidency, so I have taken the best advice I can find to help make my decision.

'With immediate effect, I resign as President of the Coalition of Earth Planets and designate Jason Thomas Abraham as my successor, in accordance with the articles of the constitution of the Coalition.' He took a small data-pad from his robe and passed it to Jason. 'Mr. President, if you would please sign this?'

Jason read the declaration, smiled, and signed it by way of ocular recognition, before handing it back to Malik.

'Now, Madam Collard, as leader of the Council, all it needs is to be countersigned by yourself and Admiral Grogan, and the transfer of power is complete.'

Madam Collard took the pad, repeated Jason's ocular signature, and handed it to Sam, who did the same. 'President Malik, I applaud your timely decision and thank you, on behalf of the Council and indeed, the Coalition for your dedication and tenacity in the role.' She turned to Jason. 'President Abraham, I congratulate you and look forward to working closely with you over the next twenty-five years and maybe beyond.'

Malik again shook Jason's hand. 'Thank you. I won't wish you good luck, it won't be needed; I **know** you will do an exemplary job.' Everyone took turns in congratulating Jason before they finally settled to discuss the matter at hand.

Sam opened the discussion with a summary of the last few weeks; he then turned over to Sol who gave his report as to what they found on the Raider hulks they had examined. Then it was Maalai's turn.

She, and her team, had deciphered the encrypted instructions hidden in the Raider ship's navigational data. She turned to the console in front of her and began her presentation. When she brought up the hidden, encrypted message, the room was deathly silent.

'This is the message we deciphered, as you can see it clearly shows that the Abraham compound on Caprica was the main target. Barton City was a secondary target and the other domestic compounds just targets of opportunity. It was here that one of my team found something very interesting... a second hidden message.'

The contents shocked everyone in the room as the message made it clear that Jason was the target. It even gave the reason for it; he was being considered as a replacement President by Malik. 'This message was dated six weeks ago and, as I am led to believe, long before any discussions had taken place.' She stopped and took her seat.

Crompton finally spoke. 'Surely your team got it wrong. This can't be true.' He knew the implications were enormous. If the message was authentic, then the Presidential Palace had been compromised. 'We vetted everyone who works there, the security detail is handpicked and under the control of Deputy Director Garrick, nothing gets past him... you must be wrong. Let my people take a look at it.'

Sam waved him down as Maalai stood again, shaking her head in disbelief. 'They already are. Your chief cryptologist and some of his team are with my people as we speak... you should have confirmation soon.'

As she sat back down, Crompton's comm unit chimed. He moved away from the table and took the call. It lasted much longer than anyone thought it would, with Crompton cutting the call and then initiating another. After a few minutes of quiet conversation, he hung up and returned to the table. He looked like he had seen a ghost; he was pale and had started to sweat.

'It is worse than we think. My people confirmed what you found Ms. Bakshi and I must say they are very impressed with your team. One thing you couldn't find though was the source of the information in the file, which we did. In every communication or file from CID, there is a hidden source code; that way we can identify who and where it came from. Whoever issued that message was sloppy.

'Instead of rewriting the specific information in the hidden sub file, they only did a quick copy and paste, leaving the code intact.' He took a long drink from the glass of water in front of him. 'My team is deciphering the code now... we should have an answer in a few minutes.' Crompton stopped as his comm unit chimed; this time he didn't leave the table to take the call.

'It appears that I may be wrong about some of my people,' Crompton looked deflated. 'The evidence shows that **Director Garrick** was the source of the information. I have agents detaining him as we speak.' He let his eyes pass over each person until he finally met Jason's gaze, 'President Abraham, I apologize for this and ask that you accept my resignation.' A simple statement delivered by a defeated man.

Jason's eyes bored into Crompton, like twin laser beams. Here was the man who had tried to destroy his family all those years ago, Jason had delved deeply into his younger son's sudden departure and had dug out the grubby truth, now he could take revenge if he wanted. The room waited in silence for his answer.

'Not so easy, Crompton. While it's no secret that there is no love lost between us, this is not your fault. Believe me, **that** is not easy for me to say that. I have been a supporter of Garrick for many years. I even tried to have him appointed instead of you, but since you have been at the helm of CID, this is the first real transgression we have seen. No, you need to stay and sort this bloody mess out - your resignation is **not** accepted.'

Madam Collard stood. 'I think it might be time for some refreshments. Admiral, can you arrange some?' Sam nodded and called his aide. 'Also I need to inform the Council of the change in the Presidency so we can complete the transition.' Everyone agreed and they all moved away from the table.

Amanda watched as Crompton moved to the far side of the room, away from the others. She took her husband's arm and guided him to a more private space. 'Jason, you need to do something. You need to clear the air with Crompton.'

'What?'

'Listen to me. We know what happened all those years ago, and the man we blame just placed his head on the block, you let him lift it again. You could have destroyed him, but you didn't.

'We have two sons who think they have kept a secret for over thirty years, but we know different. We know they both blame Crompton and I don't think they will be very understanding when they find out what happened here unless you find a reason. You are now his boss so go talk to him. Find out the truth and we can bury this ghost forever... do nothing, and it will haunt us for just as long.'

Jason looked at his wife. 'I somehow feel that you'd be a better President than me.'

'Bullshit, we'll do this together, like everything else. Now go, talk to the man.' She gave Jason a gentle shove and watched as he walked over to Crompton, a few seconds later they went into the small anteroom that Malik and Jason had used before. Madam Collard moved to her side. 'Amanda, I **am** pleased Jason has accepted, he will be a great President, but should I call you Madam President?'

Amanda laughed 'Yvette, how long have we known each other... don't answer! I don't think either of us wants **that** number out in the open. I know you and Jason worked well together when he was a Council member and I hope you will again, now that he's President.'

'You are correct, we did make a good team, but times have changed. Most of the Council are too involved with their own agendas and getting anything done is an exercise in ego massaging. It was such a shame that Jason didn't stand for a second term.' Collard stopped, leaving the veiled question floating in the air.

Amanda knew she had to diffuse this now. 'You know the reason; Aaron had left to find himself, and Jeffery was swamped so Jason had to step back in. He felt there would be a conflict of interest if he was still on the Council and Chairman of Abracorp.'

'A very noble stand... pity there aren't more like that, things might happen faster.'

'Oh, I think that the two of you will find a way to cut through the inertia. By the way how... is Francois, he must miss you?' Amanda deliberately inserted the reference to Madam Collard's husband.

'He is getting fatter, older, and richer. He doesn't miss me too much, he still has three mistresses to keep him occupied,' Yvette confided. 'But going home is always lots of fun.' She winked, provocatively to Amanda.

From the corner of her eye, Amanda saw Jason and Crompton exit the side room and start back toward the table. 'Looks like the meeting is about to restart,' she said and started to move back to her seat. Madam Collard followed quickly behind her.

After everyone was seated, Sam Grogan indicated for Sol to continue.

'One fortunate outcome from the Caprica attack is this,' he brought up the file on the screen. 'We now have the course taken by the attack ships, but even better' he changed the image again, 'we now know where the Raider base is, and I'll bet we find Sarclan there too.' The room was silent for a few moments, as this sunk in. Then, almost at once, everyone started talking.

'Please, a moment more,' Sol pleaded, 'before we congratulate ourselves we still have the issue of their formidable weapons. We still haven't cracked that and until we do, and we know their strength, any incursion could be disastrous. I can only assume that either: arrogance, stupidity, or plain luck saw them send some of their older ships to Caprica. My personal view is that they saw it as a soft target; no known defences; no weapons allowed on the planet or in orbit; something I don't think they'll repeat.'

Malik turned to Sol. 'Admiral, what findings have you from the Paladin vessels?'

'None that make sense to us. Our engineers and physicists are still trying to decipher the results from their investigations; as yet we have nothing conclusive.'

JT stood and addressed the group. 'I believe that the weapons they used are not from this realm. We know that two inner realm ships, one from Nileros and one from Galdor, escaped. My assumption, and fear, is that they have teamed up with the Raiders and Sarclan and have given them the improved weapon systems Paladin encountered. I have sent the initial readings from the returning ships, plus their battle logs, to Eldora for analysis. If anyone can find a solution, I believe they can. Until then, and I can't emphasize this strongly enough, we must not enter the Bad-Lands. We must ensure that we inform all colonial leaders as well as the Empire of the situation.'

Madam Collard interrupted. 'Surely, Admiral Abraham, we must try and gather more information... even survey their base now we know where it is... so we can plan an attack. We must remove their threat as soon as we can.'

Sam Grogan replied. 'If I may answer...?'JT nodded his permission, and Sam continued. 'Madam, while I understand the urgency, we cannot risk another disaster like Paladin. Each ship we sent carried 2500 crew. In all, we lost nearly 4,000 souls in that action, plus the returning ships are just scrap.

'Yes, we did destroy two of their ships, ships that were less than half the size of ours, but our losses are telling. Over the past 200 years Space Corps, indeed our entire military, has been severely neglected. We simply cannot afford to trade ship for ship against an adversary whose strength we don't know.' Sam knew this was his best chance of ramming the point home.

'General Klastok also has the same problem with our ground forces. Continual political manoeuvring and a lack of commitment from the Council has left the entire Coalition desperately short of protection. The **very** thing every Council member is elected to do has been neglected, and now all our colonies are vulnerable. This must be reversed before we can do anything, an ill-conceived venture now would be devastating.'

Sam glared at Collard as he spoke. It was well known she was one of the best players in the political game, but even she must accept some of the blame for the situation. Silence fell, and all eyes finally sought Jason out. As new President, he and he alone could seek an answer.

Jason knew the question everyone had in their mind. 'Madam, when will the succession announcement be made?'

Madam Collard glanced at the clock on the far wall - 13:45. 'At two PM, the speaker of the house will table the documents and make the announcement. At five PM we have scheduled broadcast for you and President Malik.'

'So when will I **officially** become President?'

'As soon as the announcement is made and you are sworn in.'

'And where do we do the swearing-in, and who is needed to be there?'

Madam Collard appeared baffled. 'As the leader of the Council, I can perform the ceremony... the only attendees that are required are, the outgoing President, the chief of our armed forces, and myself. Everyone is here in this room, why?'

Jason thought for a moment before calling the President's aide over. After a quick and quiet conversation, he turned back to the rest of the group. 'At five past two, please have a broadcast set up. We'll conduct the ceremony, broadcast from here, and have Graham Argort linked in, as a witness... after that; we can finalize our response to the Caprica incident.'

Jason's decision was the catalyst everyone needed and the room became a flurry of activity. An area was set up for the swearing-in ceremony with the Coalition flag draped over a tall bookcase. A lectern was set up in front of it, four chairs behind and cameras placed at each side and centre to capture the event. It was 13:58 when everything was ready and the view screen had changed to show the Council chamber. The speaker, Karon Chaktur, from Telluria stood in the centre of the Council chamber. Around him were two hundred representatives, the only ones missing were the twenty-four from the colonies that had fallen in the rebellion and Madam Collard.

Karon's deep, rich voice boomed from the speakers. *People of the Coalition of Earth Planets, please heed my words! Today I have received word that President Malik wishes to resign and return to Ummah to assist in rebuilding his planet after the recent rebellion. As per our constitution, he has chosen a replacement to fulfil his obligations as President.*

I hold in my hands the documents of accession duly signed by President Malik, his successor, and the Leader of the Council, Madam Collard. We, the Council, agree to and support this succession and duly announce that Jason Thomas Abraham has been chosen for this role. Both the President and his successor are standing by for the swearing-in ceremony to be completed by Madam Collard.

The scene changed and now the screen showed the presidential party seated behind the lectern. Madam Collard was standing behind the lectern and began to speak. 'President Malik, members of the Council, citizens of the Coalition; today is an auspicious day. For the first time, we have a President resigning and I must add that it saddens us all to see him do so. But, he is doing this for the most honourable of reasons; he is returning to help rebuild his planet and culture after the failed rebellion.

'I admire him for his dedication to his people and pledge to assist in any way we can, and I thank him for his years of service to the Coalition. As our constitution states, any President who must retire during their incumbency is required to select a successor. It is my duty, as leader of the Council, to perform this ceremony to swear in our new President.' She nodded off camera. 'Gentlemen please join me.' Malik, Jason, and Sam stood and moved to the lectern.

President Malik spoke first. 'I, Salim Hussain Malik, relinquish the title of President and transfer all duties, privileges, and authorities of that office to Jason Thomas Abraham. Do you, Jason Thomas Abraham accept?'

Jason replied. 'I, Jason Thomas Abraham, accept the position of President of the Coalition of Earth Planets.'

He turned to face Madam Collard and the entire Coalition as he spoke the pledge, 'I, Jason Thomas Abraham, hereby pledge myself to the office of President of the Coalition of Earth Planets. I pledge to carry out the duties of the office diligently, honestly, and without favour. I pledge to defend the principles of our constitution and the rights of members of the Coalition with justice and honour.' As he completed the pledge, Salim Malik moved in and handed him the Presidential seal and again shook his hand.

Madam Collard announced the broadcast that would be made by President Abraham later at 17:00 and the ceremony was complete. The broadcast was terminated and the group now returned to the table to continue the business at hand.

Duramot materialized exactly where Mondrac had requested, but nowhere near the position their authorized flight plan had indicated.

Goran-Esk stood from his command chair as Mondrac spoke. 'Captain, I suggest you proceed with caution, I don't know if my message was received.'

'Agreed... full shields,' he commanded. The Tactical Officer initiated the shield protection grid.

'Full shields operating, Captain.'

Goran-Esk turned to Mondrac. 'Now what?'

'We wait.'

Goran-Esk turned back to his Bridge crew. 'Tactical... full sensor scans... in the hologram, please.'

Mondrac was still amused by this very human operation. He had to admit, though - so far it was proving to be efficient, but much noisier than he was used to. The sensors showed nothing, and the wait began.

Twenty minutes later, the ship was already using Earth standard time - a proximity sensor sounded the alarm - something was close but the rest of the sensor suite indicated nothing. One of the other crew members, a high-level telepath, spoke. 'Sir, I sense other beings, very close.' The location was placed into the hologram and a small red icon was now close beside Duramot.

'Well done, Altara-Chaddik. Can you identify who is there?'

'No need,' Mondrac responded. 'It will be a ship of Reglaos.'

Unidentified vessel, this is Admiral Tocmal of Reglaos, identify yourself!

Mondrac smiled. 'Tocmal, this is Mondrac on the Eldoran vessel, Duramot. Please will you join us?'

Mondrac, I would love to join you, can you transport me?

'Sorry, old friend. You'll have to come via shuttle unless your ship has a transport pad?'

That is fine I will board a shuttle now. Can you give me a passage through your shield grid?

Mondrac looked over to Goran-Esk who nodded to his Tactical Officer and a path through the shields was initiated. A few minutes later, they saw a small shuttle leave the other vessel and make its way to their shuttle bay. Mondrac left to welcome the visitor, arriving as the shuttle settled to the dock floor. The door opened and out strode Tocmal, in full Admiral Garb, walking confidently through the entry port.

'Mondrac, old friend, it is pleasing to see you again. But I must admit this ship had us a bit concerned, your message said you were going to meet us here, but I wasn't expecting this.'

'Yes, it is a new design based on an ancient human craft. There are many things you will find different from the Eldoran vessels you are accustomed to. Please, come with me... we have much to discuss.'

They reached a transport pod and entered, it stopped at the level of Mondrac's quarters. For the next twenty minutes, they discussed the information Mondrac had received and its ramifications.

'If what you say is true, then Galdor will try and retake the portals. This cannot be allowed.' Tocmal spoke decisively. 'I must prepare our forces; maybe our celebration of peace was somewhat impulsive.'

'You may be correct, my friend, but I would counsel caution and stealth. I am certain they have eyes everywhere. A quick mobilization might be harmful,' Mondrac warned.

'Yes, but we must be ready.' Tocmal thought for a while. 'Maybe we could have a training exercise, a navigation and battle scenario... I don't think that would raise interest.'

'Well thought, I must get this information to the Twelfth Realm quickly... I'll leave here knowing the tenth is in capable hands.' They stood, said their farewells, and walked back to the shuttle bay.

Mondrac watched as the small shuttle went back to the other ship, before contacting the Bridge 'Captain, we can proceed, at your discretion.' He watched as the Reglaos ship initiated its Displacement drive and disappeared, and then he returned to the Bridge.

Duramot was moving slowly towards the next jump point when Tactical called, 'I have an unidentified ship at extreme range.'

The icon was placed into the hologram at a point over one million kilometres away. The seconds ticked by as they watched the new vessel. Goran-Esk turned to his telepath who shook her head, she could not detect anything. The ship appeared to be on a course that wouldn't intersect with Duramot, but it was still unidentified.

Goran-Esk turned to Mondrac, 'What are your instructions?' While he was the Captain, Goran-Esk had no illusions as to who was really in charge of the mission.

After a few minutes of studying the hologram, Mondrac moved to the navigation console. He was familiar with it and interrogated the star charts for this sector of the realm. He summoned the Navigator to him, 'Can we use the Displacement drive to this point and then jump to our previous planned point?' The Navigator studied the chart and agreed.

Mondrac called Goran-Esk over. 'Unfortunately, we will need to divert.' The new course was already in the nav system, all that was needed was the Captain's command.

Goran-Esk studied the course. 'I see no problems... Navigator, execute the course change.'

The Navigator completed the program and Duramot accelerated slightly, made a minor course correction, and proceeded on the new heading. Ten minutes later, the Displacement drive was initiated and Duramot slipped into the relative safety of its wormhole.

***

Jason called Sam and General Klastok to join him at the far end of the room.

'Gentlemen, I need you both to prepare a formal briefing as to the real capacity and disposition of all our armed forces. I don't care what or where it is, I need to know and I need to know soon.'

Unlike most Abrahams, Jason hadn't served in Space Corps. Instead, he had joined the Ground forces and progressed through the ranks. He came to the attention of his superiors during two separate operations and, after some discussions, was offered the opportunity to join Citadel. In its heyday, Citadel was an elite fighting force, getting the most dangerous and, sometimes impossible assignments. This unique group had a history spanning nearly 900 years and only the very best of the best were ever recruited.

Today, Citadel was only a memory. The last 100 years had seen its demise, but both Klastok and Grogan knew Jason's service record and secretly hoped he could reinvigorate the military. 'We also need to somehow get eyes and ears in the Bad-Lands... see what your guys can come up with.'

'Yes sir,' they left to gather their people and start working on the problems. Sam called JT and Sol to his side and asked them to follow him. Jason stood looking at the now depleted room, quietly wondering how things could move so fast. His thoughts were interrupted as Salim Malik moved to his side.

'I wanted to say farewell, Mr. President,' Malik started. 'I can't thank you enough for doing this and I know you'll do a great job.' He bowed his head slightly. 'Should I be able to help you in any small way, please allow me?'

'Of course, I will always appreciate your counsel. Good luck my friend.'

Malik bowed again and walked to the door. He was met by two guards who escorted him to a waiting shuttle which would take him to an orbiting frigate for his journey home.

117

Crompton was at Jason's side. 'Mr. President, we have Garrick.'

'Good, I want him brought here so I can talk to him.'

'I wouldn't advise that, Sir. There may still be a danger to you.'

'Crompton, I think I can handle myself. But to be certain, run him through a complete set of scans and we'll be OK. Also, I want Ms. Bakshi and her team to go over everything you have... and I mean **everything.**' Crompton nodded and went back to his seat, picked up his communicator, and left the room.

Jason went over to the sideboard and poured himself a fresh coffee. He would have preferred something a little stronger, but he needed to keep his wits about him. Amanda joined him. 'Did you sort things out with Crompton?'

'Yes, my dear. It appears he was only the delivery boy. He had just been promoted to Assistant Deputy Station Chief when it all took place. He didn't even know what was in the files, he delivered them and made the calls... even they were scripted... Xanderlou was in charge, back then. He has undertaken to give me all the files and help investigate further if I want.'

'And you believe him?'

'Yes, I do.'

'Well now, Mr. President, you just have to talk to your sons,' Amanda smiled as she turned towards an approaching Madam Collard. 'Yvette, please join us.'

'Mr. President, my congratulations!' She said as she joined them. 'I look forward to working with you but now we must work on your broadcast for tonight. Do you have any particular thoughts you would like to give to the speechwriters?'

'No speechwriters, Madam. I will use my own words,' Jason said firmly. And before she could protest, 'No buts, that's how I want to do it. Now, how is Frank? It must be what, thirty years since I last saw him.'

Sam, JT, and Sol were sitting in JT's office poring over logistics and vessel disposition.

'I never thought it was this bad.' JT said as he scrolled down another page detailing all the mothballed ships. 'Do we have any ships that are in service?' The question wasn't rhetorical, of the 25,000 ships listed as assets for Space Corps, only 3,267 were actually in service - most of them were older than Sam. 'This is a huge fucking mess; most of the ships are old and need replacing.

'The only real force is the 25 new Mantas. The 4 ships that were Paladin were some of the most modern of our heavy units, and even they were over 50 years old. Without calling on Freebooters again, we would be lucky to stop an aggressive force of Ranger Scouts.' He slammed the data-pad down in frustration and leaned back in his chair.

'I told you we had issues when I offered you the job but even then, I didn't realize how bad it was,' Sam remarked as he called his aide, 'Get Admiral Hubbard here... pronto!' He turned back to the others. 'Ivan, I hope our ground forces are better prepared.'

General Ivan Klastok, Commander of Coalition ground forces shook his head; great sadness was written over his face. Klastok was a large man - his nickname Bear was a tribute to this. He was tall, slightly over 190cm and his frame tipped the scales at 145Kg, but he carried no excess fat. His exercise regime was brutal and he could hold his own with almost any of his subordinates in any competition, even though most were half his age. His grey eyes had a haunted edge to them as he spoke, 'I regret that we are even worse off than Space Corps.

'Back during the Krell conflict we had over 2.5 million troops; now we are down to a little over 200,000. Most of them are career men and they are not getting any younger. As for equipment, that is even worse, our armour is over 100 years old and mostly parked up. One plus though is our small arms... both side and long arms are the latest available.'

'How did it get this bad?' Sol asked.

'Politicians... we have presented several recruitment programs but they have either been delayed in committee, or simply refused. The consensus was we don't need the expense of a substantial military, and most of the politicians have their agendas and pet projects... they're damn good at making deals that get what they want. I have made several petitions to President Malik, but even he couldn't get them approved.' His discourse was halted by a knock at the door; it opened and Admiral Hubbard walked through.

'Admiral, you wanted to see me?'

'Yes, sit down Tony.' Sam pointed to a vacant chair at the table and Hubbard took his seat. 'You're well versed in the antics of the Council; can you tell me why they have let our defences run down so badly?'

Admiral Tony Hubbard was an unassuming man, tall with short red hair. He also sported a flaming red beard, cut to regulation length, and his deep emerald eyes had been the undoing of many young women in his day. He gazed around the room, trying to formulate his answer, *Where to start*? He asked himself; drawing a long breath, he began.

'Since you appointed me to this position I have been conducting an audit of how our procurement process works or doesn't, and discovered quite a bit of history.

'Over the past 200 years, since the Krell conflict, the military procurement process has gone through huge changes. To streamline things all procurement requests have been channelled through one office... now my office. There have been three Logistics Commanders to date, not including myself, and each has...' he stopped, looking for the right words.

'Just spit it out, fuck diplomacy now!' Sam snapped.

'Each of my predecessors has tied things up in so much red tape, that nothing got through.'

'Bullshit!' Sam cried out. 'What about Galileo? That got funded!'

'Yes, but that was by direct negotiation with the Council; procurement wasn't in the loop. Even a request from the President has to come through my office, and I can tell you all those have been delayed or locked up they'll never see the light of day... and before you ask, most never got as far as Admiral Morris' desk. Almost everything, for the last fifty years at least, stopped with Captain Dean, or his predecessor.' Hubbard finished and sat down.

Sam spoke quietly to JT, 'Sometimes, John, I wish you had left that bastard back at Zyralin 4.'

Hubbard continued. 'Part of this investigation was into the people who had held this office. Those prior to Dean are dead, and there are some anomalies to suggest they were fudging the books, but no actual evidence. Dean had some... interesting finances. He has properties on three separate worlds. He's also being paid regular, and substantial, amounts supposedly from some family inheritance; I can't dispute that and he had declared it in his pecuniary interests file, but, the source of the funds has been difficult to trace. Everything's in the report that I sent you this morning, Admiral.'

Sol changed the direction of the conversation. 'OK, we all know Dean was an arsehole, but where does that leave us. We're still behind the eight-ball and we need some response capability.'

Hubbard spoke, again. 'I think we can get a lot more through now. General, this morning I received approval for the new ground vehicles and air support craft you have been chasing. The orders are being sent to the manufacturers today.'

Klastok swore in Russian, but smiled, 'We have been waiting for those to be cleared for two years... finally some progress! Thank you, Admiral.' Further discussion was halted as the door opened and the aide admitted Jason and Crompton.

'Sorry to interrupt,' Jason started, 'but I need your report by eighteen hundred tonight, so I can read it before I meet with the Council tomorrow.' Without waiting for an answer, he turned and left.

***

Jason and Crompton walked in silence down the corridor,

finally arriving at the interview room. They stopped at the door. 'Anthony, give me the data- pad, I want to talk to Garrick alone, at first.'

'But, Sir, that's against protocol! What if he is a direct threat? I advise against this, Sir.'

'Your people scanned him, right?'

Crompton nodded in confirmation.

Jason continued, 'I have known Rowland Garrick for many years, I believe I'll be fairly safe, but the interview is **not** to be recorded, understand?' Again, Crompton inwardly seethed at this dropping of protocol, but he had no choice but to agree.

The room was small, only 3 metres by 3 metres, the only furnishings were a table and three uncomfortable chairs. The walls were standard drab grey; there were no windows, mirrors, or any other decorations. If a subject was claustrophobic, this would feel like a small tomb. There was light emanating from the ceiling and this could be dulled or intensified as the interrogator wished.

The man sitting in the single chair on the other side of the table was not who one would expect to find in this situation. He was well groomed, wearing an expensive suit and shoes. He was not particularly tall, or exceptional in any way. His face was unremarkable, a feature that had been one of his greatest assets during his field years - he didn't stand out and was easily forgotten. Jason noticed Garrick was cuffed to the table; he faced Crompton and demanded the key.

He turned and threw the key to Garrick, 'Rowland Garrick, been a long time,' Jason said quietly as he sat down, opposite to Garrick.

'Yeah, a long time Jason. Now what the fuck is this all about?'

Jason activated the data-pad and selected a file, 'Read this, Rowley.'

Garrick read the file, the colour slowly draining from his face. Jason retrieved the pad and selected another file. 'Read this,' and he passed the pad back.

This time Garrick's response was different, more assertive.

'My ID code, so what?'

'Well, then, tell me how your personal ID code was used to send this message?' Jason demanded.

'Bullshit... and why am I talking to **you**? What the fuck is going on, Jason?'

'There has been a change of leadership,' Jason spoke confidently. 'I am now the President and if I ask you a question, I expect a bloody answer fast. Understand?'

'What? Where is Malik?' Garrick started but then recalled the first file he read. 'You don't think I had anything to do with this, do you?'

Jason had resumed his seat. 'Frankly Rowley, I don't know what to believe. Let me fill you in. First, there was the attack on Caprica. We now know that I was the real target... three million people died in an attempt to disguise the fact, and Barton City was wiped out. Then, when we get back to Earth, Malik tells me he wants to quit and asks me to take over for the remainder of his term.

'Next, this morning, on our way to the Palace we're intercepted by a full squadron of Dart fighters and escorted back to Perth. Now I seem to have evidence that you, someone I thought I could trust, may be the ringleader. So, as you see, I'm not having the best of days and I need some answers, now, before I lose my fucking temper.'

Rowland Garrick remembered the only time he had seen Jason lose his temper. It was many years ago when they were both serving in the military. They were in an expeditionary force, looking for a Raider base on one of the Dandaro moons. They didn't find the base - it sort of found them - and they were trapped in a very bad place.

They had dropped into a shallow ravine when a group of the pirates opened fire from a hilltop above them. While their position gave cover, they were trapped and split up. They managed to form three groups, but the situation was grave, anyone who put their head up, paid an awful price. They lost three in the first barrage and four more were wounded.

They couldn't advance and they couldn't retreat. The mission was supposed to be one of Intel gathering, to confirm that the Raiders had departed; now they were in a firefight with forces that weren't supposed to exist, on that moon. They huddled under cover all day, exchanging fire when the opportunity arose, without achieving any advantage.

For a morning engagement, their adversaries had chosen their ambush location well, but as the day wore on a mistake became evident. As the moon rotated, the star that gave it light moved behind the soldiers and would be directly in the faces of the enemy. As the sun dropped, Jason made a decision, gave his orders, and moved to the left flank.

On his command, everyone opened fire at the hilltop. Jason leaped from behind cover and raced up the hill, the fire from his troops sending the opponents diving for cover. Exactly three minutes after it began, the cover fire stopped and the enemy emerged and began return fire.

By this time Jason had secured the spot he was aiming for, he stopped and caught his breath before leaping down from the rocks above the enemy emplacement, firing as he dropped. He landed in the middle of them, twelve in all, but didn't stop firing. He pivoted on his left foot and spun in a circle, his blaster firing continuously. When he completed the spin, all twelve Raiders were either dead or badly wounded.

Then he raced into the shallow cave behind the position, where he located the two leaders. One he dispatched with the last of the energy pack in his blaster, the other simply threw his weapon down and surrendered, not knowing that his opponent's gun was dry - that was the day Garrick learned that Jason was a Citadel operative.

All this flashed through Garrick's mind and he could now see the same look in Jason's eyes.

'Killing me would be bad enough, I know damned well that

there are a few who would like to see me dead, but to target my wife as well, that pisses me off, do you understand Rowland?' Jason hissed - his teeth clenched in anger.

'Jason, I didn't have anything to do with this, that is **not** my message.' Garrick's voice was adamant.

'Then how come it originated from your console, with your access code?'

'I don't know, but you know me... if I wanted you dead, I'd do it myself. You know that, Jason.' The two men glared at each other, memories now flooding back.

Jason nodded and sat back down, 'But this is damning evidence, how do you explain it?'

'I can't, those codes are supposed to be impregnable, nothing or no-one should be able to break them or access them. I have no explanation but I swear to you, I am innocent!' Garrick said with conviction.

Crompton sat in the next room, not believing what he saw. He knew Rowland Garrick - they had been on several operations together. He had never seen any fear in the man, but what he just witnessed made a cold shiver run down his spine causing Crompton to reconsider his view of his new boss.

Seems there's more to President Abraham than meets the eye, he thought. He saw both men in the other room stand, so he left his spot and met them in the corridor.

Jason said frankly. 'We're wrong here Crompton... Garrick isn't responsible.'

'I agree. But that leaves us with more problems.' He was alluding to the fact that the un-hackable codes had indeed been hacked.

'That's why I have Ms. Bakshi and her team sifting through your files, maybe she can pick up what happened.'

'What, you're having a Corps group look through CID files?' Crompton was incredulous. 'They don't have the clearance!'

'They do now. Besides, do you know who you can trust in CID, at this moment?' Jason had a point and Crompton had to agree, even so, he was unhappy.

Their discussion was interrupted by a Presidential aide.

'Mr. President, it's almost seventeen hundred, sir.'

Jason checked his watch; he had only been in the job for three hours.

Hell of a first day, he thought as he followed the aide, signalling for the other two to join him. They walked a couple of steps behind as Jason set a brisk pace, he wanted to get this broadcast over. They reached the small room that had been set up for the purpose and waited outside the door as the President entered. The door closed and a few minutes later a small red glow emanated from the annunciator panel, indicating that the room was sealed.

Crompton turned to Garrick. 'Rowland, what happened in that interview, I know you and I have never seen you show any fear. What gives?'

Garrick quickly told Crompton the story of Dandaro 5, no embellishment just the facts.

Even so, Crompton was moved. 'Abraham was Citadel, he was an operative?'

'Then yes, but he rose to Group Commander, an entire unit of six teams. What I saw in his eyes in that room, was the same as on that day. Believe me; I don't want to be on the receiving end of that.'

Both men stood silently for the next fifteen minutes, each lost in their thoughts. The light on the annunciator changed to green and Jason came through the door. He felt better, lighter as if a weight had been lifted, he smiled at both, 'I am so bloody glad that's over, Anthony, can we get some food? I'm starving?'

'I'll see what I can find,' Crompton agreed as they walked back down the corridor to the meeting room.

***

Duramot exited its worm-hole mid-way between the twin pulsar stars. Although she was constructed of the new Acrilan/Resin compound and was virtually invisible except when in close proximity to others, like all space ships, she did leave traces of her passage. Residual heat trace, ion trail, and latent energy tracks could all be detected, some a long time after a ship had passed.

Using the vagaries of the space between these two stars should mask any trace they inadvertently left. She was in the area no longer than a few seconds - just enough time to plot the course and engage the jump drive - but Mondrac was in no mood to leave any clues behind. Twenty-two hours later, she emerged in the Twelfth Realm, outside Jupiter Station.

Goran-Esk opened the Coalition hailing frequency. 'Jupiter Station, this is Eldoran vessel Duramot, please respond.'

Duramot, this is Jupiter Station, we cannot detect you, please transmit your location. Goran-Esk sighed - sometimes the new hull coating could be such a problem - he signalled his Navigation Officer to comply.

Duramot, Jupiter Station, we have scanned that location and there is nothing there, please re-transmit correct co-ordinates.

'Navigator, turn on the transponder.' When he saw it had been activated, he called the Station again. 'Jupiter Station, my apologies; this is a new vessel and we had a slight problem with our transponder. Can you see it now?'

Duramot, this is Commander Hargraves, we see your signal, what is your intended destination?

Before Goran-Esk could answer, Mondrac interrupted, cutting the comms.

'Do not reply, we need secrecy at this point. Let me handle this.' He moved to the comm station and asked the operator to send a message, then contacted the Station, 'Jupiter Station, this is Duramot. We are on a diplomatic mission and prudence dictates we keep our ultimate destination confidential; we only request permission to transit your sphere of operations.'

Duramot, Commander Hargraves, who is in charge of this diplomatic mission?

Bureaucrats are the same everywhere; he thought but instead replied, 'Ambassador Mondrac, of Eldora.' He used Mondrac's formal title, hoping it would speed things up. As he spoke the Tactical Officer beckoned Goran-Esk to his console; they conferred for a couple of seconds and then Goran-Esk pointed to the Navigation hologram.

Ambassador Mondrac, please transmit your validation code.

Mondrac swore. This Hargraves was a "by the book" man, as he had heard A-Bra-Ham describe certain officials, but he complied. The hologram showed three new vessels entering their sensor range; Tactical was desperately trying to identify them.

Slowly an image began to form on the display screen. These ships were different from anything Mondrac had seen. They were long and sleek, the front was square and tapered slightly down and back to the body. It seemed to flow in one delicate, slightly curved line to the rear which was also squared off. There were no view ports and no external protrusions; Mondrac's sixth sense was starting to itch. He was about to speak when the Telepath caught his attention.

'Mondrac' she said, 'they are mainly human minds on those ships, but there are others I can't identify. I can feel that they are intent on stopping us, they are a danger.'

Duramot, Jupiter Station. Ambassador Mondrac you are cleared to transit our sector.

Mondrac replied. 'Jupiter Station, this is Ambassador Mondrac. Thank you, but might I suggest you inspect sector...' he looked at the hologram, now inside it held the standard Space Corps grid navigation system... 'sector G twelve? There are three unidentified ships of foreign design that I fear may be hostile. I would suggest you raise your level of alert, just in case.' As he spoke the ship was already moving away toward its next jump point.

Ambassador, thank you for the warning but Jupiter Station will make its own assessment.

Mondrac shook his head at this but was stopped from

responding by Goran-Esk. 'Mondrac, you do realize that we are not allowed to use the jump drive, in the Solar System?'

Mondrac smiled, 'I recall something A-Bra-Ham once told me. *"It is easier to ask for forgiveness than permission;"* so I say... as he would... fuck the rules, just do it.'

He felt strangely elated at uttering these words, *maybe there is something to the human tendency to curse, after all*, he thought - but his thoughts were shattered by the Tactical Officer.

'Captain, one of the ships has broken off and is on an intercept course... somehow they are tracking us.' He couldn't understand this, the ship's construction made it invisible to sensors.

Then Mondrac remembered, 'The transponder, they are following it!' He cried as he moved to switch it off.

Goran-Esk had returned to the command chair 'Tactical, power up the shields and weapons, Navigator change course to 020 by 265. Keep tracking a jump point.'

'Goran-Esk, what are you doing? We need to get to Earth urgently,' Mondrac cried.

'I know, Mondrac, but we were still over two minutes from our insertion point and that ship is only moments from effective weapons range. We're sitting ducks, as humans say. Tactical, what are they doing?'

'They are still following the original track, they can't see us now.'

'Good. Navigator, do you have a solution for our jump?' Goran-Esk asked.

'Yes, course 105 by 085 and we jump in 2 minutes and 40 seconds, at .5 light speed.'

'Authorized!' The ship changed direction, again. They remained at high battle readiness, until, the jump drive engaged. Duramot slipped quietly into subspace when shields were powered down.

It was a shallow insertion and seventeen minutes later they emerged back into the Solar System, behind Earth's moon. Mondrac asked for a hailing channel to be opened and was rewarded with the response he wanted.

Duramot, this is Condor Junior, we have you on visual. We are 500 metres off your port quarter and 4 degrees above your horizon. We will close to 100 metres, welcome to Earth.

Aaron slowly moved Junior to within 100 metres of the larger vessel; he led them, via a stealthy route, to an old Abracorp base on the Moon. Once they had both landed and Duramot was safely hidden in one of the more remote hangars, Mondrac transferred to Junior for the trip to Earth. Captain Goran-Esk and his crew stayed aboard in case they needed a quick exit.

'A-Bra-Ham, Man-Nix, it is pleasing to see you again, but I would prefer the circumstances to be better,' Mondrac said as he walked onto the Bridge.

Petra embraced Mondrac as Aaron initiated the yacht's drive system. 'Always lovely to see you, Mondrac.'

Aaron moved Junior away from the umbilical and turned toward the exit portal. The hangar was located deep underground away from other structures and the other three bases on the Moon, their incursion should go unnoticed. The force field flashed white, then green as the small vessel left, quickly traversing the 200 metres to the surface. Here it stopped and waited as the remote sensor array adjacent to the ground opening gave the area one last sweep.

Receiving the all clear, Aaron urged the ship forward and out of the tunnel. The hangar complex had been built in the times of the Second and had been the base for Abracorp Salvage during the operation to clear Earth's orbit of space junk. It had been used for various purposes over the years but now was in a care and maintenance role and rarely visited.

As per Mondrac's request, Aaron had programmed the nav system with a very circuitous route to avoid any visual detection. The hull coating should protect them from any sensors until they reached the atmosphere. Once there the new ground systems could detect atmospheric Displacement, potentially rendering their present efforts useless. He turned the ship over to the nav system and finally welcomed his friend.

'We are now on our way but I must say, all this secrecy has tweaked my interest. What's up, Mondrac?'

'Much my friend, much... I have the analysis from the data you sent me and it is not good... I need to get it to Gro-Gan urgently and quietly. That is why I need all these precautions.' He was serious, more than Aaron could remember from their past exploits.

'Mondrac much has changed here also. I'd better fill you in before we land.'

Aaron familiarized Mondrac with the current situation, as he understood it, and suggested he should try and contact Grogan to set up a meeting. Mondrac agreed and Aaron placed the call. It took a few minutes for Sam to be located and when Aaron told him he had Mondrac and the data, Sam asked him to go directly to Perth Space Port, hangar 6.

Aaron took control of the yacht and changed course for Perth. Seven minutes later, they were on final approach to the hangar. Aaron kept Junior a few centimetres off the ground until the hangar door slid down, giving Junior access. Before he could rotate and settle the craft, the door had closed and twenty security guards had entered the hangar. In front of them was Sam Grogan.

Aaron grounded the yacht and lowered the boarding ramp; Grogan hastened aboard. He was met at the top by Mondrac who, in un-Eldoran fashion, greeted Sam with a firm handshake.

'Welcome Ambassador, if you would follow me.' Sam turned and led them down the ramp with the security guards splitting, half-forming a cordon around the ship, the other ten escorting the group to the elevator.

The elevator stopped five floors below and the door opened; Sam exited first and led them at a brisk pace down the corridor. He stopped at a door on his right, entered a code into the keypad and a thin red light washed over him. Satisfied as to his identity, the door opened; they were now in the same conference room that had been used all day. Mondrac smiled as Jason stood to greet him.

'Ambassador, welcome,' Jason said simply.

'President A-Bra-Ham, I am pleased to see you again,' Mondrac handed the data-pad to Jason, 'If you could integrate this with your system, I will show you my findings.'

Jason handed the pad to an aide and directed Mondrac to take the seat to his right. The aide quickly activated the system and looked up; the pad was now matched to the system and Mondrac began his presentation.

'This information came from an old and trusted source in the Galdoran Hierarchy, someone I trust and have worked with for many cycles. The weapons used against your Task Force were of Galdoran origin and are a system they refer to as *spear and shield*; I believe the translation is correct.' He referred to his grasp of Basic English.

'The shield is the new, almost impenetrable ones you encountered. They are the same shield systems but they use a random frequency and harmonic modulation, making them almost impossible to penetrate. The spear is a new directed energy weapon that focuses an extremely narrow energy beam of immense power; I believe this was able to cut through your shields like they were not there?'

He glanced across to Sol who nodded. 'Fortunately, there is a way to protect against that weapon; the shield, though is another story. We cannot find any way to actually penetrate it, and our best scientists and engineers are still working on a solution. My contact did tell me one thing, however; the shield uses immense amounts of energy. One possibility is to overload it, force it to shut down, but I don't know if your, or even our weapons can do that.' He stopped to allow everyone in the room time to digest the information.

It was JT who broke the silence. 'Mondrac, is this the same system they used to protect the portal power supply?'

'No... that used a regulated shield modulation... it did

constantly change but it was to a set pattern. This one is completely random, that is why it uses so much energy.'

'Yes, but we almost broke through the field on the portal with Sling Shot; maybe it would do the same with this.'

'And that almost destroyed us in subspace,' Petra added.

'My point exactly,' JT agreed. 'The shield system couldn't deflect or absorb that amount of energy so it diverted it into the portal system, causing the subspace equivalent of a tsunami, but we could have more than doubled the energy with our next barrage; that may be enough to destabilize the shield system. If so, we may have a way to counter their shields, but the spear, how do we counter that?' He turned to Mondrac, hoping for a simple answer.

'There are two possibilities. The first is simple but not readily available. The resin from Reglaos when put over your Acrilan is able to diffuse the weapon, but we have not trialled this in battle. The problem is the ability of Reglaos to supply this resin; it is only able to be produced in very small amounts, as you are aware.

The second possibility... but again we have not tested it... is to modify your shield generators to diffuse, not deflect, the energy beam, make it less focused and therefore, less powerful. If that can be achieved, then your absorption field may be able to negate the weapon, at least for a short time. Those are the only options we have been able to come up with.' Mondrac finished his explanation and sat down.

Jason turned to JT. 'Admiral, who is heading up the Manta program now?'

'Amy Rodregas.'

'Can you have her liaise with Ambassador Mondrac? Let's see if we can make these modifications quickly,' Jason suggested.

'Yes sir,' JT immediately left to contact Amy.

hillip Hargraves was incensed.

Eldoran Ambassador or not, that ship didn't have any right to use their new drive system when he had **specifically** given them instructions on how they were to transit the Solar System. Adding to this, the three new ships - now in his sphere of control - were not responding to any hails. Two were still on an intercept course to the Station while the third was accelerating towards the Eldoran vessel. When the Eldoran vessel vanished, one of the unidentified vessels did the same, he knew he would have to file a complaint and lay charges against both Captains. His thoughts were interrupted by one of the operators.

'Sir, the two vessels on approach, they've raised shields and are powering their weapons.'

'What? They are not permitted to do that, hail them.' Hargraves yelled, he was tired of the flagrant disregard for procedures he was seeing here, 'warn their Captain that we will lay formal charges if he doesn't power those systems down immediately!'

'Sir, I don't think they will worry about charges.' To his left, the Defence Officer was busy raising the Station's shields and initializing weapons and, simultaneously transmitting a warning, to all ships in the area that the Station may be under attack. Hargraves noticed this and exploded.

'Why are you doing that, I didn't give the command!' He screamed at the younger Officer.

While the Defence Officer was young, she knew how to deal with bureaucrats like Hargraves.

She spoke calmly. 'Commander... Space Corps' manual, section seven, paragraph three, *"in the event any ship or Station is approached by any vessel that indicates it has hostile intent, the response must be to initiate appropriate defensive measures to negate any threat, real or implied,'* " she quoted the operations manual verbatim. 'I'm only following standard operating protocols, Sir.' Hargraves knew she was right, but it had been a long time since the weapons systems had been activated in response to any threat, 'Sir, shall I sound General Quarters?'

'Yes, I suppose we should,' Hargraves capitulated, petulantly.

Alarms began wailing throughout the Station followed by the announcement... *General Quarters, all crew man your Battle Stations! All civilians proceed to the closest emergency shelter, this is not a drill!*

The message repeated itself and the alarms kept screaming for three minutes, then silence. The Station's weapons and shields were at full power and the two ships had closed to within 50,000 kilometres, almost within weapons range. They split and moved to divergent tracks, now offering two distinct targets instead of one. Their approach speed didn't change.

Again, Hargraves tried to hail them. 'Unidentified vessels, this is Commander Hargraves on Jupiter Station! You are ordered to return to the outer mark, immediately. Any further approach to this Station will be considered an attack and we will respond accordingly.' Hargraves' voice showed the stress of the situation; he'd never been in a real battle situation, the closest he had come was simulation training at the Academy, many years ago.

Jupiter Station, this is Coalition vessel Valkyrie, do you require assistance?

Valkyrie was the latest Manta to be commissioned and she had completed her final weapons range trial. Commander Colin Bryant, former Defence Officer on Valiant, was in command; he waited for a response.

'Valkyrie, this is Commander Hargraves on Jupiter Station. Yes, we could do with your assistance; I will transmit the tactical data so you can assist.'

***

135

No need, Commander, we can see well enough from where we are. Valkyrie had just entered Jupiter Station's sphere when the call came through, the Comms Officer was about to contact the Station for clearance when Jupiter had called for help.

'Guns spin everything up, just in case,' Colin called and activated the red alert function on his console. 'This is the Captain,' he began to broadcast to the entire ship. 'It appears that there is a problem at Jupiter Station, it may be nothing but we will take no chances. Everyone get to your Battle Stations pronto; let's see what the flap is about.' He turned towards his Tactical Officer. 'Anything?'

'Two unidentified ships, both exhibiting weapons active readings on attack course to the Station. I can't identify them... they aren't in the database.'

'Shit! Helm, full power to the drive... let's get there quick.' Colin ordered. The Manta surged forward, she had the latest Gravitron drive from Greenbach Technologies, and her acceleration was far better than her predecessors.

'Shields at max, all weapons initiated and the Sling Shot's online Sir,' the Weapons Officer called.

'Sir, both bogies are firing on the Station, direct hits, their shields didn't work!' Proctor called back. 'Station returning fire, no effect, these bogies seem tough.'

'How soon to firing range?' Colin called.

'Ten seconds.'

'OK, prepare a full spread of torpedos, target the starboard ship, blasters to the port vessel, fire on my command,' he called and started counting the seconds to himself. No point in firing too soon, all that would do was waste energy.

Colin waited, ten seconds, twenty. On his count of thirty, he called. 'Fire!'

Immediately six mark nine torpedos spat out of their cradles and the forward blaster bank erupted, spewing raw energy towards the second ship. Both weapons found their targets, with no spectacular results. The shields of both bogies flared as the energy from the weapons impacted on them but suffered no damage.

'No effect,' the Weapons Officer Sharon Carmody reported. She was young but had trained with Helen Tradeski, a legend in the weapons community, and someone Colin had served with on Valiant.

'OK, bring the big guns out. Three spread from Sling Shot, 50mm shots.'

Sharon smiled. She loved nothing more than using Sling Shot, it gave her a sense of total power and dominance; after all, it was supposed to be the most powerful weapon in the galaxy. She spun up the three shots her Captain had ordered. 'Sling Shot ready, Sir.'

'Sir, the starboard ship has turned, heading straight for us,' Proctor said.

Colin swore to himself. 'Put everything in the Bubble, use Sling Shot on the port ship, torps, and blasters on the starboard one... fire at will.' The Bubble now showed the battle scene, the two bogies, his ship, and the Station. The bogie to port was firing on the Station again, its weapons sending devastating energy blasts to the structure.

It was as though the Station didn't have any shields; the bogie's weapon tore into the structure causing incredible damage. Sling Shot fired, the indicator in the Bubble showing the track. The other bogie was being slammed by torpedos and the blasters, with no effect. It fired its weapons and they slammed into Valkyrie. Alarms screamed, consoles went dark, even the Bubble failed. The amount of energy hitting the ship was huge, too much for the shields to deflect or the absorption field to absorb.

'Damage, number one... helm, evasive action!' Colin called.

First Officer, Andrea Coulton worked her console. 'No hull breaches. Absorption battery full, that one shot overloaded it!'

'Tactical, where is it? The Bubble's down?'

'Bubble re-initiating; the bogie is coming up behind us,'

'Helm, come to course two-one-five by zero-six-seven... execute.' This brought the ship to a violent turn to the left and increased their vertical attitude, just as the enemy fired. The manoeuvre caused it to miss, but allowed them to see the result of Sling Shot on the other ship. It had been hit, and pretty badly and was yawing off course away from the Station.

'Their shields are down,' Tactical called.

'Guns, ready another spread of torpedos, and work Sling Shot again, this time for the other bastard.'

'Torpedoes, ready... Sling Shot in ten seconds.'

'Fire torpedos,' Colin said in a calm voice. The torpedos flew from their cradles, speeding towards the target at over half the speed of light. Each found the target. The rear section of the ship suffered catastrophic damage, the primary reactor was breached and all power was lost; without their reactor, life support wouldn't last long. 'Now where is the other one?'

The Bubble finished its power-up cycle and the images began to coalesce. The other bogie was turning away, heading out of the battle zone. 'Guns!' Colin called. Sharon Carmody smiled as she fired Sling Shot.

'Sling Shot fired, sir!' The three invisible balls of antimatter sped toward the enemy at the speed of light. The bogie was attempting to initiate a Displacement field when the first anti-matter sphere struck momentarily overloading the shields, but it didn't stop the Displacement initiation. Before any more damage could be done it disappeared into its wormhole and was gone.

'Damn,' Carmody hissed, as she tapped the destruct icon. Immediately both of the two remaining spheres exploded, harmlessly, 'Sorry sir, we missed it.'

'Doesn't matter... we stopped the attack, that's the main thing. Comms contact Space Corps and fill them in. Number one let's see if we can help the Station.'

'Yes Sir. Helm set course for the Station, one-third power on the drive.' Valkyrie changed course to a normal Jupiter Station approach, temporarily placing them between the Station and the now unpowered enemy vessel.

'Jupiter Station, this is ECS Valkyrie on approach. We request docking clearance.' Valkyrie's course was taking her on a direct track toward the hangar section of the Station, an area that hadn't been targeted by the bogies.

Earth Coalition Ship Valkyrie, docking permission granted, and thank-you for your assistance... Please proceed on your present course... you are cleared for bay seven-alpha.

'Jupiter Station, Valkyrie on course, we confirm docking in bay seven-alpha.' Colin confirmed and turned to the Helm. 'Helm, bay seven-alpha if you please.'

The Comms Officer spoke 'Sir, I am getting no response from the enemy ship.'

As soon as the battle had ended, comms had started hailing the stricken ship. One of the sacrosanct rules of space is, you never leave anyone stranded, so by the tradition of Space Corps, she had been trying to contact them to offer assistance. 'Sir, I have a priority call from Admiral Abraham, video.'

'Put it on the view screen.' Immediately, JT Abraham's face appeared.

Well done, Commander. Your new ship seems to have succeeded spectacularly... any damage?

'Surprisingly none, but their weapons were incredible... we managed to cripple one but the other got away,'

You mean 2 got away... we had a report of 3 bogies from the Station? JT cut in.

Colin shook his head. 'No Sir, we only had 2 bogies here.'

*Colin, whatever you do, **don't dock**. You don't want to be tied up if there is another bad guy out there and get a security team from the Station to that other vessel. We need to know what we are dealing with'* JT stopped, listening to another conversation. *Wait-one!* He turned away from the camera to speak to someone else, *Belay that last order, the Station Commander is on the line now... we'll get the security boys moving. You make sure the* *ship is secured...* Abraham out.' The comm ended abruptly.

'You heard the Admiral,' Colin called to the Bridge crew. 'Comms inform the Station of our new orders. Number one, get a team ready, full hostile environment gear; Helm, come about. Put us a couple of hundred metres off that ship's bow Guns, load everything. Let's move people!'

Everyone sprang into action and carried out their assigned tasks. The First Officer selected ten crew members for the expeditionary team, the Pilot brought the ship to a complete stop two hundred metres off the bogie's bow and comms confirmed their actions to the Station.

The Bridge crew studied the enemy craft on the view screen. It was larger than Valkyrie, by about half and a shape they had never seen before. It had a rectangular front that was the width of the ship; it curved slightly on the upper surface but the lower was completely flat. There were two ports on the front section, presumably weapons housings. The outer upper edges of the superstructure were raised, forming a ridge that ran the full length of the ship on each side.

'Still no life signs, Skipper.' Tactical had been scanning the vessel constantly. 'They must've had a total environmental failure the instant we hit it.'

As they were all watching their shuttle came into view, slowly heading to the other craft. It changed course and did a complete pass over the vessel and came back under it.

No signs of any life... there is a large hole at the rear; looks like the primary reactor blew. We are taking radiation readings... there seems to be some anomaly... The voice of the First Officer trailed off. *Valkyrie, we are getting some residual Trisidium readings, can you confirm?* Everyone knew how deadly this could be, so precautions would be paramount.

'Helm, move us to the rear, where the reactor used to be,' Colin spoke, and the ship started to change position. 'Tactical, scan the whole area thoroughly.' He called the shuttle, 'Number one, stand by, make your distance two hundred metres.'

The shuttle complied and began moving away. Valkyrie approached the rear of the ship, the result of the battle displayed. Most of the rear, port side, was missing - a huge, jagged hole remained where this section used to be.

'Skipper, I confirm trace residual Trisidium radiation. I have sent the data to the Med Bay... see if they can work out the danger. I think we should send in a remote before we board,' Proctor suggested.

'Good idea Alain... do it!'

Almost immediately, a small remote probe left Valkyrie's hold. It headed directly to the huge hull breach. Lieutenant Azargo, Valkyrie's Science Officer was handling the probe. Skilfully he sent it into the open wound on the side of the ship, its video feed showing the damage. The bogie's construction was different and they could only guess what was supposed to be in the missing section. Slowly, and with great care, Azargo moved the probe around twisted metal, over crumpled consoles. Finally, he stopped.

'Trisidium readings are decreasing. I believe our people could enter here, but they'll need radiation suits.' He moved the probe a little further forward and reached what was obviously the main corridor - the door was open. He tapped at his control console and an intense light blazed from the probe, lighting up the corridor. There before them was the open corridor. No bulkhead doors were closed; everything was open.

'Sir, this doesn't make any sense. They should have sealed each section before they engaged us... what's happened is unbelievable. When we breached their hull it initiated an explosive decompression.' He panned the probe's camera to emphasize the damage.

'With all these doors open,' he aimed the camera to the bulkheads forward of the probe, 'the atmosphere would have blown out the rear of the hull, where we breached it... this doesn't make any sense.' He repeated himself, quietly, in total disbelief.

The truth of his words hit Colin like a sledgehammer. No Commander in his right mind would ever go into any battle with his ship so open, in fact, Coalition Space Corps' regulations, and common sense, dictated that a ship must be sectionalized and sealed at all times. To leave it this open was insane.

'Mr. Azargo, can you see if any sections still hold atmosphere? Maybe there are some survivors?' Colin asked solemnly.

'Aye Sir, I'll check.' He moved the probe deeper into the ship, testing every door to see if there was any atmosphere left in the ship.

'Number one, have your team don radiation outers. We detect some radiation but the suits should protect you long enough.' Each time a team left the ship for one of these missions, they always carried extra equipment, as a precaution.

The **rad suits**, as they were affectionately called, were thin material designed to protect the wearer from hostile radiation. It was also durable and could take quite a bit of abuse before it tore or abraded. The team unpacked the suits and put them on over their battle suits.

Expeditionary team ready, Valkyrie, Coulton announced when they were suited up.

'OK number one, I'll have the feed from the probe sent to you... be careful, and record **everything**. We'll be sending this back to Earth.'

Colin watched the feed from the team. First, they entered the ship via the damaged hull section. With all power now gone there was no artificial gravity so they were all moving like bulbous puppets, safely ensconced in their battle and radiation suits. One thing he didn't envy them was the zero-grav work; he still remembered how his stomach reacted the last time he had to do this.

The team split into three units as soon as they had passed over the debris field; all that remained of the engineering section of the ship. Two hung back, to act as both safety sweep and rear guard; the others formed into two groups of four. The first group headed directly to where they believed the Bridge to be, the others performing inspections of each room they encountered. First Officer Coulton led the Bridge-group while Security Chief Sam Maxwell drew the grizzly task of inspecting the various spaces they passed down the main corridor.

Affectionately known as "**Goliath**", Sam was a huge guy with hands that everyone thought would be able to strangle a bear. He wore his hair long in a non-regulation ponytail that no one ever made any jokes about. Normally quiet and seemingly gentle, Goliath was the sort of guy you wanted on your side if things went downhill.

He led his group to the first door as Andrea and her three followed the probe forward. 'No time like the present,' he whispered as he disengaged the door lock and used his impressive strength to slide the heavy door aside. The second in his group shone his torch into the room, the scene inside was straight out of a horror film. Six humans, grotesquely arranged, each still looking like they were gasping for their last breath.

Maxwell shook his head. 'Poor bastards, this's no way to die.'

Stowing any emotions deeply, he and his team completed their initial survey of the room before leaving for the next. Maxwell closed the door, trying to preserve some dignity for the victims. Room by room, they cleared the corridor. Almost an hour later, they reached the Bridge and re-joined the other team. The Bridge was the same as the rooms they had inspected; the Bridge crew were dead, all showing the same signs of a catastrophic decompression.

Everyone tried to ignore the sight as they finished the inspection, not an easy task as bodies floated and seemed to follow wherever they moved. Finally, Andrea called a halt and ordered everyone back to the shuttle; they were reaching the limit the Med-tech had indicated was safe for exposure to Trisidium.

One by one they entered the airlock and went through the decontamination process. Only when the residual Trisidium reading reached zero was any one of them allowed to re-enter the shuttle. The process took a full 55 minutes before everyone was safely back inside; and the pilot turned the craft for Valkyrie.

As they were executing their final approach, Andrea entered the cockpit, surprised by what she saw: three of the Station's four heavy salvage tugs, standing off to port a few kilometres away. These were ugly in the extreme - square and boxy - with only one purpose, to drag large vessels through space. She shook her head and walked back to the passenger compartment.

Andrea hadn't even left the shuttle when she was hailed over the comm system; the Captain wanted her in his ready room. She hastened through the walkway into the waiting pod, and it sped her forward and up to the Bridge. She pressed the annunciator button and was immediately admitted.

'Damn good job, number one,' Colin congratulated her as she entered, 'but we now have somewhat of an urgent assignment. It appears that there were three of these ships... one left before we got here, chasing an Eldoran ship. JT wants us to haul this wreck back to Mars base... he's sending a recovery ship to meet us there. Getting back in one piece is our task.'

'But why three tugs? One could haul this baby.'

'Yeah, but with three we can spread the load and energy consumption. Remember tugs aren't designed to go fast. If we use two pulling and one pushing, we can maintain nearly .75 light which should get us there in a little less than 7 hours. Also if the other bad guy shows up, we can certainly take it out but one, or more, of the tugs, might be hit... three gives us some insurance.'

'OK, I've got to get to medical and be checked out... when do we leave?'

'As soon as those tugs are connected.'

Andrea made the med-bay in record time, finding a tech waiting for her. She was pushed through the various tests, prodded, poked, jabbed, and scanned. This was all in twelve minutes; the rest of her team would take substantially longer.

She arrived back on the Bridge as the three tugs started to accelerate away, the dead ship now securely in tow.

***

'Commander Hargraves, when did the first bogie leave your control?' JT was about to lose his temper with this bureaucrat.

Admiral, I assure you, it will be in my report.

JT cut him off, 'Hargraves, **I don't give a flying fuck about your bloody report**; I need to know details **NOW**!' He was shouting at the comm-link by now. 'Have your sensor logs transmitted this instant... **do I make myself clear**!'

Perfectly Admiral, Hargraves replied. *They're being transmitted as we spea*k.

JT was about to explode. 'Bloody pencil pushers,' he muttered, 'An unidentified ship chases the Eldoran Ambassador's ship, and disappears in his sphere of control and all he wants is to file a report.'

He turned to see the data stream from the Station's sensor logs going up on the view screen. The two sensor analysts were sitting in front of their consoles and racing to crunch the numbers, knowing full well that their boss was breathing down their necks. Five minutes later they called JT over.

'Sir,' the senior analyst began, 'the sensor trace indicates they went to Displacement over thirty-five minutes ago, and from the data, went to Displacement factor seven. At this stage in the orbits of both planets, they would arrive at Earth, assuming that is their destination, slightly over an hour later.' The young officer was nervous; he hadn't done anything with the new Admiral before and didn't know what his expectations were.

'So if they are heading here, we have about thirty minutes before they arrive?' JT concluded.

'Yes sir, that's what my calcs show.'

'Thank you, well done,' JT thanked the analyst; then went back to the others. Mondrac and Aaron were deep in conversation with Sam Grogan as he approached. 'OK, we believe the third ship is on its way to Earth. We have about half an hour to figure out what their target is and how we stop them.'

'I believe I know their target Jay-Tee,' Mondrac began. 'So far their attacks have been directed towards the new President... Caprica told the story. These three weren't here to intercept me... no, I believe they have a different target. I have been studying this Sar-Clan, a most interesting person, but I believe he is not trying to do much real damage, at least not to your infrastructure. I believe his goal is to terminally destabilize the Coalition and allow him to offer the colonies an alternative Government. That is why he has had his spies operating so close to the President and the Council. I believe the target for the ship coming here will be the Presidential Palace and the Council itself.'

Sam shook his head. 'Just what we should expect from Sarclan.'

'Yes, but we need to stop the attack. If it is successful, even destroying the Presidential Palace would send huge political shock waves throughout the Coalition, and that wouldn't be a good thing at this stage.' JT acknowledged the delicacy of the political situation now facing the Coalition.

Jason joined the group. 'A few buildings aren't an issue... we can work through that. The Council is another matter. Can we evacuate the Council in time?' .

General Klastok answered. 'I believe we could. I wouldn't advise an airlift but we do have three submersibles in the area. We could have all the Councillors transported to them and dispersed.'

'Can you do it in time?'

Klastok thought for a second, 'it won't be easy but we should make it.'

'OK, no more talk. General, you sort out the Council. JT, Sam... see what defence we can mount.' Jason's words galvanized everyone to action.

They leaped to their tasks. Klastok was barking orders into his comm unit, arranging the airlift and subsequent transfer of the Council to submersible vessels. Three heavy-lift transports were always close to the Council buildings for just this type of emergency and once initiated, the slowest part of this exercise would be getting all the Council and staff on board.

There would always be someone who believed this would be a great time for a press release or to grandstand for their ego's sake. This time, however, there was no opportunity. One of the first things Klastok did was to order all press members out of the area and while there were the usual protests about *military strong-arm tactics*, it went smoothly.

Concurrently Sam, JT, and Sol were working on the defence strategy. During the Krell war, Earth had built a formidable orbiting defence screen made up of permanent satellites that were heavily armed. While most were still in orbit, only a few were now active; of these, six were kept updated.

These were placed on red alert and others around the globe were brought back online. The main problem was the lack of definitive data on the attacking ship they had received from both from Jupiter Station and Duramot's sensors. This meant that Coalition ships could not operate in the operational zone of the satellites, or they might be mistaken for an aggressor.

'Do we have any ships we can use?' Sam Grogan asked.

'Two Morgan class frigates, Asgard and Dietrich plus Valiant, but only Valiant is Sling Shot equipped. We can place the two frigates above the poles and Valiant lower, in the atmosphere close to our predicted target. Above the target we have a few squadrons of Darts but, from all we have seen, only Valiant has the weapons to hurt the enemy.'

JT was correct; only one ship in Earth orbit could have any chance of inflicting damage on the enemy. He had already mobilized Valiant and it was about to exit the dock complex when its Captain Jarad Cross' voice boomed from the comm system.

ECS Valiant calling Admiral Abraham.

'Valiant, this is Abraham; proceed to these coordinates,' JT said as he transmitted them, 'Wait there for further instructions.'

Roger, Valiant out.

Everyone watched the view screen as the deadly dance unfolded . The two frigates moved into geosynchronous orbits 3,000 kilometres above each pole; Valiant sped to her holding point directly above the Presidential compound at a height of 500 kilometres, and the defence satellites came online 10,000 kilometres out in space. There was nothing more that could be done - all that remained was the wait.

At three minutes, Klastok confirmed that all Councillors and staff had been evacuated and were now all safely on board the subs. The seconds seemed like minutes, two, one, zero - nothing.

Zero plus 1 minute - no sign of the ship.

Two minutes, five minutes - still nothing. JT was getting restless; maybe they had decided to run? The thought was tantalizing but deep down he knew that wasn't happening.

At 10 minutes and 37 seconds past their estimated arrival time, one of the operators called out. 'Tranquillity base detected a Displacement signature... we're analysing it now.'

'Where?' JT was already sitting at one of the consoles.

'Behind the moon... the dark side.'

'Clever, very clever,' JT said through gritted teeth. 'Do you have coordinates?'

'Coming through, now,' the operator sent the data directly to JT's console. He quickly integrated them into his program and sat back to watch the simulation. A few seconds later, he had his answer.

'Zyralin... they are using the Zyralin manoeuvre... sneaky bastards!' JT had called up the training program for this operation, fed in the data from the moon base, and used his calculations to fill in the gaps.

'A bit thin don't you think?' Grogan asked. 'Why do you think they are going to use that?'

'Because it's exactly what **I'd** do. Besides, they can't know what ground defences we have, and this type of attack offers them the best chance of success and survival.' JT turned to the analysts. 'What passive sensors do we have up there?' The two techs attacked their console and quickly brought up a grid map detailing the sensors. 'OK, let's get these things working, passive only... we don't want our guests to twig to what we are doing.'

Slowly the sensor arrays powered up and a few minutes later the screen changed. There it was - centre of the screen, only 70 metres off the surface - the distinctive shape that had been described by Jupiter Station. It was running cold, barely enough power being generated to keep it moving and for life support.

JT stared at the image, 'Can we superimpose Earth on screen? We need to see this in perspective.' The scene changed and Earth filled the screen with the moon showing through the transparent wire frame image. 'Now, put in the Government complex and the bogie... confirm the relevance.'

A couple of seconds later the enemy ship, the Coalition Government complex, the moon, and Earth were all now shown in true relativity. JT spoke to one of the analysts and they started working on the console. When they had finished the screen again changed.

'This is what I believe they will do,' JT said as the scenario he had programmed began to run. 'Watch the bogie.'

The scene changed as the compressed time play progressed. The Earth rotated, the bogie moved towards the edge of the dark of the moon, and finally, it stopped. 'This is when they will initiate a high Displacement micro-jump; only about a second and then this is where they will exit.'

The scene changed again showing the ship now inside the Earth's defence ring. 'They come in on this trajectory, fire everything here and then escape before we can do anything.' He ran the scenario forward, showing all details and the subsequent actions, 'The scenario estimates total destruction of the complex.' JT stopped and rewound the simulation. 'This is the only time we have to take them down; the full ten seconds they will need for this operation.' He re-ran the simulation this time with Valiant in the frame. The enemy ship materialized out of its wormhole, began accelerating toward Earth and just before the simulation fired its weapons, Valiant hit it with multiple Sling Shot bursts.

The bogie was destroyed but not before it managed to fire its weapon a couple of times, the complex simulation suffered considerable damage. 'Unfortunately, we can't guarantee any of this. The best case is that we stop them before they do any damage; the worst, we don't and they succeed. But this is the only scenario that fits with what they're doing now. So if anyone has a better idea, please speak up... we'll only get one chance, so we'd better be right.'

Sam operated the console to his left. He ran and re-ran the simulation, 'I can't think of any other explanation.'

JT continued. 'Admiral... this is what I'd do. The approach vector, the attack profile, and the exit course give them the greatest chance of doing the most damage and still surviving. What we need to do is move Valiant to **this**,' he pointed to a spot on the screen, 'position; it means taking her away from the complex, but I don't think we have any choice.' He stopped and waited for any objections.

All heads turned towards Jason. At the end of the day, **he** was the Commander in Chief and the decision should be his. He turned to JT, 'Admiral, I know you can't guarantee anything but what do you see the odds as?'

'Mr. President, if we don't try something, we could lose the Capital and that will give Sarclan a huge boost; even if they only do some damage and we destroy their ship, he still gets bragging rights. Either way, he comes out on top. But I'd rather he comes out of this with a bloody nose if nothing else.' JT stopped and waited as his grandfather considered the situation.

Jason considered the scenario once again before he finally answered. 'OK, make it happen.'

JT called Valiant and discussed his ideas with Jarad. The sensor data and battle scenario were transmitted and he agreed that it was the best option, with a few minor changes. Valiant moved, spun up Sling Shot, and went dark - now to wait.

When the bogie did finally appear, Jarad's changes proved to be correct. He and his crew had worked on the assumption that the enemy would use a shallower trajectory so they could bounce off the Earth's atmosphere, increasing their escape speed. The ship appeared very close to where Valiant's crew had predicted. They waited - the enemy accelerated toward Earth - still they waited; Jarad was glad Helen Tradeski was manning the weapons console.

'Detecting an increase in their energy output... they're getting ready to fire,' the Sensor Officer called, but still, Helen waited. Five seconds later and almost if synchronized, both ships fired their primary weapon, the bogie directed a huge, concentrated blast of energy down toward the planet, Valiant firing Sling Shot at the attacking ship. The path of the enemy energy blast was easy to follow, the brilliant white-hot beam slicing through the planet's atmosphere.

The beam was hot, hotter than the surface of the sun and as it passed through the atmosphere it caused the gasses it contacted to boil and separate. As it went past, the vacuum left by its passage was filled explosively by the surrounding air. A massive, rolling thunderclap that could be heard many kilometres away.

Sling Shot, was invisible and silent. Less than a second after the three balls of antimatter left the gravimetric accelerator, they impacted the bogie, exactly where and, more importantly, when Helen had planned them to. The data from the Jupiter Station incident indicated that these ships had a shield vulnerability around the engineering section, particularly on the port side This is why she had waited, so she could have the best chance of stopping this ship. And it worked: the first shot overloaded the shields, not enough to cause a failure, but enough to weaken them.

The second impacted a millisecond later and this one caused the shields to fail. The third shot found its mark and blew the rear of the hull apart. The engineering section, the primary reactor, and the drive all vaporized instantly. Thankfully the matter/antimatter reaction was so intense that all Trisidium on the ship was also vaporized, negating any problem with residual Trisidium radiation.

'Well done, Valiant,' JT called through the comm. 'We got the bastard.'

Yes, but we have a problem. The ship is still largely intact, and heading towards the planet, it can still cause more damage, Jarad replied.

There was only one possible alternative. Everyone knew it but still; it wasn't what anyone wanted to do. Although there could still be survivors, there were only seconds before the ship would enter the atmosphere and begin its fiery journey to the surface. It would partly break up but some of the pieces would be large enough to cause significant damage.

'No choice, Commander. Hit it again; destroy the rest of that ship before it reaches the atmosphere,' JT answered, his voice betraying his feelings.

Roger, Command.

Jarad ordered his weapons officer to fire. Helen used Sling Shot again, time was short and it would guarantee success. She sent another three 75mm shots across the void between the two ships. They all hit exactly where she had aimed and the enemy ship vaporized in a spectacular explosion. It was close enough to Earth for anyone who was looking skywards to see, a huge explosion followed by millions of tiny flare trails. Any remaining pieces burnt up harmlessly in the atmosphere.

In the Command Room there was no cheering, no slapping each other on the back; only silence, as the enormity of what had just happened and what might have happened; sank in. JT called Valiant and again congratulated them, also asking them to do a sensor sweep of the dark side of the moon, in case the bogie had left anything untoward there. The others shut down their consoles and quietly left the room.

Sam walked across the room to JT. 'Now you know why I wanted you for this job. No-one else, me included, would have seen that. Well done.' He held out his hand. JT took it and welcomed the firm grip of his boss and mentor. 'I mean it JT that was a bloody good job.' JT nodded without speaking, and they left the room.

he rest of the day was spent sorting through the aftermath of the attack.

The fact that Sarclan had been able to reach Earth changed everything. For an enemy to be able to breach the Coalition defences so easily and attack the home of the Human race demonstrated how much things had changed.

Throughout the whole Krell/Human war neither side had breached the other's Capital. But now a bunch of pirates with few resources had done just that. The news would spread like wildfire through the Galaxy so even though the attack had failed, politically it was a huge victory for Sarclan. The ramifications were the topic of discussion long into the night.

'Mr. President,' Madam Collard addressed Jason, 'you must address the Council as a matter of urgency. We must diffuse any rumours, rumours that I assure you will already be starting. There will be stories circulated in the colonies touting this attack as a huge victory... you can guarantee that is what Sarclan and his agents will be calling it.'

Jason cautiously studied the room; he knew she was right. 'Madam Collard, if people want to believe that we are weakened by this, there's not much we can do to stop them. But we can show solidarity, we can show we stand with all colonies against this anarchistic rabble. So far, all they have been able to do is attack lightly defended targets.

'Caprica, for example, is the softest target and still, they failed. Their battleships were defeated by a private yacht. Let them try and spin that in a positive light. Yes, they have destroyed two bases... but, again bases with little or no defence capability.' He noted that the mood seemed to have lifted. 'But you are right.

Have the Council assemble tomorrow, I will come and address them at eleven.'

'Where, where can we hold a full Council meeting?'

'The Council Chamber, Madam, where else?' Jason turned to General Klastok. 'General, have the Council members returned to the Parliament complex immediately. Tomorrow, I want this meeting to be covered by every News operation... I want it to be broadcast throughout the galaxy. We will show Sarclan that he has failed.'

He stopped speaking; a rumbling in his stomach telling him it must be way past dinner time. He pulled out the ancient pocket watch he carried, flipped the lid open, and noted the time; 10:30 PM.

'Look, we can't achieve any more tonight and, as we haven't eaten I suggest we adjourn till tomorrow at the Council meeting. I don't think we have to worry about any further attacks... for the time being. Amanda and I will be going home for the night, if any of you need somewhere to stay, I'm sure we can accommodate you.'

Mondrac was the only one who accepted the offer, and within minutes, the group had dispersed and were heading home. The Abraham group was the last to leave; now, as President, Jason was restricted in his movement. Whenever the President of the Coalition went anywhere there was always security. The shuttle would be accompanied by a flight of six Darts and a full 20 man security detail, and this took time to mobilize. It was a little after midnight when they finally left the secure site in Perth.

Mondrac settled into the comfortable leather seats of the Presidential shuttle, Jason and Amanda sitting opposite him.

'Mondrac, I take it you have news from the inner realms?'

'Indeed I do, President A-Bra-Ham. I was able to obtain all the technical data of the new weapons you are now facing, weapons brought here by both Galdor and Nileros. I hope that we can find a way to neutralize their advantage.'

'Wonderful news. Our technicians will find a way to negate

them... they always do. But, I sense that there is something else?' Jason could see that Mondrac had more information.

'You read people well, President A-Bra-Ham. I discovered something that I do not understand. It appears that Sar-Clan has another weapon, a weapon that we have no experience with, something referred to as a **Nano Virus**. Do you know what this is?' Mondrac stopped for an answer.

Jason sat back, thinking. 'Mondrac, humans have been using things called Nano Machines for centuries. They're in everything we use. From medicine to waste disposal... most things humans do have Nano-technology attached to it... but a Nano Virus? No, I've never heard of it... I'll call Silas, this is more his area of expertise.'

He asked the new aide to place a call to Silas and ask him to join them at Lucknow for breakfast, 7.00 AM tomorrow. The aide returned a few minutes later and confirmed Silas' acceptance.

It was 1.45 AM by the time they had returned to Lucknow. Phillip had a light supper ready for them. Soon the house was quiet and all had retired for the night. A short night, as everyone needed to be up in a few hours.

Amanda rose first, 6:00 AM showing on the clock. Quietly she went to the kitchen area and started making coffee. She returned to the bedroom as Jason was coming out of the bathroom.

'Hell of a first day,' he said gently kissing his wife's forehead.

'Rubbish, you loved it! Once again you were totally in charge, just as you have always wanted.' She smiled as she went into the bathroom. 'Coffee should be ready in a couple of minutes,' she called.

Jason dressed and went to the kitchen to finish the coffee. He had poured two mugs when Amanda joined him.

'Well, Mr. President, what are you going to tell the Council?'

'The truth... we have allowed ourselves to become soft and weak but, we still won the day. I'm going to lay the blame where it belongs, in **their** laps. The Council has, for too long, been more about egos and image than actually doing its job. Well, it's all about to end. We face the greatest threat ever and all their petty politicking is going to stop, permanently.' Jason's vocal tone emphasized his commitment. The sound of a shuttle passing over the house interrupted any further discussion - Silas was arriving.

Jason and Amanda opened the door to leave their apartment - across the hall was one of the three security operatives on the floor. She greeted the President and signalled the other two that their boss was approaching.

'Do we really need them outside our rooms?' Amanda grumbled, slightly put out by the intrusion.

'Sorry, my dear, protocol. We are going to have to live with it, for a while at least,' Jason answered as they approached the stairs and the second agent. Using the stairs was one of Jason's idiosyncrasies, and it gave him some exercise. On each floor, two more agents were watching the staircase and another was stationed outside the elevator. Finally, they made it to the first floor as Silas exited the pod.

'Morning, **Mr. President**.' Silas seemed slightly amused at the new status he had to accord his old friend.

'Morning Silas,' Jason responded, a wry smile crossing his face.

Amanda grimaced, 'Good morning Silas. Please don't encourage him... I have to live with him.'

Jason shook his head and guided them to the patio where he had Phillip set up a table for four. 'Ambassador Mondrac will be joining us shortly.' They sat, gazing out over the garden to the paddocks beyond. The recent rain had done its job, the paddocks were green and lush and the garden showing new growth.

'Looks like I will have to do some gardening now,' Amanda said as she studied her prized plantings.

'You could do that today, my dear; the Council thing will be very tedious.'

Amanda gave her husband a knowing look, 'and who, may I ask will keep Yvette Collard at bay... you?' Thankfully Mondrac arrived at that moment accompanied by two androids carrying breakfast.

'One of the things I am truly grateful for; our return to a mixed diet. If there is one thing that Eldorans did wrong it was our diet... artificially constructed... it was truly a mistake.' Mondrac waited till the others had uncovered their food, before attacking his serving with gusto.

'Ambassador, can you please repeat the information you have gleaned, to Silas?' Jason asked.

Mondrac returned his knife and fork to the plate and began. He recounted his meeting with his old Galdoran contact, the information on the new weapons that Raiders suddenly had, and then repeated the Nano virus information. 'Sadly, Green-Bach, we have no knowledge of this technology or what this means.'

'I understand, but before I go further... what did your contact **actually** say?'

'Not much more, except that this Sar-Clan person believed it could be the one weapon to bring the Coalition down. Both the Galdorans and Nilerans seemed to discount it as nothing more than a fantasy.'

Silas thought for a moment. 'Unfortunately, Ambassador, what Sarclan believes could be the truth... let me explain. Human technology for centuries was built on silicon-based electronic technology, but it proved to be holding us back. This is where Sarclan first came to our attention.

'He developed a bio/chemical computing system. This system transferred information and did calculations so fast we couldn't measure the speed, initially. It revolutionized everything, but had one vulnerability... it could get sick. I know that sounds strange but the systems could develop biological illnesses. Short of placing everything in totally sterile environments, there was nothing we could do.

'Meanwhile, others at Clo-tech... one of our companies... had been doing incredible things with... what we called, Nano Droids; microscopic machines designed to do specific tasks. These have been instrumental in our obtaining such longevity. Not only did we manage to isolate and control the so-called death gene, but we also developed Nano Droids with specific tasks in the human body.

'I won't bore you with details but I doubt if there is a human alive today that doesn't owe part of their life to the technology. Plus, and this is the most important piece of information, no human alive today, doesn't have Nano Droids in their body. They are placed there at birth and help to protect us from disease.

'If Sarclan has developed a **virus** to attack Nano Droids, then not only is our entire technology at risk, but the life of every human is also in danger.' The silence from the others told Silas that his analysis was indeed a cause for grave concern.

Mondrac summarized. 'So, in essence, all humans in this realm are part machine?'

Silas considered this and answered. 'I hadn't thought of it like that, but yes, that is a fair analogy. I'll give you an example of what they do. Centuries ago we had an insidious disease; cancer. It killed millions and the treatments of the day were crude and sometimes more destructive than the disease.

'One of the first Nano Droids developed was programmed to find and destroy pre-cancer cells. I can't say that it was a total success... at first, there were many failures... but over time the system was perfected and now that disease is gone. This is only one of many types of Nano Droids we have in our bodies; if these were destroyed it would... well, I don't even want to speculate on that.'

'That's not all,' Jason entered the conversation. 'Nano Droids form part of our standard computing systems... all control systems; in fact, every piece of technology we have relies on Nano Droids. If these were destroyed, we would lose all our technology... and quickly we'd be back in the Stone Age.' Jason's voice was heavy with sadness. 'A damn pity we didn't finish Eugene when we had the chance; now his revenge may be total.'

Phillip returned at that moment, noticing that very little food had been eaten. 'Is there a problem with breakfast?' he asked politely.

'No Phillip, breakfast is fine; some bad news, is all,' Amanda answered.

She resumed eating with the others following her lead. When they finished, one of the androids brought a fresh pot of coffee and poured each a mug. Jason again consulted his pocket watch: 8:05 am. They would soon need to leave.

Mondrac noticed the watch. 'President A-Bra-Ham... that instrument... what does it do?'

Jason smiled. 'It records the passing of time, we call them pocket watches. This one has been in the family since John Abraham the First. Evidently, he acquired it at an antique auction centuries ago, and, traditionally, it is handed down to the eldest son every generation.' He unclipped it and handed it to Mondrac.

Made of gold, the outer case was finely engraved and inlaid with emeralds and rubies. The lid opened to show a clear internal structure with only the hands and time divisions interrupting the view of the internal workings. 'It was made in a time when we greatly valued the craftsmanship of the construction,' Jason explained. 'Unlike modern units, it relies on a mechanical movement that utilizes a spring to provide the operating energy. It has an automatic winding function; every time I move it, the spring is tensioned and thus keeps the unit operating.'

'Fascinating! And how long ago was it made?'

'The makers mark inside shows it as being from 1925, making it over one thousand years old. Fortunately, we have kept complete engineering data on it and I have it serviced regularly on Caprica... or I did up till now.' Jason turned to Amanda. 'I haven't thought to check if Andrew survived.'

Amanda smiled. 'I'm sure he would have been OK, his home is a long way from ours.'

Mondrac returned the watch and Jason clipped it back into his trouser pocket.

'Time to go; it'll take around two hours to reach the Council Chambers. Silas, will you please start investigating what possible virus Sarclan may have developed? He turned to the others. 'And not a word about this to anybody... is everybody clear?' The others nodded their agreement. 'We'll meet here in ten minutes.'

He turned to Mondrac. 'Please Ambassador, I would like you to attend also, there may be some questions I can't answer.' Mondrac agreed and they left the table. On the way back to the staircase, Jason and Amanda greeted the other family members in the dining room. They were finishing breakfast and would follow the Presidential Flight; no-one wanted to miss Jason's first address to the Council.

Silas stood outside as the others filed out; he waited until Aaron walked through the door. 'Aaron, a word if I may?' he guided Aaron to the patio. 'I trust everything went well with Argort?'

'Yes, better than either of us expected. Means more work for Henry, but I'm sure he'll have it covered. But that's not why you got me here, is it?' Aaron could sense the tension in Silas, recognizing the signs of worry.

'No it isn't,' Silas turned toward the garden. 'Mondrac has brought some disturbing news about a possible weapon Sarclan may have. I need to come up with some sort of analysis and solution, but I fear that if I use any of our systems, it may alert our enemy.'

'You believe Sarclan has access to Coalition computers?'

'Possibly. What I would like, is to utilize your ship's brain. From what I've heard and seen, it's more than capable of the analysis we need. I know this is a lot to ask, but could we start working on this problem straight away?' Silas knew it meant Aaron missing his father's inaugural speech to Council but, if Sarclan did indeed have some sort of Nano virus, every second counted.

'That urgent?'

'I believe so. I'm sorry, but I think Jason will understand. After all, he's the one who gave me this task.'

'Well, it's a good job I've transferred George to the yacht. I'll tell the others and meet you in the hangar in ten minutes.'

***

Jason's speech was hard-hitting. The reaction was, initially, incredulous - some even drew insults from his words. But they eventually saw the truth of what he said.

It was Hiro Tanaka who took the floor. 'Mr. President, fellow Council members, these words are hard to hear but they are the truth. We, are all complicit in this situation; we have let our petty differences cloud our purpose. I, for one, am embarrassed by what I have just heard; if it were our children behaving as we have we would have disciplined them. But now that we are faced with this problem we **must** drop these games. We must **all** work together, or else we will fall and I do not want to see our Coalition destroyed by this madman. So...' he paused as he constructed his next sentence. 'I, Hiro Tanaka, representative of Nippon, move that we the members of the Coalition Council grant full emergency powers to President Abraham.'

Angus Roy - Representative of the Gaelic Federation - leaped to his feet. 'Aye to that! I second the motion!'

The leader of the Council, Madam Collard stood. 'As the leader of this house, I call for a vote. All those in favour, please move to my right, those against to my left.' The chamber divided to vote. It took some fifteen minutes for the division to settle: 150 moved to the right: 20 to the left: and 30 stayed put, indicating they were abstaining from the vote.

This wasn't the outcome Jason foresaw or wanted. While the granting of emergency power effectively disbanded the Council and gave Jason total control, it also had the effect of absolving the Council members of any responsibility arising from the situation. All responsibility would fall on Jason and his family.

Collard resumed her seat. 'I hereby declare that the motion to grant emergency powers to President Abraham has been resolved in the affirmative. As is required, I now declare this Council dissolved.' She turned to Jason. 'Mr. President, do you wish to say anything?'

Jason stood and approached the dais, still not believing what had happened. In two short days, he had gone from retired to effectively Dictator of the Earth Coalition of Planets. 'Council members, Madam Collard, while this outcome is not what I was seeking, I thank you for your confidence in me.'

Jason was playing the game. He knew that all these politicians were trying to protect themselves; the well-being of the Coalition was the last thing they had on their minds. But he wasn't going to let them walk away from this fight so easily.

'In the coming days and weeks, I may need to call on you to assist in defeating this insidious enemy.' He let his eyes traverse around the room; everyone who caught his gaze knew he was on to them. 'I thank you in advance for your support.' He left the dais to subdued applause as those present pondered what this would mean for each of them.

***

Aaron and Silas had been locked in the yacht for hours; George had been given all the information they had and they began building scenarios. They were struggling to determine what the word **virus** actually meant.

For centuries, it had been a generic term used for many computer maladies. Back when silicon ruled, the hacking industry had generated millions of computer viruses, making the authors extremely rich. It had become a massive industry, both in designing the malady and then in detecting and eliminating it. The advent of the bio-computer, however, had eliminated this industry almost overnight as the new programming was biological and genetic - not digital. Now, what Sarclan had devised was new and unknown to Coalition technology. But they knew they had to figure it out as quickly as possible.

Aaron was tired and his mind felt numb. 'Silas, we're getting nowhere. I think we need to call in some fresh brainpower. We have a guy back on Argos, with a brilliant mind who has even impressed the Eldorans. I think we need to go and see him.'

'I agree, we do need a new perspective. Who is he?'

'Leonard Fraslok,' Aaron said quietly.

Silas smiled, as the Professor's reputation was widely known. Silas excused himself, citing the need to contact people to arrange for his absence, leaving Aaron to do the same.

Aaron's first call was to Petra. 'Hello, darling.'

'Hey, you sound flat, what's wrong?'

'Nothing I can discuss now. Where are you?'

'On our way back, we should be there in half an hour.'

'Great, we'll talk then.'

He sat back and started to recall what the last year had seen. The release of the jump drive technology was proving to be an interesting undertaking. Decisions as to who would be allowed access had become bogged down for months and to date, only 10 ships had been equipped. Abracorp had begun fitting the Sling Shot system to all Coalition vessels and licensed it to AA Engineering, Aaron's Argosan engineering operation.

So far, Condor, Albatross, and Junior had all been retro-fitted, but it hadn't all been smooth sailing. Sling Shot created huge demands on each ship's antimatter generation, leading to substantial redesign and refitting of each vessel. As most were individual designs, each refit was different. But with each retro-fit, the engineering challenges were met and the work continued.

Many trips had been taken to the inner realms and trade had begun in earnest; everyone seemed to be benefiting from the arrangements. Sarclan's attempts to destabilize the Twelfth Realm had a huge ripple effect through the inner realms, and this had resulted in Galdor and Nileros being sidelined in many inner realm dealings.

Aaron's position as Twelfth Realm Ambassador had placed him in a challenging position. He held no love for either of the two antagonistic planets but was aware - from human history - the consequences of punitive actions of the nature he was seeing now. He had led a number of delegations to try and find an amicable solution, but emotions were still high and no one wanted to give any ground. Effectively, Galdor and Nileros were given pariah status and shunned by most, but Aaron persisted with his efforts and was hopeful this could be reversed. The sound of a shuttle overhead broke through his thoughts; they were back.

Aaron was waiting as the shuttle grounded in the hangar. Jeff, Sonia, and Petra were first off the craft with Petra leaping into Aaron's arms and smothering him with a kiss.

'Will you two get a room?' Jeff laughed. 'Sonia, 'how come I don't get greeted like that?'

'Jeffery Abraham, are you complaining?' Sonia spoke with mock indignation.

'No, not at all, my love, besides it, wouldn't get me anywhere if I did.' This comment was met with a loving punch to his arm. It was at that moment that Silas joined them.

'Silas, Dad told us of the problem... any ideas?'

'None... Aaron suggested we go to Argos and have Leonard Fraslok look at it.'

Petra's face beamed. 'Home, we're going home!'

'Yes, for a few days. I contacted Henry, and he has a candidate for your Proctor... they'll be here soon. If she's acceptable, we'll be off tomorrow, providing it's OK with Silas.'

Silas smiled. 'I've set things up for the next week, so yes I'm in.'

'How about us?' Jeff interjected. 'To be honest, I've never been to Argos. David can sit in for me for a week... do you mind if Sonia and I invite ourselves?'

'No... sounds great!' Aaron said as he led them through the doors to the pod.

They arrived back at the house Aaron and Jeff heading straight to the study. As the others entered, the face of Leonard Fraslok greeted them from the view screen on the wall.

'Professor,' Aaron spoke to the image on the screen, 'this is Ambassador Mondrac and Silas Greenbach.' He waited until introductions were completed. 'Professor, we'd like your take on a problem we have... I'll let the Ambassador explain.'

Mondrac recounted his information to Fraslok, with Silas covering the more technical details. They finished and the Professor sat, quietly thinking and processing what he had just heard. Finally, he stood and moved across the room to an old filing cabinet.

This is something I've been concerned about for years... I hate the little buggers running around inside me. I have tried to warn the authorities time and time again, but no-one listens... now they might have to. He was rummaging through an old cabinet as he spoke. *Here it is. I ran a simulation ages ago on how this could be done... believe me, it isn't easy.*

The problem of corrupting existing Droids in humans is genetic. Their program is flexible until they are matched to their host, or more correctly, the host's DNA. Once this has been done, it is impossible to infect either the host or the Droid.

To have any real effect on our population, any so-called virus **must** *be included in the initial program of the Droid. Once it is inserted into a body, the program will be locked... but any deviation in the Droid's behaviour will be detected by other Droids and the virus-infested version will be destroyed. I had many failures before I discovered the only viable program.*

New Droids must be programmed as hunter-killer units... their only function is to find and destroy other Nano Droids in the body. Once this is done, then that body can be subjected to any number of diseases... even simple ailments will be killers.

'And you did this with success?' Silas guessed.

'Yes, it worked every time. The problem Sarclan faces is getting enough of the new **Virus Droids** into the population. I can see only one way: he must deliver his program to the Nano Droid Program Stations **before** any Droids can be infected,' Fraslok surmised.

The threat was now laid bare. Nano Droids had a finite life, after this, they went dormant and were absorbed by the body. The life cycle was about 30 years so, at that time the Droids needed to be replenished. This meant every human and every computer Bio-Gel pack, needed to be resupplied with Droids.

Jeff broke into the conversation 'But it would take decades to infect everyone? The logistics are impossible for Sarclan.'

Are they? It seems to me that he has been able to infiltrate the most secure systems in the Coalition, Space Corps, and Parliament. Breaking into the Droid Program Stations should be relatively easy for him, I would think. Fraslok's voice was condescending; his dismissal of those he considered inferior could be infuriating... but he had a point.

'OK Professor, what do you suggest?' Silas asked.

It was Aaron who replied. 'This is brilliant... he doesn't need to infect everyone, only some of the people. The Nano Droids are infected; some people will succumb, others won't, but every single Human will be uncertain of their immune system. Then Sarclan comes out with a cure, but the cure comes with conditions... follow me or die. The Coalition would implode in days and Sarclan becomes the Supreme Leader as he always wanted; everyone would obey because they could never know when he would repeat the process... bloody clever.'

Aaron's words came like a slap in the face, the simplicity and totality of the scenario fitted Sarclan's profile perfectly.

I may have a solution, Fraslok announced. Immediately all eyes returned to the screen.

'Please Professor, continue.' Aaron said.

The Droids have a critical flaw, one that took me years to discover but they can be defeated.

'So tell us... what do we do?' Silas was standing now.

Fraslok shook his head. *Not over these comms. I don't care how secure you think they are, Sarclan has proved how effective his Sedition is. No, bring the information and some samples of infected Gel Packs and I'll show you what we need to do.* Fraslok's demeanour showed his resolution in the matter.

'And how do we get infected Gel Packs?' Aaron asked.

Simple, I would suggest that any of the current packs at Space Corps HQ will be infected. Bring some of them and some of the spares on hand. How soon can you do this?

Aaron started some calcs; total jump time to Argos was 12 hours. He looked at his watch then back at the screen. 'Professor, we'll be there about this time tomorrow.'

Excellent, I'll be waiting. Fraslok smiled and cut the connection.

Jeff shook his head. 'Aaron, how in hell do you think you're going to get through all the red tape and have the packs there in twenty-four hours?'

'Easy... your son... Admiral Abraham... is head of Space Corps. Get him on the comm to get things moving.'

Jeff nodded and made the call. Three hours later JT called back with the news that everything had been arranged and that he was bringing the packs to the house himself.

Aaron had everyone on board Junior when JT's shuttle landed. He opened the cargo section of the shuttle and extracted two containers, both equipped with antigrav supports.

'The blue container is filled with replacement Gel Packs and the other has ones we just removed from service,' JT explained. "They're from different systems and areas so we should have a reasonable cross-section of the problem if there is one. Only a few trusted people know about this; I'll inform the President tomorrow. Now get going and sort this out.'

Aaron nodded. 'As soon as you clear out we're out of here.'

'I've authorized you to jump as soon as you pass the moon. That way there will be no trace; don't contact control... just launch and go,' JT advised.

'Thanks, Admiral,' Aaron turned and walked back into the yacht. By the time he was back in his command chair, JT's shuttle had left. He looked around the Bridge, the determined faces of his companions giving Aaron confidence. 'Time to go,' and he initiated Junior's drive system.

The next morning, JT met with Amy Rodregas, his old chief engineer on Valiant.

She was now heading up the R&D team investigating the new weapon technology Sarclan had obtained. She had put together a team of engineers and scientists to assist including the brilliant Phillip Harper, the man responsible for the new sensor programs.

'Morning Captain.' JT welcomed Amy as she entered his office.

'Morning Sir... and thank you for the promotion.'

'Amy, if anyone deserves this, you do... it was long overdue. Now, what progress have you made?'

Amy motioned toward the console, 'if I may Sir?'

JT agreed and she handed him a data drive.

The screen came to life and diagrams started to appear. 'As you can see we have worked out their new particle beam weapon. They're not that different to our blasters but they use a much more tightly confined beam. The energy released is around five times that of ours but the beam constriction is much tighter. That's why it causes so much damage... it literally slices through our shields.

'The absorption field can take some of the energy, but the intensity soon overpowers it. The Reglaon resin can withstand some hits and, combined with Acrilan, should give a hull strength that can, at the least allow a ship to escape. Nothing so far can deflect, withstand, or negate the beam, but we have been able to replicate it. This may even up future encounters.'

'OK, so we now both have similar weapons... what about the shield?'

Amy smiled – a self-satisfied smile if JT had ever seen one. He started to relax a little as she began.

'That's another story. Up until yesterday, it had us beat; the randomization program was simple and we can do the same with our shields. It was the way they independently randomized the shield frequency and magnetic resonance that had us stumped. Then Harper made his breakthrough... sometimes that kid scares me, he's so damn smart.

'Anyway, he's worked out the algorithm and is now building a new shield control system. We should be testing later today. With the Sling Shot, we know it can defeat their shields but it takes huge amounts of energy. Most of our ships equipped with it just don't have the energy capacity to fully utilize it. We may have a solution, at least for the Mantas. We propose installing additional crystal storage and anti-matter processing system, to feed Sling Shot. This way, we can generate enough anti-matter to defeat their shields.'

JT lifted his eyes from the console. 'What's the cost?'

'We lose our secondary hold,' Amy explained. 'It becomes the new conversion and storage area. Other than that, if you look at the next screen we have a cost breakdown.'

JT read the numbers, scrolling down the page till he reached the final cost. 'I don't think this is an issue.' He called up his overall project costings and scanned through it. 'As I thought, we have funding left; with each conversion, costs are coming down. We have about twenty-five Mantas completed. Start with Valiant; upgrade her systems and put in the new generators. How long will each upgrade take?'

Amy looked uncomfortable. 'That's the unknown. Abracorp is flat out with the Manta project; they have five docks working on that. Greenbach Technology is pushing hard to keep up with deliveries, and now we are bringing all twenty-five back for the jump drive upgrade. Adding this will stretch things too much... there just isn't the capacity here on Earth.'

JT's mind was in overdrive. The Coalition needed these ships urgently and delays could prove disastrous. 'OK, leave that for the moment... do you have enough resources to do your upgrades without the new power systems?'

'Yes, we're using part of the Galileo dock and we have the personnel for two conversions at once, so we're good on that. But I'm concerned about Harper,' Amy divulged. 'He's not Space Corps and I think he wants to get back to Argos.'

JT smiled. 'That may be the best option we have. We'll leave it there; I've got some calls to make. Get all your data ready, we may need to send it to a different facility.' He stood as Amy turned for the door. 'I'll call you later today, hopefully with a solution.'

***

Aaron sat in the command chair; Junior was mid jump and the view screen in front of him was pitch-black. He thought back to sitting in his lounge aboard Condor watching the beauty of a Displacement flight unfold. The swirling matrix of colours delineating the edge of the wormhole - the heavenly bodies, planets, stars - everything flashing past, outside the cocoon. He missed and longed for that view again.

Jump drive was great, travel time shortened to almost nothing, but it was also boring; boring and depressing. The trip between Earth and Argos usually took around four days but that was the old Displacement way. Now, it took twelve hours utilizing two fairly shallow jumps into subspace.

He checked the time again - 02:35. They had left Earth a little after 22:00 and had initiated the first jump three hours ago. He took a last look at the console - everything was functioning perfectly. Realizing there was nothing to do he stood and left the Bridge.

Mondrac was in the dining room making more coffee. Jeff and Silas were sitting in a corner discussing something in hushed tones. Aaron decided not to enter; instead, he took the stairs down to the accommodation level. His cabin was forward and he turned that way at the bottom of the staircase.

His master suite was directly below the Bridge and also had

a full-width view screen; as he walked through the door he saw a generic ocean scene playing. He closed the door and Prince trotted up to him, he bent and picked the cat up and was immediately rewarded with the sound of loud purring. It seemed that even the cat was glad to be back in space. The living room was fully illuminated as was the corridor leading to the bedroom. He quietly walked to the door and heard the gentle hum of the Spa; a wicked smile crossed his lips.

Quickly he stripped off, threw his clothes on the bed, and walked into the bathroom. Silently he slowly opened the door and tiptoed around the screen. His final move, meant to be an entrance, proved to be a mistake. He stepped from behind the screen naked and announced his presence.

'Hey babe, want some of this?'

He was greeted with shrieks and peals of laughter; sitting in the spa were Petra and Sonia enjoying the bubbling water. Aaron was dumbfounded. Although he knew he should get out of there, he was unable to move.

'Well brother in law, if you'd brought Jeffery with you this might have been an interesting evening!' Sonia blurted out between her giggles.

'Shit, sorry... bloody hell!' Aaron gasped.

While looking rather proudly at the picture before her Petra added. 'Now that you've made such a grand entrance, did you want to join us?'

'What? No! Sorry! I'll leave you alone.' He ran from the room, accompanied by more laughter.

He quickly threw some clothes on, poured himself a huge whiskey, and sat on the lounge. Prince immediately settled on his lap, purring contentedly. He had finished his drink when Petra and Sonia entered the room, now wearing fluffy bathrobes.

'Don't worry Aaron, this isn't the first time I've seen **you** naked... nothing has changed,' Sonia needled at him.

Petra, feigning indignation spoke. 'What! You've seen my fiancé sans clothes before?' Aaron groaned tonight was proving to be a disaster.

'You remember Aaron,' Sonia began, 'you brought that busty blonde home for the weekend? Jason and Amanda were away. We had a great night. A little too much to drink and we all ended up in the lake, skinny dipping.'

'OK, OK... no more,' Aaron protested.

'No... the best part is still to come.' She turned back to Petra.' While we were swimming someone was nipped on a very sensitive part of their body by an eel... poor thing... must have thought it had a big worm.' With that, they both lost control and burst into fits of giggles.

Petra stopped laughing and moved to Aaron's side. 'Does it still hurt?' She asked, faking sympathy, 'Maybe I should kiss it better?'

'Very funny... not right now thanks! Damn, that was a long time ago. I don't think you and Jeff were even married then,' Aaron quipped back.

'What was a long time ago?' Jeff's voice came from the door.

Sonia began to explain. Aaron shook his head and poured them all a whiskey. When she finished Jeff was also laughing. 'Come on Aaron, you have to agree it was pretty bloody hilarious?' He added.

'To you maybe, but I had to drag the bloody thing off, you lot were enjoying it way too much.' Aaron's feigned indignation fooled nobody, as Petra smiled and snuggled up to him.

'Come on, admit it, it sounds awfully funny,' she cooed.

Aaron had to admit, it did make a good story and now, after his *Grande Entrance* this evening, it'd be many years before this night was forgotten. They finished their drinks, and Sonia spoke again.

'OK... now we are alone and have time, why did you two clowns fight? Aaron, why did you leave?' Her tone was determined; there was no way she was going to be fobbed off.

Jeff answered. 'Sonia, I don't think this needs any revisiting. Aaron and I have sorted it out... the matter's closed.'

Sonia stood and glared at her husband. 'Not likely! Something monumental happened... it tore our family apart! Look at what it did to Johnathon, it devastated him. No... you two aren't getting away with this any longer. Jeffery Thomas Abraham, either discuss it here and now or face the consequences!'

Aaron answered. 'Alright, remember Jeff was about to complete his tour in the Corps while you and I were trying to have the replica of his ship made?' Sonia nodded, suddenly looking worried. 'Well, someone in CID was following us. They took photos and started to work on Jeff.' As he completed the story, Sonia's eyes widened, angrily.

Sonia interrupted, her voice filled with quiet rage, 'And you fell for it?' She glared at her husband. 'You thought I was having an affair... with your **brother**?' Her voice quivered; anger, pain, and indignation coming to the surface. 'Jeffery, how could you even think that?'

Aaron jumped in. 'In Jeff's defence, it did look bad. Remember, I used to stay at the Hilton in Sydney a lot. Whoever was behind it set up long-term surveillance! They recorded lots of images and used them to force Jeff's thoughts in a specific direction; and it worked. Jeff confronted me, I took a swing at him and the rest is history.'

Jeff remained silent; deep in thought.

'Well, Jeffery, what do you have to say for yourself?' Sonia demanded.

'I thought it was Crompton... he was the one who delivered the photos... but that sort of operation was way above his pay grade back then. It's now clear... it had to be someone at the highest levels of CID... maybe the director.' Jeff stood and started the familiar Abraham pacing.

'But even if it was the director, what benefit could that have for CID or the Coalition?' He continued pacing, back and forth while the others kept silent. After a few minutes, he stopped, as if something had suddenly blocked his path.

'The truth is,' he said quietly. 'It couldn't benefit the Coalition...

it was exactly the opposite. I think I know who was behind it all those years ago.'

Almost in chorus the others spoke, 'who?'

'It all makes sense now. Abracorp was going through a particularly strong period; Dad was pushed to the limit, and growth was quickly outstripping our ability to fund it. It was then that I decided to leave the Corps... my decision... no-one forced me. With Aaron and me both in the company, things improved; shareholder confidence rose and funding became easier.

'Then we fought, you left and suddenly things went bad... very bad. We even had to dump a couple of good contracts. But gradually things improved, again after a couple of years, but I never saw it until now. Sarclan was still influencing things from far away. He must have had several operatives deep in the administration and what better way to destabilize the Coalition than to cause confidence in one of its biggest companies to falter? It had to be him.'

Aaron stood still, unable to fully comprehend the words. 'So you're saying that Sarclan has had a finger in the Coalition pie all along?'

Jeff nodded. 'Sounds unbelievable, but who else could pull something like that off?'

The conversation followed this course for a couple of hours until they decided to call it a night. Jeff and Sonia left for their cabin and Aaron headed for the shower. Petra was sitting up in bed when he came back in.

'Interesting evening,' Aaron observed as he joined her. 'I've tried to pick holes in Jeff's logic... but I can't. I believe he's right... Sarclan has been manipulating things for many years, and nobody picked it up. Hell, for all we know, he may have been running CID all these years.'

'Well, who's running this ship?' Petra asked, trying to change the subject. She'd had enough of the Sarclan conspiracy talk for one evening.

'George. Everything's programmed and he'll call if there's a problem.'

'Then you better come here, let me inspect where the nasty eel bit you.' Petra teased. 'Don't worry, I'll be gentle.'

12

The two guards by the door snapped to attention as Jason approached. The door slid silently into the wall and Jason Thomas Abraham walked into the office for the first time as President of the Earth Coalition of Planets. He stopped as the door closed, taking in the room. Although he had been in here many times, this time it was different. Slowly he approached the large oak desk that dominated the room. He walked behind it, pulled the solid leather chair out, and sat in it for the first time.

It felt surreal. Sitting on this side of the desk, the room appeared different. He shook his head and chuckled to himself. *Stop dreaming, you've got work to do*. His thoughts were interrupted by a knock at the side door to his office. The door opened and in walked his chief aide.

'Good morning, Mister President, I'm Courtney Hollingsworth. I was President Malik's Chief of Staff.' She was tall, tall and elegant with long dark hair neatly held back behind her head.

'Good morning, Courtney; President Malik advised me to keep you in the position, how do you feel about working for me?'

'Thank you, Sir. I'd like that.' Courtney smiled and placed a data drive on his desk. 'First thing each day is this.'

She activated the drive and a view screen moved up from a concealed spot in the desk. Together they went through the data, actioning each item as it came up. Thirty minutes later the task was finished. 'Sir, I am still working on the previous administration's timetable. If you want to change anything, tell me.'

Jason shook his head. 'No, Salim seemed to have things running well; I'm not going to change anything unless it needs changing. Now I think I should meet the rest of the staff. Can you round them up and bring them in here?'

'Of course, say about ten minutes?' She suggested as she disconnected the drive.

'Ten will be fine. Thank you, Courtney.'

Ten minutes later she returned with the senior staff - all twenty-three of them. Jason greeted each in turn, taking time to learn as much as he could about them; all the while he wondered if any had been compromised. Although every member of the administration had been vetted and vetted again, Jason still had some doubts.

The door opened and Courtney entered; a worried look on her face; she moved quickly through the gathering until she reached the President.

'Mister President... a word please?'

They moved to a far corner and she spoke. 'Sir we have had a communication from the Mechanista... they are asking for an urgent meeting with you... and the Emissary's shuttle is now approaching the compound.'

'A Mechanista... here? They never leave their planets,' Jason said with total surprise. 'How long?'

'He should land in around five minutes.'

'OK, we need to break this up, can you please reschedule,' Jason motioned towards the gathered staff, 'for later this afternoon?'

'Yes Sir,' Courtney moved away and began to circulate through the group, quickly dispersing them. Within minutes the room was empty.

Jason was impressed, 'Well done, I've never seen a room cleared so quickly.'

'It's not that hard, everyone here knows how quickly things can change, besides, I told them all to come back at four and we'll continue the meeting. Now, where do you want to meet the Emissary?'

'Please excuse my ignorance, but where would you suggest?'

'Sir, this is a surprise visit; the fact we only learned of it five minutes prior to him arriving is somewhat problematic. I would suggest that there is no need for ceremony. Treat it as a business meeting and receive him here in the office. If you require I can sit in... it's up to you.'

'Thanks, but I think I should sound him out myself, at first.'

Courtney touched her left ear 'He's here, in the waiting room, I'll bring him in.'

She turned and quickly left the room. A few minutes later the door opened and in strode the Emissary followed by Hollingsworth.

'Mr. President may I introduce Wu Chan, tenth-degree Game Master of the Mechanista,' Hollingsworth said, and then retreated through the door.

The man standing before Jason was nothing like what he expected. He was tall with long dark hair. His body appeared to be powerfully built and he moved with effortless grace. . He extended his hand, which Jason took.

'Emissary Chan welcome to Earth. I apologize for the lack of reception but we have only just found out you were coming.' Jason greeted his guest warmly. He moved them toward the lounge area, where they both settled, into the comfortable leather armchairs.

'Mister President, you could not have known. I did my best to keep my trip here secret; there are many things we need to discuss,'

'I must confess,' Jason admitted, 'you've caught me off balance. You're not at all what I was expecting.'

Chan smiled, as he nodded his head. 'Yes, I can believe that. You were probably expecting something totally different, but it has been centuries since we have had contact. We have changed, somewhat?'

Jason smiled in reply. 'That Emissary is an understatement.'

Chan continued. 'Much with the Mechanista has changed. About three hundred years ago we started to see a reduction in the number of gamers. As you probably know our society is based on virtual gaming, with all citizens connected permanently; so any decline in numbers can easily be noticed.

'What we discovered was a turning point for us. We had become so sedentary, so inactive our bodies could no longer be kept alive; even with all our technology, we were dying out. A radical solution was required. Some turned to cloning, but the success was poor... others decided to transfer their consciousness totally into machines.

'The rest of us decided to try a different approach. This body,' he indicated with his hands, 'is the result of some ingenious design. It is part biological and part mechanical... but the brain is mine. We have developed a process where we can take the brain of one of our people and incorporate it into a body like this. We are truly now Biomechs.'

'Amazing,' Jason was fascinated, 'So you are now part of the unit? I mean... your actual brain is inside?'

'Yes, this is the real Wu Chan. Unfortunately; it allowed some of our people to transition back to the real universe too soon. They still craved the excitement of our gaming... of our virtual battles... but they wanted their new freedom.

'Sadly some have come under the spell of your enemy, Eugene Sarclan. I'm afraid that his new virus is something some Mechanista have developed for him.' He took a breath, his face showing his sadness and embarrassment. 'Fortunately, we have been able to severely limit their potential, but we have not been able to eradicate the threat. Believe me, I would rather not have come here with this news; it is a dishonour we will have to bear for a long time.'

'You are not alone, Chan. We have had a long list of traitors as well. Perhaps we can work together and find a solution.'

A knock at his side door interrupted their conversation. His aide entered with a tray and poured both of them a cup of tea. As they sipped the tea Jason spoke again.

'Emissary Chan, please can we dispense with formalities? I

know your rank is of the most senior in your culture, mine is the same so please; call me Jason.'

'Agreed but please return the favour. Call me Wu.'

With formalities completed, they settled back to discuss how both cultures could co-operate against their common enemy.

***

Junior approached Argos from the star side, brilliant daylight illuminating the surface.

'Beautiful as always,' Petra was clearly happy to be back home. 'I thought you had been here before, Jeff?'

'Well yes and no. I have been here for a couple of meetings but they were always in orbit, I've never been to the surface. Now, when I look down there, I can't for the life of me understand why,' Jeff mused as he took in the vista of the approaching planet.

Even Aaron, who had made this approach countless times, was enthralled by the beauty before them. It was with some reluctance that he took the pilot's seat and commenced the re-entry and landing procedure. He quickly obtained clearance and soon they were entering the atmosphere.

AA Trading, Aaron's premier company, maintained its spaceport and industrial complex, to the north of Central City. Ship repair, engineering, and transport operations were all run from here. Even though he was the major shareholder and CEO, Aaron still had to wait his turn to land.

Once on the ground, they decided on their course of action. The four men were heading to the Academy and Professor Fraslok but when Sonia asked if she and Petra would be going to Aaron's house he revealed he didn't have one.

'In truth, I've never needed a home; I've always stayed at the Morgan or on my ship.'

'Well, I think that Petra and I will do some house hunting while you boys go and meet with the Professor,' Sonia suggested as they left Junior.

They made their way to the transport hub, Petra and Sonia

taking a pod to the centre of the city and the others a different one to the Academy, fifteen minutes later they were met by Professor Fraslok. He was just as Aaron remembered; long unkempt grey hair and a constantly startled look on his face.

After a short walk through the main gardens of the facility, something that the Professor seemed exceedingly proud of, they finally entered one of the buildings and a comfortable lounge. Here he began to outline the process they were about to see. Next, they went to the lab viewing area. No one was allowed into the lab as it was a super sterile area - any stray microbe could destroy years of work.

'The trick was to find a way to force the Nanos to accept the virus and the answer was simplicity,' Fraslok was explaining. 'In the end, we grafted the virus DNA to the ID of the Nano and it worked. This is the **only** way Sarclan could get a virus into the host Human.'

'So, what you're saying is he doesn't have a virus to destroy the Nano Droids but rather a way to program them to carry a virus into the hosts?' Silas suggested.

'Yes, that and a way for the other Nanos to ignore the virus. It can only be done during a replacement process, which happens every thirty years or so, giving Sarclan a constant supply of potential victims. They will be from different colonies too... hell, if he was discrete enough he could infect half the human race in a few months!'

'But infect with what? Most of the old viruses have been eradicated?' Silas spoke absently, to no-one in particular.

Fraslok took up the challenge. 'They may have been eradicated **but** their DNA structure is known. It wouldn't take much for a competent cloning operation to develop a new strain... and a new strain might be able to evade the older Nanos if the DNA was mutated.' His words hit the group like a hammer blow.

Mondrac was the first to speak. 'You Humans never cease to amaze me. You are the only species that has constantly delved deep to find the most horrific ways to exterminate itself... this makes no sense at all!'

'Unfortunately, my friend, it makes perfect sense to Sarclan,' Jeff began speaking. 'I remember from my days in the Corps where one of our lecturers espoused an ancient battle theory... this theory stated that it may be better to injure or cause illness in your enemy than to kill him. You see, an injured or sick enemy takes a lot more resources than a dead one, tying up your enemy's logistics and personnel. A dead enemy, on the other hand, can be simply left or quickly buried, very little resource allocation needed. What Sarclan is doing, if we are correct, could devastate our ability to respond to his advances.' His voice trailed off as Silas' communicator began to chime.

'Jason, what can I do for you?' Silas listened for a few seconds before switching the call to a speaker function, 'now everyone can hear.'

Jason began speaking, confirming what Fraslok had told them. He was even able to identify the viruses that Sarclan had been working with.

'Mr. President, you're saying that Sarclan has been working with Ebola and Smallpox?' The Professor queried.

Correct, Professor. Our information is that he has already sent a few batches of infected Nanos to two colonies; we're expecting epidemics to break out... soon and, if our assumptions are correct, the existing Nano Droids will not be able to stop it, Jason replied.

Fraslok broke in at that moment. 'Mr. President, it is entirely possible that if he is using such an ancient pathogen, none of the Nano Droids will even recognize it; there will be no defence and the death toll will be horrendous.'

'Then what can we do to counteract this?' Aaron asked.

We're working on something, but I can't divulge any more at this time, Jason was still not trusting the Coalition encoding or comms systems. *What I can say is thank you, Professor. Your work and advice have been invaluable in helping decide on our next course of action. I'll leave you now and see you back on*

Earth soon. With those words, Jason cut the comm-link.

Aaron stood and walked to the view window. The room they were in was grey and sparsely furnished; two rows of lecture-style seats and not much more. The lab he was now looking into was a huge contrast, with many machines and data consoles. Coloured screens were everywhere, with a very large one now slowly moving toward the view window.

'I have brought up the old virus DNA sequences; this is the enemy we are now facing,' Fraslok said as he directed their attention to the screen now in front of the window.

'Is there anything we can do? We brought heaps of Nano samples... can they help?' Aaron remembered the containers they still had on Junior.

'Not for this. What you see here is an old data stream; the virus we will be facing will be far more advanced and probably totally different,' Fraslok revealed. 'What I wanted the samples for is something else.

I think I know how Sarclan has been able to so easily tap into the whole Coalition network. I'll bet he's using a type of infected Nano in the packs. Probably take a couple of days, but I think I can solve that problem and give you a way to eradicate his intrusion.'

He turned and led them back to the lounge, where a light lunch was waiting. He took the Nano samples and called one of his assistants in, before returning to his guests. 'Please enjoy... I need to get to the lab and get things moving.' He said his goodbyes with a promise to call as soon as he had any progress.

'Come on,' Aaron said to the group, 'nothing more we can do here, except wait. 'Let's head back to the hotel... at least the wait will be more agreeable there.'

Jason looked at the time display on the screen, 15:33; realizing that he and Wu Chan had been talking for most of the day but now he needed to prepare for the staff meeting.

'I didn't realize the time. Emissary Chan, I must ask your indulgence; I have a meeting shortly that is very important. May I offer you accommodation for the night? We can continue our discussions in a more informal setting, this evening.'

Chan smiled. 'That would be acceptable, thank you.'

'Excellent, I'll make the arrangements,' Jason summoned his aide.

Courtney entered the room and stood to the left of the two men. 'Courtney, could you please arrange for my wife to accompany Emissary Chan to the compound in Orange? I'll join them after the meeting.' Given recent events, Jason was still not comfortable spending too much time in the Presidential or Parliamentary compound.

Hollingsworth agreed and turned to Chan. 'Emissary Chan, if you would come with me?'

Chan stood and nodded to Jason. 'Until later, Mr. President,' he followed the Chief of Staff out of the office.

Jason's first call was to Amanda - he should be the one to break the news of visitors to their home. As he expected, Amanda took the news in her stride. She had been the wife of the CEO of the largest corporation in the Coalition for many years and was used to sudden changes in routine. Extra house guests didn't cause her any problems.

His next call was to Sam Grogan to invite him to breakfast as well. Usually, Sam had to check his schedule, to have time with old friends but now, with Jason the President, schedules had little meaning. They discussed this, with a degree of humour until Jason finally decided that Sam should come for dinner as well. That settled, Sam agreed to collect Jason at 17:30; Jason returned to his console and the staff files.

At five minutes to four, Hollingsworth returned. She informed Jason that Amanda had collected the Emissary and they were now on their way to Orange. Also, the senior staff was gathering in the conference room, at 16:00 if he would like to join them.

'How long do you want this meeting to go?' She asked.

'I hadn't thought about that, what do you suggest?'

'About half an hour,' Hollingsworth spoke confidently. 'If I may, Sir, just make this a basic meet and greet like this morning. You can interview each individually later.'

'I can see why Salim got so much done. I'll be relying on you heavily at least for the next few weeks... thank you.' Jason stood and accompanied her to the conference room.

The meeting went well, though Jason still had some concerns. CID had pointed out that some of the staff must be compromised; they couldn't pinpoint exactly who. For now, Jason was in the position of having to allow these people into the most sensitive areas of his administration, just so it could function. He was glad to keep the meeting brief and retreated to his office to record his impressions.

Shortly after, Hollingsworth announced that Admiral Grogan had arrived and was waiting in his shuttle for the President to join him. Jason thanked her and left for the hangar area of the compound.

Sam Grogan had arranged for his official shuttle to be completely stripped, as soon as the possibility of Sedition infected Gel Packs was discovered. He had all the packs replaced and before every trip, the shuttle was completely scanned. While this was no guarantee of total privacy, it was the best that could be done at the moment.

As soon as Jason boarded and the door closed, Sam spoke. 'Sorry for the cloak and dagger shit, Jason, but we can't be too cautious.'

'I agree. I've had a meeting with my senior staff, and it was hard, not knowing if any of them were who they're supposed to be, or if they had been turned. Life certainly is interesting now Eugene has raised his ugly head, again. Anyway, I've had an interesting day.' Jason described his meeting with Wu Chan to Grogan. Sam listened intently, it had been a long time since there had been any contact with the Mechanista, and he didn't want to miss a single detail.

'And you think he has more to say?'

'Yes. Look... Wu Chan is as aware of how deep Sarclan's fingers go into the Coalition as we are. He knows how the infected Nanos in the Gel Packs work so he was very circumspect in his information. Tonight, we'll meet again in the Bunker; we know that is **totally** safe from Sedition spying.'

Sam shook his head. 'How can you be so sure?'

Jason smiled at his companion. 'Simple. All data transmission and comms in the Bunker still use old fibre optic systems. Sarclan can't connect to them, making it the one place in the whole Coalition we know is his blind spot. Even the interface between the Bunker and the new systems is impossible for Nanos to breach and, as there is no direct connection to any outside system, it cannot be compromised. From now on until we can secure our Gel systems, all sensitive meetings and planning will be done down there. It's the only way to keep our plans from Sarclan.'

Sam could see the reasoning behind the move. Secretly pleased that the Abraham family had decided to restore the Bunker to its former glory - no more could it be called a Folly. Now it was the only secure facility in the Coalition.

The flight took two hours and it was after 6.30 pm when the lights of the complex came into view. By 7 pm they were all sitting in the study, informally getting to know each other.

'One thing I am glad of,' Wu began, 'is this body's ability to utilize normal human food and drink. Although technically it isn't necessary, it is still one of our species' greatest joys... good food, good drink, and good company.' Wu raised his glass in salute to his hosts.

Amanda was intrigued. 'Please Emissary, if I am being too inquisitive just say so, but your body is, in fact, a machine, of sorts?'

'Correct Madam, I will answer any of your questions.'

'Does it have all normal human functions?' Amanda's curiosity was peaked.

'Pretty well; some are different, but all do similar tasks to normal human physiology. For example, although I do not breathe as such, I still need oxygen for certain functions. This is extracted from air or water as required. Although food is also unnecessary, I made the decision when we designed the first vehicle that it should have the ability to utilize nutrients from food and drink as an energy source, and yes, that means the normal human bodily functions take place.' Chan was trying to address the information as delicately as possible.

'As for other things, I feel the same way, the skin is sensitive to many things; the eyes are as close to human design as we can make them. Although I do have enhanced low light vision and I can adjust what I see through a much-expanded spectrum. But one thing we have incorporated is a simulation of the reproductive function; in short, I can again enjoy sex.'

Amanda held her hand up, thinking her inquisition had gone too far. 'Emissary Chan I apologize, I didn't mean to intrude.'

Chan smiled. 'No intrusion has taken place. In reality, we are not so different. I am part human, part machine. You are the same thanks to your Nano Droids. My body cannot exist without my human side, and my human side is dependent on my mechanical components. Humans are similarly symbiotic with their Nanos.'

Phillip entered and announced that dinner was served. They all stood and adjourned to the dining room. Dinner was a simple affair, consisting of a fine seafood chowder followed by poached trout and salad with individual apple strudels for dessert.

Wu Chan nodded his thanks, as he pushed back his plate. 'That's why we designed the body as we did; one of the greatest joys any person can have is sharing a wonderful meal with pleasant company. I thank you, Madam.'

'My pleasure Emissary Chan; I hope that we are now at the start of more contact between our races. I know you three have things to discuss, so I've had Phillip set up coffee and port in the conference room. Please go and enjoy.' Amanda smiled and left the room.

Jason led them through the study, where they entered the old elevator and down to the Bunker. As Amanda had said, there on the table in the conference room was a decanter of port, glasses, and a steaming pot of coffee. Jason poured the port as they all helped themselves to coffee.

'Now Wu, we are in the only secure place we know of. I take it you have more to tell?'

'You are indeed astute,' Chan said. 'I couldn't say more this morning as I don't know how compromised your office is.'

'I agree. We don't know ourselves, but I can assure you that there is no way this place is compromised. We have no Gel Packs or Bio-computer systems here; everything is run on optical communication.' Jason spoke reassuringly.

'Excellent, as I said earlier, I am ashamed that some of our people have sided with Sarclan, but his tendrils have corrupted most of the galaxy. The information I have is very delicate as it involves Mechanista citizens and I do not want to compromise their safety.

'But by siding with Sarclan, they have put all in our galaxy in danger. One thing I must insist on is your **absolute** assurance that every effort will be made to protect our citizens. Even though to your people, they have sided with the enemy, they are Mechanista and as such, not under Coalition rules.' He stopped to allow this to sink in. 'Mister President, what say you on this?'

Jason stood and started pacing, the Abraham tell that he was thinking deeply. At length, he stopped and spoke. 'Emissary Chan, I also do not want any more death or destruction. Sarclan has already done too much of both... but, if there is to be any sort of relationship between our peoples, I must be honest. I cannot give any guarantees, except that I will do all in my power to ensure our people act responsibly.

'I emphasize this. **I will not** ask my people to put themselves in unnecessary danger. If anyone supporting Sarclan confronts our forces, they will be met with reciprocal force.' Jason stopped pacing and sat back down.

Chan sat, considering the answer, his eyes fixed on Jason. 'Mister President... Jason... I appreciate your honesty and dedication to your people. I have details of where Sarclan is manufacturing his Nano Virus Droids.' He handed over a data drive.

Jason took it, placed it into a security scanner, and, when the scan was negative for any intrusive measures, inserted it into the console. Immediately the screen activated. Displayed was a huge space Station.

'This is the facility Sarclan is using,' Chan spoke as the images scrolled through on the screen. 'Please understand... this is a Mechanista facility and those who own it are contracted to Sarclan to manufacture his Nanos. But it is also one of the facilities we use to make the proper Nanos for the Coalition. If we can take control of this facility, we will not only stop production, we will gain access to the virus that he is using. In one action we should be able to stop this threat.'

'You use the word we?'

Chan smiled. 'Yes, Mr. President The one condition to me revealing the true location is that I am part of the intrusion force.' He saw that Grogan was about to protest. 'Please Admiral, if I go, the possibility of success is far greater. There are at least four level-nine masters on that facility; your troops would be at a great disadvantage against them... allow me to demonstrate.' Chan changed the file and brought up one of the Mechanista battle games; this one was an infiltration program, very much like the scenario they were currently discussing.

'The goal of this game is for the Master to infiltrate the compound, defeat the opposing force, and take control of the Command Centre. What you do not know is that this takes place in **real-time** and against **real adversaries**... now watch.'

Chan started the recording. It was shot from the head of the invading Master; it showed all the battles, all the strategy, and all the action. When the recording ended, Chan closed the file.

'That gentlemen, was the scenario that elevated me to the tenth level. What you saw there was recorded from my eyes and all the action was real. Mechanista no longer lay back on a lounge and vegetate. If any of us wish to progress through the ranks we must compete in reality, as I did there.' He unfastened his tunic. 'These are some of the wounds I suffered.' There in front of both humans was the evidence. Several deep and ugly scars ran across his torso; scars that showed where Chan had been seriously injured.

Grogan was impressed. 'And with all this, you **still** won? Well for my money, you're more than welcome to come with us, but any final decision will be made by Klastok... after all, the troops are his.'

'Do you mean General Ivan Klastok?' Chan smiled when Sam nodded. 'Excellent. It would be my great honour to serve under such a brilliant strategist. I will await his decision.'

With that sorted, Jason contacted Klastok and asked him to join them, first thing in the morning. While Jason was talking with the General, Chan, and Grogan were studying star-charts trying to find the most direct but covert route to the facility. In the end, Sam stood, defeated.

'Sorry Jason, I can't seem to see any way we can get a force of any size there without being detected and ending up in a full-scale battle... maybe we need younger eyes? I suggest we call JT and Sol, see if they can suggest anything.' Even Chan appeared despondent at what they had discovered.

Jason made the call and arranged for the other two to join Klastok in the morning.

'Well, that's all we can do tonight. I suggest we get some sleep, I take it you still need sleep, Emissary?'

'Indeed I do, and it would be gratefully accepted.'

'Well, it's settled.' Jason added as he led them back to the elevator, taking the data drive with him.

***

The readout showed 02:12 - the numbers seemed to float. With consciousness slowly returning; the fog of that place between sleep and awake slowly dissipated. Amanda turned to her left, that side of the bed was empty; she also noticed that the two cats that usually occupied the foot of the bed were missing. She gave herself a few moments for her mind to clear before rising. She donned her gown and went to the door, the faint sound of someone walking reaching her ears. Taking a deep breath she opened the door and stepped through.

'If you need some nocturnal exercise, I'm sure I could arrange something a little more enjoyable,' she said, her voice both sarcastic and inviting.

'Sorry, did I wake you?' Jason shot back, a little too quickly.

Amanda shook her head; sleep was not on his agenda now. 'Jason Abraham, we have been married a long time. Do you believe I wouldn't notice your preoccupation? Now, I'll make some tea and we'll discuss this.' There was no diverting her once she made up her mind.

Amanda went to the kitchen and started brewing a pot of Earl Grey. She returned with a tray holding the teapot and a plate with a few slices of lemon and two fine china cups. She went through her usual ritual of turning the pot before pouring. She placed a slice of lemon into each cup and handed one to her husband.

'Now talk... what's bothering you so much you get up in the middle of the night?'

Jason knew he had no choice, in all the years they had been together he'd never been able to keep anything from her. 'It's Wu Chan,' he confessed. 'There's something he's not telling us... something he's holding back. I've been trying to figure it out but I just can't get it.'

'And you decided to ruin a night's sleep, over that? Why not simply ask him?'

'What if I'm wrong? I've got no evidence, just my gut.' Jason was on his feet, pacing again.

'How many times have we been in a situation where everything was riding on your gut? How many times have we been to the brink of ruin, only to be saved by your gut? And now you're the President you suddenly feel you should doubt that? Bullshit!' Amanda was now standing, blocking Jason's path. 'Call him into the study before breakfast, and tell him how you feel. Remember honesty is a two way street.'

Jason gazed into her eyes. The strength of the woman never ceased to amaze him, she always seemed to have the right answer at the right time. He nodded.

'You're right, as usual. I did offer total honesty... maybe I should demand the same, in return.' He raised his cup and sipped his tea. 'You always make the best Earl Grey.'

His smile told Amanda the crisis was over. In a few hours, Jason would ask the questions and get his answers.

'Right, now come back to bed. We've still got time for a few hours rest... or not.' She winked seductively, placed her cup on the tray, and walked back into the bedroom. Jason smiled, his heartbeat increasing, and followed her.

By 7.29 am Jason was sitting behind the study desk. At 07:30 there was a knock on the door.

'Enter,' Jason called. The door opened and Emissary Chan entered.

'You wanted to see me, Mr. President?' He closed the door behind him.

Jason carefully studied the man before him. Every part of him cried trust him, but there was the smallest nagging doubt.

'Yes, Wu; please sit.' Jason waited until his guest was seated. 'Yesterday I told you that for any relationship between our societies to develop, there must be total honesty, so I'll be blunt. There is a nagging doubt in my mind that you aren't telling us everything about this situation. I feel there is some important detail you're keeping from us.' He stopped and sat quietly, allowing Chan to think.

Finally, Chan smiled. 'The stories about Jason Abraham **are** true. You are indeed insightful and direct. You are correct, but the omission was for no other reason than my own embarrassment. Please allow me to complete the picture.

'Many years ago, a representative claiming to be from Eugene Sarclan approached our then leaders with an offer of friendship and mutual benefit. They were intrigued, as the rest of the human race had written us off as a lost cause. Sarclan was impressed by our ability to design and manufacture exceptional machines. His offer included much wealth and support for us, plus a promise that, eventually, the human race would be forced to recognize us as an individual species.

'At the time, I was a lowly level-five contestant. As such, I had little input on policy decisions. Many of our senior warriors were enthralled by the offer but, thankfully, sense won the day. As we did with the Coalition, we agreed to test the relationship on an ad hoc basis... they would request something, we would analyse the request, and then decide if we wanted to be part of it.

'This seemed to work well at first, but there were dissidents who wanted more. In secret, they built a separate agreement with Sarclan, eventually incorporating some of his refused requests into our normal business. This worked for them for many years and if any of the senior warriors knew, they turned a blind eye... until I ascended to the highest level. By then it was too late, several of our facilities were working exclusively for Sarclan and nearly fifty level-nine masters were involved.

'A purge, of sorts, was undertaken and all but four level-nine masters have been neutralized. All facilities except for this one are now back under our full control. I must face these traitors and either bring them back or dispatch them. I apologize for any deception you felt... that was never my intent.'

Jason sat back, digesting the information. Finally, he made a decision and spoke.

'Emissary Chan, I fully understand your position and I thank you for trusting me with this information. It appears we are more similar than we first thought. Both our people are susceptible to greed and the seduction of Sarclan's promises. It will be our honour to work with you to rectify the situation. What you have told me, will remain in this room. Now, shall we adjourn for breakfast?'

Chan smiled stood and bowed his head slightly. 'Thank you, Mr. President.'

***

The shuttle touched down effortlessly, the pilot completing the power down procedure quickly to allow his passengers a quick exit. He watched them walk down the access ramp - now he could relax. The two Admirals walked across the apron and into the hangar where they were met by Sam Grogan. They both snapped to attention and saluted their Superior.

'At ease, gentlemen. It feels strange, me welcoming you to your home JT. We're heading into the Bunker,' he said as he turned and led them away at a brisk pace. They entered the newly reconditioned secure elevator that serviced the hangar. Sam selected SB 5 on the control pad and the doors closed. They rode down in silence, with JT and Sol wondering why they were here and why their Commanding Officer was greeting them. The elevator deposited them at the correct level and again, Sam took the lead.

JT couldn't help himself. 'You seem to know your way around here, Sir.'

'Have to. This is the only secure site that we know of.

Everything will be done from here until we can sort out the mess that Sarclan has set up.'

He turned down another corridor and walked up to a guard stationed outside a door. The guard inspected their ID and ran them through a scan before allowing them into the conference room.

Already present were Crompton, General Klastok, and, much to JT's surprise and delight, Maalai Bakshi, Coalition Space Corps' chief Cryptologist. With the greeting formalities complete, JT took a seat to the left of Maalai.

'The only time we can catch up is at some formal briefing. How are you?' he spoke quietly.

Maalai chuckled to herself. 'I am well and you are correct... we don't seem to be able to get the time for that coffee.'

JT noticed the coffee service on the sideboard. 'Well, I'll fix that,' he said, quickly standing and going over to it. He filled two mugs and returned with them and a tray with milk and sugar. 'The coffee problem is now solved.'

Maalai smiled. 'Thank you,' she spoke quietly, accepting the mug. She was about to say more when the door on the far side of the room opened. In strode Jason Abraham and a second person, nobody knew.

Everyone leaped to their feet but Jason waved them down. 'Forget the ceremony... we have a hell of a lot to do and not much time. I would like to introduce Wu Chan, Tenth Degree Games Master, and Emissary of the Mechanista.' Chan nodded. 'Emissary Chan has brought us some vital information and has pledged the Mechanista to assist us. For those of you who don't know Mechanista society, Wu Chan is my equivalent in their government.'

Chan stood apart from the President and greeted all. He stood as tall as Jason but seemed to have a cat-like stance. He gave the appearance of being constantly on guard. Chan seemed to read their minds, curiosity, wariness, even some fear, he quickly moved to quell these feelings.

'What your President has said is true,' he declared. 'The Mechanista will work with you to defeat this **Sedition**, as it is called. In our society, our rank is gained through our gaming, most commonly war games. I know many of you will have an image of us as semi-human blobs, sitting around playing computer games. Sadly, that was true many years ago. We have changed and we now want to throw off our self-imposed isolation and re-join the rest of humanity.

'What I am about to show you is indicative of how alike we are. As you have seen, Sarclan can be very seductive, and he has seduced some of our senior ranks, as he did yours. We must work together to finally defeat this menace!' As he finished, Chan bowed slightly and took his seat beside Jason, who rose to address them.

'Let's clear up some housekeeping details. As I have been given total control by the Council, I've decided to run things from here, till we can find a solution to Sarclan's eaves-dropping. Also, I will be bringing on some new staff, as we still don't know who in the Presidential Office we can trust. Ms. Bakshi will be my Chief of Staff at this location and Ms. Hollingsworth will continue to run the other office. Now, I'll hand the meeting back to Emissary Chan so he can bring you up to date with the situation.'

For the next two hours, they discussed the problem, analysed the location, and pored over the plans for the orbiting facility. They also took particular note of the planet the facility was stationed over and the defensive capability that was based there. It was formidable. With over one thousand troops, fifty fighter craft, and three KL10n cruisers, any attack was going to be a daunting assignment.

'We need more Intel,' JT said. 'I suggest we send a recon ship and deploy some mini probes to see what they are doing. We need to know what forces are patrolling before we do anything.'

'Yes,' Klastok concurred. 'If we **are** to send in a full assault team, we need to know what they will face. They might not even reach the target with all that firepower.'

'I also agree,' Chan added. 'I have sent a few of our people to the sector to monitor and report back... I should have their report later today. Then we will have a better idea of what we will face. But General, I do not think we will be able to send in a large force initially. I have a strategy... based on your assault on Hadrian's compound... that may work. But I can't be confident until we have the data.'

Jason checked the time. 'Well, I think we should break now, we can't do much more until we have the data. I have arranged for lunch to be served two floors up. We'll reconvene at 15:00.' He looked at Chan, who nodded his agreement.

They stood and Chan approached General Klastok. 'General,' Chan bowed, deeply. 'It is an honour to meet you. I have used some of your campaigns to build the strategies that have helped me to reach my position... I could not have done it without them.'

'I'm flattered, Emissary Chan. I'm glad some of those old battles have been of use to you. Come, let's discuss them over lunch.'

Klastok beamed as he walked out with a new friend.

ow goes it my friend?'

The words were soft, so out of character for Eugene Sarclan. He was standing in a hospital suite, the subject of his question lying on the bed in front of him, but separated by the glass panel.

'I have my moments. Memories are incomplete and I seem to have lost some time, but all things considered, I'm doing fine; just one thing... why Eugene why?'

Sarclan stared at the person on the bed as if he was seeing him for the first time. The man was fairly tall, well built with long dark hair. His face was a mass of stubble as he hadn't shaved for days but his eyes were alive, constantly darting around the room.

'Why? Because you died,' Sarclan's voice almost cracked with emotion.

'We have been together for many years... you are my right hand and I didn't want to carry on without you. I have never had friends... you are the only person who qualifies as that. Only you, Hiro, of all the people I've ever known, are a true friend, I couldn't let you die.' Sarclan spoke softly but with real conviction.

'And these gaps in my memory, what's that about?'

'An unfortunate side effect of not being able to record your brain regularly,' Sarclan said, almost pleading. 'If you'd only let me do that, there would be no gaps.'

'I told you at the beginning I didn't want to be cloned and that when my time came I was prepared to die. Why didn't you let me go?'

'Because it wasn't your time.'

Hiro Nakamura... or this version of him... stared at the stark white ceiling. The external window was shuttered and everything in the room was either white or gleaming silver. Even the viewing window that Sarclan was behind was opaque white. The technicians hovered over him, fussing with their instruments and machines, he hated it; even they were white, covered head to foot in white coveralls.

The head technician picked up the comm handset. *Mr. Sarclan, everything is good. His muscles are well developed, his organs are functioning perfectly. He's ready to get up.*

This was the moment Sarclan had been waiting for, the moment when Hiro Nakamura, second in command of Sarclan Sedition was back from the dead; twelve months of work – building the body, watching it grow, and finally inputting Nakamura's recorded brain. Memories, abilities, desires, hopes, and fears all placed carefully into the new brain. All Hiro had to do was accept the gift, get out of that bed, and join the fight again.

'Hiro, you are ready? Get up, stand, and take stock of your new life.' Sarclan spoke with enthusiasm. Would this be the one? Fifteen attempts and all ending the same way - would number sixteen be better?

Slowly Hiro sat up, swung his legs off the bed, and gingerly stood. The technicians rushed to his side, assisting him to walk; he pushed them away. 'If I have to do this, I'll do it myself,' he said.

Slowly, he took his first step, then another. Soon he was walking with confidence; he approached the window and stood before Sarclan, shaking his head. 'Fifteen times, Eugene... fifteen times you have resurrected me. When will you give up?'

The viewing window changed, now Sarclan was visible to his friend. 'Never, my friend, never!' Sarclan almost spat the words. 'I'll never stop trying.'

Nakamura sadly shook his head. 'Then I'll have to accept this time; I'm sick of dying.'

He turned to the techs - most of who were almost trembling with fear. They were recalling how each time Nakamura had been resurrected; he had killed himself and some of the techs with him. 'Stop fretting! He said. 'If it is my fate to live, then so be it.' He moved back to the bed and sat down in resignation. 'Can someone get me some clothes?'

Usually, the only emotion that Sarclan expressed was anger, but standing there watching Nakamura finally accept this gift of life was an intensely joyful moment for him. He had succeeded in the most important venture of his life. He had brought back to life the only friend he ever had, the only person whose advice he ever listened to, the only person he truly cared about. The techs may not have seen the single tear run down his left cheek, but Nakamura did.

***

Task Force Paladin was officially a disaster. Four Coalition cruisers had entered the Bad-Lands to search for Balerophon and the unthinkable had happened; they had been attacked by Raider ships and given a royal flogging. One ship was destroyed and the three survivors had limped back to Coalition space only to be scrapped. But they achieved one thing; they left hundreds of micro-probes and - more importantly - a viable relay network. The probes were the latest design, with guidance and a basic propulsion system that could keep them on a specified course.

For much of their life they were dormant, they drifted - being propelled along by inertia and the natural forces of the galaxy. When the gravity field of a planet captured them, it triggered their systems, and they came to life. They had a limited life; eventually, the orbit they had achieved would decay and they would burn up harmlessly in the planet's atmosphere. Before then, each probe would orbit; running sensor sweeps of the planet below, hopefully in this case, locating the rebel base. With luck, each tiny probe could complete up to one hundred orbits before they succumbed to their inevitable fate.

Three of the units were now approaching their final target

in the Bad-Lands - Betanna. The problem with Betanna was that most of the time there was some form of cloud cover with violent storms. Clear days were a rarity so capturing images was highly unlikely.

After five days, the first probe succumbed to the force of gravity and made a small but spectacular show in the sky; something that was common for Betanna. Four hours later, the second probe transmitted data to both the relay Station and the remaining probe before it too became celestial pyrotechnics.

Inside the last unit, the tiny micro brain analysed the data it received and changed course. It followed the path of the previous probe, constantly recording data and images and sending them to the relay Station. Finally, it also signalled its death with a brief, but colourful spectacle.

The relay Stations were recording and transmitting data from hundreds of these tiny spies and this was being monitored on Earth. All this data was then compartmentalized and sent to the Abraham Bunker, where it was further analysed for any evidence of either Balerophon or human habitation.

***

Back on Earth, Sol's alarm screamed and he leaped out of bed. It took him a few minutes to figure out where he was and what the bloody noise meant. Quickly he shut it down, grabbed his clothes, and dressed.

Three minutes later he was in the analysis room looking at the images on the screen. The data from the Betanna probes had finally arrived. It had taken six weeks for it to traverse the distance and be processed, but the computer recognized one of the parameters it was searching for in the images it received. As it was programmed to do, it immediately set off an alarm in Sol's communicator.

'Well, I'll be... we found you! **Yehaa**!' he yelled as he jumped up and punched the air. '**Fuck you Sarclan, we've found you!**' Immediately he reached for his communicator and made a call.

A sleepy voice answered. *What's the emergency?*

'JT, get your sleepy arse down here... we've found Balerophon!' Sol shouted.

What the fuck are you talking about... are you dreaming?

'No, my friend, just come to the analysis room now!'

He cut the comms, walked over to his desk, and opened the top right-hand drawer. He pulled out two glasses and a bottle of Bourbon, poured two drinks, and took one back to the console. He stared at the screen. There in all her glory was the hull of Balerophon, unmistakable and intact. The last probe had flown over at precisely the right moment, the cloud cover had dissipated for a few seconds and it was able to capture a crystal clear shot.

'Talk about a one in a million shot,' Sol whispered. He drained his glass, not taking his eye off the screen for a second. The door opened and JT walked in.

'Now, what the fu...' he stood still staring at the screen. Sol went back to his desk, refilled his glass, and brought the other back for JT.

'There, old man. This'll start your heart again. Ain't she beautiful?'

'Where... how?' JT stuttered.

'Micro probes... we dropped **hundreds** of them in the Bad-Lands... set up a relay system and left them there. This was picked up on Betanna. John, we've found Sarclan... he has to be there!' Sol's voice was filled with excitement.

JT regained his composure and drained his glass. 'Sol, start a full analysis... we need a precise location.' He picked up his communicator and called Sam Grogan. Ten minutes later he and Jason entered the room; no words were needed, the image on the screen told it all--Balerophon had been found.

In the three days since the Abraham group had returned to Argos many things had transpired.

True to his word, Fraslok and his team had discovered the secret of how Sarclan was using Nano Droids to spy on Coalition installations. It was inevitable that Sarclan would realize his spies were being defeated so, in the interests of victory, Fraslok set about developing a remedy - one that would remove the threat without alerting the enemy too quickly.

While this was going on, the Bunker back on Earth was transformed into the Headquarters for the entire Coalition operation. Plans were made and discarded as better Intel was received. With two prime targets, it was imperative that the execution of both operations took place simultaneously. But the information coming back was not encouraging. The Mechanista facility in orbit around Delgado 6 was proving to be a real problem. Every scenario they developed failed dismally

'The trouble we face here is they are expecting a Coalition attack. Their defences are impressive and we simply can't break through them,' Wu Chan said, the frustration showing in his voice. 'I think we need a completely new approach... a direct attack won't work.'

Sam Grogan stood to stretch his tired muscles. They'd been at this for three days straight and every time they were defeated. 'It's a simple enough scenario... attack the facility, capture, or destroy it... so what are we missing?'

It was Klastok who made the first breakthrough. 'Clearly the facility knows either we or the Krell are coming, and they're ready for that. Maybe we need to look at an initial covert infiltration? A small force might be able to talk their way into the facility, disable it and call in the troops.'

'I know how to disable the facility, but how do we get there? Every scenario we use is detected. We need something else...' Sam stopped, lost for an answer.

'I've got it! Chan finally announced. 'No Mechanista would ever refuse to assist a ship in distress... it is against our code and punishable by death. Suppose we were aboard a small private yacht and it develops some problem with the drive? The facility would be called on to assist; and believe me, they will. The small force then disables the defences and captures the rebels.'

The voice of Jason Abraham stopped them in their tracks. 'Sounds like you have a solution?'

He had entered via the door on the far side of the room and had been listening to the conversation. 'I believe that might work, but I would like to bring someone else in on this.' He moved to his left to reveal his companion, as he strode across the room. 'Before I introduce you all, please put these on, it's a translator Emissary Chan.'

With translators now in place, Jason made the formal introduction. 'Emissary Chan of the Mechanista, please meet Admiral Tocmal of Reglaos. The Admiral may be able to assist in this matter.' Jason handed the room to Tocmal.

'Emissary Chan, it is my honour to meet you.' Tocmal bowed, as best as his body would allow.

'Admiral,' Chan responded, warily. This was the first time anyone from the Mechanista had met a real alien and Tocmal's insect-like appearance was totally new to him. He was completely lost for words.

Tocmal clicked, but Chan heard the words. 'Emissary Chan, do not be embarrassed; I have this effect on most Humans when they first meet me. But we must get past this awkwardness quickly. What I heard of your idea intrigues me, and I think we may have the ability to assist. President A-Bra-Ham,' Tocmal turned to Jason, 'I think the small force needed is on Argos. I would like to take the Emissary with me to discuss this with the others. How much time do we have?'

Jason deferred to Grogan, who replied. 'No more than four days. We've sent a force of Mantas into the Bad-Lands to set up a more sophisticated monitoring system; it should be coming online later today. Admiral Radchak is coordinating the Bad-Lands operations with Admiral Abraham handling Delgado 6 Maybe he should be part of your planning team.'

Once all had agreed, Sam called JT and they arranged for a ship to be readied. Two hours later, the small group was transferred to Valiant for the trip to Argos.

***

On Argos, things were moving fast. Sonia and Petra had organized to view a property that Petra was interested in. Aaron had no choice but to comply, even though his mind was focused elsewhere. Coming back had shown him just how much he relied on Henry. After his first day here with the Professor, he'd been corralled in his office with so much to do that his workdays seemed almost never-ending. Any excuse - even looking at this house his fiancée and sister in law had selected - was a welcome relief.

The house turned out to be similar in many ways to the family compound on Earth, though smaller. The location was a real surprise, being less than a kilometre from a beautiful meandering river which formed a substantial lake in front of the house; the whole area felt familiar, welcoming and relaxing.

There was a functioning vineyard and two thousand hectares of prime grazing land as part of the package. Jeff immediately saw the potential and was soon deep in discussion and planning with Aaron as to what could be achieved. In the end, after several hours of looking at every aspect of the property Aaron spoke.

'How much?

'Does it matter? Do you like it or not?'

Aaron gazed deep in her eyes; they seemed to sparkle in a way he hadn't seen for months. All the pressure of their situation had dulled everything. For most of the past year, they had been absorbed with business and diplomatic issues and hadn't had much time for each other. Finally, it dawned on him; this would be their refuge, a place they could call home; the one place where they could be themselves.

'Yes, you're right. It is a beautiful place and **I love it**!' he answered honestly and with real enthusiasm. After over thirty years of living in space ships, hotels, and worse, the idea of finally settling down intrigued him.

Buying a property on Argos was a simple matter. All Aaron and Petra needed to do was agree on the price, action the finance and everything else, engineering reports, title searches, and other mundane matters took place within days. In this case, it was even quicker as the current owners had already moved to their new home and completed the formal process to sell. Now all the agent needed, was the funds to be transferred and the property would be theirs.

Jeff was stunned. 'Just like that, you're buying the place?' He watched as Aaron transferred the funds and he and Petra signed the purchase agreement. The agent ratified the deed transfer and they were the new owners of this magnificent home.

'Now you see why I'll never leave Freebooters. Little or no bureaucratic intrusion... no land tax, no transfer fees... nothing. Buying a house has nothing to do with the government, so why pay them for doing nothing?' Aaron smiled as he authorized the deed copy into his private account. 'Tomorrow, we need to set up our joint accounts,' he said to Petra. 'You're registered as the joint owner but we should get everything else sorted while we're here.'

'Sounds perfect, now... time to celebrate... how about dinner at the Flame Grill,' she beamed. Aaron made the call and reserved a table. Next, he called Mondrac to see if he and Silas would like to join them but the invitation was declined, they were both engrossed with Fraslok and the work at the lab.

While Aaron was finalizing all the details, Petra and Sonia

started taking inventory. Although the house had most of the basics included, being over two hundred years old it needed a lot more individual pieces of furniture than more modern homes. Things like beds were included in all homes as these were all gravity neutral systems, but chairs and lounges were individual. Almost an hour later Aaron had to remind them that their reservation was for seven-thirty and it was already six forty-five; they still needed to get back and change for dinner. Petra's hands were shaking slightly as she took the security control Aaron handed her.

'You OK?'

'Yes, a little stunned... we've just bought our first home.' A tear gently caressed her cheek as she spoke.

Aaron brushed it aside, 'yes; the first in many things we're going to do. Now, let's get going, I'm bloody hungry.'

Aaron had booked the same table he and Petra had sat at on the night they met and everyone had the Carnivore Plate; a bottle of vintage Champagne and a couple of reds completed the meal. It was after midnight when they all returned to the Morgan Hotel, agreeing to meet for breakfast at eight.

Once back in their room, Petra started the shower and dropped her clothes into the sanitizer; she was soaping herself when she felt Aaron, now, naked himself, step up behind her. He ran his hands slowly down both sides of her body, gently folded his arms around her, and nibbled her ear. She felt the first tingles of desire and reached her arms up to join his.

She knew this was where she belonged. Turning around, she cupped his face into her hands. 'I'm so incredibly happy. Can I show you just how much I love you?' Her pent up emotions from the last few days were desperate to be released. She kissed him with ever-increasing passion, his response firming between her thighs. She began to bite his neck --teasing, tantalizing--wanting all of him.

'I'm yours!' Aaron whispered, as his passion rose. He could sense this was going to be fast and furious and this excited him even more.

Petra pressed herself up against him parted her thighs and began rubbing herself against his growing erection. He groaned with delight and felt her wetness. He knew she was ready, so he lifted her, and she wrapped her legs around his hips. He grabbed her butt cheeks firmly as he entered her slowly; savouring every millimetre, then pushed her backward pressing her against the wall, for extra support. He gave two more strokes then together, they began to thrust and grind in unison, as their hunger surged.

Finally, Petra cried out in pleasure with Aaron following her a few moments later. Their passion now satisfied, they stood, holding each other close while the water cascaded over them. It seemed like an age before they moved apart, finished showering then stumbled into bed and were soon fast asleep, cradled in each other's arms.

***

The first order of business at breakfast was to complete the outfitting of the new house and for this Aaron produced his data-pad with the details of home ware suppliers in the city. Sonia and Petra studied them and decided on two; one they thought could supply everything and a backup, just in case. Aaron smiled to himself; they had chosen the one his company used to outfit all their ships.

Next, arrangements were made for Petra's things to be moved from storage, and for Aaron's clothing to be collected; living aboard his ship had negated any need for furniture. They finished breakfast and were leaving the dining room when Aaron's communicator chimed. He looked at the screen and shook his head; the face of Allen Grainger was displayed.

'Hello Allen,' he answered.

Good morning, I hope I'm not intruding?

'Not at all, we just finished breakfast and are off to do some shopping,' Aaron answered, wondering what the Freebooter Prime really wanted.

Ah, yes... I hear you bought a home yesterday. Congratulations!

Grace is back and is keen to meet your fiancée so I was wondering if we could catch up?

'Of course... we'll be at the new house later today. How about you meet us there around four? Aaron paused for an answer, 'It's above Lake Camargue on the Hough River.' Aaron cut the connection and turned to Petra, 'Well you're in for it now, Grace Grainger wants to give you the once over. Better be on your best behaviour.' Aaron chuckled.

The expedition to outfit the new house went much better than anyone could have thought. By twelve, all purchases had been made and Petra was making final arrangements for delivery and any installation for this afternoon. Aaron was watching as Petra harangued the poor logistics guy when his communicator again chimed; this time Mondrac's face was displayed.

'Mondrac, hello; how's everything at the lab?'

Mondrac's voice was tense and firm as he spoke. *A-Bra-Ham can you talk freely?* Aaron looked around, moved half a dozen steps away from the others, and answered.

'I can now!'

I am sorry my friend but things are about to get problematic again... where can we meet?

Aaron didn't like what he was hearing, but he gave Mondrac the location of the new house and agreed for him to be there around two in the afternoon. The hackles on the back of Aaron's neck were standing to attention, *first Grainger and now a very serious Mondrac. This is not good* he thought.

He moved closer to Petra and entered the conversation about having goods delivered and installed. They agreed this afternoon would be fine and the arrival was planned for midday. With that settled they returned to the hotel where Aaron settled the account for the two rooms, leaving instructions that the account for Mondrac and Silas' room be sent to his office. Finally, with all this taken care of, they left the hotel for the last time and pointed their shuttle away from the city.

***

Wu Chan, Tocmal, and JT were sitting in the wardroom on Valiant. JT was finding it difficult staying away from the Bridge; his new rank and position carried certain protocols, one being that the Captain of a ship must invite an Admiral to his Bridge. This annoyed JT, he had been instrumental in the creation of the Manta class; while rank did have privileges, it also carried some downsides, these protocols being one.

Wu Chan addressed Tocmal. 'Admiral, you said that the ideal team may be on Argos... what do you mean?'

'Emissary Chan, I have fought beside the people we are about to meet and I can assure you there are no finer allies in all the Realms. Besides, the problems you experienced in your battle simulations were due to utilizing a Coalition frontal attack; I'd like to propose using a subterfuge, we should be a little more underhanded. I agree that a ship in distress is a smart idea but a neutral ship in distress will be even better.' Tocmal stopped to take a long draw from his coffee mug.

'You're thinking of using a Freebooter trade ship? Most have formidable weapons but if it goes bad, what then?' JT had grave doubts about this idea, and he wanted to voice them.

'That's where this vessel comes in. It is one of the upgraded units, is it not?'

"Yes, Tocmal it is. We've finally broken their shield randomization and installed it in Valiant,' JT admitted.

'Well then,' Tocmal replied, 'Valiant is our back-up. I have also contacted Prime Grainger and Mondrac... they'll already be with the others when we arrive. I suggest we relax, it may be a while before we have this luxury again.'

***

At midday, a freight shuttle touched down at Aaron and Petra's new home accompanied by a smaller unit with the installers and craftsmen aboard. Petra and Aaron were there to meet them and quickly gave instructions on what was required.

'Let's leave them to get on with things; in the meantime, I have something you haven't seen yet, in the basement... follow me.' Petra led them to a door beside the stairwell, opened it, and revealed another staircase leading downwards. Lights automatically came on, and they started to descend.

'This first landing is what I want to show you, these stairs continue for two more levels, first to a storage area and finally house services, power supply, and other things.' Petra smiled as she opened the door. Before them was a long well-lit room, divided by a transparent panel; one side was a sparkling pool, ten metres wide and about thirty metres long; The other side was a gym, with the usual array of equipment, both mechanized and manual, but two-thirds were vacant, with a magnificent wooden floor.

'The previous owner was a ballet dancer, this was his practice area.' Petra grinned as she led them onto the floor. There was a long mirror down one side with a support bar running along it.

'What... are you going to learn ballet?' Aaron was bewildered.

Petra had a slightly sheepish look on her face. 'No, I'm not but there is something I haven't confessed to. I'm an exponent of Tharis Gha, Vargan martial arts... similar to Kung Fu. My mother was the holder of the fifth level... I'm at level four and this will make a great workout area.'

'Only a level four... that makes you one of how many?' Aaron asked.

'I 'm not sure... probably no more than six.'

'I'm sorry' Sonia broke in, 'what is Tharis Gha?'

'Well for most, an exercise routine and meditation technique, but also a way of fighting. We are taught to use many weapons from sticks and stones through to blasters and disruptors. The focus is on personal defence and spiritual growth; using your mind and body in concert with your surroundings. It really keeps you fit, both mentally and physically.' Petra smiled.

Aaron stood beside Petra, disbelief etched on his face, 'and here's me thinking that you were going through a Yoga routine each morning. I'll have to always be on my best behaviour,' he mumbled.

Petra moved closer and kissed him gently 'As you're discovering, Vargan women are incredible lovers, but we also have a dark side; it might be better if you didn't push those buttons.' She giggled as she turned towards a door at the far end of the room, opened it, and revealed a roomy elevator. 'This should do nicely. Come on Aaron, I need some muscle.'

Aaron and Jeff followed her into the elevator. Fifteen minutes later they returned with several boxes, which Petra directed them to place at specific locations in the room. The two men repeated the trip a further three times, each time with more boxes. While they were doing this, Petra and Sonia started to assemble some of the components in the boxes.

'What does Tharis Gha mean?' Sonia was curious.

'Loosely translated, it means warrior of light; a master can enter a battle, defeat their enemy and leave no trace of being there. My mother always told me that a true master could fight on a floor covered with feathers, and never move a single one. Once when I was much younger she was instructing me, and I wasn't doing so well. She told me I was too slow and heavy, that I had feet like a Saradoc, something like an Earth bear. I got angry and challenged her to do better.

'When we entered the training room the next day, she had a huge bag of feathers; she spread them around the room and covered the entire floor. She then told me to make sure I knew where each one was; I did, and even recorded the image on a data-pad.' Petra paused, gathering her thoughts before continuing, 'she went through one of her normal routines, first slowly and then much faster. I didn't see a single feather move, it was amazing.

'Then it was my turn; it was like we were in a feather storm. It was then that I realized I had a lot more to learn; so from that moment on, every chance I had I'd drag out the feathers, spread them around, and practice. I kept at it for years; I was determined I was going to prove myself her equal. Eventually, I thought I was ready and only a few weeks before she died, I brought her to that room and went through the routine, certain I would progress to the next level. While she was impressed to see how far I had come, I still failed; one feather had moved.'

Their conversation was interrupted by Aaron and Jeff racing down the stairs, 'the last crate was too big for us to fit in the elevator with it... and bloody heavy. Thank heavens the guys upstairs had an AG sled.' The door on the elevator opened to reveal the huge crate. Petra walked over to it as it slid effortlessly across the floor on the sled. She took a small device from the side of the crate, pressed a button on it and the crate separated from the sled. She tapped a command into the unit in her hand but nothing happened, she tried again.

'Damn,' Petra shook her head, 'the battery is low.' She scanned the room and saw a power outlet close by, opened a port in the base of the strange unit, and pulled out a cord. This was connected to the power outlet and the unit began to charge. She saw the confused looks she was getting. 'This is Moril, my trainer. I'll give you a demo later when she's charged.'

Aaron's communicator chimed. 'Mondrac's here.'

Mondrac was waiting in the entry, his face a mask of concern. 'A-Bra-Ham, we must talk.' He moved towards Aaron revealing he had brought Fraslok with him.

Aaron tried to lighten the mood. 'Morning Professor, this must be something to get you out of your lab.'

'Indeed it is... a new problem has been discovered,' Fraslok answered.

Aaron nodded and led them to the front of the house, away from the activity and craftsmen. 'OK, what's so serious?' He asked when they were out of earshot.

'Prime Grain-Ger is on his way here and he has others with him. He is bringing your nephew, Tocmal, and some Emissary. They... in conjunction with President A-Bra-Ham are planning to attack the facility manufacturing the Droids. You must convince them to abandon this course of action; it would only spell disaster for your species.' Mondrac seemed awfully agitated, more than Aaron had seen before. It was the Professor who clarified the problem.

'What Mondrac is referring to is the virus. We've been able to isolate the delivery mechanism... even create a defence... but until we know what virus we are dealing with, it's all useless. We must get someone onto that facility and download the specific genome of the virus, or viruses before we can do anything.

'If I were Sarclan, I'd have a fail-safe; any attack and the information would be destroyed and the infected Droids released. This would be a disaster of massive proportions, especially as we have no idea how many tainted shipments have been made or where they have gone.'

'I have spoken to The Prime... he understands and is trying to do what he can, but this is essentially a Coalition operation so he has doubts about his influence,' Mondrac added.

Aaron replied. 'And as the President's son, you think I should have some influence?' Mondrac simply nodded and turned to take in the landscape, giving Aaron time to consider his advice.

He stood still, gazing long at the beauty before him. They were standing on the front veranda of the house, it stretched across the entire length and wrapped around both sides. Directly in front was a well-maintained garden, nothing like the one at Orange, but still beautiful. Past the garden fence was a field with several head of Dab Korac, Argosan cattle, grazing. The field sloped down to the shore of the lake, or more correctly, the river Hough.

Lake Camargue had formed millions of years ago by the river eroding a deposit of soft sandstone. What was left was the lake, three hundred metres across, over a kilometre long and one hundred metres deep at the far shore. The water was a deep blue and, in sections, quite fast flowing. But for the most of it, it was part of a gently meandering river.

'You have chosen a beautiful place to live, my friend. A great place to raise your offspring,' Mondrac offered.

'Providing we live long enough,' Aaron responded, now deep in thought.

The sight of a Coalition warship landing on Argos was unusual, but not unprecedented.

An official shuttle from the Prime's office settled beside the visiting ship, and JT, Wu Chan, and Tocmal boarded it. Grainger greeted each as they entered.

'Sorry we don't have time to show you our planet,' he apologized, 'but I thought it prudent we get things up and running as soon as possible. I've arranged for a security cordon around your ship. While we occasionally get visits from aligned ships, warships rarely land, and there might be some who are a bit too curious.'

Grainger took his seat, as the shuttle lifted off and headed away from Central City. Twenty minutes later they were hovering to the south of the house, waiting for the last of the delivery vessels to leave.

JT smiled, 'it wasn't that long ago that those delivery vehicles would have needed roads to bring goods here.' As he spoke, the vessel lifted off and tracked away to the east.

'Not on Argos, Admiral.' Grainger replied. 'When Jones and co settled here they rarely used ground vehicles, never made any roads, and except in the cities, there are no ground vehicles. It costs the same to manufacture a ground car as it does an atmospheric shuttle. Quite honestly, I can't envisage a place that has roads running everywhere.'

As they spoke, the shuttle settled gently to the ground. Because there were no hot jet or rocket exhausts, landing was possible anywhere.

The ramp extended and Grainger led the group off the shuttle. Aaron and Jeff were waiting and introductions were made, while

Fraslok and a couple of techs moved quickly to place spear-like objects around the house.

'What's your new partner doing?' Grainger asked, sarcastically.

'Lenny wants to make sure that there's no way anyone can eaves-drop on this meeting and I agree,' Aaron answered, seriously. 'Come on, I'll give you the full tour while the boys finish.'

'Aren't you forgetting someone?' Grainger asked. As he did, an elegant woman walked down the ramp - Grainger's wife and First Lady of Argos.

Aaron smiled and walked to her. She threw her arms around his neck and hugged him. 'You're looking great, Aaron! Life must be good.'

'Grace, it's wonderful to see you... yes, life is pretty darn good.'

Next Petra waited, fidgeting nervously. Meeting Grace Grainger was important, not only was she someone central to Aaron's life, but she was also the wife of the Prime, the First Lady of Argos. Her trepidation was unfounded as Grace stood in front of her.

'You don't remember me, do you?' She asked.

Petra shook her head, 'no I don't believe we have met.'

Grace smiled, 'it was a long time ago, but we can talk about that later. For now, I am so pleased to meet the woman who has stolen Aaron's heart.' With those words, she reached out and embraced Petra. The three women excused themselves and went to the veranda; Sonia had a table set for afternoon tea.

Aaron led the others to the lounge area and, once everyone was settled, Emissary Chan began detailing his people's involvement. He was profound in his embarrassment and disdain of the situation and started the discussion down the path of taking the facility out. It was here that Mondrac interrupted.

'Emissary Chan, please understand... we must first gain the information we need to counter this virus. As yet, we don't know what it is, how it's being incorporated into the Nano Droids, or how it's being distributed. The first action must be to infiltrate so one of our technicians can find and capture the data we need. Doing anything else would only trigger Sarclan into releasing the virus... we **cannot** risk this.' Mondrac was most insistent in his presentation.

Chan replied. 'Ambassador, while I understand, please be aware there are four level-nine Game Masters in that facility. Infiltrating while they are there is impossible. Add to that we cannot use any directed energy weapons on the facility... it is too sensitive. The only weapons we can use are traditional and some sonic disruptors - nothing more.'

'What do you mean, traditional?' Aaron asked as Petra entered the room.

'Swords, staffs, fighting sticks and, of course, one's body... are any of you trained in any of these?' He paused as, one by one, everyone answered. Except for the usual hand to hand training, everyone gave negative answers, until Petra spoke.

'I am trained, in all you mentioned, and others,' she said quietly.

It was well known that Mechanista had a dismal view of human females, treating them as second class creatures. Mechanista females were warriors like males.

'No human woman can equal even a level one Mechanista, you are wasting time!'

'Then let me prove it to you if you have the balls!' Petra fired back as she turned and walked towards the stairs. 'Are you coming or do you want to sit and talk?'

Chan stood and followed her, down the stairs into the exercise room. He stopped dead when he saw what was in the centre of the room. Petra had continued to a cabinet which she opened. There displayed were many different ancient weapons: swords of many types, daggers, sticks, and other items that defied imagination.

'Is that a Moril?' Chan asked, glancing at the contraption to his right.

'Yes. Unfortunately, the power supply is depleted... I'm

charging it now.' Petra turned away, 'do you wish to select your weapon? I'm going to change.' She moved behind a screen in the corner of the room.

Chan moved to the cabinet, mesmerized by the weapons he saw. 'Lady, I meant no disrespect! I was unaware you were **Vargan**... my apologies.' He held one of the swords, examining the crest on the blade, above the hilt. He studied it almost reverently.

'This symbol... this is the crest of Aeiysta, first among Vargans... or was until she disappeared.'

Petra stepped out from behind the screen, now dressed entirely differently. Gone was her normal attire. In its place, she wore what resembled a bodysuit, a small tunic, and a gleaming breastplate. Her shins were covered by the same material and melded completely with her boots. Her forearms were clad in a sturdy-looking black sleeve.

'She didn't disappear... she chose to leave and marry my father.' Petra said with pride. 'I am the daughter of Aeiysta.'

Chan dropped to one knee. 'Again Lady, I apologize for my insult, I beg your forgiveness.'

Aaron stepped forward, confusion written all over his face. 'What's all this? Where did it come from?'

Petra replied, simply. 'This is the protection I wear when fighting. The bodysuit is extremely resilient and durable as well as having a self-healing property. If it's cut or pierced, it can self-repair. The metallic bits are made from a special ore only found on Varga, again extremely tough. Now stand aside, I need a workout. Chan, are you ready?'

Chan had removed his top clothing and now stood similarly clad, except his lower body was covered with loose-fitting trousers. 'No weapons, Lady,' he suggested.

Petra agreed and they commenced. For the next twenty minutes, they fought, almost like they were dancing - whirling, leaping, punching, and counter-punching; each testing the other's limits. Then, suddenly Petra pressed her attack and in an almost invisible blur, bringing Wu Chan to the floor. Even with his mechanically enhanced body, he couldn't break free from her hold. He acquiesced, knowing he had met a superior opponent.

As they stood and paid tribute to each other he spoke in admiration, 'You are indeed the daughter of Aeiysta. I am honoured to have been beaten by you. If you accompany me, this mission may just succeed.'

Petra held up her hand. 'On one condition, Wu Chan... I will go only if Aaron is with me. We fight together or we stay here, together.'

'As you wish.' He turned to Aaron and formally invited him on the quest. 'Aaron Abraham, I would be pleased if you would join me in this venture. How say you.'

'Yes, I'll go, but you two have missed one thing!'

'What's that?' Petra asked.

'How do we get on board undetected?'

Aaron's question hit like a bullet. He was right. Fighting like this was great, but if the team couldn't get into the facility, it was no more than fancy dancing. It was Grainger who had the answer.

'McLeod,' he said. That one word made Aaron freeze.

'Yes... Angus McLeod,' a sardonic smile crossing Grainger's face as he spoke. 'He has the transport contract, and he has a freighter due to dock at the facility next week. So, my friend, you have two days to fix things and to get Angus on board. I've asked him to meet me at the residence tomorrow around noon... I'd suggest you be there.'

Aaron looked like he'd been punched. 'Fuck, not McLeod! Why don't you just shoot me? Same outcome.'

Grainger chuckled. 'Bullshit! Look at what you and your brother have done... mending a rift over thirty years old. Sorting things out with Angus should be child's play. Look, if this infiltration is to work, you **need** Angus. I know him, and so do you; first and foremost he's a Freebooter he'll do whatever is needed to protect our way of life... don't forget that.' The two men stood, almost glaring at each other until Aaron finally nodded.

'You're right...' he agreed quietly. 'I'll be there at midday.'

'Then that's settled.' Grainger turned to Mondrac. 'Ambassador, could I trouble you to make one of your famous coffees everyone else talks about?' Mondrac agreed and everyone started back up the stairs; everyone except Petra; she held back and turned to Sonia.

'Sonia, you know where everything is in the kitchen... would you help Mondrac? I think I need to talk with Aaron.'

'Yes of course.' Sonia turned and quickly reached the stairs. Aaron was standing at the stairs when he saw Petra beckon him. Slowly he walked over to her, reaching her as Sonia closed the door at the head of the stairs.

Petra took a deep breath. 'You want some answers?'

'That's one way of putting it... when were you going to tell me?' Aaron asked his voice flat and unemotional, his jaw set tight.

'And what was I supposed to tell you, that I am a trained fighter and some fantasy about my mother being a Queen or something like that?' She watched his face, seeing bewilderment in his eyes. 'Aaron I haven't lied to you, I haven't kept anything of importance from you. What my mother was before, and I emphasize that word, **before**, has no bearing on me or us. Anyway, what do you know about Vargan culture?'

'Not much... it's a Matriarchal society and there is a caste or class system.'

Petra led him to the seats on the other side of the room. 'Partly correct, it is Matriarchal and there is a warrior class. My mother was the leader of this class. Being the only level five gave her that honour... but there is much more. Unlike most human societies, we have no religious ideology and no marriage.

'When a Vargan woman wants to breed, she selects a male to father her child and they make a personal pact, a promise, to the care and nurture of any offspring. They may... or may not live together, but any children of that relationship are their prime responsibility and they will share that equally, much like what we see here on Argos. People may marry... or not... but the thrust of any Freebooter partner contract is for the raising and protection of any children.'

Petra paused while Aaron digested this; his countenance softening as understanding began to dawn.

'Now, for my mother, it was somewhat different. Her title, roughly translated, was **Warrior Queen**, and, as head of the warrior class, she had many duties and responsibilities but one thing she or any Warrior Queen has never been able to have is both the position and children. Warrior Queens are forbidden to marry or bear children they don't have to remain virgins, but they cannot do both jobs of leader and mother.

'When my mother met Colin Mannix, everything changed for her. She told me that the day she met him she knew she would have to relinquish her title. She did this and two weeks later they were 'married.' They made their own secret pact, left Varga for Argos, and two years later, I was born... the rest you already know.

'Everything except the fighting,' Aaron deliberately pointed out.

'I never saw it as fighting. To me, it was merely our way of exercising. Honestly, I've never used any of the gear in anger... until now... and it scares me,' Petra's reply was tinged with emotion.

'What scares you?'

'What I may be capable of; what Vargan warriors can do. I don't want it, but I may have it anyway. Aaron, I want what my mother had. I want a home, a quiet life where we can raise our own family but this fucking arsehole Sarclan keeps getting in the way.' Petra spat out the last words and burst into tears.

Aaron held her, desperately searching for the right words. 'Well we better make sure we fry the bastard this time, hadn't we?' Petra looked up to him, her eyes glistening with tears. She smiled, nodded, and planted her lips on his. She hugged him tight until Aaron broke away.

'Ouch!' he cried, 'I do love your tits against me but that armoured bra you're wearing bloody hurts.' He smiled, rubbing his chest. 'And before you get any ideas, we do have guests.'

'OK, if that's what we must do.' She stopped speaking, turned away, and started walking towards the changing area, removing the armour as she walked. Aaron groaned as he stood, unable to take his eyes off the double vision he had, both of Petra walking away and the frontal view in the room-length mirror. Slowly, as she removed the last piece of her garb, Aaron turned toward the opposite wall; *we do have guests* he told himself.

***

It was a little after midnight, Earth time, as Sam Grogan and Solomon Radchak finished analysing the data from the new sensor probes in the Bad-Lands. The initial readings were promising, indicating that Balerophon was still exactly where the original data had shown. The huge ship had been grounded, but the new images showed that it was now actually part of a complex. It looked like several hundred buildings were close and connected by power ducts.

'They're using the old girl as a power Station,' Sam offered.

'Yes,' Sol replied. 'But we can't determine any life signs on board, only in the other buildings. They must be using those machines the Mechanista designed... it's the only way they could run the Station. So what do we do?'

'A full ground assault over that terrain is foolhardy, at best.' General Klastok had been sitting quietly in the background, giving the other two a free hand with the data. 'We have no data as to their strength or capability, but I would assume they are well entrenched. We need better Intel before we commit to anything.'

Sam and Sol agreed and started to work on a plan to send probes even lower, some even to the ground.

'We need to inform the President about this, and see what JT and the others are planning for the Droid facility,' Grogan decided. He downloaded the information to one of the old data drives needed for the Bunker's system. 'We better get some sleep... I'll arrange for a shuttle at zero seven hundred. Be ready.' With that, he stood and walked out of the room. Sol shut the system down and followed.

They arrived at Orange and had just finished setting up in the conference room when Jason entered. 'Sorry to keep you waiting but I got caught up with a couple of things,' he said as he took his seat.

'No need to apologize, I should have let you know we were coming,' Grogan apologized. 'We have the latest data from our surveillance of Betanna. It appears that Balerophon is a power hub for a sizeable installation.' Sam produced the data drive and began to initialize the connection to the Bunker's system.

The old systems were much slower than the Bio gel systems used elsewhere, but they had the advantage of being invulnerable to Sarclan's spy systems. It took a few minutes for the drive to be scanned and the data loaded.

Klastok waited until all had settled before he began the briefing. 'From these images, we can see exactly where Balerophon is located, what the terrain around it is like and the size of the compound it is part of... not much else. We need to get a closer look to see more details... we can't attack until we have better data.' He paused giving a moment for the information to sink in. 'At the moment there's no way we can see where a large scale attack could be carried out.'

Jason studied the images before speaking. 'It took the three of you to bring these to me?'

'No, Sir. We have a plan, but we need your approval,' Sol announced. 'We need to divert Sarclan's attention away from Betanna so we can land an expeditionary force; one that can find out exactly what we will face when we attack. We know that the Mechanista facility is to be breached and we think that we could use that attack as cover... after all, Sarclan has a lot tied up on that facility.' Sol sat back, rather pleased with his plan.

Jason shook his head. 'Sorry, there will not be an attack, only a covert infiltration. No more than five people will be in the group.' Jason saw Sol's jaw drop and anticipated the question he was going to ask. 'No need to say anything, this is a condition placed by Emissary Chan. We will not attack the facility... destruction of it would be our worst option.'

'Why?' Sol began, but he saw the steel in the President's eyes, so he stopped there.

'If we destroy the Nano Droids and the production facility, we lose any chance of discovering what virus Sarclan is using and more importantly, where he's sent it. This is the greater of the evils we face and that is what I intend to stop. Now if you wish to send a force, either expeditionary or more punitive, you have permission to do so but I suggest you coordinate with Admiral Abraham so the operations don't clash.' The words closed the discussion, now it was time to devise their action against Betanna.

**ugene Sarclan stood at the huge arched window.

It stretched twenty metres across the room, curving back at each extremity so he had a one hundred and eighty-degree view of his domain - at least the above-ground part. In the distance was Balerophon, gently nestled in its purpose-built rock cradle; no longer a space ship, she had finally realized her true potential, as a power and manufacturing hub of his operation. Closer to the cliff face was the compound - over one hundred buildings housing the final finish and research facilities. But even that was only a small part of the operation, as over six hundred metres down and one thousand metres into the mountain, protected by rock, lay the most secret and sensitive part of the operation.

Sarclan turned from the window and gazed at the view screen showing the detail of the complex. Both above and below ground, there were over one hundred levels for research, training and accommodation, and massive hydroponic gardens for food and enjoyment. He smiled; a self-satisfied smile. His thoughts were interrupted by the door sliding open and someone entering.

He turned. 'Hiro, glad to see you, how are you feeling?'

'Somewhat better, for a dead man; the memory gaps still annoy me but mostly much better, thank you,' Nakamura's voice was soft and calm.

'Don't be so melodramatic, you're not a dead man. You're definitely alive, my friend... come look at this. Our friends, the Mechanista are incredible. Their machines dig and burrow better than anything I have ever seen. We now have enough accommodation for the last batch of sleepers... it is time to awaken them.'

Sarclan smiled as he walked to his only true friend. 'Hiro,

don't look so glum. We have done it... we have finally found a home! From **this** protected place, we shall exact our vengeance on the Abrahams and the Coalition.' He gloated as he led Hiro towards the pod. 'Come on, seeing for yourself will put a spring back in your step.' They entered the pod and left for the new accommodation sector.

***

Nefaris lay back in the pool, the steaming water, and the bubbles easing away her tensions. She turned to her left and there on the bed was Darius lying there, watching her. She felt tired; more tired than ever before. The constant effort of keeping the peace was taking its toll. Sarclan was always aggressive and keeping him, Zarof, and Darius from killing each other was a constant battle.

Darius himself was so needy, something she had noticed about human men. Their constant need for reassurance that they were the best lovers or the most handsome and intelligent was draining. She gazed over his naked body. For all his faults he was not unpleasant to look at, being nicely muscled and without the grotesque bulk favoured by some. His face, she found pleasing and his manhood was more than adequate. *If only I didn't have to keep telling him how great it is,* she thought to herself.

Then there was Zarof. Although there was never any physical intimacy between her and the Galdoran, he regarded her as his property; or at least, his to protect. While she sometimes found this necessary, it could also be a nuisance. She shook her head, to clear these thoughts and let her eyes pan around the room.

Like all other areas in Darius' domain, this room had been carved out of the living rock. The pool had been a natural depression that had been enlarged and shaped into a smooth, elegant oval. Even the bed had a rock at the base. An artisan had created the rock headboard and Darius had installed both mattress and antigrav bed systems. Nefaris had great respect for the effort and craftsmanship that had gone into the room but, it was still only a cave.

At length she sighed, stood, and climbed out of the pool, feeling Darius' eyes on her. She stood under the dryer and allowed the warm air to do its job, turning slowly to give her audience the best view.

As she stepped out of the dryer and walked towards the bed, Darius stood and greeted her. Nefaris wasn't in the mood for a long, almost tedious, foreplay session, she was already turned on from the erotic display she had given in the dryer. She reached down, took hold of his hard cock, and kissed him, almost violently.

'No Darius... use me... fuck me like you hate me!' She hissed through clenched teeth, her eyes flashing a challenge.

Darius responded, grabbed her by the throat, and flung her toward the bed. 'If a fuck is all you want,' he said, a vicious leer crossing his face, 'believe me you'll get it.' He spun her around, bent her over and started to rub himself against her - then thrust violently into her.

Nefaris let out a brief cry; pain, surprise, and pleasure all encompassed. Darius was a man possessed; he grabbed a handful of her hair as he viciously complied with her request. There was no finesse, only animal lust, just as Nefaris wanted, and it wasn't long before she was moaning and matching his thrusting. She let out a cry of pleasure only moments before Darius reached his climax. Finally sated, they both collapsed on the bed, sweat glistening on their bodies.

They lay there for ages before Nefaris broke free and kissed Darius tenderly. 'I think we both need a shower now,' she giggled as she leaped out of the bed and ran to the shower; Darius joining her at a more leisurely pace.

Darius pulled on his soft calf-length boots when the door annunciator chimed. Casually he reached for the control panel as he heard an urgent hammering on the huge metal door. He de-activated the lock and the huge door slid silently into the wall - Zarof strode in.

'Why do you lock your doors? Are you scared of assassins?' The Galdoran snarled.

Darius watched as Zarof walked through his chamber, the hair on his head standing up, his eyes darting everywhere. Darius was used to Zarof's unusual demeanour, but this was something different, he was dangerously agitated. Deciding that discretion was the best approach he simply said, 'and good morning to you, Zarof.'

As she normally did, Nefaris made her perfectly timed entrance just as Zarof was about to explode. The flimsy gown she wore did nothing to cover her nakedness.

'Zarof, how many times have I asked you to respect our privacy?' She demanded.

Her directness stopped Zarof in his tracks; he spluttered some apology before bowing his head.

'Better! Now, if you would please give me time to finish dressing, we'll meet in the audience chamber, say in... twenty minutes?'

Zarof started to protest, but one look from Nefaris stopped him, he bowed again and left, throwing a vicious glare toward Darius as he did. As the door closed behind Zarof, Darius sat in one of the chairs carved out of the virgin rock and watched as Nefaris dressed, a lustful leer splitting his face.

***

Sarclan and Nakamura exited the pod at their final destination. So far Hiro was impressed with the preparations for the last group of colonists currently in the process of being awakened from their long hibernation. They were now at one of the labs, one that Sarclan usually kept for himself and few others - even Hiro had only seen it once before. They entered the airlock in silence, waited for the decontamination cycle to complete and the inner door to open.

Hiro's curiosity finally got the better of him. 'What do you have here, Eugene?'

'Spies my dear Hiro, Galdoran spies.' Sarclan replied as he

flicked the lights on in the next room. Through the observation window, Hiro saw five Galdoran figures. They were wretched; their hair was matted and dull with their bodies showing signs of extreme exposure to the worst of Betanna's climatic vagaries.

'What happened Eugene?' Nakamura asked, quietly.

'They were found sneaking around our facilities we captured them and asked them a few questions; that's all,' Sarclan's answer was far too enthusiastic, Hiro thought.

'It appears our friend Zarof is suspicious of our intentions. He thinks we will betray him, so he sent these five to learn more. Well, he'll learn a lot more when we return them.' He turned to one of the three techs in the room. 'Revive them!' he ordered. The Techs obeyed and slowly the five Galdorans began to wake.

'These five have been a great source of information. We now have a good idea of their genetic structure, their physiology, and many other things.' He turned to the Techs again. 'Prepare them for transport, and place them in stasis pods... gently please.' Hiro shook his head, Sarclan showing any sort of kindness was something to be feared.

'But how did they get in such bad condition?' Hiro asked, knowing the truth deep in his soul. Each of the prisoners bore marks that could either be from exposure, as Sarclan had suggested or from attempts to loosen tongues. Either way, the five in front of him were close to death.

'They got lost, probably in a Black Storm... fortunately, we found them in time, now we are taking them back to Zarof. They'll confirm every detail... believe me.' The sinister tone in Sarclan's voice left Nakamura in no doubt that this was exactly what would happen. 'See, we are all working together... something else they'll confirm. We're all one big happy family now.' Sarclan sneered.

***

'You did **what**?' Darius shouted at Zarof.

'I told you, trusting this Sarclan is a mistake!' Zarof shouted back. 'I sent five of my best men to find out what he is up to,

231

and he's killed them.'

'And how the fuck do you **know** that, Zarof?'

'They've been gone for seven days, with **no** communication. They were supposed to call every day, with updates. How else can you explain it?' Zarof growled.

'Boys, please let's calm down. Zarof, what were they looking for and where?' Nefaris pleaded. Lately, her hold on Zarof was weakening. If she lost control, the outcome could be disastrous.

'I sent them to the compound; we need to see what is going on there. For all we know he's assembling his forces to attack us; we know he's been thawing more humans each day. He probably outnumbers us now... why are you so blind?' Zarof shouted again. The worst part of living in a cave was the sound, every time Zarof shouted, it echoed around the chamber.

Normally Darius loved the acoustics, but not today. Today they were almost painful. He was about to answer when one of his aides came running into the chamber.

'Sir, Sarclan is here; with five Galdorans... in stasis pods.'

'See! What did I tell you? He'll suffer for this,' Zarof spat at Darius. The door opened; Sarclan and Nakamura walked in with the five pods in tow.

'Zarof, I'm glad you're here.' Sarclan's voice conveyed sincerity. 'We stumbled across these poor wretches late yesterday, they appear to be suffering from exposure, possibly from the Black Storm we had over the last couple of days. Please, we don't have the knowledge or equipment to help them... they're in bad shape.' Sarclan's voice was perfect; the correct degree of concern and compassion emphasizing his despair at not being able to help the creatures in the pods. 'We thought it best to place them in the pods, stabilize them as best we could, and get them here ASAP.'

Zarof ran to the pods, inspected each one, and called a medical team to the chamber. After he placed the five in the care of the med team, he turned to Sarclan. 'Where did you find them?'

'About five klicks south of our old compound... they were

huddled around some equipment, like they were doing Geological surveys.' Sarclan explained.

'Yes... yes, they were part of our ongoing survey of the planet,' Zarof confirmed. 'But how did you find them?'

'Purely by accident,' Sarclan lied. 'A random sensor sweep picked up an anomaly that turned out to be their heat signatures. Luckily, our area commander sent out a team to investigate; by the look of them they wouldn't have survived much longer.' As he spoke the med team took charge of the stasis pods. 'This was not why I intended to come here. We have completed the final preparations for the last of our colonists; they are now in the final stages of waking.'

Zarof leaped into the conversation. 'Your army I presume.' His accusation finally spat at Sarclan.

Sarclan laughed. 'Army, what army... these are **colonists**, engineers, farmers, teachers, and doctors. Zarof, these people have been in hibernation for over two hundred years, now they are free... they're a threat to no one. Would you like to see what we have achieved?'

Darius saw an opportunity to dampen the situation. 'Of course Eugene, when?

'Tomorrow, say midday? I'll have the pod here to collect you.' Sarclan smiled, trying to show sincerity. 'Till tomorrow,' he turned and, with Nakamura, left the room. They entered the pod and as the door closed Nakamura spoke for the first time since arriving.

'What was that all about? Why invite them to our compound?' Nakamura asked.

'Simple my friend. I want them to think we are all playing the same game, that we are no threat to them. What better way than to invite them into our newest colony?' Sarclan laughed. 'Don't be so intense. I've left a surprise with those five dogs we returned... a surprise that will call Zarof to heel, in a few weeks. Now stop worrying, everything is proceeding as I want it to.'

General Ivan Klastok stood and stretched, his back was killing him.

He had been studying the topography of Betanna, searching for an answer, but secretly he knew there wasn't one. 'Fucking hopeless,' he muttered as he reached for another mug of coffee.

Ten hours we've been at it... ten long and arduous hours, and still no answer, his thoughts were full of gloom as he glanced around the room. Eight of the best military minds in the Coalition were still poring over the maps, environmental data, and topography holograms. They were all tired, tired to the bone; he could see it in the sore, red eyes, and in the copious amount of coffee everyone was drinking.

'Your attention, please,' he called to the group. 'We're all getting stale, let's call it a day; get some rest and something to eat.' He looked at the clock. 'We'll reconvene at zero eight hundred tomorrow.' He didn't need to issue the command a second time; the team rose and headed for the door, all except for one. Colonel Garcia stood near the hologram still studying the images.

'Garcia?' Klastok called.

Margaret Garcia stood, staring at the rendition of the planet's surface. 'Yes sir, I heard you but I have an idea. I'm trying to work out the logistics.'

'OK, but we all need to rest. Don't stay here too long,' Klastok said as he headed towards the door himself.

'No Sir, but can I present my idea first thing tomorrow?' she asked.

Klastok turned, realizing he hadn't had much to do with Garcia. She'd been a last-minute replacement for Brigadier Rodham.

She was tall, well built with a lithe athletic form. Her insignia showed she was SAS, one of the most elite of all military forces. They were the ones who got the worst jobs; the dirty jobs and the most dangerous.

Klastok moved closer. Her appearance belied the uniform she wore - in any company, she would be called attractive. When she moved it was with an economy of movement that some might call graceful, but to Klastok it showed she could handle herself.

He smiled. 'Very well Colonel. Tomorrow at zero eight hundred, the floor is yours. Good night.' He smiled again, thinking as he left the room, *if she comes up with a solution, there will be some noses out of joint.*

***

Solomon Radchak finally managed to get away from the conference room now being used by President Abraham and Emperor Dokad. The commitment from the Krell Empire, now firmly agreed, would be a game-changer; the Emperor had pledged full Krell support to the Coalition in hunting down and destroying Sarclan and any forces that aligned with him.

Sol was upbeat as he boarded his shuttle, took his seat, and instructed the pilot to head for Perth. He settled back and was pouring three fingers of Bourbon when his communicator buzzed. He pressed the talk icon and answered 'Radchak.'

He immediately recognized the voice that addressed him. *Admiral, Colonel Garcia... can we talk?*

Sol smiled and switched the call to vid capability. Margaret Garcia's face filled the screen. 'Margaret, long time,' he said.

Yes Sir, it been a while. I was wondering if we could meet, I have something I would like to discuss.

'Yeah, I'm on my way back to HQ now. Where did you want to meet?'

How about Romano's, I know how much you love their Carbonara.

Sol quickly checked with the pilot. 'Margaret, I'll be there in

235

forty minutes.'

Look forward to it, Sir, she said as she cut the link.

Romano's, interesting choice, Sol thought.

Romano's was owned by an ex SAS officer and an ex CID operative. It was one of the few places on Earth that were totally disconnected. No comms, no data access, and fully screened. Next to the Bunker, this was the best place for secret discussions - even the interior design and materials used confounded any eaves-dropping. Unless you were sitting at the table, nothing could be heard.

The last time he had met with Garcia at this restaurant, they'd ended up thwarting an uprising on Agricola. Sol wondered what she was up to tonight. *Whatever it is, it won't be boring*. He chuckled to himself.

Exactly thirty-nine minutes later Sol stepped out of the taxi, directly opposite the restaurant. Inconspicuous was the catchword of Romano's. No uniforms, no military formalities, and no official transport - show up with any of these and entry would be denied. Sol wore faded blue denim jeans with a grey shirt under a light jacket; to any passer-by, he was just another guy out for the evening. He approached the door - the doorman asked his name and checked him against their reservation list.

'Welcome back, mister Radchak. It's been a while since we saw you here. Please enter and enjoy your meal.' He held the door open.

Sol thanked him and fingered a generous tip on the data-pad. Inside, the head waiter greeted him and guided him to his table. Sol was always astounded by the lack of conversation noise. Except for the sounds from the kitchen; the restaurant could have been empty. The waiter held his chair as Sol sat down, then disappeared.

'Margaret, you look great.'

'And you too Sol... congratulations by the way,' she paused as the waiter delivered two pairs of glasses and a Holo-pad to their table. The only technology allowed in the room - owned by Romano's - the Holo-pad was keyed to the glasses - whatever was displayed could only be viewed by the people wearing that specific pair of glasses. Simple but effective, it allowed sensitive things to be discussed in complete security.

Garcia took the pad and inserted a small data drive. 'Shall we get this over before we eat?'

'Why not,' Sol answered.

Garcia powered the pad as they both put on the glasses. They sat watching the scenario being displayed - to any observer they were looking into thin air, nothing was visible. Ten minutes passed until they finally removed their glasses. Sol's face showed grave concern.

'You're serious?'

'Yes, I am... can it be done?' she asked. Before Sol could answer the waiter returned with a green salad and bread, then another brought their meal; Carbonara for Sol and Veal Scaloppini for Garcia.

'In theory, yes... but it's risky... very risky for all concerned. How many do you want to drop?' Sol asked. They continued to discuss her proposal while they ate their meal. Sol had to admit her idea was innovative - risky - but innovative.

'All I need to know now is that your ships can do it, the rest is up to us. As for the number, at this stage, I haven't worked it out. We're tasked with the job and, to be honest, we're bogged down in the wrong thinking.

'You and Admiral Abraham have taken the Corps and shaken it up, changed almost everything it does. The ground forces need the same; we're too soft and, quite frankly, old. None of the senior staff are under two hundred and fifty. There's little actual battle experience, except for Klastok. I'm only there because Brigadier Rodham wasn't interested; he thinks he's better suited to a parade ground... and he's bloody well right!'

'OK Margaret, I get the picture. But do you think this can be pulled off?'

'If I didn't, we wouldn't be talking. Can you help?' She asked almost pleading.

Sol sat back, thinking. He sat quietly for almost ten minutes then looked directly at Garcia.

'Possibly, but we need to run this by some people; time to leave.'

He called the waiter and authorized the bill. The doorman had a taxi waiting for them, which took them to the parking station where Sol had left his ground car. They took the car and headed toward the Airport, where Sol had left the shuttle. He called the pilot and told him he was taking the shuttle and would probably have it back sometime tomorrow. They arrived at the hangar, Sol parked the car inside and they double-timed it into the shuttle.

'Where are we going? I have to prepare this plan and deliver it to Klastok at zero eight hundred,' Garcia reminded Sol.

Sol looked at the time - after midnight. 'Well, we are going to pitch it to someone else first.'

He finished his pre-flight check and powered up the drive. While he was waiting for the system to auto cycle, Sol called Sam Grogan. A short, cryptic conversation followed and then they lifted of. 'We're taking a short detour, we'll be picking up Admiral Grogan and, if I understood what he was saying, Klastok as well. This could be an interesting morning.'

***

The time readout showed 13:30, as Aaron initialized the shuttle's operating systems.

Petra settled in beside him in the second chair. 'Thirty minutes, plenty of time,' she confirmed, happily. Aaron nodded as he lifted the shuttle off the apron, programming the course and flight profile for the Prime's compound into the autopilot.

Petra reached over and tapped the autopilot icon on the flight screen. 'Now, we have half an hour. Tell me... what's all this with Angus McLeod?

So far, Aaron had managed to avoid any discussion on the topic, but now they were alone and he had nowhere to run for thirty minutes. 'OK, it began not long after I started my own company. Angus and I were competing for several deals... in a friendly way, but we were competitors.

'I was on Barilum four to finalize negotiations for one of the contracts I won. We signed the agreements and I went to a bar to celebrate with Henry and a couple of others. There I met a stunning Selarian waitress. We had dinner, Henry warned me to behave; he and the others returned to the ship. One thing led to another and I ended up spending the night with her. I left the next day, but told her I would be back in a few months.'

Petra smiled, enjoying his discomfort. 'So was the night as pleasurable as you expected?'

'I'm not going into details. Henry warned me not to get involved with her, but I was unattached and Barilum was now a regular port of call for us.' Aaron could see more questions forming in Petra's head, so he continued.

'To cut a long story short, a couple of visits later Angus caught up with me and demanded I leave his woman alone. I didn't even know he was involved with her! A few words were exchanged, followed by a couple of fists and that was it. Henry waded in, dropped both of us on our arses, and dragged me back to the ship.

'He sat me down and told me some things that I didn't want to hear. He had done some research and discovered that she... shit; I can't even remember her name... was a con artist, wanted on five planets. Her game was fleecing unwary traders.'

Petra jumped in. 'Don't you mean horny and desperate traders?' she teased.

Aaron glared at her. 'I'll ignore that remark. Anyway, about this time I bought my second ship and left the Barilum contract with my first ship... I never went back. She conned Angus out of a heap and he blames **me** for it.'

'Is that all? And you two clowns have fought over it for what, twenty plus years?' Petra couldn't help herself; she burst out laughing. 'Men, I'll never understand you lot! Everything comes down to a pissing competition... yes; I have read old earth culture texts. Well Aaron Abraham, today you are going to fix it... shake hands like adults and move on. We need Angus for this mission... remember that!'

Before Aaron could reply, the auto-pilot chimed to announce they had arrived and the landing cycle had started. Three minutes later they were exiting the shuttle. On the ground to greet them was James, the Prime's PA. After the customary welcome exchange, he led them through security toward the office complex. As they approached the divide in the path, Grace Grainger met them.

'I thought Petra and I could spend some time together' she said as she gently kissed Aaron on the cheek. 'I'm sure she'll enjoy it more than listening to you and Allen.' They parted company and James directed Aaron towards the main building, through the maze of offices before arriving at his destination, the Blue Office - the room used for all official meetings. He closed the door behind Aaron and left.

***

Grace Grainger gently guided Petra toward the residence, where they moved quickly through the security screen and into the vestibule. Here she changed direction, moving to her left and a waiting elevator. They entered and she selected one of the basement floors.

'I knew your mother Petra,' Grace revealed as they reached the selected floor. Here they exited into a large, comfortable room. The furnishings were soft and feminine, as was the colour scheme. In the centre was a pond replete with fountain and exotic fish.

'I didn't know that you knew her, she always kept mostly to herself.'

Grace motioned for Petra to sit. 'Yes, I knew her very well, not just here, but also on Varga.' She saw the puzzled look on Petra's face. 'There is a lot you don't know, and now you must learn the truth. Do you remember the last time you tried the

240

feather dance for her?'

'Yes, and I failed, as I always did.'

Grace shook her head. 'No, you didn't. I was there, in the background, and believe me you were amazing; even Aeiysta was impressed. You tried it twice, that day. The first time you moved some feathers, but then I spoke to you when you were resting. Do you remember?'

Petra thought back to that day. 'No, not you, but I heard a voice, telling me to stop worrying about feathers, to think of them as rock... solid rock.'

'And?' Grace asked.

'I remember doing the routine again, thinking I was on solid rock, not thinking of feathers.'

'And you succeeded.'

'But she said I moved a feather!' Petra interrupted.

'Yes, she did. Petra... she was trying to protect you. She wanted you to be free from all the intrigues she had lived with, she wanted you to have a life she briefly had with Colin. She knew you would never have it if you ascended to the fifth level, so she blocked many of your abilities and encouraged you to pursue the career you chose. In the end, she gave her life to protect you.' Grace's voice was heavy and sad.

'Rubbish, she was old and sick... she died naturally!' Petra shouted.

'No, she was younger than me... she was murdered by the same people who killed your father and my son. Vargan fundamentalists, rebels if you like who want to force Vargans back into an isolationist stance. They plan to use an outdated and twisted interpretation of our culture, something we have kept supressed for millennia. Anyone of the higher orders was under constant surveillance and, if they left their office, that person was seen as a threat.

'It now appears certain that these rebels were used, or assisted by Sarclan. Now listen... your survival may depend on this.' Grace was interrupted by the elevator door opening.

Mondrac walked out of it and towards them. 'Mondrac, my old friend I think I may need your assistance here.'

Mondrac walked to Petra, his voice was reassuring as he sat on the chair opposite her. 'Do you remember when we offered you enhancements so you could travel through the other realms?' Petra nodded. 'Well, you didn't need any. As a matter of procedure, we **always** do complete scans of those we intend to help. But your scans showed you already had all the abilities we were considering, and far more. I had only seen such abilities in one person before: Aei-Ys-Ta of Varga, your mother. All we did was unlock a small portion of what you are capable of.'

'But what about all that time spent... in the **training**, as you called it?'

'OK yes, A-Bra-Ham needed the training. But all you did was sleep. Do you remember what happened when you both opened your minds to the crew?' Mondrac didn't wait for an answer. 'A-Bra-Ham had difficulty, he had to concentrate hard to focus on a single mind; too much interference from others, what did he call it... yes, static. You, on the other hand, had no such trouble.

'Also, the control of your molecular frequency was almost automatic for you, while again A-Bra-Ham had problems. He responded exactly as we knew he would but you, quite frankly, were an enigma, until I found out who your mother was.'

Grace knelt in front of Petra. 'Petra, search your memory, look back... who am I?'

Petra gazed deep into the sparkling green eyes staring at her, deeper and deeper till she felt as though she was falling, losing herself.

'Who am I?' Grace asked again.

That question again, echoing in her head. There just in front of her was the answer; if only she could reach it! Petra struggled, trying to stretch enough, but still, it remained out of reach. Then the voice again.

'Don't fight, think. Remember, remember it all.

Petra's mind reeled, swirled, and flashed. Colours, darkness, light; it all flew around her mind. Then it stopped, she became calm. Memories flooded back into her consciousness.

Slowly Petra opened her eyes. She was still sitting on the lounge with Mondrac and Grace still in the same positions, but something was different; she could feel so much more, she couldn't explain or understand what she felt, but it was different.

'Garawyl... you're Garawyl, my mother's sister! How, why?'

'So much needs to be said, but we don't have enough time. I met Allen years before Aeiysta met Colin, and I made the choice to leave Varga and marry him. I relinquished all my duties and came to Argos. I never imagined she would do the same with Colin Mannix.

'For some reason... and I never found out why... your parents wanted to settle here, so as I, Garawyl became Grace, Aeiysta became Anita. The first sign of trouble came when my son was killed, in an almost impossible accident. But a communiqué from Varga left no doubt as to what happened. It was a warning from a rebel faction. They were afraid that if we were allowed to join forces, then Freebooters would be the most powerful force in the galaxy.

'Then your mother had you and they tried again, this time against her. She was poisoned, a slow and insidious way to die. So she devoted her remaining life to training you and then blocked it all out, so you wouldn't know, and wouldn't seek revenge.' Grace paused, to allow what she had said to sink in. 'Your father was marked from then on.

'The rebels saw you as no more than another young Argosan and being of mixed parentage, nothing special. They believed that your abilities would be lessened by having a Human father but if your father ever told you the truth about your mother... well, they didn't want that to take place. So they engineered the attack on his operation on Varga, lured him there and killed him. But that brings us to now.'

Petra held her hand up. 'I now feel... so strange.'

Mondrac looked at Grace. 'I think you've removed all the blocks Aeiysta had installed... now you have access to all you may be.'

'And that is what's so dangerous,' Grace was now pleading. 'Petra, you must understand what you are now capable of... you must not go on this mission!'

'No! Aaron's going and I'm going with him. We were separated in the battle for the gate... never again.' Petra was adamant; nothing would change her mind.

Grace sighed. 'I thought as much... very well. What you feel is everything around you: air, water, fire, and earth. You have always been aware of them, now you can feel and interact with them. What you can't do yet, is control them, not in any practical way, this you must learn.'

She studied Petra and smiled. 'Close your eyes.' Petra complied. 'Now, clear your mind, and hold out your right hand, palm up. Now imagine a fire in your palm, concentrate, see the flames, feel the warmth? This is a good fire, a fire that will comfort, not injure, can you see it?' Grace waited. Petra smiled and nodded, hesitantly. 'Now build the fire...make it larger, warmer... make it light up the room.'

Petra's smile grew. 'I can feel the warmth... and it's gentle, not hot.'

'Open your eyes.' Grace commanded.

Petra opened her eyes. There in the palm of her right hand was a gentle orange flame dancing on her skin, without causing any damage. As quickly as she had seen it, the flame died and her hand was its normal bronze colour; no evidence that it had just held fire.

'That's what you can do, unassisted.' Grace stood and walked to a cabinet at the end of the room. She opened it and removed a small ornate box. As she did, Mondrac's communicator sounded.

'I've been missed, I must go.' He stood and walked to the

elevator.

Grace called to him. 'Tell them we're involved in some **girl stuff**, it should stop any of them from getting curious.' Mondrac smiled and nodded as the elevator door closed.

Grace returned with the box. 'This was your mother's and to be honest, I don't know if giving it to you is the right thing. But as you're so determined to go, it may be one thing that saves your life.' She opened the box, revealing a gossamer-like material - Petra gently touched it. 'Don't worry, you won't harm it,' Grace laughed.

Gently Petra lifted the material out. It was like a thin bodysuit. 'What do I do with it?' she asked.

'First, remove your clothes and put it on.'

Quickly Petra removed her clothes and very cautiously pulled the suit on. The fit was perfect and it was almost invisible.

'For it to work it must be next to your skin; that way it can amplify your actions. If you use the armour she gave you, and I strongly suggest you do, this goes on first, then the rest. Now, at the end of the room, there is a fireplace. Hold your hand out again and make the fire again.'

Petra complied and quickly there was a roaring flame in her hand.

Grace smiled. 'Most definitely Aeiytsa's daughter... now listen carefully. Look at the fireplace, see the fire in there. Can you see it?'

'Yes,' Petra whispered.

'Close your fist and throw the flame into the fireplace... **now**!'

Petra obeyed. She closed her fist, never taking her eyes off the fireplace. Then she drew back and threw the flame with all her might. What she saw stunned her. The flame leaped from her hand and flew straight to the fireplace; it hit the stacked wood which burst into flames. '**Shit!**' she exclaimed 'Did I do that?'

Grace laughed and applauded. 'Yes my dear, you did! The suit you are wearing amplifies your thoughts and allows you to control the basic elements of existence. But don't get too impressed with yourself; you need to learn a hell of a lot more before you're less of a threat to those around you... and yourself, than to your enemies.'

She saw the question before Petra asked. 'I'll explain. The suit interfaces with you at a physical and metaphysical level. It allows your thoughts to control the elements of life, fire, air, water, and earth... but it does have a cost. You need to learn control, or the suit can drain your energy. Used indiscriminately, it can drain the life force out of the wearer; it could kill you so you must learn how to control your thoughts and emotions while you wear it. For now, only use fire; it is the easiest and least taxing of the elements to control.'

Petra nodded. 'Grace, does Allen know about all this?'

'Yes, Allen knows all this, and don't worry about Aaron; most likely he'll call in a few minutes to tell you he'll be tied up tonight and probably tomorrow. We'll have plenty of time to bring you up to speed, and then we'll decide how to tell him.'

Right on cue, her communicator chimed, it was Aaron apologizing for having to go to another meeting, probably wouldn't be home tonight, possibly later tomorrow. Petra smiled and told him it didn't matter, as she was with Grace, and enjoying herself.

'Well, that's sorted. Now, young lady, you've got a hell of a lot to learn and not much time. Let's get cracking,' Grace smiled.

19

The door closed behind him.

Aaron stepped forward into the Blue Room where Angus McLeod and Allen Grainger were waiting. Both men turned as he walked forward, caution spelled in every step. They couldn't contain themselves anymore; both burst into hearty laughter.

'What are ye scared of, laddie?' Angus asked between chuckles. 'De ye think I'm gonna bite ya.'

'The thought had crossed my mind,' Aaron replied, clearly not understanding what was happening.

'So we can get on with things,' Grainger began, 'I'm going to clear the air. The issue between you and Angus was sorted years ago, but both of you were too stubborn to realize it, at the time. The lady in question was caught and all Angus' property returned, so the feud was only in your mind. Now both of you shake hands and stop behaving like two silly schoolboys.'

Angus stood and moved toward Aaron. He held out his right hand. 'I believe congratulations are in order! That fiancée of yours is one bonny young lass. You're a lucky bastard.' His smile reassured Aaron, so he gripped the proffered hand and shook it vigorously.

'Thanks, McLeod, I agree with you on that one.

McLeod began laughing again. 'Ye should have seen ya face when ya walked in, Laddie. That look was priceless.'

'OK, Grainger interrupted, 'now let's get to the business at hand. Aaron, I've asked a few more to join us.' Grainger touched an Icon on his console.

A door at the opposite side of the room opened and in strode Wu Chan, Mondrac, Tocmal, and JT. 'Events are moving quickly and we need to get our plan set and coordinate with Coalition forces, Grainger explained. 'They're planning a separate operation. JT, you've been in contact with Earth, bring us up to date please.'

JT waited as the others were seated, with a Reglaon seat brought in for Tocmal. 'Gentlemen, we have finally located Balerophon and Sarclan's base. Coalition assets have been monitoring the area and are planning an attack in a few days.'

A plaintive cry from the back of the group sounded. **'No!** It must **not** happen!' It was Fraslok, he had entered unnoticed.

Grainger looked up. 'Professor, you have something to add?'

'Prime Grainger, any attack on Sarclan **must** be delayed until we have the data we need. If he is attacked, he'll almost certainly activate the existing Nano Droids. If we don't have the data on their genetic programming, we'll never be able to stop them.' He turned to JT. 'Admiral you must delay the attack.'

Wu Chan stood. 'I agree with the Professor... if the Coalition attacks his base, Sarclan will release the virus. The result would be devastating.'

Grainger held up his hand. 'How are you so sure?'

'Because it is what I'd do and, in any case, it is the best strategic response. If he is under threat, releasing the virus will cause **massive** disruption to Coalition operations. Resources will need to be diverted to deal with it and if, as I suspect, the outbreak is on multiple planets; resources will be sorely stretched. We absolutely **must** have the data first,' Wu Chan responded firmly. All eyes turned toward McLeod, he held the key to the whole operation now.

Angus shook his head. 'Sorry, we cannae change our schedule. The facility grants us a two-hour window to dock, offload any supplies and load the cargo. The timing cannae be altered; believe me, I have tried but they're no the most flexible to work wit. Aye, even If we turn up early, they still willnae let us dock.' He shrugged, showing his frustration.

Grainger stood and walked across the room, all eyes followed him. He turned and walked back. 'Professor, how long will you need to design an antidote, or whatever you call it, to Sarclan's Nano Droids?'

'How long is a piece of string? I have no idea, Sir. If the data is heavily encoded it could take weeks to decipher it, then we have to drill down through the Droid's DNA program until we find the virus code, then we have to devise a countermeasure.' Fraslok saw the faces of the others drop; this wasn't what they wanted to hear. 'But we can't do **anything** without the data,' he added.

Wu Chan spoke up. 'Do not worry about any encoding; it will be our standard system. If anyone, me included, tries to alter our standard system, it will reject any changes and lock that person out of the system. I'll decode any data for you.'

Logistics for the mission were agreed to and it seemed like they now had a chance. JT needed to contact Earth via the secure Eldoran system so he quickly exited the meeting, followed by James. As they were leaving, Mondrac - whose absence had gone unnoticed during the in-depth discussions - returned, apologizing for his absence. He had contacted Duramot and arranged for it to come to Argos urgently.

'Duramot is a capable ship and she will be the best backup, in case you cannot complete your mission in two hours,' he told Aaron.

Everyone joined JT to discuss the battle plans. The Coalition was, at first, intractable, insisting that their attack should happen with urgency. It took intervention from the President to calm things down. After several hours of discussions, a compromise was reached.

The infiltration of the Mechanista facility was scheduled for Friday, three days hence - to allow for time to decrypt the data and analyse it, the Coalition agreed to hold its attack until the following Monday. The only proviso was that they would move into the final stages for the attack as the infiltration was to take place. The rationale was that if things went south, at least the attack on Sarclan could still take place.

Petra arrived back at the house a few minutes before Aaron landed his shuttle. She had just enough time to place the ornate box and its contents with her other weapons.

'You're cutting things fine,' she said as she greeted Aaron and the others at the door. 'According to the timetable, we have to leave in a few hours.'

Aaron couldn't help but notice that Petra seemed... different, something subtle that he couldn't quite define, but still different. 'I suppose we should get packed, then.' He turned to the group. 'Professor, come with me, I'm sure we can find you a survival kit to fit.'

'I'm not going. I'd probably be the most useless person if I did. I've sent for one of my staff, one who's better suited to this sort of thing and, more importantly, a computer specialist.' As he finished, another shuttle landed with a tall and slender figure emerging from the doorway, wearing a full deep blue bodysuit - complete with armour at strategic points. Attached to the chest area was a carry bag. At each hip a disruptor and on the figure's back, the hilts of two swords could be seen.

Fraslok greeted the figure on the steps and stood to one side to make the introductions. 'Team, this is Nathanial Jones... he's the specialist I spoke about.'

Aaron was first to shake the young man's hand, surprised at the strength of his grip.

Nathanial smiled. 'Nathanial is a bit of a mouthful, most of my friends call me Nat.'

Wu Chan was the last to come forward; he took Nat's hand and spoke, sarcastically. 'Are those swords for decoration, or can you use them?'

Nathanial smiled. 'Master Wu Chan, I assure you, I can use them.'

Now the team was complete and Aaron surveyed them. *What a ragtag bunch,* he thought. *From what most people call an intelligent cockroach, to a true cyborg, with a couple of boring humanoids thrown in.* He smiled to himself, *well if any group of misfits can save the universe, this is the one.*

He studied Nat more closely, 'Jones... the Joseph Jones family?'

The young man smiled. 'The same, Joseph was my great, great grandfather.'

Aaron smiled. 'So, Nathanial, how come you're working as a lab assistant?'

'Captain Abraham, you of all people should know, there are no free rides on Argos and besides, I not a lab assistant; I'm a systems' specialist. I keep all the computers and equipment working, ergo I'm the best for this job. And please I hate Nathanial; it sounds so old and formal.' He paused and stared straight at Wu Chan. 'I prefer Nat or to use my gaming handle Nighthawk.'

Wu Chan smiled in recognition. 'Indeed, you do know how to use those swords.' He turned to Aaron. 'I have gamed many times with Nighthawk, he is skilled and a worthy opponent. But I am in somewhat of a quandary... Admiral Tocmal, may I scan you?'

Tocmal stood and moved toward Wu Chan, buzzing, and clicking as he walked. 'You may... but why, may I ask?'

Wu Chan took a small instrument out of his case and started to run it over Tocmal. There was no reaction from the instrument. 'As I thought Admiral... you may be our secret weapon. All the facility's internal security is based on the sensor grid. The sensor grid is programmed to look for numerous emanations, readings that will alert it to intruders. But that is a major flaw in our system because you, Admiral do not register. None of the sensors will read you; in essence you're invisible.' He handed another case to Nighthawk. 'Here, you try.'

Nat opened the box and took out a pair of VR holographic glasses. He put them on and looked directly at Tocmal. 'Admiral, if you would be so kind as to move?' he asked.

Tocmal obliged and started to move away to Nat's left; then he darted to the right. Nat was searching for Tocmal, but detecting nothing. The demonstration went on for a few minutes until Nat pulled the goggles off. Tocmal was standing directly behind him, a disruptor aimed at his head.

'Incredible, I couldn't see him at all!' Nat said in astonishment. 'I had no indication where he was. You are correct, Wu Chan, this may be our secret weapon.'

The rest of the evening was spent discussing the plan; JT arrived and confirmed the timing of the attack on Betanna. Space Corps would give them from Friday until; Monday to infiltrate the facility; locate and download the data, get out, and complete the analysis. After that, the attack on Betanna would commence.

Fraslok was furious. 'Impossible, we must have more time. We need to devise a countermeasure. Please, Admiral, can't you make them see reason?'

JT shook his head. 'I'm sorry, the decision was made at a much higher level than me... it came from the President.' Further discussion was cut short as another shuttle landed. This one carried Angus McLeod and he wasn't in a good mood.

He strode purposefully up the steps to the front of the house, to be greeted by Petra. She brought him to the others.

'By the looks of ye lot, I'd say ye had trouble. Well, I willnae make it any better. I've just been contacted by the facility, they've moved our shipment up by two days and we've got to be there Wednesday at the latest. It means that we've got to reschedule everything and I dinnae have a ship that can make it there in time.' He slumped into the chair.

'But I do,' Aaron smirked. 'Condor's in dock, ready to depart tomorrow. If you like, Angus, I could charter her to you?'

'They won't allow just any wee ship. Their defences are locked to certain ships only... anything else and they'll open fire,' Angus grumbled as he eyed off the bottle of Scotch on the sideboard.

Aaron smiled, 'help yourself, Angus; all you need to do is go back to them. Tell them the problem and offer the solution... I'll bet they accept. In the meantime, Wu Chan and I will work out how to send Condor's power readings, so we can keep some weapons active and look like we're running dead. Come on, it's worth a try don't you think?'

Angus thought about the idea, sipping his scotch enthusiastically. 'Aye, it might work... I'll give them a call now; I can communicate from my shuttle.' He stood and left the room. It was only a few minutes and he was back. 'Bugger me, they agreed! All we need to do is transmit the ship specs and we're on our way.'

Aaron had contacted his engineering department and now Wu Chan was diligently working with them on the specs. As Angus announced his success, Aaron called Katie and asked her to prep Condor for immediate departure. Everything was back on schedule.

The plan was simple; Aaron and Kate had arranged for some surveillance maintenance to be conducted in the early hours of the next day; while this was underway, Junior would dock with Condor and transfer the conspirators secretly. Angus McLeod would arrive - with due fanfare - at dawn when all the surveillance equipment would be back online. To any observer, this would look normal - the hirer arriving and boarding the ship he had contracted.

***

At zero three hundred Kate Albrecht, Captain of Condor took her shuttle and left the dock, leaving the hangar on Condor open. Exactly ten minutes later, she rendezvoused with Junior, transferred herself to the ship, and left a subordinate to take the shuttle to another of the company's facilities.

'Katie's on board,' Petra announced and Aaron accelerated toward the dock complex.

Kate met Petra at the Bridge doorway, they exchanged greetings and Petra left. Kate was puzzled by Petra's reaction, her empathic senses going haywire. She approached Aaron, 'Captain, is Petra OK. She seems... distant, tense... I can't read her and that's strange in itself.'

253

'She has a lot on her mind at the moment and this crap with Sarclan isn't giving us any downtime. Don't worry, she'll be fine.' Aaron deflected the question, but Kate wasn't fooled. She sensed the turmoil in Aaron; something was wrong, something big but she just couldn't decipher it.

20

Sarclan was watching the approaching storm from the huge window in his quarters.

He smiled as he heard the footsteps approach from behind. 'Is all going well, Hiro?' he asked without turning.

'Yes Eugene. The final shipment of our Nano Droids is ready and will be collected in two days. Our contractor had a minor issue with the shorter time frame, but this is now sorted and we are on schedule,' Nakamura answered. He stopped about six metres behind Sarclan and stood, waiting for a comment.

Receiving none, he continued. 'There is something that I think you'll find amusing; the contractor had to hire another ship to accommodate our changed schedule. The ship he hired is the flagship of Aaron Abraham's trading fleet. Almost poetic isn't it, an Abraham helping you to win the day?'

Sarclan turned, a huge smile breaking across his face. He started to laugh; a deep, sinister sound, one that Hiro Nakamura had always dreaded. 'Yes my friend, this is indeed poetic justice... if there is any such thing,' he said clapping his hand on Nakamura's shoulder, 'most poetic.'

Nakamura's attitude told Sarclan that he wasn't convinced. 'What about the attack you suspect? Could the Coalition be aware of our plans?'

'Have no fear, I have taken steps to bolster the defences and I will be there to lead the way... **nothing** will stop us now. Hiro, consider where we have come from. Ten years ago we were still nomads; then last year we almost succeeded in seizing control of the galaxy. We have formed alliances with some capable aliens that have resulted in the most formidable weapons available. The Coalition is in turmoil with twenty-four colonies succumbing to our rebellions and now under our allies' control; and the coup-de-grace; in a few days we will release the most diabolical weapon ever imagined.

'Once activated, ten of the Coalition's most affluent and populous colonies will be infected with our virus. The people from these planets constantly travel and even though the incubation period of the disease is long, while it incubates the carrier is highly infectious. By the time the first symptoms start to show, **millions** will be infected.

'There is no reference for the disease, and it will kill millions before the survival instinct takes hold and anarchy reigns. Then we arrive with a miraculous cure! Humans being what they are, they'll pay **any** price for the cure. In the final scene, we will destroy Abraham and all his family. Whoever said revenge is sweet, really knew their stuff.' Sarclan completed his tirade, his eyes wide and perspiration forming on his brow. 'This time my friend, we will be victorious!' He punched the air and paced back to the window.

Nakamura's shoulders drooped, he'd heard all this before and every time they tried before, the Coalition always won. *Will this time be different?* He asked himself. He waited for Sarclan to regain his composure.

Slowly Sarclan turned. 'Come on, we need to go see the dogs, make sure they know what they have to do.' He clapped Nakamura on the shoulder as he strode purposefully towards the door.

***

The small group sat quietly in the private observation lounge on Condor. Aaron was nursing a scotch; the others simply watched the passing light show.

Wu Chan broke the silence. 'This is an amazing sight, Aaron, but I am perplexed. What happens when we are scanned by the facility? They will see where we are.'

'No, Emissary,' Aaron began, 'they won't. This section of the ship is impervious to all known sensor systems; even the

256

Eldorans can't penetrate it. The real test comes when we try and board the facility, that's where we are counting on your knowledge and assistance. Once we leave this section of the ship, we only have our personal cloak systems to fool the sensors.'

'All we need is to get on board undetected. After that, we will be in action and nothing can disguise that,' Wu Chan said and beckoned the others to join Aaron and himself. 'Let's go over the plan again.'

Eight hours later, Condor reinserted into normal space, ten minutes later she would enter a wormhole for the last trip to the facility. In those ten minutes, Junior was released from Condor, piloted by JT and Mondrac. Their role was to be the primary back up - if all else failed, she could make a last desperate jump to the facility to try and rescue the small band of infiltrators. They set their course for the predetermined rendezvous point.

'I suggest we all get some rest, in six hours we arrive and then... show time,' They all left for their respective quarters and Petra followed Arron to their room. As the door closed behind them she leaped at him, threw her arms around his neck, and kissed him. Desperation filled the kiss as she almost devoured him.

Aaron finally broke away, feeling her tears on his cheek. 'Petra what's wrong, why are you crying?'

'I don't know... I had a horrid premonition of desperate loss. Please don't come on this trip, stay on board Condor,' she spluttered through her tears.

'Hang on... I thought we were going to face everything together?'

Again she was racked by sobs of desperation. 'I don't know what to say, I have this feeling... I can't explain it.'

He tried to reassure her. 'Nerves, nothing more... hell; I have butterflies the size of Condors in my stomach. I'm scared too, we have no idea what reception we'll get but we will survive, I do know that.' Slowly the sobs faded as Aaron held her close.

'Come on, I think some rest is in order.'

'No, I'd rather a soak and some bubbly. Let's forget about what we have to do, let's enjoy this moment,' she turned and walked toward the bathroom.

***

Sol Radchak sat in the Command Chair of ECS Columbia, one of the Coalition's newest and most powerful battleships. Sol was enthralled by the size of the Bridge; he almost believed he could fit an entire Manta class boat in here. He sensed someone behind him and vacated the chair. 'Sorry Captain, I was admiring your Bridge.'

Ellen Satria, Captain of the Columbia, smiled as she took her chair and indicated for Sol to sit at her right. 'No problems Admiral, I still have to pinch myself at times to make sure I'm not dreaming,' she chuckled. 'Comms reports that all ships have reached their designated holding points.'

'Thank you, Captain... now we wait,' Sol replied, without enthusiasm; seventy-two hours just sitting in space, waiting for the right moment to attack would seem like forever. Betanna was only a short jump for the ships equipped with a jump drive. Only Columbia, ten Mantas and two of the Krell's new battleships were so equipped. For the remainder of the fleet, it would be a twenty-hour Displacement trip to reach the battleground.

The attack on Betanna was initially coordinated to take place 48 hours after the predicted time of the incursion on the Mechanista facility. But, now with that attack brought forward to Wednesday, Sol was concerned that the additional time would allow Sarclan to activate his Droids. In reality, the extra time was little more than a nuisance; but trying to change anything now would be a nightmare.

Satria completed her check of the ship's operations. 'Well, if all we can do is wait perhaps we should find some distraction? We do have a couple of holo-theatres and an excellent stock of entertainment, three gymnasiums, and many other rec facilities. What's your poison, Admiral?'

'I don't suppose you have a pool?' One of Sol's preferred ways of relaxing was swimming.

'Several actually... if you feel like a swim I suggest the Rec area on the accommodation deck. It has a full Olympic pool as well as a spa and sauna. Tell you what, I've got about an hour until the end of my watch. Go and enjoy yourself... I'll meet you there in an hour; then we can get back to business.'

'Thanks, Captain, I'll do that.' Sol smiled as he stood and left, knowing that the Captain would be only too glad to see him leave her Bridge. He smiled, *I know exactly how she feels, the last thing I've ever wanted was some nosy Flag Officer on my Bridge*. His smile broadened as he programmed the transport pod for the required destination.

***

Aaron had been sitting in the observation lounge for almost an hour when Wu Chan and Tocmal joined him. The three were sitting quietly discussing possible strategies when the door opened. Petra walked in.

She was almost covered head to toe in a brilliant red cape. Her legs looked bare except they were a dark grey colour and her boots - a match for the cape - ended below her knees. She stood for a moment looking at them then reached up, undid the cape at her neck, and let it fall to the floor.

Aaron stood, his mouth dropping open, mesmerized by what he saw. Petra's flame-red hair was tied up with gold strands that attached to a broad gold bandanna. From head to toe, she seemed to be covered in a fine grey metallic material that accentuated her figure. Her torso was further encased to protect her major organs.

At each hip, she wore a Sonic Disruptor and protruding just above each shoulder were the hilts of her swords. The belt around her waist supported the Disruptor holster, spare energy packs, and several throwing knives. She glared at the three before her and spoke.

'I certainly hope you three are enjoying this... it's a bitch putting all this stuff on.'

Aaron chuckled and replied. 'Well, it works for me. But remind me never to piss you off when you're wearing all this.'

As he spoke, Nat raced through the door. 'Sorry...' he stopped mid-sentence, 'Oh shit!' he blurted out and stood perfectly still. Like Petra, he was wearing two swords. 'This is real... I mean, you really are a **Vargan warrior**?'

The moment was interrupted by Angus announcing they would be docking in five minutes. Petra picked up her cape and as she draped it over her shoulders, she looked up into Aaron's eyes. 'Remember, whatever happens, I'll always love you.' She kissed him and turned for the door.

'For the record, all that's going to happen is we're going to get the data and save the universe... again. No heroics or bravado. Get in, grab the loot and get out... simple, OK?' Aaron pressed his hand against hers. 'And I'll always love you... just make sure you get back in time.'

Petra's reply was simple and firm. 'I promise.'

They entered the airlock and stood hard against each wall, watching the distance readout. It was like a countdown, starting at ten metres and reaching zero, then a slight shudder as the docking ring engaged.

'Everyone... engage cloak,' Aaron called. They activated the personal cloaking devices; Aaron could still see everyone but they were invisible to anyone not wearing a similar device. The outer door indicated a secure seal and the door started to open; at the same instant, Petra vanished. Aaron felt panic rise. *What was she doing*?

Her voice inside his head calmed him down. *Don't worry... get going and get the data.*

Aaron nodded and led the others out the door. They made it to the first bulkhead when they had to dive for cover as a large transport came down the corridor.

Something's wrong! Angus' voice sounded in Aaron's earwig. *They never send the transport; they always inspect first and check out the hold. Be careful!*

'Make sure they don't put something nasty on my ship,' Aaron's voice was firm at the comment.

They kept walking down the corridor, ducking into bulkhead spaces several times as more transports moved the cargo to the ship. Progress was slow until Petra's voice sounded in Aaron's head.

Take the next left and then the second right. It'll bring you to the data core, and get a move on, something is not right here. Aaron conveyed the message to the others and they started to double time in the direction Petra had indicated.

They reached the second junction as Angus again called. *We've been told to leave, I cannae stall, sorry.*

'Don't worry Angus, do as they say. Kate?' Aaron said.

Here Sir.

'Remember what we discussed, do it.'

Yes Sir.

They rounded the next corner and there before them were six Mechanista; dressed like Wu Chan but less ornate. The next thing they saw was Petra, reappearing between the six and the team. She removed her cape, drew her swords, and shouted to the team. 'You have your task, get on with it! I'll entertain these children!'

'OK, you heard the lady, let's get going,' Aaron cried and the four ran down the corridor to the data core.

Petra stood, legs slightly apart, well balanced for any attack facing the six Mechanista Gamers. 'OK boys, who wants to die first?'

The six laughed, defiantly. One managed to speak, his voice soft, as though he was talking to a child. 'What are you, some sort of warrior, bitch?'

His words, calculated to inflame his opponent's anger, had the opposite effect. Petra calmed and focused on the task at hand, her green eyes smouldering with a dark rage.

She took one step toward them and they all drew their

weapons, a variety of swords glinting in the light. Simultaneously the six rushed her, quickly covering the twenty metres between them. As they closed the distance, Petra leaped forward, took a dive to the ground and rolled under them.

As she regained her feet five metres away, three of the antagonists lay on the ground. Two had both legs missing and the third had one gone and the other badly sliced.

'I must be slipping, 'Petra smiled, coldly. 'One leg still attached.' As she spoke, she sheathed one sword.'

The last three charged, this time she stood her ground, the clash of fine swords echoing down the corridor. The first one lunged with all his weight, only to see his sword sliced in two by her. She spun and kicked him under the left ear, smashing the connection to his cerebral cortex, knocking him out.

The second to reach her was the one who had taunted her. Petra wasted no time with him - she quickly sliced through his neck, his head rolling away as his mechanical body kept running ten paces before it realized it was dead. The last one stopped, turned, and ran. Petra took one of the knives from her belt and threw it. It found the mark at the base of the skull, severing all communication between the brain and the mechanical host. He dropped in his tracks, as Petra set about the grim task of dispatching all the remaining parts.

While Petra had been engaged with the Mechanista, the team reached the data core. 'Only one door, one way in and out,' Jones commented as he set about bypassing the lock.

Wu Chan eyed Aaron and Tocmal. 'Admiral, you and I should stay in the corridor as guards. Aaron, you go with Nighthawk and protect him... remember, the data is the most important thing.' Aaron nodded as Nat finished and the door opened.

Tocmal drew his four Disruptors and walked several paces down the corridor; Wu Chan drew his swords and walked in the other direction.

Nat and Aaron entered the core and Nat immediately started working at a console. In a matter of seconds, he had accessed the database and located the correct files. He attached a data pack and began downloading the information. He also found the system reset command and a wicked smile crossed his lips. He tapped commands into the icon pad, his smile widening and looking more sinister. When the data finished downloading, he hit an execute icon, placed the data pack back in his vest, and turned to Aaron.

'Might be a good time to leave, in ten minutes this whole system is going to reboot. But it won't reboot in the same configuration, more like a total system purge, if you get my drift.' Nat smiled as he stood. 'Shall we go?'

As they left the core, the sound of Disruptor fire and swords clashing reached their ears. To Aaron's right, Wu Chan was battling five Mechanista; to his left; Tocmal was firing down the corridor at an advancing group of guards. Aaron leaped out of the door and sent several shots towards Wu Chan's adversaries, dropping to one knee, he took better aim. This time he was accurate and one of the assailants fell to the ground. As he did, Petra leaped past them.

'Aaron, get to Tocmal, he's in trouble. I'll help Wu Chan!' she cried.

Aaron and Nat turned and raced toward Tocmal, activating their shields as they did. The shield was designed to absorb part of any blast, to recharge the power supply, but they had the disadvantage of not being able to take too many hits without overloading. Tocmal's unit was close to the limit as Aaron and Nat dropped beside him.

'Like some company, Admiral?' Nat grinned as he drew his weapon and took aim at the right side of the corridor intersection.

'Yes, I was getting lonely,' Tocmal responded, one of the guards poked his head out, Nat fired and the head exploded. Aaron leaped across the other side. Now they could cover both sides of the corridor.

Suddenly, four guards rushed into the corridor. Aaron, Tocmal, and Nat returned fire and the four fell in their tracks. Tocmal stood and rushed to the next bulkhead with Aaron following his lead.

Again four more rushed into the corridor, this time firing where Tocmal and Aaron had been. Tocmal waited, four more rushed to support their comrades as Nat started firing from his position. Aaron and Tocmal were about to open fire when Petra and Wu Chan ran into the midst of the melee. Swords flashed, body parts and blood splattered everywhere, and the eight were quickly dispatched.

Aaron and Tocmal raced to the corridor intersection and fired several volleys down each direction, then surveyed the intersection. The corridor was empty. Petra, Wu Chan, and Nat joined them.

'Nighthawk told me what he has done, we've got to go. The purge reboot will dump all protocols; there won't even be life support!' Wu Chan cried. As he spoke, several weapons fired from each direction, sending the small band scurrying for cover.

They all searched for any target opportunity but Petra shook her head. 'We don't have time for this, I'll handle it.'

She stood, holding her hands in front of her, flames starting to rise from them. She concentrated and the flames grew until they seemed to engulf her hands. Then she walked into the centre of the corridor and threw her hands out on each side.

The flames shot out from her, growing magnificently. Suddenly they erupted in a spectacular display of pyrotechnics. Nothing at either end of the corridor survived.

'Let's get moving. Duramot and Junior are on their way!' She turned and led them towards the airlock.

They all raced after her, leaping over or crunching the burnt remains of defenders under their feet. At the next turn they were stopped; there standing between them and the airlock door were the four, level-nine Game Masters Wu Chan had spoken about. They drew their swords and adopted their attack stance.

'Aaron, get Nat to the ship... nothing else matters. Wu Chan and I will take care of these!' Petra called as she drew her swords again. She and Wu Chan approached the four, Wu Chan's swords still sheathed.

'My brothers, there is no need for this. Allow passage and your transgression can be adjudicated,' he said as the two groups stopped advancing, now only metres apart.

The rebel leader laughed. 'What is wrong with you Chan, you need to hide behind a woman, a Vargan witch, at that? Can you not deal with four lowers yourself?'

'I'm sick of being called a witch,' Petra shouted, 'so put up or die!'

'Quiet, witch, I am talking to the coward Chan.'

Petra turned to Wu Chan. 'Are all lowers such empty blowhards, or can some actually fight?'

That was enough for the leader. In one lightning-fast movement, he bounded at Petra screaming in fury. 'You will die for that insult, witch!'

He was fast but not fast enough. Petra deftly parried his attack and sliced through his sword arm. The sword hit the ground, still tightly held in the now severed hand.

Petra didn't stop. She immediately engaged one of the others; swords flashed and clanged against each other. This one, a female, was more controlled; she moved with grace and economy, knowing full well the opponent she faced had skills. As they danced, Wu Chan had engaged the others; the corridor now filled with flashing blades and whirling bodies - an elegant but deadly ballet. There was nothing Aaron or the others could do except watch; trying to pass this performance was impossible.

Petra and her opponent traded thrust and parry each looking for any weakness; any opening would end the dance for one of them.

Then Petra saw a chance - she feigned a slip. This was enough for her opponent, who thought she had the advantage. She surged forward and thrust her sword directly at Petra's left side.

The blade missed - as Petra had calculated. It went between her left arm and her back.

This was her chance. She clamped her left arm down and spun to her left at the same time, drawing her opponent closer. Petra's right arm flashed and her sword neatly sliced through the opponent's throat. She thrust out and the sword cleaved its way through the Mechanista's spine.

Her opponent slumped into Petra's arms, her final death rattle the last thing Petra heard from her as she flung the body away. As it dropped unceremoniously to the ground, Petra jumped into the battle Wu Chan was fighting. She separated one of the opponents and began the dance, again.

This time it was much shorter. This Mechanista found out quickly he was massively outclassed, and within a few seconds, Petra had disarmed him and knocked him to the ground. Wu Chan dispatched his opponent and joined her.

'What shall I do with him?' Petra asked.

'Nothing, I'll finish it.' Wu raised his sword and swung it down, removing the head of the rebel. 'Now it is over.'

The airlock was only twenty metres away and Duramot was already docked. Disruptor fire from behind the team snapped them back to reality. Aaron dropped to one knee, aiming at the newcomers. 'Get Nat moving; get the data out of here. I'll cover you!' It was clear that he had the best position so the others quickly followed his orders. Once they had Nat secured on Duramot, Tocmal and Petra took station either side of the airlock door.

'Aaron, come on, we'll cover you,' Petra called as she sent a volley down the corridor. Aaron broke cover and ran. He ran as he had never run before.

Unexpectedly, ten metres from the airlock door a bolt of energy came from an access tube to his left. It hit his shoulder and flung him into the sidewall.

An almost maniacal cry burst from the tunnel. 'An Abraham...

finally, I get to kill one!' Eugene Sarclan stepped into view, raised his weapon, and fired again. The energy bolt hit Aaron in the chest, blowing a hole through him.

Petra screamed, a strangled cry of pain, like an animal wail filled the corridor. '**Aaron, Noooo**!'

'Sorry, was he some sort of pet, witch?' Sarclan sneered.

Petra stood and started towards Sarclan. Her green eyes were blazing furiously, but her face seemed curiously bereft of emotion. Her arms by her sides with the palms facing back.

First a flicker, then a definitive flame erupted from them, as she turned her hands toward Sarclan.

Still, she walked, purposefully on. Sarclan turned, laughed, and fired his blaster. The air around Petra glowed red and the flames in her hands grew.

Again and again, Sarclan fired, with no effect. He began walking backward away from her. No more taunts came from him, his eyes showed fear; fear like Tocmal had never seen before.

Petra reached Aaron's body, tears streaming down her face. 'For you my love,' she whispered and she threw her hands out in front of her. The flames shot out, growing each millisecond, filling the corridor.

She started to advance, the screams from Sarclan becoming a terrible cacophony, guttural and filled with agony. Still, she advanced.

Later, Tocmal swore she deliberately controlled the heat of the flames, to inflict the most pain she could. The screams grew and grew until they lost all semblance of being human; becoming the tortured and agonizing howls of a dying animal. Finally, Petra stopped, the screams had died and the flames extinguished. She stood silently over the charred remains of Sarclan.

Petra turned. Twenty armed Eldorans were lined up along the corridor, and Mondrac was sealing Aaron's body in a stasis pod. Two of the guards took the pod and headed back to the airlock as she reached Mondrac.

'Goran-Esk!' Mondrac called frantically. 'Get him to Eldora, I don't care what you have to do, get him there as quickly as possible... Eldrac-Tar will know what to do.' Goran-Esk left and the airlock sealed behind him. Mondrac turned to Petra. 'Man-Nix?'

She collapsed in his arms.

T he wet fog was starting to thin. She felt the cold damp air on her skin.

She could see shapes in the mist, trees, shrubs, all familiar but somehow strange. Then she saw a human shape, it walked toward her, one arm extended, trying to reach out to her. She heard her name - *Petra* - it was almost a whisper, but familiar. She still couldn't identify the person approaching her.

Petra - louder this time, the shape was closer, still no face to see. She reached out her hand, trying to connect with the shape. And then the fog cleared. Standing before her, reaching for her was Aaron.

Petra, she heard again. A flash of light from her right, maniacal laughter, and Aaron was gone.

Petra woke with a start, the dream-memory fresh in her mind. Tears flowed freely as arms reached for her, held her, and comforted her. It took ages for the wails of desperation to subside. Petra moved as the arms lessened their hold and released her. She opened her eyes; Grace Grainger's face was the first thing she saw.

Grace smiled warmly. 'Welcome back.'

'How long?' Petra asked.

'Twenty-seven hours, or so,' Grace offered.

Petra sat silently, 'They killed Aaron,' her voice was almost a whisper. 'Where is he... his body?' she asked.

'On Eldora. Ambassador Mondrac arranged it; I think they wish to honour a friend. You can ask him yourself, tonight.' Grace spoke gently. 'Do you remember killing Sarclan?

'I killed a Sarclan, but not **THE** Sarclan.' Petra's voice was cold with hate.

'And how do you know that?'

Petra thought for a moment. 'I don't know... I have no words for it... I **know** it wasn't the real Sarclan.'

Grace moved to her side again. 'Tocmal told us what you did. He said you were controlled, as though you were deliberately trying to cause as much pain to Sarclan as you could before he died. Did you?'

'Yes, I suppose I did.' As she spoke, Petra threw off the bed covers, discovering the grey fabric of the bodysuit still clinging to her body.

'One thing I should tell you... that suit can only be removed by you. Others did try but you defended yourself. This is the one thing your mother didn't want for you. Now you understand the true power you can unleash, or are starting to... but you need to learn how to control it, or it will control you.' Grace paused, studying her niece intently 'Are you ready to remove it?'

The look in Petra's eyes told her what she didn't want to know. 'Not yet, I still have some unfinished business,' Petra responded, standing beside the bed. 'Where's the rest of my gear?'

'In the gym... why, what are you going to do?'

Petra glared directly into Grace's eyes.

'Finish it.' The words came with such venom; they almost froze Grace's blood.

Although Grace knew Petra better than anyone realized, knew the real abilities she was just beginning to discover, that look chilled her to the bone. Nothing would deter Petra from this course. Grace felt the cold hand of fear grip her heart as Petra gazed deep into her eyes.

Petra left the room and could hear voices as she passed the lounge area but managed to avoid any contact and quietly descended the stairs towards the gym. She found the rest of her gear, quickly put it on, drew the swords, and felt their weight. She tested the edge - though unnecessary as Vargan swords never dulled - threw the red cape around her shoulders and turned towards the stairs. There, standing on the landing was Mondrac.

'Going somewhere?' he asked.

'Yes,' she answered, 'to finish the job.'

'You won't be alone.' Tocmal's clicks and buzzes came from behind her. She turned and started to say something, but he stopped her. 'I'm coming with you... either that or you have to kill me to stop me.' His eyes were turning slightly pink, a sign of his intensity.

'And you'll need a ship and a pilot,' JT's voice appeared from the top of the stairs.

'No way, JT this is a private operation... you **can't** come,' Petra spoke forcefully.

'Bullshit,' JT fired back. 'Do you see any rank insignia? I'm a civilian; I've taken some leave due to me. I think a little cruise to Betanna is on the cards. But, before we go, there are a few people upstairs you need to see.' Petra knew he was right, as much as she didn't want to, she knew she must speak with the others.

She climbed the stairs slowly, finally reaching the door. JT smiled as he opened it for her. The looks on the faces of those gathered, in the lounge staggered her. Everyone was gathered and the sight of Jason and Amanda caused Petra to stop, the President of the Coalition was now on Argos, and she had lost his son. Shame and grief slammed into her like a hammer, they must blame her for the loss of Aaron.

As she entered, everyone stopped talking and came to her. Embrace followed embrace, each holding her and whispering their secret thoughts. Petra held herself together until the last person - Amanda. The tiny woman held her tight; Petra lost all her composure, sobbing desperately on Amanda's shoulder. 'I'm so sorry... I couldn't save him.'

Amanda pulled back and locked eyes with Petra. 'Nonsense... you did everything you could and between the two of you, you may have saved the human race.' She took hold of Petra's left hand, the Firestone ring glowing brightly.

'This stone shows how much you love each other, while ever it shines, that love is still alive and don't you forget that.' She paused, fighting back her tears. 'Now get going and kick Sarclan's skinny arse, but remember; you have a family to come back to.' She grabbed Petra and held her tight for a few seconds. When they parted, Petra left the room with Tocmal and JT.

'So... which ship are we going to borrow?' Petra asked.

'Junior... she's easy to operate, robust, and has teeth,' JT replied. Together they walked down the path to Junior, noting that already the reactors and drive were at idle. As soon as they stepped off the boarding ramp, it started to close. The door to the Bridge opened and revealed the fourth member of the crew, Mondrac. He had bypassed the family farewell and started the ship's systems.

'We should get going,' he advised. 'I've already obtained the necessary clearance.' He handed the data-pad to JT.

'Hang on Mondrac... this says we're going to Earth?'

'Oh, I must have selected the wrong destination. Still, we don't need to cause any problems; we'll sort this out when we get back.' Mondrac smiled and went back to piloting the ship. Once they left orbit, they changed course, it would take twenty minutes to reach the optimum insertion point. Mondrac placed the ship on auto and turned to the others. 'Jay-Tee-A-Bra-Ham, please can you tell us your plan?'

'No plan, as such. Firstly, we jump very close to Betanna... then we'll sort of ad-lib. Our travel time is about seven hours and the Coalition attack will start in five so we'll be running directly into a war zone.'

'No matter,' Petra interjected, 'we're not there for a holiday.'

They reached the insertion coordinates and made the jump into subspace.

***

Sol Radchak was pacing the Bridge. Five hours until they arrived at Betanna and he was edgy. He stopped, taking note of the people around him.

If the guy calling the strategy is this nervous, then he's not helping anyone else, Sol thought, but out loud, said. 'Captain we've got five hours till zero. I think I'll go down to the gym, nothing like a workout to pass the time.' He hoped that his casual, almost nonchalant attitude would help others to relax as he quickly left the Bridge.

On the way, he decided on a swim and found the pool in the gym. Designed as a zero-grav concept, the pool was a tube. Down the centre ran a modified gravitron system, this generated a gravitational field and kept everything in place. The pool itself was thirty metres in diameter, with the centre taken up by the gravity system. No matter where you stood on the side you were always diving into a flat surface.

It felt strange to swim and look down to see the underside of someone else swimming on the other side of the pool. He was completing his twentieth lap when he saw someone standing at the end of the pool, exactly where he would turn. He stopped and looked up. It was the Captain.

'Sorry sir, but you have an encrypted message from Admiral Abraham.'

Sol nodded and climbed out of the pool. 'I'll look at it in my quarters, thanks.' He picked up his towel and headed for the showers.

Ten minutes later he was sitting at his console, entering his encryption code. He read the message, and read it again. 'Fuck me,' he whispered as he glanced at the countdown timer on the screen and made the mental calculations. 'Shit... they'll arrive right in the middle of the invasion!' He called Satria and asked her to meet him in the operations' room immediately as he ran out of the room and stepped into the pod.

Moments later, Sol rushed into the operation Command Centre, from where the entire Betanna operation was being coordinated. He moved towards the operation chief's position. Currently in the chair was Commander Mariel Cabot, a native of New Gaul and one of the Coalition's best strategists.

'Admiral, you look like someone with a problem?'

'You could say that, Commander. I have been made aware of something that may affect our whole operation.' He brought the operations' chief strategist up to date.

'Are they mad?' she asked. The look on the Admiral's face said he was,. 'We better let all the Commanders know.' She quickly built the heavily encrypted message and showed Sol, who read it and agreed. Then she activated the comm system, instantly transmitting it to all the Coalition and Krell vessels.

'So, Admiral, what is this special Commando group, and what the hell are they doing in this action?' Cabot asked as Satria joined them. As she did, her communicator chimed. She looked at it and then at the two in front of her.

'OK, who is on FTS Condor Junior... and what is a Freebooter trade ship doing here?' Satria asked.

Sol took a deep breath. 'As you are aware, this isn't only a Coalition problem... hell, it isn't even only a Galactic problem. There are forces from other realms here and Junior has a Commando unit aboard. Their objective is to nullify these inter-dimensional forces, although Admiral Abraham was circumspect in his mission profile. All we need to do is continue our attack but be aware there is another operation in progress as well.'

***

'Yes!' The cry came from Fraslok standing in front of a microscopic analyser, 'we've done it! That's the twentieth success... now we have the answer.' For hours, ever since they received the data from the facility, his team had been working on the infected Nano Droids, trying to find a way to deactivate them. Another team was trying to identify the actual virus from the DNA found in the chemical program of Droids.

Leonard Fraslok turned toward the observation window and activated the intercom. 'We have a solution... we can stop the Droids!' He looked at the faces behind the transparent partition, hope now evident on all. 'All we have to do is transmit this coded signal and they will go dark. Once that happens, the healthy

274

Droids will see them as a foreign body and destroy them... the virus will never be released.' His smile revealed the elation he was feeling.

The meeting that followed set the plan for what they called *sterilization protocols* to be enacted. Nat had been able to decode all the infected manifests so they now knew, with a degree of certainty, which colonies were in danger. The plan was simple: they would send ships to the infected planets; these would circle the planet, at low levels, transmitting the coded signal. Once complete, they would move on to the next world. According to the data, the staggering enormity of Sarclan's plan was now evident, over half of the colonies had been infected, to some degree.

Grainger pulled Jason aside. 'Mister President, you may need to place these planets in quarantine. Also, we will need to track any of their people who may have been infected. Who knows **where** they have travelled since receiving the tainted Droids.' As he finished one of the technicians entered the room and walked up to Fraslok. A hushed conversation followed.

Fraslok turned to the others. 'The viral team has also triumphed. They have isolated and identified three separate viral DNA strands but at this stage, we don't know which will be activated and they are completely different.' He sounded puzzled by his announcement.

'Well,' Grainger spoke, 'can we design a defence for them?'

'That's the strange part. Two are easily removed by the normal Droids... they're only a couple of variations of the old influenza virus. One would show symptoms in a day or so of release, the Droids would quickly eradicate the virus. The victim would only notice a slight sniffle for a day or so, most likely it would go unnoticed. The second influenza strain is somewhat worse. It could take a week or more to incubate and may put the victim in bed for a couple of days; usual symptoms. But again, within days of the victim becoming ill, their body's defences would kick in and either the Droids or the natural immune system would destroy the virus. Apart from being a nuisance, these two are nothing to worry about.

'But the third?' Grainger asked.

'This is one we don't want to get out… a haemorrhagic fever. A mutated strain but related to the ancient Ebola virus, extremely nasty, the incubation period is around four weeks and during that time it is extremely contagious. This is the real problem and one we **must** develop a defence to. None of the normal Droids will even recognize it, and our natural body defences are no match for it. Once someone is infected, death is inevitable.' Fraslok seemed to shrink even smaller than normal.

Jeff Abraham interrupted, 'and I bet the other simple influenza attacks would mask any symptoms?'

All eyes turned to the young virologist who had brought the information to Fraslok, slowly, and with sadness, he simply nodded in agreement.

Grainger slowly shook his head. 'Sarclan has used this before. Zyralin Four, it's all in the report on that incident. The Science Station was used as Sarclan's test for the virus, and it was one hundred percent effective. What an arsehole… he's been planning all this for years.'

'Fucking Sarclan' Jeff continued. 'What a devious bastard… I think I know what he was up to. Professor, you need to check the delivery schedule, where were the first units sent to, and what was the delivery sequence after that.'

He turned to Jason and Allen. 'First he has to allow time for delivery, then time for distribution… they will activate after that. Consider this: people start to feel ill, with symptoms nobody has had for centuries. Next, people start to die in horrible ways. Our best minds and advanced technology fail us. What would frightened people do if, suddenly, someone materializes with a cure? We all know the answer; they'd **flock** to him, do anything he demanded. Anarchy, the end of the Coalition, everything Sarclan wanted. Genius, diabolical… but pure genius… he'd quickly take control of everything.'

'Well, it's not going to happen!' Fraslok said rebelliously. 'We have the solution: we make all the rogue Droids dark and the normal body defences will take over. Once the alien Droids are turned off, they can't do anything, so it doesn't matter **what** virus DNA they carry, it simply won't do anything. We must get the ships to those planets immediately and start transmitting.'

***

'Five minutes until reinsertion, better gear up,' JT called.

Behind him, Petra donned the antigrav pack, strapped an emitter to each ankle, and the power pack to her belt. Tocmal didn't need to bother with any of this. Instead, he opened the back-plates of his body and flexed his gossamer wings.

'These will do me,' he clicked.

The seconds ticked by as Petra and Tocmal entered the secondary airlock.

On the Bridge, Mondrac manned the operations' station while JT watched the reinsertion countdown. This must be timed meticulously. Reinsert too late, and they'd crash into the planet; too early and they would be visible to defenders for too long.

He'd set the system to deliver them just outside the atmosphere. From there he would descend fast to a height where he could safely drop Petra and Tocmal. Then they were on their own, while he and Mondrac would begin to strafe the surface, doing as much damage as they could to cover the infiltration.

In the airlock Petra felt the momentary disorientation of reinsertion, 'Almost time, Tocmal,' she said. She felt the door begin to open below, then together they held on to the rail above their heads. JT's voice came through the comm.

'**Drop, Drop, Drop**!'

Together they released their hold and fell through the now open outer door towards the ground, several thousand metres below. Petra had worn a glide suit and could almost fly; Tocmal had no problem, being a creature designed to fly. Lower and

277

lower they fell. Still, the visibility was zero, clouds and mist obscuring everything.

At one thousand metres Petra flared her glide suit. The display in her helmet now showed rugged terrain below, some of the jagged peaks almost at their level. Tocmal's eyes were glowing so he could see through the clouds - another natural advantage he had.

Follow me, Man-Nix, he called over the comm as he changed course. Petra followed and quickly they broke through the blinding mist only a few metres away from a looming sheer rock face. Tocmal effected a quick right turn with Petra close on his heels. Down they plummeted, now Petra could see the compound and troop emplacements.

Galdoran scum, Tocmal yelled ***time to die***. He drew his blasters before Petra could say anything. He peeled off to the north and she continued south. If the defenders saw either, the other should get through.

At fifty metres, Petra engaged the antigrav system and dropped the glide suit. She fell quickly and landed in one of the troop emplacements. She took the defenders by surprise, drew her blasters, and began firing, killing most of them before they could react.

Now so close that blasters were useless, she drew her swords. One of the Galdorans grabbed a spear and lunged toward her - she pirouetted and deflected the lunge. The Galdoran turned too slow, - her sword sliced through his neck. He was dead before he hit the ground.

She had no time to gloat; four more were coming toward her. She had noticed before that Zarof and his subordinates carried swords and thought they were ceremonial only. Not so; each of these four drew their weapon and advanced, flanking her.

Petra stood perfectly still, her swords by her sides, waiting. The Galdoran to her right was the first to move. He sprang forward, slashing at her as he did. Their swords clashed as he passed to her left.

She dropped to her knee and sliced through his trailing leg, he dropped howling in pain. The other three sprang toward her, trying to force an error. Skilled as they were, the battle was one-sided.

Petra dispatched another, severing his sword arm. One got a couple of good strikes on her armour, sparks flying from his sword as it struck her arm piece; the blow put him off balance and his death was quick.

The last Galdoran standing knew he was outclassed but to his credit, he stood his ground, sword in one hand, and a spear in the other. That was his biggest mistake; the unwieldy spear slowed his reactions. The fight lasted only a couple of thrusts and he too fell, his head landing a couple of metres away.

Petra sensed something behind her; she spun only to face Tocmal. 'I see you don't need any help,' he buzzed as he backed off a little. 'So, where to now?'

Petra turned to look at the cliff face a couple of kilometres to the west. She pointed at the huge window two hundred metres above the ground and the huge door at ground level, and hissed a single word; 'Sarclan.'

***

The space around Betanna was chaotic. Coalition ships of various types and five of the huge Krell cruisers battled the rag-tag forces of Tragarian Raiders being flung at them. The battle was far from one-sided - the new shields and weapons installed in the Raider ships gave them some advantages - but it wouldn't be enough.

In the central chamber of Darius Tragarian's lair, Nefaris and Zarof watched the battle above. It appeared both sides were evenly matched - for the moment.

'Why am I standing here like a coward? I must take our ship and enter the battle. I can win!' Zarof screamed, as the door to the chamber opened. Darius entered and confronted Zarof.

'No, let my crews fight this battle, you will be needed later!'

Zarof growled and stormed from the room, just as another

279

human entered.

'Darius, there has been some ground action at Sarclan's compound.' He moved to the console and changed the security view - it showed two of the defensive positions but nothing was moving. At both sites, twenty or more Galdoran guards lay dead.

'I see no other dead, only the Galdoran...' Nefaris mused.

'This was quick and hand-to-hand. Whoever did this must have a huge force. I don't care, it's Sarclan's problem,' Darius dismissed the scene, changing the view back to the battle in space above them. What he saw took his breath away; several of his ships were reduced to a mass of mangled metal or glowing balls of radiation. As he watched, a call came from the Commander.

Betanna, this is Commander Ralok... what do we do now? They're smashing us... We need more ships! The sight was evidence enough; three more ships were engaged in battle with the new Coalition Mantas, the new weapons having no effect. Suddenly, two of his ships exploded with no discernible weapon trace from their attackers. The battle had turned, the Coalition forces now outnumbering Raiders and they appeared to have superior weapons.

Darius turned to Nefaris. 'You said your weapons would be the deciding factor, now look! The Krell and Coalition are carving my ships up. What's going on?'

Nefaris stood - a look of total disbelief on her face. 'I have no idea. There is no weapon that I know of that can penetrate the shields,' she said in horror as they watched the last Raider vessel in this battle fire on the closest Manta, to no effect. 'That can't be! Their shields can't stop our new Blaster technology, it's impossible!'

'Well, I've got bad news for you... it can!' Darius spat as the last of the three ships also exploded. 'Commander Ralok, regroup and withdraw, no point in losing more ships... regroup at the alternative base.' He turned to Nefaris as Ralok acknowledged his order. 'I don't know about you, but I'm getting out of here; it appears that the Coalition has bettered your technology.'

Petra and Tocmal stood in front of a huge door.

It stood over ten metres high and twice as wide. 'This could prove a problem,' Tocmal said as he paced the width of the door.

'I may have a solution,' Petra said as she unclipped the power supply to her antigrav units and started to open the control panel. 'This antigrav unit is powered by a small MAM system.' The top of it came off and she started to change some of the internal circuitry. 'A small system like this, modified the right way, can become a lethal explosive device. This should let them know someone is visiting.'

She changed the last connection and placed the pack near the centre of the door, slightly off to the right. 'Now we run!' She yelled as she started to head for the opposite side of the doorway. Tocmal needed no encouragement; he spread his wings and flew straight to the rocks in front of them. Petra dived behind the same outcrop as the scream from the power pack reached a crescendo.

The explosion tore a huge hole in the ground in front of the door and blew the opposite side of the door open. Rocks and glass from the massive window crashed down on the path. They waited until the dust started to clear before leaving their cover. Blasters in hand, they edged toward the ruined door. As they approached, Tocmal rose into the air and flew through the opening. Silence followed him, then the unmistakable sound of blaster fire.

Petra crept closer; Tocmal reappeared. 'Coast is clear,' he clicked triumphantly. 'There are a few casualties though.'

Petra climbed over the last few pieces of rubble and entered the huge cave. 'A few casualties?' She observed as she surveyed the scene. There were dozens of bodies, mostly Galdoran soldiers but, scattered through their ranks were a few Humans as well. 'I think we better get moving; this won't go unnoticed.'

Deftly she plucked a small instrument out of a pouch on her belt and used it to scan the area. She frowned. 'We'd better hurry; we have quite a bit of Trisidic radiation here.' She started toward the rear of the cave. Halfway down it split with a smaller drift moving away to the left and on a slight incline.

'This way,' Petra called, moving silently into the new corridor. Another few metres and it divided again. She pointed to a window. 'This must lead to Sarclan's quarters.' She led the way, her steps quickening. About one hundred metres further along they came to a series of doors cut into the rock. Symbols and writing told the story.

'What does this mean?' Tocmal asked.

'Cloning... **this** must be where Sarclan clones himself and others.' Gently she opened the door and let Tocmal through before silently closing it. The room was dimly lit, but they could see half a dozen figures moving around, working at consoles and other machines. They crept closer, the room opening out into a huge cavern.

'No!' Petra whispered. 'This isn't possible!'

'What?'

'Blanks, Sarclan cloned blanks. He must breed them and activate them when he needs to.' She edged even closer. Before them were fifteen cylinders, over two metres high and one metre wide. Every cylinder had a clear front, and inside each was a human body, all copies of Eugene Sarclan.

'This is what you killed on the facility?' Tocmal asked.

'Yes,' Petra said as she stood. 'And we're going to destroy **all** these.'

She stepped out from behind her cover and approached one of the two armed men in the room. He heard something and turned round directly into the full force of her right foot. Petra spun as he turned. She kicked, her right foot connecting with his jaw, snapping his head back and breaking his neck. He dropped noisily to the floor, alerting the other guard. He spun to the source of the noise but had no chance as Tocmal's blaster sent him to oblivion.

Pandemonium erupted with technicians running every way, but as there was only one door, they couldn't get out.

'**Stop!**' Petra shouted, and they all obeyed, fear in every eye now directed toward her. 'Which one is in charge?'

A tall slender woman stepped forward. 'I am, Alanna Petrova. Who are you?'

Petra's eyes bored into her, she recoiled from the stare. 'To those who help me a friend; but to those who oppose me... death,' Petrova's bravado vanished and she stuttered something incomprehensible. 'Alanna, may I call you Alanna? This is extravagant even for Sarclan. So many copies of himself, you must admit, even for a total narcissist like him, this is a bit over the top. What gives?' As she spoke, Petra drew one of her swords. The effect was exactly what she wanted and Petrova started talking.

Her story was not what Petra had expected - Sarclan was dying. His love affair with Trisidium had deformed his DNA to the point where he needed to regenerate regularly.

Petra was intrigued. 'But if he clones himself that often, he's already passed the tipping point.' She was referring to the problem with DNA degradation. Each time a clone was made, the DNA was slightly degraded, or mutated from the original.

Between five and ten cloning cycles was all that could be achieved, but Sarclan had been doing this for some time now. 'And with the number of blanks stored here,' Petra stopped and turned to the technician. 'He's been using his original DNA... that's the only answer.' The look of fear in Petrova's eyes told her she was right. 'Where is it?' she asked, her voice cold and menacing.

Petrova's shoulders sank. She stood and led Petra to a safe built into the cave wall.

'Open it!' Petra demanded, raising her sword to emphasize her intentions. Petrova complied. The safe door opened to reveal one small bio-stasis unit on a pedestal. It was only fifty millimetres square, the clear sides revealing the contents, a small section of flesh.

'That's all we have left; only enough for five more cycles.' Petrova held the container with reverence. Petra took it from her and turned to Tocmal.

She scanned the room and pointed to the cylinders. 'Tocmal, destroy all these abominations.' She turned to Petrova. 'Are there any more?'

Petrova peered back at Petra, then at the sword in her hand. 'No these are all.' Her voice held sadness and resignation.

'I suggest you and your people leave, this place is not going to be safe anymore.'

'And what are you going to do?'

'Kill Sarclan!' She spun back to face her ally, 'Tocmal?'

'Yes?'

'Once you've destroyed these things, show the technicians the way out.' She didn't need to say more, he knew exactly where she was going. Tucking the small stasis unit into her tunic, she stepped through the door; five Galdorans were running toward her, spears raised. Five others were standing behind as a second wave. Swords drawn, Petra sprinted at her adversaries.

There was no battle. Petra's mind had only one objective - Sarclan. The five running toward her died quickly and bloodily - it was more of a hacking frenzy than a battle. As the last one fell she turned to face the others now aiming their weapons at her. She sheathed her swords, held her hands in front of herself, and started walking. Immediately the next five soldiers started firing, the air glowing from the energy released. But nothing touched her.

As she walked forward the area in front of her became hotter and started to glow a strange blue colour. It kept building with each energy bolt shot from their blasters until finally, Petra released it. She sent the huge ball of energy down the corridor, instantly vaporizing anything in its path.

Petra kept walking. The corridor was long and kept ascending. Eventually, it started to level out revealing another group of bodies the energy ball had destroyed. Carefully she stepped over them.

To her left was a huge door, now charred and hanging off its hinges. She kicked it open and stepped aside. A volley of blaster fire came from the room, impacting on the far wall of the corridor. Three new large holes appeared where they impacted.

Petra took a deep breath and dived through the door, rolling to her left; more blaster fire, but straight through the door, again. She stood, again holding her left arm out in front of her. With her right, she took the stasis unit out of the pouch.

'Sarclan!' she shouted. No blaster fire greeted her this time. She stepped into the middle of the room. There at the other end stood two figures, one in a full black robe, the other - Eugene Sarclan.

'**Nakamura, kill the bitch!**' Sarclan shouted. But Nakamura didn't move.

'What's the matter, Sarclan?' Petra called as she advanced. 'Scared to face a woman alone? Your clones are much braver, at least the one I killed on the Mechanista facility was. But he died. The blanks down the corridor; well they couldn't fight... not activated... they died as well.'

'But at least I killed one Abraham,' Sarclan sneered. 'Your lover, I believe. How did that feel, to watch me tear a hole through his body, to vaporize his heart?'

Petra didn't flinch or show any emotion. She kept on walking slowly towards Sarclan, speaking confidently. 'It felt horrible, you know that. You killed him purely for your pleasure, like any common psychopath; but all it did was to convince me to wipe **every memory** of Eugene Sarclan out of existence.'

She held up her right arm and opened her hand, revealing the bio-stasis unit. 'See this Sarclan? This is all that's left of you, this and that diseased body you now inhabit.' As she spoke a flame started in her right hand. Slowly it grew and encircled the stasis cube.

'**Nakamura, kill her!**' Sarclan screamed, his voice had an edge of madness to it now.

Petra glared at Nakamura, her eyes almost challenging him.

Nakamura removed the power supply from his blaster and dropped to his knees. He threw both the weapon and the power pack behind him through the now destroyed window.

'No Eugene, this time you're alone; this time you must fight your own battle.' He bowed his head in resignation.

Petra advanced, the flames in her right hand now flaring over a metre into the air. 'This is the end Sarclan. This is **MY** vengeance. You killed my future, now I will kill you and all who stand with you!' As she spoke, the cube in her hand reached its flash point and burst into flames. Petra threw it into the air as the flames engulfed it. The air was hot and the flames grew, totally covering the ceiling. The wall coverings began to ignite as did some of the furniture; the room quickly becoming an inferno.

'**Noooo!**' Sarclan cried desperately. He leaped at Petra holding a sinister curved blade in his hands.

Petra spun to her left, drawing her two swords as she did. She parried Sarclan's frenzied attack, ducking under his blade.

'Now you will learn the futility of your actions, Vargan whore! I have had two centuries to study, to perfect my fighting skill; I have fought and bested the best of the Mechanista; yes, even your friend Chan.'

He stopped talking and advanced. He lunged, but Petra easily deflected the blow, kicking out at Sarclan's left leg as she did. The move caught him and he fell to the ground, rolling out of harm's way, as Petra sliced the space where his head would have been.

'Good, excellent move, but are **you** enough?' Sarclan hissed as he spun and sliced at Petra. This time his blade found the mark, but the Vargan chain-mail protected Petra's body.

'Ah, the venerated Vargan chain-mail; will it save you now?' He lunged again, spinning as he did; his blade a blur as he attacked. Petra parried but was forced back. As she rolled away, the flames appeared to form a circle around her, protecting her.

'So, Vargan witchcraft is your answer!' Sarclan spat toward her as the heat forced him back.

Petra dropped her guard, the flames obeying her and retreating. 'Do I scare you that much?' She called as once again she advanced to battle.

They continued their dance, thrusting, slicing - both trying to find an opening. Petra spun to her left, barely evading Sarclan's attack. She rolled away and stood, now framed against the window opening.

Sarclan sprang forward, ignoring the flames now licking at him.

Then Petra saw an opening. She dived to the ground and rolled away, behind Sarclan.

He sensed victory and let out a bloodcurdling cry; turned and attacked. Petra stood her ground, forcing Sarclan to alter his advance. Now she pressed her advantage; her twin blades leading the way.

Sparks flashed as Sarclan reached her, their blades singing their deadly opera. Petra slipped under his attack, spun to her right, and sliced viciously. When she regained her feet, Sarclan was standing still, a look of surprise and horror etched on his face.

Petra moved to his side and whispered. 'Now you die.' She gently nudged him and his body fell into three pieces. Two clean blade cuts had separated his head from his neck and his upper torso at the waist. It fell into a bloody pile of torso and entrails on the floor. She stood, her eyes flashing in the firelight as the flames slowly engulfed Sarclan's remains. 'I told you I would wipe every memory of Eugene Sarclan out of existence; this is the beginning of my promise.'

Petra turned to Nakamura, her swords still in her hands.

'What's your story, Nakamura?'

Nakamura stood and studied Petra. 'I have no story, other than I am already dead. I died over a year ago.' He looked sadly at the body now in pieces, burning intensely on the floor before him. 'Eugene wouldn't let me go. He was convinced he could build a better civilization, but the poison of Trisidium destroyed his dream.'

Looking around the room he saw a clear path to the door. He looked back at Petra, his eyes signalling his understanding. She was controlling the fire, the flames her willing servants. Finally, he continued.

'Eugene worked tirelessly to try and find a solution but, in the end, he couldn't. Then the insanity started. He blamed the Coalition... in part... but the Abraham family was the target of his rage. So sad, they were once so close; he trained Jason Abraham. In times past he had a great affection for the man.' Nakamura gestured toward the waiting flames, 'I think we should leave.'

He turned and beckoned Petra to follow him. They walked down the corridor, as the fire suppression system activated in Sarclan's chambers. Nakamura led in silence until he turned into a viewing room. It looked down into a massive chamber. There below them was the underground colony.

'This was his vision,' Nakamura pointed to the scene below. 'To build his own colony but the drug of power seduced him. He became obsessed with the Coalition and destroying it. Now here is his colony, and he still couldn't see it.'

'There are over two million of them, but they won't last long... Trisidium. Most will die within a couple of years. They are no threat, I can guarantee that.'

Petra stood, swords at her side watching the people below, people going about their normal day. They were oblivious to what was happening above, also not knowing they had very little time left to live.

'Two hundred years sealed into a colony ship, only to be poisoned by the energy source that was driving them on.' Petra spoke quietly, the sound of her sheathing her swords louder than her words. She turned and started to leave. 'I'll see what I can do; at least they should have a place to die.'

'Thank you, daughter, of Aeiysta of Varga,' Nakamura said reverently.

Petra stopped at her mother's name.

Nakamura continued, 'I know who you are, and I knew your mother. She was a Warrior Queen, as are you and so will be your daughter. But there is something you need to know. Your father was also half Vargan, so Vargan blood runs strong in your veins. That is why you can master the Vargan arts, both physical and metaphysical, so well.'

Petra stopped, looking deep into Nakamura's eyes. She sensed no deception. What he was saying he believed to be true.

'Have you ever met your paternal Grandmother?'

'No, I always thought she died many years ago, on Earth. My father never mentioned her.'

Nakamura smiled. 'You need to go to Varga; she still lives. That was the reason your father went there, after the dissident attack, to check on her. But be warned there are forces on Varga that will do anything, go to any lengths to kill you. I will say no more, but the Krespah are real and growing in strength. You are the only threat they can see.'

She turned again to Nakamura, trying to see any deception, but she found none. 'How... how do you know all this? And who are the **Krespah**?

'Vargan dissidents, the ones who killed your father; Eugene was trying to work with them, but they are fiercely independent.' He placed his hand on her shoulder. 'I was not always a servant to madness, and now, as I die I think I shall be my former, true self. I can say no more, because I know no more... just be warned.' Nakamura turned back to the scene below, those below would now need him to help them through what was coming.

Petra smiled, 'yes... they will need all the help they can get.' She walked until she reached the massive entry then called Junior. JT responded.

'It's finished JT... call off the attack on the planet. There is nothing more to be gained here.' She stepped through the door, the gentle flapping of wings alerting her to Tocmal's presence. She turned to watch the small creature approach. He landed and walked up to her. 'I am pleased to find you intact, Man-Nix.'

'As am I to see you still here, my friend.' She scanned the path before them and saw something move then another. Within moments the path was filled with troops in Coalition uniforms. They stopped twenty metres from Petra and Tocmal; one officer continuing to advance. She stopped as she reached them and surveyed the scene.

'Colonel Margaret Garcia, Coalition Special Forces,' the woman introduced herself. 'I take it you're part of the Freebooter Commando force? Did you leave anything for us?' Garcia was keen to join the battle.

'Mostly bodies, Colonel, and a couple of million colonists that I advise you to leave alone.'

'And why should I do that?' Garcia asked belligerently.

'Two reasons: they are dying, most won't last more than a year.'

'And the second reason?'

'Because I gave my **word** they would be spared.'

'And who are you?' Garcia inquired.

'Petra Mannix, now I suggest you check with Admiral Radchak before you do anything I might consider provocative.' Petra waited as Garcia followed her advice. Finally, she turned back to her troops and they retreated.

'I thought we might have had another battle, Man-Nix. She is not happy that she missed all the action,' Tocmal clicked.

Petra smiled. Together they stood, watching the sky as JT slowly brought Junior in to land.

***

'Captain, two unidentified ships leaving Betanna.'

Ellen Satria turned to her Tactical Officer. 'What do you mean unidentified?'

'Sorry, ma'am, but the energy signature is not recognized by the system.'

'They'll be the two alien ships we've been looking for,' Sol offered. 'What's their projected course?' The Tactical Officer worked her console and the course of the fugitive ship appeared in the Bubble.

'Heading straight for the Krell Flagship... as effective as Dokad's ships are, I don't think one is a match for two of these.' Sol walked round the Bubble as he thought. He activated a pointer and a red dot appeared in the hologram. 'Captain, how quick can you get here?'

Satria consulted her Navigator. 'At maximum Displacement, nine minutes,' she answered as she put the proposed course change into the system. At the same time, the Tactical Officer compensated for the target ship's position. The Displacement hop would put Columbia slightly behind but between the two target ships.

'Excellent, that should give them something to think about! Make it happen and call Dokad... tell him what we're doing.' Sol smiled as he resumed his seat. 'Do we have any Mantas spare?'

Satria called the operations room. 'Four are currently not engaged in any action.'

'Have them form up astern of us... give them the coordinates and tell them to arrive ten seconds after we do. We reinsert and fire the first volley... that should cover the Mantas... they arrive and let loose with their Sling Shots. Between that and the Roharg, we should be able to handle these two. Remember, no quarter... as soon as we reinsert, start firing on both of them.'

Satria gave the orders and Columbia changed course and accelerated. Minutes later the Displacement drive activated and Columbia disappeared into the wormhole.

***

292

On board the Galdoran ship, Zarof was busy abusing Darius for being a coward. The comm system carried his abuse to the Nileran ship, where Nefaris and Darius patiently waited till Zarof ran out of alien expletives to use. At last, it happened and Darius had a small window to speak.

'Zarof, you're wrong. We are better to retreat, regroup, and fight another day. We're simply outclassed.' Darius tried to keep his voice calm, as Nefaris had advised.

'**Run away!** That's all you puny humans can do. No, we should stand and fight, take as many of these Coalition scum with us as we can!' Zarof continued with a few more expletives.

'Listen, Zarof. We're losing three ships to every one of theirs we damage. We simply are now outnumbered and out-gunned. Standing our ground is suicide. Do you want to die for **nothing**?'

Zarof answered with a growl. He stood at his Command Station, one of the junior officers tried to get his attention. The young male was rewarded with a fist to his face. 'Why do you interrupt me, what do you want?'

The junior officer stood rubbing his jaw and faced his Captain. 'Sir some of the Coalition ships have broken off the attack and jumped to hyperspace.'

'So? They're running away, as all humans do!' Zarof spat back.

'I don't think that is the case.' The young officer entered data into Zarof's console. 'This is the course they took. It is possible they intend to intercept us.' He brought up his projected interception point.

Zarof studied the screen. 'Nonsense! They would never attack two of us, we're too powerful. Get back to your station.' Zarof dismissed him. 'May the Gods protect me, now my crew is starting to see humans as a threat!' He sat down, anger still boiling in his veins.

On the other ship, Nefaris turned to Darius. 'You did well... he can be such a fool when I'm not there to control him.'

Nine minutes after insertion Columbia reappeared, exactly where Sol wanted her to be. It took a few seconds for the systems to lock the targets, but then all hell was unleashed.

Columbia had every latest weapon except for Sling Shot. Her Blaster banks unleashed massive amounts of energy, her forward torpedo tubes launched twenty mark-nine Anti Matter tipped torpedos and her four forward plasma cannons opened fire. The amount of energy released should have been enough to vaporize a small moon, but the effect on the two was far less.

'What's going on?' Zarof shouted.

'Those are the Coalition ships that were running away' the young Tactical Officer replied. He was entering his firing solution when there were three massive energy bursts at the rear of the ship.

'Shields are failing... engineering is exposed.' His words were lost as three explosions slammed the huge ship into an uncontrolled yaw.

'Engineering has taken a direct hit!' Again words were lost as more explosions rocked the ship. 'Life support in engineering and all aft sections has failed. Hull breach in engineering, the primary reactor is overloading!' Alarms were screaming, relay panels showing damage throughout the ship.

'Do we still have weapons?' Zarof screamed.

The Tactical Officer replied. 'Yes but only enough power for one cycle.' The ship was spinning, totally out of control, 'I can't get a lock on them; the system can't compensate for our damage!' As he spoke another six Sling Shot impacts put any thought of retaliation beyond contemplation.

Three again targeted the engineering section, slamming into the reactor core, the other three impacting behind the Bridge. The hull buckled and tore apart. 'Zarof you arrogant fool, you have killed us all,' were the last words Zarof heard as death finally claimed him.

The Nileran vessel fared a little better, but Darius and Nefaris realized they were outclassed when Roharg sent a volley from its massive Plasma Cannons. Darius immediately stopped his engines and transmitted the surrender transmission.

'Good work,' Sol spoke to the Bridge crew. 'Good work everyone! We destroyed one Alien vessel and I'd say we'll capture the other.' The battle, if it could be called that, had lasted less than ten minutes. All that remained of Zarof and his Galdoran vessel was a quickly dissipating energy cloud.

***

JT brought Junior in low and fast. He flared at the last minute and dropped gently to the ground a few metres from Tocmal and Petra. By the time they reached the ship, he had extended the boarding ramp.

Mondrac greeted them as they entered. 'Welcome back. It is pleasing to see both of you in one piece. I take it your mission was successful?'

Petra nodded. 'Yes, Sarclan is well and truly dead. I'm glad I got to see him take his last breath. That evil son of a bitch will never harm another person again! If you'll excuse me, I need some time out.' She headed immediately for her quarters.

Once inside, she removed her armour and stowed it in its container. Next, she stripped off the rest of the garments until she finally stood clad only in the grey bodysuit. This was the last piece separating her from reality. Slowly she reached behind her and unfastened the interlocking seam. The garment slowly peeled off.

Now it hit her. A crushing weight of pain and grief; all-consuming grief, a pain she didn't think she could ever bear. The tears started, and she wailed like a wounded animal. He was gone, the only man she knew she could ever love. Her life partner snuffed out in an instant of insanity and hatred. The grief overwhelmed her and she dropped to the floor. She knelt there, sobbing uncontrollably until a tiny head filled her vision.

'Prince!' Petra had forgotten he was on board. He gave a soft meow and stretched up asking to be picked up. Petra reached out and scooped the animal into her arms, hugging him close as he started to purr. She stood and walked to the bed, lay down, and within seconds was fast asleep.

***

Slowly the veil of sleep lifted, consciousness washing away the muddle in her brain. Petra opened one eye. The surroundings were familiar; she recognized the bedroom as being on Junior. How long she'd been here, she didn't know.

Now both eyes were open as she took stock of where she was. The time readout showed 16:45 but that didn't help as she couldn't remember when she had lain down. Then she remembered the cat. She scanned the room again, 'Prince?' she called tentatively. She was rewarded with the sound of softly padding paws and then she felt him jump up onto the bed. He climbed onto her and started purring.

'No, not now; I need a shower.' Petra smiled as she gave the cat a quick rub. Quickly she left the bed and went to the bathroom.

Twenty minutes later, freshly showered, she emerged and opened the wardrobe, some of her clothes were still here but still, she took time to decide. In the end, her standard company uniform won the day. *After all, I'm still on a company ship* she said to herself. That thought sent a wave of grief through her. *Company; Aaron's company; what'll happen to it now*? She shook her head shaking these thoughts away.

As she turned for the door, Prince started rubbing against her leg, 'Food... of course, you're hungry!' She said, quickly she opened the stasis larder. There she found a small choice piece of Argosan Salmon; minutes later it was being devoured by a grateful cat.

Petra closed the door behind her and headed for the Bridge. She was surprised to find it was empty. Also, nothing was powered up - Junior was dark. She left and went to the access ramp. At the bottom was a guard in Coalition Army uniform.

'Ma'am, please follow me.' He turned and led the way away from Junior.

'Excuse me but where are we?' Petra asked, totally puzzled as to where she was.

'On board Columbia, ma'am; I was told to escort you to the

others when you woke.' Petra shrugged as he stood aside to allow her to enter the transport pod first. 'Deck three, conference room,' the guard said and the pod sealed and shot off. The trip was short and the guard was soon opening a door to the conference room for her. 'In here, ma'am.'

Petra entered and was surprised to see who was already there. Everyone seemed to be in high spirits, so she knew something good must have happened. Grace Grainger walked up to her.

'How do you feel?'

'Fine thanks, Grace. How long was I out?'

Grace smiled. 'About fifteen hours... you were quite exhausted. Now, we'll fill you in on what's happened.'

Grogan came over to greet Petra. 'Yes, congratulations are in order, we have confirmed Sarclan's demise... not much left though.'

'What do you mean?' Petra asked. 'He was on the floor in three pieces when I left.'

'Apparently something started a fire. When you left it burnt furiously and destroyed everything in the room. We found charred remains, but enough to confirm identity. 'Great job.' Grogan added. 'It was strange, even though the fire suppression system activated, the flames seemed to keep burning.'

The next hour was spent with various people telling Petra what had transpired. From their words, she gleaned that the Raiders were either destroyed or scattered to the ends of the galaxy. Zarof had died when his ship was destroyed; Darius Tragarian and Nefaris had been captured.

The plague Droids that had been delivered had been largely rendered inoperative by Fraslok's team. Damage to the Mechanista facility, though substantial, had yielded much information on the rebellion. Now the Coalition had the intelligence it needed to put down any Sedition plots that were still operating.

Condor had jettisoned the cargo picked up at that facility just in time. They dumped it as they passed behind one of the planet's moons and made an instant jump into hyperspace. Good thing they had - the cargo was nothing less than a huge bomb.

Mondrac was hovering in the background watching the proceedings. Everyone was very animated, as humans can be, but it was evident to him that Petra was drowning in it all; he sensed the grief and pain she was hiding. The pain built and just when she felt she couldn't contain it, he acted.

He walked behind her and gently touched her on the shoulder; instantly she collapsed. Mondrac caught her and gently laid her on a couch. He turned to the others. 'She's been to the place you call hell, and worse... to do what she has done has taken a huge toll on her... she needs rest! I'm taking her to Eldora where we can help her through this.' His tone told everyone it was useless to argue.

Grace glanced to her husband, who simply nodded. She turned to Mondrac 'I'm coming with you,' and she moved to Petra's side.

Mondrac bent and picked up the unconscious form and he and Grace walked out of the room. Tocmal also took his leave and followed them.

Once again, she felt consciousness returning. Part of her psyche screamed for it to stop.

Petra partially opened her eyes; she sensed her surroundings were familiar. She felt something beside her; she reached out her hand touching a warm furry body. *Prince!* She thought. *I'm on Junior, but how?* The last thing she remembered was being on Colombia and in a discussion with others, but what was it about?

She suddenly became aware of someone else in the room: her eyes shot fully open.

'Grace! What are you doing here? Where am I?'

'We are on Jok-Tar's ship, on our way to Eldora.' Grace's face was impassive. 'What's the last thing you remember?'

'The meeting, we were discussing what happened on Betanna; then I woke up here. What happened?'

'Mondrac saw the emotional distress in you, saw the exhaustion, so he put you to sleep. Petra, tell me exactly what happened, on Betanna.' Grace's voice was firm.

Petra propped herself up and began, starting at the moment Aaron was killed. Her words were broken, and her emotions ebbed and flowed as she remembered all the details of the past few days. It felt cathartic to finally be able to talk about it.

A few hours later, Grace was still patiently sitting to the left of the bed as Petra swung her legs over the side. She grimaced, pain coursing through her body.

Noticing the look on Petra's face, Grace spoke. 'How about a nice long soak in the spa? I'll get it ready for you.'

Petra knew better than to protest. Moments later, the water was perfect as she stepped into the tub.

She lay there for ages, allowing the water jets and bubbles to gently massage away the aches in her body. Eventually, she began to feel refreshed and another sensation crept into her world; Petra was hungry; ravenous in fact. 'Grace, how long have I been here?'

'Thirty-six hours. Petra understand this, if Mondrac **hadn't** acted as he did, you would, in all probability have died.'

'Why? I felt fine.'

'Don't you remember the warning I gave you back on Argos? *To use the suit you must control your emotions...* but you didn't... you went berserk. Do you know how many you killed on Betanna?'

Petra was puzzled, then memories of her actions started to return. She sat in the tub as the realization came flooding back, accompanied by shame and tears. 'When I saw all those people I wanted to destroy them all but something... no, **someone** said something that stopped me. Nakamura... he said they would all be dead within a short time... I remember sensing loss and hopelessness for them, and I stopped.'

'That's when sanity resurfaced in you and I'm glad it did. Now,' Grace directed, 'you need to get dressed and regain your strength. Start by having something to eat.'

Petra quickly dressed, again in her Company uniform, and went straight to the kitchen. After a hearty breakfast, she was almost normal again. She noticed Zal-Tar standing in the lounge area.

'If you are sufficiently refreshed,' she spoke quietly, 'we should join the others.'

Zal-Tar had waited till Petra had eaten to speak. She handed a small round disk to Petra. 'This is part of a technology we are considering offering you... please place it around your neck.'

Petra took the disk and examined it. It was heavy and made of a gold-like metal; it was warm to the touch. Gingerly, she placed the cord attached to it around her neck.

'Now, if I may, I will show you where we are going.' Zal-Tar touched Petra's temples with both hands. Instantly Petra saw a room with comfortable lounges and several people in them. She only recognized Mondrac. Zal-Tar broke the connection. 'Now Man-nix, can you still see the room?'

Petra paused, recalling the scene. 'Yes, I can.'

'Then touch the disk I gave you.'

Petra slowly placed her left hand on the disk. Everything swirled for an instant and then she was standing in the room. She turned but Junior was no longer there.

Mondrac's voice boomed across the room. 'Well done Man-Nix.' He left his chair and came over to greet her. 'How do you feel?'

Petra tentatively took a few steps. 'A little disorientated. What just happened?'

'Sit and I'll tell you.'

Petra saw that the others had left. Now only Mondrac and Zal-Tar were present. She sat in one of the large armchairs, grateful to be off her feet - she was quite dizzy.

'The disorientation will pass and, as you become accustomed to the transport system, it will not bother you. Now where to start?' Mondrac paused, gathered his thoughts, and began his explanation.

The transport system she had used was installed in all Eldoran vessels and had been for some time. Mondrac explained that it converted matter into an energy signal and transmitted that signal to another place, where it reformed as matter. The disk around her neck was the key. It held Petra's matter signature so when she arrived at her destination, her body could once again reform. 'I remember some of the old science fiction vids that my brother has. Your race has imagined this type of transporter for centuries, but has never been able to make it work.'

At that moment Jok-Tar appeared. 'Man-Nix, welcome, we have arrived at Eldora.'

As he made the announcement the wall in front of Petra changed and became transparent. Eldora was similar to so many

M class worlds: abundant water, huge oceans, and landmasses ranging from tiny islands to continents. It could have been anywhere in any realm of the multiverse but something about it struck a chord in Petra.

'It's beautiful,' she whispered. 'But where are the cities?'

'We have few cities; most Eldorans live in clan communities. You'll see when we arrive at the Tar compound. Come, we will show you.' Jok-Tar started to leave.

'Prince... what about the cat?'

Zal-Tar laughed. 'Do not worry... he will be well catered for. Your companion animal has become a favourite of most of the crew. Such an interesting creature, so primeval and yet so intelligent... believe me, he will have no end of companions while we're gone.'

They transported to another part of the ship. Here they found a blank wall and a console. Mondrac explained. 'We have rules in the use of the transport system. One is never allowed to transport wherever one wants, to do so would impinge on the freedom of others. To protect these freedoms, we have dampening fields on each planet and designated transport pads.

'To transport to the surface you must identify where you want to go... we are going to the Tar compound. Approach the console, touch your disk and announce you are travelling to the Tar compound. There you will arrive.' As he spoke Jok-Tar followed the procedure, instantly he vanished. 'Now Man-Nix, your turn.'

Petra cautiously approached the console. She placed her left hand on the disk and simply said, 'Tar compound.'

The room she was in disappeared; instantly another room appeared. Jok-Tar was waiting but this time she felt better, the disorientation less than she expected. The room was similar to the one they had left; round with a slightly domed floor and the console in the centre. As she surveyed it, Zal-Tar and Mondrac appeared.

'How do you feel now?' Mondrac asked.

'Pretty good... that was much easier.'

'Excellent! Now welcome to the Tar Clan compound,' Mondrac said and opened the door. 'But I must warn you: Eldrac-Tar is something of a fanatic on ancient Earth art and architecture.'

The sight that greeted Petra was astounding. Although she had never seen any of Earth's ancient buildings, she had spent much time in the archives, hunting through old data files. The room was actually a separate building, built on one side of a municipal square. Petra turned to look at it and was astounded at the ornate structure. It was circular and around the outside was a portico supported by huge stone columns; they reminded her of ancient scenes from Earth's past.

'These columns were modelled from something called the Acropolis,' Zal-Tar pointed out. 'The building opposite is from an ancient city called Rome, I believe. Our Clan Sire has taught us about his constructions but, in honesty, I don't find it as exciting as he does; the fountain...'

Before she could finish Petra interrupted. 'The Trevi Fountain and the Palazzo Poli, I don't believe it. How could it be here? As far as I am aware it is still on Earth and under several metres of ice.'

Jok-Tar laughed. 'Our Clan Sire had it built from old data files, images in books... anything he could find on the subject. The building behind the fountain is where we are going.'

The rest of the square was bordered by many different Earth architectural styles, in all a journey through most of old Earth's cultures. They quickly crossed to the left of the fountain and up a set of stairs. They entered the palace and things changed. Gone were the Roman influences, now the interior was different.

He led them to a set of huge wooden doors, knocked and pushed them open, and ushered Petra inside.

'Sire of the Tar Clan, I am pleased to introduce Man-Nix, of Argos.' Jok-Tar announced formally. An old Eldoran stood from behind a massive oak desk. As he moved forward Petra's eyes wandered over the room. From floor to ceiling each wall was covered in bookshelves and, as she gazed up, there was a mezzanine holding many more rows of shelves stacked with books.

Eldrac-Tar reached them. He bowed in the Eldoran fashion and offered his hand to Petra. 'Man-Nix, I am pleased to make your acquaintance.' His voice was deep and sonorous and formal. Eldrac-Tar smiled. 'Do you like books?'

'I do, as a matter of fact; but I've never seen so many in a private collection! I wasn't expecting it here in the Fifth Realm.'

Eldrac-Tar smiled again. 'Well, I have A-Bra-Ham to thank for most of it. It was his company who found most of this for me.' He beamed as he opened his arms to emphasize the grandeur of the room. Petra's heart sank at the mention of Aaron; the wound was still very raw. The elder of the Tar clan saw this and gently guided her to a sofa.

He took her hand. 'My dear Man-Nix there is much we must discuss.' He beckoned Jok-Tar over and a quick conversation ensued. Jok-Tar quickly withdrew and returned a few moments later carrying a tray that held a bottle of ruby-coloured liquid and several glasses.

Eldrac-Tar poured Petra and himself a glass, before indicating his offspring to do the same. Once satisfied everyone was settled, he spoke again.

'Man-Nix, there is much that has happened and there is a debt the whole multiverse owes you... and A-Bra-ham. It is a debt we all feel and will always try to honour. But, we have done a small thing to help.'

He stood and walked to his desk; operated some control and a hologram started to form. It was a stasis pod; one like Mondrac had placed Aaron into when he was killed.

'Man-Nix, do you remember when you first came aboard Jok-Tar's ship?' Petra nodded. 'Do you remember having some *"enhancements"* while you were there?' Again she nodded.

'While you were having that process we also did a definitive scan of the two of you, partly to see if your DNA and molecular structure would be compatible with our transport system. Thankfully it was.' As he spoke the hologram moved, now it was moving over the clear cover, there was a body inside.

Petra froze, *surely not, they wouldn't be so cruel*, she thought.

Eldrac-Tar continued 'What it also gave us was a complete recording, if you like, of both of you.' Petra felt her heart racing like it was going to burst out of her chest, she still heard the Eldoran's voice but it now seemed like miles away. 'When A-Bra-Ham was damaged, Mondrac had his body sent here, in stasis, so we could try and repair the damage.'

The hologram now showed the upper torso, a complete human male but the face was still obscured by frost on the cover. A ghostly hand appeared in the display and wiped it away.

'Aaron!' Petra wailed.

'Yes, Man-Nix and he will live.'

She heard someone say the words but her mind couldn't grasp it. 'What... what did you say?'

Zal-Tar moved to her, took her face in her hands, and turned her gaze away from the image floating above the desk. 'Yes, Man-Nix... A-Bra-Ham will live!'

'But how...? I saw the damage, his chest was blown open.' Petra mumbled through tears that were now flowing freely. Eldrac-Tar was about to explain but the look from his female offspring made him think twice.

Zal-Tar looked at Petra. 'Man-Nix, how doesn't matter now... all that can come later. Now you need to see him... **you** need to be there when he wakes.' She took Petra's hand, gave her Sire another withering look, and led her out of the room.

They took an old elevator down several levels. The doors opened and they entered a clinical white room; in the centre was the stasis pod. Technicians were attending to various consoles as Petra slowly and cautiously approached the pod. Finally, she stood looking at the body inside.

'Aaron!' she whispered, emotion welling up again. She turned to Zal-Tar. 'Is he...'

'Alive?' Zal-Tar completed her sentence. 'Technically, the pod is sustaining him but his brain activity is normal. We're confident that life can be restored.'

Petra gazed at the perfect body before her. No hole in the chest, no damage at all - confusion gripped her 'But I saw him die, he had a hole **clean through** his chest... how can life be restored?'

Eldrac-Tar entered the room. 'As I was trying to explain,' he said, moving closer to Petra. 'I was insensitive, I apologize. Sometimes I can get caught up in the technology and forget the emotion.

'As I said, we took the earlier recording of A-Bra-Ham's molecular signature and used it to reconstruct the damaged section of his body. That was relatively easy for our Technicians... what comes now, however, is far more difficult.' He led Petra to a chair at the side of the room. When she was comfortable he continued.

'A-Bra-Ham will resume life, if we are successful, at the precise moment of his demise so you and Tocmal have the most important role to play. The two of you must, and I cannot emphasize that enough, **must** be the first he sees.' He could see that Petra didn't fully understand. 'Man-Nix, understand this: he will remember being shot and the impact of the energy blast. He may even recall a few moments after that but no more. When he wakes, you must be here to help him back, can you do this?'

Petra looked into Eldrac-Tar's eyes. 'Of course, I can... all I want is Aaron back!'

'Good, let's start. We have recreated a holographic representation of the scene, complete with your reactions.' He indicated a point at the far end of the room. 'We need both you and Tocmal to stand back. Do not say anything and stand perfectly still. Allow the scene to play out... I will signal you when to move. Man-Nix, this is of **utmost** importance.'

Petra nodded her agreement, 'Eldrac-Tar, has this been done before?'

Eldrac-Tar lowered his head. 'No this is the first attempt. We have been theorizing for many years but this is the first attempt. But I believe we owe this to A-Bra-Ham; he has proved to be a most honourable and valued friend.' His voice was soft as he placed his hand on Petra's shoulder. 'Now Man-Nix, we begin. Whatever your emotions tell you; **do not** move till I say so.' He turned and left the room, leaving Tocmal and Petra alone with the pod.

The two stood still as things began to happen. First, the ceiling started to glow; then a broad beam of light formed around the pod. It emanated from the centre of the ceiling. The intensity began to increase, slowly building into a kaleidoscope of colour and shape which all concentrated on the pod. Suddenly, it stopped and was replaced by the scene in the corridor.

Petra relived the moment, almost suffocating on the emotions it dragged up. She saw Aaron turn and the blast come from her right, from down the intersecting corridor. She saw herself walk towards the now lifeless body of Aaron, saw Sarclan emerge; heard his maniacal laugh as he gloated over his handiwork.

She saw him turn and the look of shock and fear in Sarclan's eyes as he saw her. She watched as Sarclan turned and started to run toward his guards, she heard her words to Aaron as she walked past his body and then watched as she incinerated Sarclan and everything in the corridor. Tears flowed freely down her cheeks. Then...

'**Aarrghh**; fuck that hurts!' Aaron's voice filled the room.

Eldrac-Tar's voice entered her head. ***Not yet***, *be still, Man-nix.* She watched as slowly Aaron sat up in the pod, he turned to watch the hologram, watch his fiancée coldly destroy Sarclan and his guards.

Now *go to him.*

'Aaron!' Petra's voice was a wail of pain and emotion, it echoed around the room as she ran to the pod. She threw her arms around him, sobbing uncontrollably. 'You're back,' she said through the sobs.

Aaron held her tight, confused as to what he was experiencing. 'What do you mean back, I haven't gone anywhere?' Those few words broke the spell and Petra started to laugh, an almost hysterical laugh of relief. Aaron was perplexed at the crying, laughing almost hysterical woman in his arms.

***

The next few days were intense, as Aaron was subjected to tests and more tests. Finally, the Eldoran Technicians agreed he was in perfect health. Then came the hardest time: four days where he was completely brought up to date with all that had transpired, everything including Petra's account of what happened on Betanna.

Aaron sat quietly, digesting what she had just explained. 'I remember seeing what you did on the facility. But you went to Betanna to kill Sarclan?'

Petra nodded defiantly. 'Yes. I did.'

'No Man-Nix, **we** did,' Tocmal spoke from the doorway. 'While she did kill Sarclan, and the entire Multiverse is forever in her debt for doing so, she was not alone in the venture. Your nephew piloted the ship, and I accompanied her to the surface. We were involved in the battle and the subsequent victory.

'Understand this, A-Bra-Ham, if Man-Nix had not acted as she did, many more would now be dead and the threat to the very existence of the realms would still exist. Do not judge her harshly.' His tone indicated he was extremely proud and protective of Petra.

'Judge her? Hell no! I'm so glad she did what she did... what **both** of you did. Now we are free of Sarclan and his madness.' Aaron smiled. He reached for Petra and looked directly into her eyes. 'I'll never understand how you can do what you do, but I'm so grateful you can.' Then he smiled cheekily. 'But I know never to annoy you when you have **that** gear on.'

'Don't worry. It'll take another Sarclan for me to put that on again, so you're relatively safe.'

Aaron smiled again. 'Now is there anything I can do for you?'

'Yes, take me home. I believe I have a wedding to attend.'

End Book 3

Reviews from my readers are important and always welcome, if you wish to leave one please go to our Contact Us page at **www.gregmutton.com**. If you want to know what's coming up join our Sci-Fi community, via the Join page on our website.

This trilogy is now complete. I hope you enjoyed the adventure and want more. Is this the end of the 12th Realm? Certainly not: this is our realm, our universe and there are many more adventures to be told.

Coming in early 2021:

FREEBOOTER FOUNDATION

The story of the beginning of the Freebooter culture in the 26th century.

A meteorite the size of a tennis ball, an old space ship, an exposed fuel nacelle and old shield relays - all come together in a catastrophic event, an event that will change the course of human history.

Hi, I'm Greg, you've just finished my first trilogy, so I should tell you a bit about myself. I live on the mid north coast of New South Wales, Australia in a quiet bayside village with my wife, son and our 2 cats.

If I'm totally honest, I began writing 30+ years ago, for my own enjoyment. I have spent most of my working life in engineering and management. When I retired I began writing in earnest, and in 12 months had a manuscript to send to an editor. The first response was "it's too long and should be a trilogy". Another year later and Chronicle of the 12th Realm was born.

I like to write about people who are forced to tackle situations – people just like you and I who rise to the challenge. I believe that no matter how advanced, no matter what technology we invent, human beings will always define their existence by their actions, both individually and collectively.

I don't have superheroes (I've never actually met any) but I explore the real physical and metaphysical abilities people have. I take examples from life – emotions, love, despair, romance – and infuse these into my characters and plots. I enjoy using literary license to enhance my stories, design alien species, and describe future technologies. After all, I am a science fiction writer.

I hope you enjoy reading my books and, being part of this journey with me.

9 780909 497170